DIM SHORES PRESENTS

Second Dim Shores Original Edition, February 2022
ISBN 978-0-9991430-8-7
DS-027TP

Cover art by Russell Smeaton
Frontis image by francescoch
Layout by Sam Cowan

Dim Shores
Carmichael, CA
DimShores.com

Printed in the United States of America

DIM SHORES PRESENTS
VOLUME 2 / SPRING 2021

CONTENTS

GUSTAV FLOATS

J.W. Donley

Thoughts of infection and contamination percolated in Gustav's mind. An unidentifiable decapitated body had splattered on the sidewalk before him. His muscles tensed, ready to run, when the red bubble forming on the severed neck popped. He felt a droplet land in his eye and mix with his tears before he gained self-control. He leapt over the body and sprinted down the sidewalk.

Only a few blocks from home, he'd worked up a heavy sweat. It flung from his arms and legs as he ran full sprint. He briefly considered jumping into the nearest house before the contagion took effect, but he feared confronting the inhabitants. The civilians of Hilldale were well armed and would not hesitate to fire buckshot into a perceived threat.

He abandoned the root riddled sidewalk and continued his sprint down the center of the street. Up the road a mother frantically corralled her children indoors and abandoned a basket of laundry she'd been hanging on the line. As Gustav bolted past, she sneered out at him from beneath the lifted corner of a heavy curtain.

Ahead, Gustav saw his home. He knew he would float off at any moment. Tears streamed down his face as he crossed the unkempt grass, each step striking the yard with less impact. He nearly reached the covered porch before lifting from the ground. A sinking feeling tugged upwards at his innards much like going over a hill on a speeding coaster. His forward momentum carried him along just enough to grab the trim of the porch roof.

"Jon! Help me!" he screamed, his voice becoming ragged. Inwardly, he pleaded Jon had not carried out on his threat to attempt breaking through the quarantine border. His body flipped, feet now hanging skyward, as he struggled to maintain his slipping grip.

"Jon!" Through his cries he heard the storm door open. Jon stepped out from the porch and scanned the yard for the source of Gustav's pleading. "Up here!"

Jon looked up, "Oh shit! What the hell did I tell you?! We should've run!" Jon's face was red with anger. In his right hand he held their shared carry-on luggage with a shirt sleeve hanging through the zipper.

"This is not the time. Do something!" *Shit. He's doing it. He's leaving me.*

"Fuck this! I'm done." Jon stomped off towards the garage as he jangled a set of keys from his pocket.

Gustav expected to hear the old green bean station wagon roar to life before watching Jon back down the driveway, leaving Gustav hanging towards the sky.

He attempted to pull his arms over the edge of the porch ceiling. Straining, he pulled one elbow down but it slipped as the plaster edge broke. He scrambled to reestablish his grip as the bits of plaster fell and shattered on the stairs below. Gladly, he would've taken a broken arm or a sprained ankle over whatever horror waited above.

Jon walked back to the front of the house, the luggage no longer in hand. Instead he carried a ladder and a roll of duct tape. He propped the ladder up against the porch and wrapped the tape around it and a porch banister.

"Oh, thank you Jon. Thank you." Gustav's tears returned and fell up to the sky as he tried to climb down to reach the ladder.

"Stop right there! You will wait until I am out of the driveway and gone before you climb down."

"What are you saying? You can't leave me like this." More tears streamed toward the clouds above.

"Good luck." Jon again turned and walked to the garage. This time the engine did sputter and start. Gustav watched his partner of three years back the station wagon from the garage. Jon stopped at the end of driveway and glanced over to Gustav. Gustav silently pleaded for Jon to stay, but Jon broke eye contact and cranked the wheel, swinging the station wagon onto the road.

Gustav didn't know how long he hung there watching the empty road before he grabbed the top of the ladder. He pulled himself down each rung and listened to the duct tape creak as it threatened to fail and send him sprawling upward. The tape on the right side started to unwrap from the banister. Gingerly he continued to pull himself down to the next rung. "Please hold," he whispered between grinding teeth.

In a quick snap, the tape on the right unhitched from the banister. The ladder jolted upward, eliciting a shriek from Gustav. The tape on the left side held, leaving him and the ladder to dangle and jostle as he regained his composure. Once settled, and convinced that the left tape might not fail, he continued pulling himself down, fully expecting the remaining tape to give way.

After much effort he pulled himself over the edge of the porch ceiling and collapsed next to the yellowing light fixture. His sweat collected and soaked into the rotted wood and cracked paint. He stared into the fixture as he tried to ease his breathing, hating the crowd of dried bugs collected within and how gravity still held sway over them, even in death.

"Dammit! How did your dumb ass get infected?" Gustav looked down to see Taylor standing beside the skewed ladder with Dodger, her trained capuchin monkey, seated before her feet. She stood with a fist on one hip and a battered Louisville Slugger studded with rusty nails hanging from the other hand. A silver star charm, hung from neon green laces, bounced with each tap of the bat against the side of her bright purple tennis shoe. Dodger squeaked twice but took no notice of him sprawled on the ceiling as he gnawed on a walnut.

Gustav sighed in exhaustion and stared down at the concrete floor of the porch.

"The car is not in the garage. Stolen? Or did Jon skip town?" Taylor stood up straight, adjusting her weight, moving her fist from her hip and hooking her thumb into a denim pocket.

"Jon wouldn't come near me."

"Well, you know what they say, 'if they can't handle you at your worst' and all that shit. I only put up with that asshole because you liked him." She stepped onto the porch beneath Gustav and stared directly up into his eyes with a scrunched face. "Let's get you inside. I don't want the government goons taking you." She propped open the storm door, straining the metal spring and chain at the top. Dodger bolted into the house. "Come on now. You've got to do this under your own effort. I don't want to catch that shit either. Who would go and pick up the rations?"

Gustav's mind still roiled with thoughts of Jon's abandonment and the possibility of Taylor doing the same as he crawled on all fours over the threshold. The living room ceiling creaked with his weight but he was surprised at its rigidity. He felt a tinge of comfort at being inside and out of sight. He was home, and not likely to float away as long as he stayed beneath the roof.

"Thanks," he said working to stand upright. Some of the popcorn plaster crumbled and fell around him as he fought his vertigo. Gustav didn't feel like he was upside down, but seeing the inverted world around him made him nauseated.

Their home was old and the ceilings were lower than most. Gustav's head was less than a yard from the floor and he had to walk around the couch and television in order to not bump his head. He reached for a picture frame from the coffee table. It was of him and Jon at a park the year before.

Taylor let the storm door latch shut behind her and stood her bat up against the door jamb before she closed the heavy wooden door and engaged the deadbolt.

"The Jon in that picture is not the Jon that drove off today," said Taylor before leaving Gustav alone to process everything that had happened.

⋅•━•⋅

Days passed. Jon never returned and Gustav became more acclimated to life on the ceiling. Sitting cross legged above the television he shed gravity defying tears and hoped Jon made it through the quarantine border, but knew it was improbable. They'd been through a lot together: keyed paint jobs, refused service at local restaurants, the loss of Gustav's mother.

Before the shit hit the fan, Gustav came across a small red box with a ring hidden in Jon's underwear drawer. Gustav tried it on and admired himself in the armoire mirror, practicing his smile for the day Jon would propose.

That day never came.

Jon changed when the disease took over and the government put everything on lock down. Gustav never brought it up.

The night Jon first mentioned running, he, Taylor, and Gustav were sitting on the couch getting drunk on their last box of wine.

"They already have the cure! We're all just part of some fucking test. Gotta make sure the shit works before they use it in the field," Jon ranted. "They're not going to let us out. We're lab rats! We've still got gas in the car, and a few gallons from the mower. I say we load up the Green Bean and make a go at busting through the barrier. Then we haul ass to California."

Gustav and Taylor could not help their drunken laughter at Jon's enthusiasm.

Jon stood and threw his wine glass into the fire. "Won't need that now that the wine's all gone." He went to bed without another word. This only stirred further laughter from Gustav and Taylor who stayed up to finish the box.

So far Taylor had no problem collecting the rations for her, Gustav, and Jon. He wondered how she convinced the distributors to give her all three portions. Then he imagined she was very convincing with Dodger perched on her shoulder and a battered baseball bat studded with rusty nails on her back.

They established a protocol to keep him hidden from the government patrols and those who would turn him in for the reward. All over town there were posters promising money and priority evacuation to those who provided information leading to living carriers. Mostly, Taylor's protocol involved keeping the curtains closed at all hours.

Last week, Robert, a middle-aged man who lived a few houses down, and his yappy Jack Russell terrier confronted Taylor and Dodger on their way back from picking up the rations. Gustav didn't witness the incident, but Taylor filled him in on the details. She'd tossed the rations into the grass and unslung her bat from her homemade back holster. Dodger immediately leapt onto the Jack Russel screeching his monkey battle cry. In shock at the nail studded bat waving before his face and shrill Dodger's screech, Robert dropped the leash and abandoned his dog to a losing fight. The Jack Russell broke free and ran after his owner, whimpering and tail tucked between its legs. Dodger clenched a chunk of the terrier's ear in his mouth and screeched victoriously.

"It was a mess," Taylor said and slapped her knee while she and Gustav watched Dodger run laps around the trees in the yard through a gap in the living room curtain.

"I wish you wouldn't risk picking up the extra rations. What if they catch on?" Gustav paused for a moment. He leaned back against the wall. "If Jon was caught, you'll draw attention."

Taylor twitched then said, "Not picking up the rations would draw attention. According to the papers you've been there every few days for the past three weeks. My friend Sherry works the food bank and ticks your boxes. I've got it covered." She winked and clicked her tongue twice as she fired a pair of finger guns at Gustav.

Gustav was glad she wasn't threatening folks in the food-banks swarming with armed guards.

"What about Robert? Aren't you worried that he'll report us?"

"Nah. He's a cowardly little shit." Taylor went quiet while she sat down on the musty couch. "I think they did catch Jon," she said without looking up at Gustav.

Gustav's stomach sank skyward, but he said nothing.

"Sherry said that Jon's name was no longer on the checklist."

Gustav squirmed at the thought of what they were doing to Jon, even if he did deserve it. What would he tell them when subjected to enhanced interrogation techniques?

"Oh," said Gustav, trying to feign disinterest.

"He was a shit-head for leaving you hanging from the roof, but I don't think he'd rat you out." She tore open one of the rations and fished out the chocolate pudding cup and a plastic spoon. "He did love you."

Gustav took note of her use of past tense.

"I'm a bit pissed that I won't get his rations anymore. No more extra pudding cups!" She put an upside-down spoonful of pudding in her mouth and pulled it down and out leaving behind the sugary chocolate before swallowing. "Damn! Those government factories make a better pudding than store bought."

"Does Sherry know about me?" asked Gustav still staring at his denim covered knees.

"I'm sure she's figured it out. But don't worry. Me and her have been flipping off government buildings since high school. She hates authority figures more than me."

Gustav sighed; his fingers twined behind his head. "I don't know what I'd do without you."

"Well, at this point, I don't think you'd do much." She smiled and sat the empty pudding cup on the battered thrift store coffee table. Dodger, done playing outside, bolted into the house through the dog flap in the back door and leaped into Taylor's lap. "Don't worry, I'm not going to leave you high and dry like Jon-boy did," she said while she scratched Dodger's back, soothing him to sleep.

"That's just it. Don't you worry about getting infected?"

"Oh, that's a possibility. But I'm fine with it. What about you, Dodger?" Dodger squeaked at the mention of his name, but did not stir.

"See, Dodger's fine with it too."

⸺⸱⸺

Later that evening Gustav enjoyed a cup of coffee after finishing his dinner. He left his plate on the high shelf Taylor'd put up the week before. It had taken him the better part of three days to figure out how to drink upside down from a cup. He'd severely burned the roof of his mouth on the first attempt. They had no stock of straws in the house, and Taylor could not find them anywhere in town. Soon he became accustomed to swallowing liquid and food against the gravity still trying to pull it all back down and out of his mouth. After anything made it to his stomach the pull would stop.

His waste, both fluid and solid, also floated. He would open the back door and toss out plastic Wal-Mart bags containing his shit and gallon jugs of piss. He and Taylor hoped that whatever was up there killing everyone was choking on his fecal balloons.

He finished his coffee and sat the mug on the shelf before getting up to go relieve himself. Even though he didn't use the toilet, it was a small touch of normalcy to at least use the bathroom.

As he stood, he lost his footing and grabbed the shelf to catch his balance. It wasn't screwed down and the side he gripped easily lifted away as he fell back to his ass on the ceiling. His empty mug and plates flew at his face knocking a tooth from his mouth. The tooth rose and bounce on the ceiling followed by a few drops of blood while the cup and plate fell to the floor and shattered. He could see some of his blood staining the shards.

"Shit!" Gustav yelled.

"You okay?" asked Taylor from the living room. She'd gone to lay down while he stayed behind to finish his coffee. He could hear her rustle from the couch before she entered the kitchen with Dodger bounding ahead of her. "Oh, you klutz."

She pulled on the pair of yellow dish gloves from next to the sink.

"Be careful," said Gustav.

"I'll be fine," she said while she plucked the shards from the linoleum floor one by one. Dodger busied himself with foraging along the counter for cans of trail mix. After a couple trips to the trash with the larger shards Taylor was almost done picking up the final and smallest porcelain bits when she let out a yelp.

Sweat slicked Gustav's skin. He'd infected his friend and last connection to any semblance of a normal life. "Are you okay," he said in a whisper.

Taylor pulled off the cut glove, exposing a fresh pearl of blood forming on the tip of her finger. She didn't look away from it as she responded, "Well, it looks like there's a possibility I won't be able to get our rations anymore."

He did not know how to respond to her calm acceptance. "What are we going to do?" His voice was still a whisper, afraid to trigger any contained rage Taylor held back somewhere deep within. Dodger had popped the top off a small tube of trail mix and was busy munching and pawing for his favorite bits.

Taylor continued to study her finger in silence for what felt like an eternity to Gustav before she said, "Dodger can carry a note to Sherry for us. She'll find a way to get supplies to us." Careful not to let her injured finger touch anything, she used the palm of her hand on the seat of a nearby chair to pull herself up. Still, she stared at the remaining shards on the floor. "I'll finish cleaning this up tomorrow. Come on Dodger, time for bed," she said before grabbing the last two pudding cups from the fridge and a plastic spoon from the sink.

Dodger abandoned his can of treats on the counter and they left the kitchen. Gustav heard her bedroom door shut in the other room as he continued to sit in silence on the ceiling.

After an uncomfortable amount of time alone in the silence he went to his own room and pulled his sleeping bag off the coat rack he kept in the corner. As he slipped into the padded cocoon, he thought about how everything had turned out and how it would've been better for him and Taylor if he'd not made it back to the porch. He wouldn't have experienced Jon abandoning him and Taylor wouldn't be infected. He would be another headless body obliterated by impact at terminal velocity. Slowly his wakeful worries transitioned into nightmare as he tongued the bleeding hole in his gums. He tossed and turned above the bed he and Jon once shared letting the blood drip from his mouth and onto the pillow he'd stapled to the ceiling.

The next morning Gustav woke to the smell of cooking bacon. The sound of a metal spatula scraping a cast iron pan rang through the house. He rubbed the dried blood from his cheek, crawled from his sleeping bag, and let it fall to the bed below. A wave of relief rushed through him. Infection never took affect more than a few hours after exposure. He turned the bedroom door handle and walked into the darkened living room; the thick curtains were effective at keeping out morning light and prying eyes.

A wedge of yellow light streamed over the couch from the kitchen where he could hear Taylor whistling 'It's Raining Men'. He fought back an urge to run in and hug her head and moved into the kitchen with caution. He stood clear of the spinning ceiling fan they rarely turned on anymore. It swung just above ankle height and the first time one of the wood slats maliciously struck his fibula he let out a yell loud enough to spook Dodger. The little monkey ran screeching through the house before he bolted out the dog door.

"A little inappropriate, don't you think? It's raining women and children out there to," said Gustav testing the waters.

"It's the first song that popped into my head this morning. I thought it extremely appropriate, given our circumstances." She snickered; not her usual boisterous laugh.

"Taylor," said Gustav. "I'm glad you're still on the ground."

"Yep." She flipped an egg cooking next to a few strips of bacon. "You want this over easy?"

"I'll take whatever you're cooking." Gustav sat on a crate he'd nailed to the ceiling the week before and watched Taylor cook. He could not stop smiling.

Dodger came in from the back yard holding a gold watch.

"I think Dodger's been going through the neighbor's houses again," said Gustav.

Taylor scolded Dodger, "We've talked about this. Give it!" She held out her hand as the capuchin sulked forward. With a tiny paw he dropped the watch into her hand. "No more of this. We don't want any more trouble with Robert and his damned dog."

Dodger bared his fangs in a monkey smile and backed away wringing his hands before zipping back out the dog door, most likely to pilfer something from another neighbor.

It wasn't until Taylor was setting a plated strip of bacon and fried egg up on Gustav's high shelf that they could hear the barking out back. Gustav stretched his neck to get a good view out the kitchen window. First, he saw Dodger zip past, closely followed by Robert's Jack Russell terrier at full sprint, nipping at the end of the monkey's tail.

"That rat bastard!" she yelled as she sprinted toward the back door, grabbing the her bat leaning nearby before bursting out into the yard. She ran after the dog, chasing Dodger in circles. Gustav soon saw Robert closing in on Taylor.

No longer caring if he was seen, Gustav went to the open back door to warn her. The dog yelped sharply, and their fight ended with the dog running off whining and missing the rest of its ear. Dodger screeched in victory as Taylor ran to him, arms outstretched. Robert approached, unseen, from behind holding a shotgun aimed for her head.

"Taylor! Behind you!" yelled Gustav.

Robert turned, distracted from his target and losing his aim, giving Taylor a chance to appraise the situation. Dodger ran up her arm and gripped her shoulder as she stood and swung the bat. She screamed a battle cry as the bat knocked the gun clattering to the ground. The nails impaled his palm.

Robert let out his own scream in anguished pain as he attempted to claw at the bat with his other hand. The nails hooked into his skin and, in his panic, he was unable to gain a strong enough grip to yank it out. Taylor pulled the bat, not hard enough to free his hand, but enough so to cause maximum discomfort.

Then Taylor lifted from the ground.

Her shock filled face turned to Gustav.

"No!" yelled Gustav, inching closer and closer to the back door.

She lifted higher, still gripping the nail studded bat embedded in Robert's hand. Dodger screeched and ran from the back of one of her shoulders to the other. Frantically, she attempted to pull herself down the length of the bat, hand over hand. Robert screamed in pain with each yank and the added weight of Taylor's body.

Robert gripped the bat with his other hand, his blood slicking the wood and nails. He tore the bat from his flesh with a roar. Gustav could see the sweat streaming over Robert's grin. He held absolute power over Taylor's life.

"Just help her! Bring her to the house! Please!" pleaded Gustav.

Robert did no such thing. Taylor continued to slip back up the grip of the bat, her feet dangling straight up and into the air.

She stopped and locked eyes with Robert. Dodger latched to the back of her shirt, she looked over to Gustav once more, her eyes wide, searching for any source of hope, but found none. She let go. Falling feet first toward the clouds, she flipped the bird with both hands aimed towards Robert. Then, more than twenty feet above the ground, she reached down over her head and pulled Dodger away from his solid grip in her shirt and tossed him screeching to the ground. Dodger landed on his feet and bolted for the house, zipped beneath Gustav's head, into the kitchen, and disappeared.

Standing over the back door and leaning his head out, Gustav wept as he watched Taylor float far enough above that he could no longer make out more than a diminishing spot.

Bleeding profusely from the massive open wound on his right hand, Robert dropped Taylor's bat and picked up the shotgun with his left. He stood and walked toward the back door with a finger on the trigger.

"She can't save your floating ass now! I was just going to turn you in for the money, but now it's personal!"

Gustav backed into the kitchen and pulled a stick of gum from his pocket and began to chew. He then reached down under his head for a nearby chair before pressing his back against the wall next to the door where Robert wouldn't see him.

Robert stepped into the doorway and Gustav swung the chair with every bit of strength he had, shattering it on Robert's back and knocking the gun away. Robert, quickly recovering from the blow, scrabbled for the gun.

"Don't you dare touch it!" the ferocity in Gustav's voice shocked even himself. Robert froze. "You make another move and I will fling as much blood, spit, and snot at you as I can muster before you move an inch. I swear I will!"

Robert remained still as he considered Gustav's threat. "I'll leave, but I'll be watching and laughing nearby when they come for you."

Gustav spat his wad of gum. It struck Robert between the eyes and a stream of spittle ran down his face from the pink blob.

Shocked and shaking from blood loss, Robert stood and backed toward the door his eyes wide in disbelief. "You fucker," he whimpered and nearly tripped backward over a chunk of the shattered chair. Dodger tumbled into the room at full speed snarling a little capuchin snarl and leaped at Robert's face.

"Dodger. No!" yelled Gustav. But the monkey clawed at Robert's face trying to get at the bastard's eyes.

Robert tore Dodger from his head and threw him against the kitchen wall before running out the door bleeding and screaming. Dodger bounced back from the impact and ran after Robert, screeching with rage.

Gustav jumped to reach the gun on the floor and moved into the living room. He attempted to catch his breath while gripping the sawed-off shotgun in one hand. With his other he slammed a fist repeatedly onto the cracking ceiling, raining crumbled paint and plaster onto the couch. A slight breeze blew in through the open storm door window and cooled his tear slicked cheeks. As his pulse softened, the silence of the house overtook him. He really was on his own and he damned himself for his part in Taylor's infection.

He was nearly asleep from exhaustion and mourning when a heavy thud shook him awake. He dropped the shotgun onto the couch and sat up to look through the storm door window. His tears blurred his vision and, at first, he saw nothing. But on the path leading from the front porch sat a bloodied tennis shoe, purple with neon green laces. A sparkling star charm glinted in the late afternoon light.

Taylor's dead hand hung over the edge of the porch roof, blood dripped from the fingers and pooled on the concrete steps below. This was his fault. He'd caused her demise.

Anger boiled up from deep within warming his face to a burning red. He jumped down from the ceiling to grab the shotgun from the couch. The plaster ceiling almost gave when he came back up. Then, shotgun in hand, he bolted for the door.

"This is for Taylor!" he raggedly yelled as he shoulder-checked the storm door, shattering the latch and ripping an explosion of splinters from the door jam. The door flew from its hinges and fell to the ground beside Taylor's shoe.

Gustav leapt from the porch ceiling, flipped, and dove headfirst into the sky, continuing his battle cry and brandishing the shotgun, pumped and ready to fire. He wanted to blow away whatever was up there even if it meant joining the decapitated bodies re-introduced to gravity.

Gustav's free-fall into infinite sky further fueled his hatred of whatever awaited him above. He approached and passed through a small cluster of clouds. He worried the moisture would cause the gun to misfire but still did not want to drop it and lose any semblance of the uncharacteristic bravery that had boiled over from within.

He continued to rise. The clouds blew by and allowed him a view of Hilldale shrinking beneath him. In the distance he could see Oklahoma City, a large gridded blotch on the landscape. The sun dipped into the curved horizon and soon night would come. The spots and blotches below would glow with sodium vapor lamps and headlights would stream along the network of roadways.

Above him wisps of altostratus clouds approached, reflecting beautiful hues of pastel sunset. But beyond that, something new caught his eye. The sky beyond was flooded with, what looked like, the largest murmuration of starlings he'd ever witnessed. It undulated, ebbed, and flowed, breathing as one giant opaque predator stalking the sky. The individual specks grew as he rose. Each had too many limbs to be birds, and they had no wings. These black creatures of stretched, unnatural shapes, wielded nine, no fifteen, spindly and jointed legs.

His earlier gained bravery began to melt away as the true size of the horrifying beings became apparent. Their glistening forms slid over one another, crawling like gigantic malformed subterranean insects with legs ending in white edged biological scythes. They clawed at the sky to gain speed when they did not gain purchase in the bodies of others.

Bile rose in Gustav's throat in disgust. With extreme willpower he tore his attention away from the nightmare above. He saw Robert to the west and higher up than himself. Gustav could hear Robert's screams carry in bursts across the chill high-altitude winds and did not look away from the bastard's approaching fate.

Gustav wondered what the creatures did with all the heads. He assumed they consumed them, but, now that he was even closer, he saw that some of the beasts had large flopping clear bags attached to their backs, carried like spider egg sacks. In them were collected a multitude of human heads, no longer floating, but piled at the bottom. From a distance he could only make out the different tones of flesh, the general shape of faces, and varying clumps of hair styles.

An image then flashed through his mind; a pyramid of severed heads built upon blood-soaked dunes beneath an infinite and starless oblivion. Other pyramids stood like spikes from the rolling dunes and seemed to call to him in one voice. A psychic invitation whispered over the dead sands. This unwanted impression filled him with an icy dread.

He shook his head to rid himself of the nightmare and began to prepare. He did not plan on dying without a fight.

Gustav looked back over to Robert, whose screams continued to stutter across the winds, only to witness his final moment. A nearby black beast, in a single motion, sheared off his head with a bone scythe. It then lifted the head up and over its back with its other pointed legs. It pressed Robert's head through the wall of the membranous bubble to join the others. Gravity retook the body as it fell back to earth, spouting blood. Gustav steeled himself, knowing that he'd just witnessed a very likely version of his own fate.

A monstrosity hovering directly above took no notice of him. Gustav assumed the nub away from the sack was its head. Its black skin glistened in the setting sunlight as it bent a number of its legs up and around the top of its body, fiddling with the portion of the mucous bag still in contact with its back. Like an air bubble on the bottom of a near boiling pot of water, the mucous bag of heads lifted. Streams of slime stretched in long drooping strands until they snapped from strain. A smattering of head bubbles lifted from the backs of a multitude of beasts across the sky. The orange glow of the setting sun illuminated them like a vast field of floating candle lanterns freshly released.

The fore nub of the creature took note of its approaching prey, but carried on with its work. Gustav positioned the butt of the gun against his shoulder, barrel aimed upward, while it busied itself with pulling a new deflated mucous bubble from one of its many back pustules.

Gustav pulled the trigger. His body bolted downward. Buckshot ripped through the beast's skin like stones through wet paper towel. Black blood bubbled from its wounds and, instead of falling, ran up and around the sides of its body.

The beast thrashed twice, then went limp.

Gustav pumped the next round into place, ejecting the spent shell. He hoped that there was a next round.

Another beast, much longer and still carrying a head sack, swam over, bone scythe legs reaching forward ready to swipe. Gustav again pulled the trigger, jolting himself sideways and blowing off a part of the creature's fore body. The shot popped the bag on it's back, freeing the contained heads which rolled and fell ground-ward. Not yet dead, the creature continued to swim after him as he continued to rise. The other beasts in the immediate vicinity took notice and began to lift in a vortex as he aimed the shotgun at the rising storm. He pumped and fired, rocketing his own body further up and blowing away a portion of the injured beast's back. It stopped moving and lazily floated to the side as another rose and took its place.

Again, he pumped and pulled the trigger, but there was only an empty click. Inspired by Taylor and her Louisville Slugger, he wielded it like a bat, ready to swing into the next bit of soft tissue. He had no hope of survival but took some solace in the dead beasts now orbiting far above the clouds. That was his doing. He created those corpses, not them.

A new monster swung a bone scythe at Gustav's abdomen. The metal of the shotgun clanged in collision with the bone. The point of the blade tore away a swathe of his shirt and missed spilling his guts by only millimeters. He felt heat behind him, emanating from the body of another beast, trying to ambush him while he reeled from his near death. He lifted both feet and kicked into its body, launching himself forward into another aggressor.

He smashed into and started clawing at the salamander flesh. It was soft enough for his fingertips to rip through and reach for any important bits within. The body felt like fresh plucked, raw chicken. He bit into the bitter meat and spat a floating wad of black-blooded filth into the surrounding air. He bit again and again, screaming between each bite to eject the flesh to clear space for another assault. It would be over soon.

A nearby creature caught Gustav off guard and snatched him up, shoved him into an empty mucous sack, and set him loose to float further up. He slammed his fists, covered in sludgy gore, against the bubble's walls while screaming in anguish at his interrupted rage. The image of bloody pyramids and forever dunes again filled his mind. A deep voice rumbled over the vast desert, but he could not make out the words.

He shook the horrifying impression from his mind. The surviving beasts returned to their business of waiting for more victims from below. Gustav shuddered as a wave of exhaustion ran through his body. He struggled to breath. He was quickly depleting the small amount of oxygen trapped with him in the bubble. Gustav tried to conserve what was left.

Another beast approached and slithered around the outside of his mucous bubble like a python preparing to wrap its prey. It paused and reached above its back with a few of its spindly legs and pulled out a mass of black dripping flesh from one of its pustule humps. The hump flap plopped shut after the mass cleared the opening. The creature slammed the mass into the side of the membrane. Two sets of circular teeth extruded from the wad of meat and chewed holes into the membrane. Gustav stared, horrified, yet ready to accept whatever new nightmare they were unleashing upon him. Instead the air became easier to breath and he felt it begin to circulate.

The beast attending to him fell away and returned to its normal duties as he floated up into the further reaches of Earth's atmosphere. He wondered what they had in store for him, but he didn't really want to think about it, and settled into a cross legged position on the floor of the mucous bubble. His breathing slowed as he watched the sun dip below the far curvature of the Earth.

He was starting to doze off when his bubble jostled. He'd bumped into a slower moving bubble filled with more severed heads. He wanted to quickly look away from the atrocities within, as he'd seen enough carnage for an eon of lifetimes within only the last few minutes, but was unable when he saw Taylor's angry face. All around her were other faces frozen in shock, unbelieving of what had happened to them. But hers was pure fury. Gustav wanted that fury to be directed at him. He wanted her final hatred to be of him.

His bubble slid by with a squeak like rubbing wet rubber balloons, causing it to vibrate at a frequency which made his teeth hurt and eyes wobble in their sockets. He watched as Taylor's bubble slipped further and further away and still felt her eyes glaring into him.

"I'm so sorry," he said before a tear fell to the membrane's floor. His tear fell to the floor, not the ceiling. He should have been on the ceiling of the bubble, but he sat on the bottom and his tears fell down. He wanted to feel joy at the revelation, but only felt sadness.

As he stared out the bottom of the bubble, Gustav expected to see the lights of cities spread across North America. The land was dark and there was no vast web of light. Hilldale and its surrounding science camps was the only glowing spec on the continent. Gustav scrambled back and forth across the floor of his bubble on hands and knees, squinting. Trying to see anything else. Where New York should shine like a beacon was nothing. Los Angeles, nothing. Seattle, nothing. Dallas, Miami, Mexico City. Nothing. It was all dark.

Gustav vomited the bile he'd swallowed while fighting the creatures. The mix of black sludge and stomach acid pooled in the center of his bubble as he stood and leaned his forehead against the outer wall near the breathing holes.

His bubble continued to rise and he looked up expecting to see stars, but instead found something blocking out the cosmos. Something which tickled at the switches holding Gustav's last bit of sanity in place.

Why didn't he attempt to escape with Jon when he had the chance? he thought as he stared into a colossal sky of flesh. Sunlight illuminated its hodgepodge surface of horrors. Tendrils, eyes, and mouths from the tiny to the monstrous, in all possible forms, crowded its surface. There were large yellow cat eyes the size of moons and rat tails larger than busses. There were fanged baboon mouths and perfect smiles filled with tombstone teeth. There were babies' arms that would rival Everest and octopus tentacles reaching and grabbing the floating mucous membranes.

Its appendages pulled the bubbles towards its many mouths and sucked them in like wet wads of jello. Gustav imagined a nauseating slurping that did not carry through the vacuum of space. He began to laugh, at first only a giggle, but then it grew to an uncontrollable guffaw with spittle flying from his teeth and tongue.

A miles long monkey's tail pulled his bubble toward a car salesman's grin. The gleaming teeth parted revealing blood-soaked dunes rolling into eternity. The image of Taylor's fury he held within mutated into a farce of three thousand Taylors manically laughing as the burning heat of a black sun called to him, inviting him to forever, and scorched the remainder of his sanity.

THE SOUL OF A NEW MACHINE

Jennifer Loring

Lilian Albunea had forecast the exploding mountains, beginning with the great Tambora in the Dutch East Indies; the fog that dimmed and reddened the sun; and the gray snows that persisted for three years. She had predicted the Legatus' ascension; he had brought order back to their world, dragged them from chaos when the crops failed and the livestock died beneath ceaseless dark skies. In gratitude, he housed her in a temple she remembered as a library and bestowed her with the title of the White Sybil. "There will arise a king," she told him. "He will be tall of stature, of handsome appearance with shining face, and well put together in all parts of his body."

A woman named Maria will rise, murmured the voice in her head. *He who will be born from her is the true God.*

But what god was made of metal and gears?

———

Not that the Legatus hadn't built and employed an army of copper men and women to do the menial tasks of running a city-state, and whose infernal tick-tock of their clockwork hearts invaded Lilian's mind even behind the library's stone walls. She already knew what he wanted when he visited her that morning. He strode in wearing his gleaming armor; the large, leaf-shaped blade of his *pugio* flashed at his side. Two centurions flanked him, as always, and guarded the door when he closed it behind him so that he and Lilian could speak alone. Only a few years ago, it would have been indecent to grant a man audience in her bedroom. How quickly worldwide starvation rendered the old social mores antiquated.

Lilian wore a white dress, classically draped and high-waisted, her arms and one breast bare. He'd had it made for her. The barber had shaved her head to rid her of lice. She reclined on her bed, her visions occurring most frequently while she rested—mainly out of sheer boredom. She ate little, lest digestion interfere. Sometimes, she dreamed of a faceless girl dying in the streets; the red-brown liquid running through her veins wasn't blood but laudanum. Her sister, or perhaps a friend. That she didn't know, couldn't remember, troubled her.

The Legatus genuflected and sat on the edge of Lilian's bed. Carmine sunlight glinted on the edges of his armor, embroidered the coverlet and her naked arm with bloody threads. "We have no influence beyond the city," he said. With so many deaths, he could not field an army large enough, not even with the addition of the clockwork men. Not enough people to build the numbers he required. He had conscripted nearly every man and woman over the age of thirteen as legionaries, but they were not enough for his fantasies of total conquest. "They are a threat to us."

She had witnessed the fates of those who resisted. For weeks afterward, those ghastly, broken bodies haunted her nightmares. It was for the good of the city, the Legatus assured her; how else would they restore order?

"You want the preacher. I have seen him in my dreams."

"Then you have seen what he has built."

The tall man with the shining face—shining because it was brass. The clockwork man who did not live or breathe, think or move. The preacher had not yet solved that problem.

Words flittered like moths in and out of her head. Half-recalled dream conversations, or snatches of real ones. But two words stuck in her mind, outshouting the rest: *human error.*

"I have," she said.

"Tell me, Sybil, what is its purpose?"

This information remained hidden from her. Some magic contained within the mechanical man, perhaps, lifeless though he was. "I do not know, Legatus."

He expected her to regardless. "Are you withholding something from me, Lilian?"

"You know I would not."

"You're trembling. You fear I will harm you if you don't tell me." His stare lingered on the rosebud tip of her breast, and he ran his tongue in a slow, prurient line across his lips as if he could taste her.

She turned one shoulder toward him. "The enemy of weakness need not be cruelty," she said softly.

"Have I been cruel to you?"

He had rescued her from a hard life, given her what passed for wealth and comfort now, and treasured her as he did no other. He wished to make love to her—this knowledge required no spiritual ability—but he would not violate what he believed divine. Or he would not allow himself to succumb to the power of a woman's body, understanding how easily she might manipulate him with the promise of her sex as a reward. An old story.

"Of course not."

"We will journey tomorrow morning into the countryside. They need to see you. You must convince them of our good intentions."

"And if they will not hear it?"

A shadow skimmed his face. "You know what we must do. We would wish them to submit peacefully. Fear, however, is a persuasive motivator. We will make examples where we must."

"You intend to execute Marshall and take the clockwork man. What will you do with such a thing?"

"You're the prophet." The Legatus smiled and rose to leave. "I'm sure you already know."

⬥

In the dull, red morning, cold though the perpetual snow had at last stopped falling several months ago, the Legatus arrived at the temple with his entourage and an enclosed carriage. The trains had stopped running just after the Cataclysm, the tracks harvested for wood to burn. The assemblage put on their double-canister, half-mask respirators—a requirement for even the shortest amount of time spent outdoors.

The *frumentarii*, who had gone ahead days ago on a scouting mission, sent word that the five-hundred-man *centuriae* should expect opposition and even violence from local warlords employing guerilla tactics. Neither this anticipated news, the respirators, nor his silent vow to protect her sanctity prevented the Legatus from dancing his fingers lightly along Lilian's arm to her naked breast, his explorations obscured by velvet curtains from the guards riding alongside the carriage. He was a man, after all, with a man's appetites. He had no wife she'd ever seen or he had spoken of.

Lilian stuck a finger between the curtains and peered outside as the carriage jolted along the broken asphalt, heralded by the *aquilifer* bearing the legion's standard, the *centuriae*, and six tribunes serving as the Legatus' high-ranking staff officers. A peaceful mission whose purpose was clear, more so if those resisting saw what bordered the road into the city.

A forest of Tau crosses, with small signs stating the crime nailed above the heads of the dead and dying, lined the highway. Right feet pressed over the left and a spike driven through the arches into the wood. Wrists bound by rope to the crosses' arms. Emaciated bodies sagging. Those still living struggled to push themselves up for a single breath. The women were turned away from the road so none could see their nudity but still look upon the evidence of their scourging with terror. Backs, buttocks, and legs reduced to raw ribbons of flesh where the *flagella* had ripped them apart. Insects had burrowed into eye sockets, ears and noses, and open wounds. Birds of prey had pecked at the lacerations and flown off with eyes, the tips of noses, earlobes—even nipples and penises. Beyond the crosses lay coalmines abandoned when the ash began to fall, their rusted, crimson-limned machinery huddled on the horizon like dead monsters. The remaining trees were blackened, naked, lifeless.

She did not oppose to the Legatus' attentions; truth be told, she craved them. Sybil or not, she was a woman, and a woman possessed appetites no less prodigious than a man's. While she gazed out the window, he discreetly gathered the folds of her plain white chiton until it pooled around her thigh and between her legs. He slid his large, rough hand over her skin. A finger, then two, into her. He did not look at her as he pretended that his cock, which he was ironically too timid to ask her to touch, was inside her instead. She didn't look at him as she relived a memory of someone else inside her.

Arrows and sling-launched missiles pelted the carriage and the *centuriae*. The copper men and women, unaffected by the projectiles, led the counterattack. As the Legatus leaped out of the coach with his shield over his head, Lilian flattened herself face down on the seat and covered her head with her arms.

"Trebuchet!" someone shouted. The horses whinnied and reared. The carriage rocked as if caught in an earthquake. She smelled something burning.

"Find their leaders!" the Legatus ordered. "Slaughter them! Take the rest as slaves!"

The carriage door opened again. Someone grabbed her arm, hand coarse from the toil of basic subsistence. She screamed.

"I mean you no harm," said a male voice muffled by a ventilator. "I've been waiting for you. Come with me. Please. Hurry!" A man with a mop of greasy brown curls peered at her through the door.

"No. No, I am here to deliver the Legatus' message of peace—"

"Peace? Why would he come with five hundred armed men if he intends peace?"

"Marshall, you must understand—"

"You do know me. Then what they say is true after all." He glanced over his shoulder. The clash of weapons and the heat of fire drew closer. "All the more urgent you come with me. Now!"

"How do I know you won't simply hold me hostage to get what you want? Or murder me?"

"You know I won't. You know why I need you. Please." He tugged on her arm like a child demanding a sweet. "Let me show you the face of God."

━━◆━━

They took advantage of the chaos to flee while the *centuriae* engaged guerillas in hand-to-hand combat, pushing them back toward a makeshift fortress that, judging from its ornate iron fence, had once been a manor house. Not Marshall's stronghold; it was too close to the city walls to be safe. They scurried like rats through a grid of narrow streets paved with shattered cobblestones and choked with the detritus of collapsed buildings and human waste, until they reached an imposing stone secondary school. An iron fence and gate fortified this as well. Lilian and Marshall passed through it and between the armed guards at the door, who nodded as they entered and whose eyes instantly drank in Lilian's exposed breast.

Respirators removed, she gratefully swallowed a draught of filtered air. "He'll know it was you who took me. And he will come."

"He'll lose many more. I expect he'll shortly be returning to the city to lick his wounds. He underestimates the resistance. The desire to be free." Marshall unlocked door after door, each one guarded. The last revealed a sort of laboratory—or more accurately, a workshop—lit by oil lamps, with gears, levers, and metal scraps of all sizes littering the tables and floors. Parchment scrawled with alchemical symbols, most prominently the *tria prima*, and an alembic also cluttered the table. Lilian's pulse quickened. A white bedsheet strung over a closet on the far end obscured its contents, but her mind's eye disclosed the shining face. The clockwork heart that did not tick.

Human error.

Marshall cast his gaze in that direction as well, and smiled. "All he needs is to be born. He needs a mother. Someone with your gifts."

"You're mad. It is an inanimate object. No one can give it life."

"You don't believe in your own abilities. Do you really think the Legatus chose you for your psychic visions alone? Spiritualists were a dime a dozen before the Cataclysm." Marshall smoothed the sheet in an almost loving manner. "No. It's because he intended to use you for the same purpose. To give the Everliving consciousness. Only he would have my son subjugate these people."

"Your son." A chill raced through her. "Then I am to be what—your wife?"

"Novi Maria to my Joseph. The mother of God, who calls Him into this eternal body to lead us into a new age. The age in which human and machine become one. *Novus homo.*"

Lilian backed toward the door. "No. I must go. I cannot help you."

Marshall snatched a rag from the table and polished a bizarre, free-standing suit of copper and iron, plates, and gemstones. "You're not the first to think me mad. If I told you I built all of this on the instructions of the dead, who encouraged me to carry out God's will, what would you say?"

"I would say you're unsound."

"But what if I'm right?"

"The delusional always believe they're right."

His smirk crawled across his face like a lizard seeking sunlight. "Indeed, they do. But is my 'delusion' much different than your claims to see the future?"

Lilian clenched her fists. No one had questioned her talents since her arrival at the temple. "I know what I see—"

"And I know what was revealed to me. Tell me, Lilian, what happened to Christ the first time He came to Earth? What happened to that fragile human body?"

Images of the Tau crosses and the tortured bodies upon them flashed through her mind. "He was scourged and crucified. He died."

"But promised He would return one day. And why would the Divine choose such a body again? Why, when I have built Him this indestructible form, would He not choose it for His Second Coming? The apocalypse has already happened. Now we await Him. He will create a new world, and we will have no need of light because He will shine upon us all."

With his shining metal face. Lilian tried to rub the chill bumps from her arms. "Supposing you did somehow grant this…thing…consciousness, how do you know whose it would be? What if it only pretends to be the Divine?"

"That"—Marshall folded his hands over his chest in a display of piety and flipped his gaze to the ceiling—"is where we must have faith."

"I want no part of this. Subjugating people under the banner of religion is little different than what the Legatus is doing."

"People can choose to follow the Everliving or not. I will not torture them or put them to death. Anyone here can come and go as they please. Their choice will not prevent the inevitable. To survive, we must evolve." Marshall swept his fingers over the suit. The lantern light reflected a rainbow from the gemstones onto his face, but no one had seen a real rainbow in years. In only a short time, Lilian had forgotten what even the stars looked like. "This is what I know will happen, Lilian. You return to the Legatus. Sooner rather than later, he will succumb to his desire for you. He will take you by force. But what use will you be then, a sacred vessel corrupted by a man?"

"Stop it," she whispered.

"He will cast you out. He cannot take you as his wife, because then he would have to admit that you were not divine after all. Or perhaps he will crucify you to send a message that even his beloved is not safe—"

Men would never know anything but manipulation and violence to get what they wanted. "All right! I will do as you ask!"

Marshall smiled again, but it was sad rather than victorious. "Your work shall be rewarded, Lilian. Come, now. Rest until tomorrow morning. Then we have much to do."

———◆———

Every part of the building bustled with activity in helping its occupants survive, down to the south-facing windows that maximized heat intake. Marshall showed her the water plant, where men and women—some of them copper too, only treated as actual people and not machine slaves—filtered collected rainwater through handkerchiefs, into large storage tanks. The water settled out impurities.

"We can even make tea," he said with pride. A simple but much-missed comfort that could sway any Englishman to his cause.

Food production consisted of honey traps to lure protein-rich ants; hunters dressing rats and pigeons to prepare them for smoking, salting, and dehydration; and the preservation of vegetables. Marshall's people defended the school against the various warlords who had once been police, politicians, gang leaders, and trained in the gymnasium using techniques familiar from their previous society: weapon use, unarmed combat, interrogation, and codes.

He saved the infirmary tour for last. Men, women, and children lay on piled quilts and blankets or woven straw on the cold stone floor. Lilian recognized scabies rashes, abscesses, and skin infections of stye and impetigo. But worse, some of the patients bore the thousand-yard stares of those not long for the world.

"We give them what we can to ease their suffering," Marshall said.

"Yes." Lilian passed between the rows of sick and dying. "Ginger for their stomachs. Tea infused with white willow bark to relieve pain and fevers. Garlic for the infections." There weren't enough of any of those remedies anymore, not without sunlight in which to grow. But metal bodies running on clockwork needed no such therapies…

She shook her head as tides of agony broke against her. "There is nothing anyone can do for them. It's up to fate now."

"I suppose you would believe in fate. Seeing the future means that future must be unchangeable."

"And you mean to tell me you believe in free will? The one your god claims to have given you, even though he threatens punishment if you don't do as he says?" Lilian dug her fists into her hips. "What sort of cruel joke is that?"

"What you know of my god"—Marshall took her arm and led her from the infirmary—"comes from a very old book written by very flawed men."

"God talks to you through the dead. I forgot." She yanked her arm away. "Don't touch me."

"I won't keep you here against your will, Lilian. But I pray you'll at least stay until tomorrow morning. Whatever happens afterward, you are free to go. Please." He held out his hand. "Let me show you to your room. I had a private space prepared for you."

No harm in staying the night. Where else would she go? To return to the Legatus consigned every one of these people to death or enslavement. She followed him up a flight of central stairs to the former classrooms. Marshall opened the first door and set to work lighting lanterns. The room faced a small garden fertilized with compost, in which grew only the hardiest roots and leafcrops. Against the dreary sky rose plumes of black smoke from those trying to stay warm by any means necessary. Sometimes they set entire buildings on fire for one night of warmth.

She thought of the Legatus. He would not discard her. He loved her, if something so frivolous still existed. And in her own way, she supposed she loved him.

"Make yourself comfortable," Marshall said. "Someone will be stationed outside if you need anything."

"Thank you," she muttered but did not look at him.

"You're not a prisoner, Lilian. Please don't think of yourself as such. You're free to go where you wish. I'll come back when dinner is ready."

The door closed. On the sleeping pallet, she found a utilitarian outfit of patchwork leather pants and a wool shirt, along with simple leather shoes. She put on the ill-fitting clothes and in the hallway nodded to her guard. Lilian returned to the lower level and peeked into one of the production rooms. A cluster of people knitted new clothes from yarn made of hair or patched them together from the serviceable scraps of old ones.

In another workshop, Marshall's "tinkerers," the people who attempted to improve efficiency and quality of life, created new machines and systems or bettered the existing ones. They also produced the clockwork humanoids.

Dinner took place at trestle tables in the cafeteria and consisted of smoked rat seasoned with onions and garlic, served with parsnip soup and steamed cabbage. The rats, at least, were faring well. Nearly half a meter long, fat with the meat of the dead. The circle of life.

Marshall directed her to the head of his table. "Brothers and sisters, please welcome Lilian to our home. She will be helping us in our experiment tomorrow morning."

"Welcome, Lilian," they said in chorus.

"You're the Legatus' prophet." A teenaged girl with matted blond hair and sallow, mottled skin sneered at her. "What future do you see for us?"

"Don't be rude." Marshall tried to force a smile, but it wouldn't take. "This isn't the carnival, and she's not a sideshow freak."

"I see nothing. I'm not under the proper conditions to do so." Lilian pushed her plate away. The cook had forgotten to cut off the rat's tail. "To be honest, this is more than I usually eat—"

"I can tell!" The girl uttered a cruel laugh. "You're a porcelain doll, thin and white, so fragile you might crack if we touch you. Is that how the Legatus keeps you?"

"Rachel, you're excused."

Her sharp, cold gaze pierced Marshall. This, Lilian thought, was one who would defect to the perceived comforts of the Legatus' city. Young and disillusioned. Sick and exhausted. "You're enamored of the Legatus' plaything, but she'll bring ruin. You watch."

"Good *night*, Rachel."

She shoved away from the table. A lantern tottered dangerously as she stormed out of the cafeteria.

"So you see," Marshall said, turning to Lilian, "I force nothing upon these people."

"Nothing but hope, when you can't promise them that, either. You've put all your faith into a mechanical man that doesn't even function."

"No, Lilian." He chewed thoughtfully on a piece of rat, frowned, and plucked a tiny bone from between his lips. He laid it on the edge of his chipped plate. "I've placed all my faith in you."

"I didn't ask for it."

"True, and I realize the difficult situation I've put you in. Betraying your benefactor. But if our experiment tomorrow works, you'll have anything you desire."

What she desired was the world as it had been, if not improved. One in which men realized that their endless games of aggression and conquest accomplished nothing. Perhaps one in which women were at last given the opportunity to prove their intelligence and capability. Peace, for the first time in human history.

No man, not even Marshall, would ever grant a woman such power.

———◆———

The rhythm of stomping feet as the colony danced to a violin's sweet melody rose through the floor. Afterward, natural silence smothered the countryside, a deeply unsettling sound for someone who had spent her entire life in the city. Used to hooves on cobblestone and the lilting voices of whores selling their wares, the mechanical hum of the factories that shut down only a few hours each night and the coal-fired locomotives bellowing as they clattered along the tracks.

Marshall entered the room when only the lantern beside her pallet remained lit and the wings of the school visible from her window had gone dark.

"What is the metal suit for?" Lilian asked.

"The spark will not come unless I show my willingness to become machine. To be as he is. Or will be." Marshall knelt beside her. "I must know what you see."

"Some questions are best left unanswered."

"I'm not afraid. The Legatus will kill me, won't he?" He stared across the room, unfocused. "But I'll die a martyr."

"Is that your endgame? Bask in your own glory as you rot upon the cross?" She curled her lip in disgust. "As your people are flogged nearly to death and left to rot alongside you?"

"I'll do what I must to guarantee the Everliving doesn't fall into his hands."

"Then you know what he intends. And either way, I'm the pawn. The one on whom its 'life' depends. The only difference is that he'll ensure its consciousness is anything but divinely inspired."

"You hate me, don't you? All of us." Marshall's shoulders bowed over his chest, and he clasped his hands in his lap.

"My so-called 'gift' has only given me unwanted attention. I could fight; I could scavenge. I did these things almost better than anyone.

Now I lie in a room, barely eating, never again to know how it feels…" The tips of her ears burning, Lilian caught herself. She flapped a hand toward the door. "Never mind. Good night."

"Very well." Marshall walked to the door but stopped before he opened it, his back to her. "I had a wife, before the Cataclysm. Had I been given the instructions before that, perhaps…" He shook his head and said, almost to himself, "Perhaps she would still be here."

"You would've transferred her consciousness to a robot."

"But then she, and others, told me it was meant for God, not for a mere human mind. I must try to save us, not pine away for her. And so here we are. Now you know everything you need to. I hope you'll trust me enough, one day, to tell me why you let the Legatus take you rather than doing what you really wanted."

She rolled onto her side and propped up on one elbow. "And what did I really want, Marshall?"

Not looking at her, he twisted the knob. "To die."

Lilian doused the light and stared into the shadows on the ceiling. She had been mostly successful at suppressing her urge to brood, but Marshall's words triggered a fresh bout of anxiety over the curious memory gap between the time she first saw the Legatus and her awakening in the temple. She thought instead of a young man with hair like Marshall's, only he was taller, stronger. Handsome like the Legatus, who knew the only thing more powerful than fear was adoration. She and the young man had paired for scavenging runs. After a time, they stole moments alone that had nothing to do with feeding and arming their colony. Fucking in the dark or in the ruins like animals because of the very real possibility that they could die at any moment.

He'd been gone for months when the Legatus found her. Conscripted, run off, or dead, she didn't know. The sight remained black where he was concerned, perhaps for her benefit. She never mentioned him to anyone. Might have forgotten if not for Marshall.

The robots' clockwork hearts ticked so loudly, she could hear them through the door. She pressed her fists to her eyes. Crying changed nothing, and she never wept for anyone.

Except tonight.

Marshall strapped himself into his peculiar metal suit with the assistance of two of his tinkerers. He then attached to Lilian's forehead a conductor that would feed information back to him. His colonists, lining the laboratory's walls, observed.

"Take this," he said softly, holding out a bottle of red elixir and a surgical scalpel. "I need you to prick your finger and place a drop of your blood in it."

Lilian backed away. "What is this?"

"The Great Work," he replied with no trace of jest. "The philosopher's stone. He will drink it, and be granted eternal life."

Impossible. No one had created the Magnum Opus in nearly six hundred years—and even then, Albertus Magnus had never actually confirmed he'd done so, either. Only the Flamels, their reputations as alchemists invented posthumously and barely more than a myth. "Your God complex has gone quite far enough, Marshall."

"God it is, yes, but not me. *Through* me. Do you still not believe what I told you?"

The stares from dozens of sets of eyes burned into her. "Very well," she murmured. She had no choice. She never had choices. Lilian set the bottle on the table, then pressed the blade against her fingertip. As blood welled up, she held her finger over the vial and let it drip. Another of Marshall's people bandaged her.

"Lilian, would you raise the curtain? Slowly, please."

Her throat burned. She grasped the sheet's edge and pushed it aside centimeter by centimeter. A gleaming arm. A hip. A leg. Marshall closed his eyes. He took small steps forward as though entranced.

A handsome, shining face. A body perfectly assembled and sculpted. Her face heated when her gaze fell upon its anatomically correct manhood. It reminded her of her baser instincts, no different from the need for food and shelter, which the Legatus had sought to erase when he declared her Sybil and thus too holy for human desires. But not for his hands.

She pretended to ignore the pleasant tickle in her belly and finished opening the curtain. Marshall stopped moving.

"Do you see it?" someone whispered loudly. People pointed to the empty space between him and the metal man.

"A cord! They're linked together!"

"Lilian, do you see it?"

A sharp, bright pain cut through the voices and through her abdomen. She clutched her stomach and dropped to the floor as cramps radiated from her belly to her back in excruciating waves. Dear God, the pressure was unbearable. She squeezed her eyes shut and pushed as if in labor to force out the pain. Something was crawling out of her. "What is happening to me?" she screamed, but Marshall didn't stir, and no one dared aid her. They stared, hands over mouths, as she expired from some sudden and violent ailment she'd failed to predict. She separated from her body and witnessed the proceedings from somewhere near the ceiling, which further persuaded her of her impending death.

But the colonists were right. An ethereal cord made of light, not the manufactured ectoplasm of many a would-be "Spiritualist," linked Marshall to his metallic creation. Father to son. But that link did not quicken the gears and gadgets inside the brass façade. That demanded a mother's touch.

At once, she understood her pain. She had soothed many others who endured the same agony. With this awareness, she tumbled back into her body, into the suffering that abated shortly thereafter. Marshall's head snapped back. His assistants helped free him of the suit. Lilian squirmed along the floor, seeking something with which to pull herself up. Her fingers encountered a brass foot. Five metal toes.

That wiggled.

She screamed and toppled backward. Gears whirred into life, and something began to tick, louder than all the others. The familiar rhythm of a clockwork heart.

"Mother," it said.

Every man, woman, and child in the room fell to their knees.

⸻

A full day elapsed. Lilian lay on her pallet at least that long, while people came in to change the cool rag on her forehead, encourage her to eat, or to empty the chamber pot. Marshall had the sense to stay away, until she opened her eyes to him sitting on the floor beside her, legs crossed like a child and brow furrowed.

"He's growing weaker. He asks for you."

She said nothing.

"I've given him the Great Work, but he needs his mother."

Lilian rolled toward the windows. A trick of the eye, perhaps, but for an instant she though she saw the moon's craggy face, a stranger for so many years now. "I am *not* that thing's mother."

"Please, Lilian. Go to him, even for a few minutes."

She scoffed. "Shouldn't a robot be self-sufficient?"

"Even God needed a mother."

She could imagine the patronizing smile on Marshall's face. "He's clockwork, is he not? Can't you just wind him?"

"Then he's nothing more than a toy. By the way…"

She turned back to him. The tone of his voice was cautious now; he feared he'd upset her further.

"We have a new arrival. He's eager to meet you."

"Tell him I'm ill and will entertain no visitors. Especially if he's seeking a prophecy."

One of Marshall's eyebrows edged up. "You can't anymore, can you?"

"I don't know what you mean," she lied, but it was true. Her visions had gone as dark as the day ash first congested the sky, as though his clockwork man had drained them from her. She was useless to the Legatus now. And once he discovered that…

He grants your wish.

"Lilian…"

"I will go to the metal man. I'll see this 'new arrival' of yours. And then I am leaving. Do you understand?"

"Of course." Marshall removed the rag from her forehead and assisted her to her feet. "He's this way."

━━◆━━

She didn't know why she expected the brass man to be lying down; why would such a thing need to? It stood by the windows that, like hers, overlooked the garden. He wore the same simple clothes as the rest of Marshall's people did.

"Already I am strengthened," it said.

Her knees trembled. She could hear it humming and clicking from across the room, such an unnatural sound. Yet its metallic surface seemed to soften before her eyes, to become more like skin.

"You are troubled, Lilian. By many things."

"You might say that."

"You don't revere me as they do." He faced her, his mouth pulling into an appealingly human smile. "This pleases me."

"You don't want to be worshipped? Aren't you supposed to be the Messiah?"

"I don't rightfully know. Perhaps it's simply too early for me to possess that knowledge."

"You don't know who you are?" Lilian scraped her hands over her bristly scalp. "Then Marshall doesn't know if he infused your body with the Divine, or if you were just some lost soul seeking a new home."

The Everliving stood with his shoulders back and chest thrust forward, hands clasped loosely behind his back. "In some ways, that makes me the perfect Messiah, don't you think? Knowing the frailty of the human body, having experienced its death... And now, in this, ready to lead you to your destiny."

"Marshall has programmed you well."

His laugh boomed. "Marshall, whatever you think of him, is no villain. He simply misunderstands many things."

"Such as?"

"Human nature. *My* nature." The brass man stepped closer, but Lilian held her ground. "Many people have gotten on just fine without a mother. Some of your greatest historical figures and literary heroes have been orphans."

Her stomach plummeted. Her heart rammed its way into her throat.

"But what is history without the tales of its greatest lovers?"

———◆———

His voice still rung in her ears as she scrambled down the central staircase. *It is not nurturing I need, Lilian; it isn't lullabies and chaste kisses on the forehead.*

It is love, physical love. I need what makes living things alive.

She snatched a respirator from a coatrack upon which half a dozen of them hung and flung open the doors to the garden. She must get away—from him, from the Legatus. Far away. Throw herself into the mountain if she must.

"Are you all right?" A man's voice, roughened by frequent shouting or the poor air quality, synthetic through the canisters.

"Leave me be."

"I cannot."

She glanced at the fence, which she could probably climb if necessary. Few ventured into the weed-choked alley beyond it for fear of cutthroats. She turned slowly, anticipating a blade, even a pistol. But it was only a man and, under the circumstances, an average human man should have relieved her.

Not this one.

Tears of rage boiled in her eyes. "Where have you been? You bastard!"

"You have every right—"

She kicked at him. "You left me behind to become the Legatus' pet freak!"

His body language obvious, he wanted to embrace her but did not move. If he touched her, she would shatter. "I wanted a better life for us. I didn't know he would… He wouldn't let his own men see you. Do you understand how awful it was, knowing you were in that temple and helpless to do anything about it because he kept you under lock and key?"

"Liar!" she shrieked, because love was fondest of cruel words. "Coward!"

"We can start again. He sent me here to get you and bring you back, but I won't. We'll go—"

"You fool," she whispered. "And you take me for one. You're either lying to me because he tortured and brainwashed you, or he knows our past and is using you as bait."

The bridge of his nose, all she could see of it beneath the leather ventilator mask, crinkled. "I'm the Primus Pilus now. He wouldn't—"

"He would. He'll do as he pleases. I imagine there are soldiers all around this building, waiting for you to emerge with me in tow."

"Yes," he conceded, contemplating the gray earth.

"Tell me what the plan was." Lilian balled her hands, the name poison on her lips. "William."

His blue eyes widened, and he struggled to invent whatever words would not anger her further. "Take you alive. Make an example of Marshall. Leave the metal man unharmed. Kill or enslave the rest."

"And then?"

"He would reprogram the robot. He only said he would deal with you himself, if you had betrayed him."

"Do you intend to return to him?" Lilian stabbed her finger at his face. "Tell me the truth, William. I know a liar when I see one."

"Now that I know you're all right," he said softly, "I'll go anywhere you wish. What must I do to earn your trust?"

She stared at the thick, leaden clouds hanging low in the sky, the sun's monstrous captors. "Kill them."

"I'm…sorry?"

"Kill your men. Give us a real chance to escape. And bring me proof."

William carved one hand through his hair. "I…Lilian…"

"That is the only way I'll trust you. I don't want to stay here, nor can I go back to the Legatus." Such emptiness, now that she had admitted it. Such keen understanding of her predicament that it physically hurt. "My visions are gone."

He laid his hand on her shoulder.

"Bring me the proof tonight." She wrenched away from him. "And don't let anyone know we're…acquainted." She looked to the second-floor windows.

A polished metal face glared down at her.

———◆———

Lilian skipped dinner and locked herself in her room. Marshall pounded on the door, insisted from the other side she tell him what was wrong and what the Everliving had discussed with her, until he gave up and went away.

In the deepest hours of night, a softer knock sounded. She peered through the small, square window and, after some internal debate, unlocked the door. She slid the latch into place behind him.

"They trusted me." William escorted her to the window. "And this is how I repaid them. The rest of the men won't act without their officers."

Four men in black clothes slumped over the top of the garden fence, their backs run through with spears.

"Are they dead or just pretending?"

"I had a feeling you wouldn't believe me." William pulled a rag-wrapped bundle from his pack and tossed it onto the floor.

Lilian plucked at the cloth and exposed a severed hand. She jumped back, her fingers pressed to her mouth.

"I have betrayed my men and the Legatus. Now there's a death sentence on my head. Are you sure you have no visions anymore? What will become of me?"

"They were never really visions." Holding her breath, she opened a window and lobbed the hand out, then shut it against the noxious air. "They were dreams, and people took from them what they wished, or I told them what I knew they wanted to hear. Even my dreams were never my own." Lilian gripped the windowsill as if she would topple out otherwise. Perhaps on purpose. "The Legatus. Marshall. That metal…thing. My only worth is in what I can do for others." Much, as she was reluctant to admit, like that metal thing.

"But you predicted the Cataclysm. Everyone knows—"

"I said, 'The skies will go dark for many days, and the darkness will cover everything it touches.'"

He quirked an eyebrow.

"A bad London fog, William. That's what I 'predicted,' because they happened all the time. We got what we needed out of my so-called prophecies, didn't we? Then the Cataclysm happened, and everyone thought that's what I meant. That's why the Legatus chose me."

William put his arms around her for the first time in countless months. He smelled of sweat, and the coppery scent of blood clung to his clothes. Such primal odors stirred in her those instincts the Legatus wanted her to feel for him and yet would not act upon. And William must have sensed them, because he crushed his mouth to hers, forcing her lips apart with his tongue. Her scalp and skin itched. Her blood screamed.

"Don't think of such things just now." He hauled her onto the pallet with him, his cock blossoming against her.

Until dawn flushed the iron sky, William filled her as she had dreamed of at least once a night since his disappearance. And she forgot, for a little while, that he had further complicated an already impossible knot.

⎯⎯◆⎯⎯

"What do you want from me?"

The rest of the colony, William included, was downstairs eating breakfast. The clockwork man paced his room but said nothing.

He knows what happened last night. He must. She was still throbbing with the primitive intensity of it. "With proper maintenance, there's no reason you cannot function. Unless you choose not to, now that you have consciousness. And the Great Work inside you."

"You want so badly, as I do, to believe we matter. To Marshall, I am the means by which he can fulfill his vision of eternal life. To the Legatus, I am a machine with which to rule all others." He stopped and faced her. "You are merely a machine to him, too."

Lilian averted her eyes. "How are you any different than the others? You would use me as well."

"No. I *need* you, Lilian. That is the difference."

She tilted her head, startled that so much of her animosity had bled away. "Who are you really? What have I helped Marshall do?"

"Not what he intended, but there is no harm in letting him believe. Not when I can do exactly as he wished. As aspirations go, his isn't so bad."

"You're changing every time I see you. You look more…real."

"It's the life you gave me. Your essence working through me." A smile flitted over his lips. "Living machines, able to replicate. A new species, capable of surviving anything. It has already begun." He scrutinized her with such fascination that she felt naked. "He was very clever, cleverer than people think. A true alchemist."

Shots reverberated from downstairs. Lilian gasped and spun around as footsteps thumped up the stairs. William appeared in the doorway. "We must go." He flicked his gaze to the metal man. "You. Come with us. We cannot save Marshall."

"What are you talking about? William—"

He yanked her arm, pulling her into the hall.

Dozens of soldiers flooded into the main entry. So many broken bodies littered the floor in a tarn of cooling blood. How odd that not a single soldier, despite William's alleged crimes, turned their swords upon him. Lilian glanced over her shoulder at the Everliving. The amber gems inserted into his eye sockets silently expressed all-too-human anger.

"You planted those bodies. They were Marshall's people. You and your men murdered them in cold blood."

"I can't sacrifice everything I've worked for. I do love you, Lilian."

She cursed her stupidity. *Human error.* "I don't want to hear anything else."

"I'm sorry," he muttered but didn't loosen his grip. William thrust a respirator into her hands and led her into the front yard.

Marshall had been stripped, his hands tied to a post. Two soldiers bearing *flagella* with iron balls attached to braided leather thongs stood on either side of him. "You are obsolete!" he shouted.

The first *flagellum* anointed his back, leaving a deep contusion. He clenched his teeth but did not cry out. The second soldier took his turn. Beside Lilian, the Everliving tightened his jaw. He said nothing.

Blood seeped from the veins just below Marshall's skin, spurting as bruises broke open like rotten fruit and vessels in his muscles ruptured. Iron lashed his back, legs, and buttocks, splitting his tattered flesh until he was awash in crimson. His knees gave out.

"Please stop this," Lilian whispered.

"I can't save him. But this will never happen again." The metal man grasped her hand, his fingers startling in their similarity to hers. "Do you trust me?"

"I have no one left to trust."

One soldier hurled Marshall to the ground and balanced a crossbar on his shoulders before tying his outstretched arms to it. The other flipped him over, positioned a six-inch rail spike in the center of his wrist, and drove it in with a hammer. More blood spewed forth. They repeated the process on Marshall's other wrist then raised him onto the short cross before nailing his feet into place. Marshall abandoned his stoic pretense and screamed as his wounded back scraped over the stipes, coating them in red. His fingers froze into claws. His feet strained against the spikes and he shrieked again, forfeiting precious air on the altar of pain.

"Why are you making me watch this?" Lilian demanded.

William glared down at her, his eyes as flat as graphite. "You went with him willingly, did you not?"

"We were under attack. Was I to sit in that carriage until it caught fire or someone killed me? Isn't it your job to protect me? *Primus Pilus*," she spat.

His face darkened. A vein in his neck ticked as though an insect were trying to burrow out of it. "The Legatus decimated us as punishment for losing you. Would you see me tortured or executed?"

Soldiers shoved Marshall's closest associates into tunics doused with naphtha and lit them. People who had worked so hard to survive and to ensure others' survival now flailed manically, almost comically, across the yard like human torches. A burning ballet. The stench built layer upon layer: frying beef and greasy pork, with the mineral nuance of blood. Scorched liver. A sweet, pungent musk. Then, finally, the sulfurous stink of burning hair.

"Now? Yes, I would."

William bowed his head.

"You left me behind. You lied to me and betrayed me. I don't know who the man I loved really was, or is. Perhaps he was just another dream."

The clockwork man still clutched her hand as he witnessed his father's exquisitely harrowing death. No one else would have recognized the rage sparking in his gemstone eyes nor found any trace of emotion at all. But Lilian knew what to seek.

She was his mother. Or his lover?

A chill ripped through her like a spike of ice. The Everliving did not return her gaze but tightened his fingers around hers.

"This…thing." The Primus Pilus— "William" was dead, if he ever existed at all—narrowed his eyes at the mechanical man. "He'll do as you say?"

"I could have him tear you to pieces right now if I liked."

His stare transformed into something more malevolent. "We lost a hundred soldiers in the battle. Forty more in decimation. That's still three hundred sixty to two. Do those sound like good odds to you?"

Lilian scratched her wrist beneath the itchy, woolen shirt until her skin was as bright red as the molten liquid that had shot out of Tambora. Out of Marshall. Her fingers wandered to her scalp and rubbed the stubble. She encountered a thin scar above her forehead but couldn't remember how she'd gotten it. "You don't love me. There is no point in loving me. The Legatus won't let you have me, even if he rejects me. So tell me again why you chose this path, and try harder to make it believable."

Charred corpses smoldered in the yard. Her stinging eyes watered.

"Out there," she said, "you have underestimated them. You've forgotten, but I haven't, because I dream of them. They see you—him—flaunting what you have. They're desperate and hungry."

The pleasure slaves, along with valuable assets like the tinkerers and any goods the soldiers could carry, were loaded into wagons. Her captor sank his fingers into her arm.

"Come. I would prefer not to bind you."

"He's forgotten how his beloved empire fell. And why. They will come. They will scurry over the walls like the rats they're forced to eat."

"Get in the carriage."

"The barbarians were betrayed, as these people are every day. Why should they think you have their best interests at heart after what you've done here?"

"They can believe what they wish. As can you." The Primus Pilus shut the door. Lilian watched through the window as he kicked the Everliving's shin and scoffed before summoning several soldiers. "Find someone who can reprogram him. In the meantime, do not let him out of your sight."

"You are obsolete," she murmured. "The Legatus clings to a world doomed from the start."

"You can tell him yourself. No doubt he longs for your…insight, such as it is." He slapped the side of the carriage. "Go. I'll ride right behind"

⬥

Her former lover marched her into the old town hall, where slaves buffed the floors and dusted furniture, and in hidden rooms attended to the Legatus' tribunes with any physical desires they demanded satisfied after a job well done. The Legatus sat in the main room on an elaborately carved wooden chair bearing a red cushion. A complement of guards stood immobile in even lines along the walls. He had set aside his helmet, but the scarlet cloak fastened at one shoulder and matching waistband tied in a bow over his armor denoted his rank.

He viewed the dancing slaves with disinterest, having never been one for petty amusements. He craved action. Problems to solve. People to subjugate. What had he been before, Lilian wondered. A policeman? A politician. Someone suffering a kind of moral insanity, that he would aspire to emperor and let it so thoroughly subsume the rest of his personality.

Or a good man, who with the best of intentions had sought to fill the power vacuum only for that authority to feed on him, parasitic, leaving behind someone even he no longer recognized. The memory of law and order crooned in his ear, but its words had become as warped as a game of Chinese whispers.

He directed his attention to Lilian, and smirked. "Thank you, Primus."

"The metal man will be brought shortly." The stone-faced Primus assumed his position at his commander's right side. He stared at Lilian until she made eye contact, then darted his gaze away.

"I'm glad you've returned, Lilian."

"As if I had a choice." She folded her arms and glowered at the Legatus.

"Was that freedom to you? Constant warfare and insecurity. Poverty and disease. Scavenging for life's basic necessities." He rested his chin in his hand, his tone even and supercilious, as if imparting a lesson to a child.

"Answering to no one but themselves."

"I ask only for loyalty, and to perform a few tasks to earn one's keep."

"Conscription? Slavery? Prostitution?" She winced at the forceful echo of her voice.

"Food. Shelter. Protection." A sinister tenebrosity resided beneath his expression. "Do not pretend you were any freer with them than you are with me. The preacher only wanted you to take care of his creation. I will, of course, need you to shut it down so I can have it reprogrammed."

"I cannot. He's imbued with consciousness; I can no more 'shut it down' than I can a human being."

"Interesting." The Legatus uncrossed his legs and leaned forward. Lilian glimpsed his leather loincloth and the fine, dark curls on his muscular thighs. "Tell me, Lilian, you had no intention of coming back, did you? You wouldn't have been so quick to sleep with the Primus Pilus otherwise."

Color bled from the Primus' face as if from a fatal injury. Lilian's voice clicked dryly in the back of her throat.

"I understand now why he was so eager to earn those promotions and become my trusted advisor."

"Legatus, I—"

He lifted a hand to silence him. "Your betrayal will be dealt with appropriately. And you… If you are no longer my Sacred Virgin, what am I to do with you?"

"I wasn't a virgin when you found me. I haven't been for many years. William and I…knew each other before. Before you came. He used that to gain my trust."

The Legatus shifted in his chair again as though he could not wait to escape its confines and perhaps the burden of his decisions. "Is this true, Primus? Is *she* the one who betrayed me?"

"It is so, Legatus." The Primus' lips twitched with the unspoken words behind them trapped like birds inside his mouth.

"How disappointing. Well. It appears I have a great deal of thinking to do. Primus, please escort Lilian to her quarters so she can thoroughly understand what she has given up."

"*Ave*, Legatus." With a curt wave, he bade Lilian to follow him.

Ashen air permeated her lungs despite the ventilator. Ashes from burning buildings, from burning people, all fuel for the dreams others plundered from her as prophecies. She was a great wound in the earth, excavated until her resources were exhausted. "Is he going to have me killed?"

"No," The Primus yanked her toward the neoclassical building.

"Then I will be his slave."

"No." He saluted the guards stationed at the entrance and the pair outside her quarters. Once inside, he wrenched off his respirator and gestured to the bed. She chose to remain standing. "You have no reason to trust me, but all of this—including the more…unfortunate parts— has been to secure your freedom from him. *Our* freedom."

Lilian bit her lip and twisted away from him. "Our time has passed."

"I love you, Lilian."

"You must." She laughed bitterly. "Only a fool would devise such a Byzantine scheme to deceive a man like the Legatus, and so carelessly throw away the lives of others. Only love is so selfish."

"We can get away before dawn. I'll come back for you when it's time." He stood behind her with his hands on her shoulders and kissed the back of her neck. "I've done what I had to," he whispered. "But always for a future with you."

Lilian fixed her eyes on the silent square beyond the window. If she looked at him, she'd believe him, and she could no longer afford to be so imprudent with her emotions. She was not the Sybil, soft and sighing with the weight of other people's expectations, nor was she some battle-hardened soldier scarred inside and out. Where did she fit into the Legatus' world now? Or the one beyond the walls, from which he'd shielded her for so long and so methodically she had almost forgotten it. The daily struggle to survive was perhaps another form of slavery after all.

"A few hours," William said, his whisper laced with longing. "Be ready."

Lilian observed from the window as he hurried back toward the barracks or the town hall; she lost him in the darkness. Prostitutes lurked in the spaces between gaslights, enticing potential customers with a wave of a pale arm or the nod of a head topped with an extravagant wig. Girls, really, still growing into newly rounded breasts and hips, their identities muted by makeup and laudanum. Names erased and new ones bestowed. The prettiest, most popular whores were ensconced within brothels and did not have to earn their keep behind gasmasks. How dare he speak of freedom?

Was there a rest of the world into which to escape? Or nothing more than thousands of fractured city-states run by men and women with the Legatus' same delusions.

She sank to the bed but did not undress or sleep. The sky was black, starless, as though the universe had disowned this unfortunate planet. But then, that had been typical before the Cataclysm, too. Men carrying torches to warn others of their approach as the fogs drifted down and coated the world with their stinking coal soot.

The clock tower above Town Hall tolled the hour, and she counted each sonorous chime as it pealed across the barren square. She watched for William. He did not come.

It was just as well. This world offered no domicile for love, when every waking moment must be devoted to scavenging or building, reinforcing or fighting. The poison air had damaged everyone's reproductive capabilities. Almost no children were born anymore. They scavenged and built, reinforced and fought, conquered and enslaved for a future that did not exist. And what a sudden, terrible sense the Everliving made now, as they stood on the precipice of extinction.

When the door opened, when the sky behind the coagulated clouds was still the color of grease and concealing the neglected stars, it was not William who stood there but the Everliving.

Lilian peered around him into the corridor. "Where are the guards?"

"I dispatched them as necessary."

"And William?"

"They've taken him. Now is our opportunity to escape."

"'Taken him'? What do you mean?"

The face that seemed to her earlier to be transmuting into a more human façade went robotic again. "He is lost. We must go, Lilian."

"No. I won't leave him." *So I do believe what he said. I believe all of this will be different one day.* "The Legatus will hunt us—both of us," she continued. "I know him."

"William cannot help us in our quest. He is purely biological."

"So am I."

He slid his gaze away. He had become as bad at deception as any human.

"What do you intend to do with me?"

"We haven't time, Lilian; we must—"

She twisted her arm away and rubbed her wrist. "I will go nowhere with you until I know."

"If you hope to save him, then we must go now." He was learning quickly. Adapting. Reading her emotions and deciphering what she needed of him without explicit instruction. "They've taken him to the wall, so he can serve as a warning."

Lilian fastened her respirator into place and pushed past him. The guards slouched against the wall as though they'd fallen asleep on the job. Whatever method the Everliving employed, it had been quick and bloodless. Same with the guards outside. Lilian nicked one of their swords. She stormed through the square, the clockwork man at her heels, until she reached the edge of the city and the massive stone wall.

William hung naked from a Tau cross, his lean and sinewy body smeared with stripes of blood, his quivering thighs gleaming in the gas lamps' light with what stank of urine.

"Let him down!" Lilian cried. "Let him down, and I'll do as you wish." Her heart was chipping off in little pieces. Flaking like a burning body. His pain, his vulnerability, infected her with the memories of what once was.

"No," he croaked. "Is this the proof you need? I have always loved you."

Tears streamed down her cheeks, puddled at the edge of her mask, then seeped beneath it. "*Do* something," she said to the Everliving, but the Legatus was striding toward them, his eyes crinkled at the corners.

"Ah, the clockwork man. Did he give you a proper name? Did she? Did they not care enough to grant you an identity?"

"I have one, with or without a human name."

"His god, when all others have deserted us. Tell me, are you God?" The Legatus jabbed a finger into the metal man's chest. "Because to me, you look and feel no different from Lilian. His wondrous creation, his marriage of science and spirit, the very same thing I had made myself." Lamp flames flickered in the dark pools of his eyes. A good man in another life, the kind of man evil most loved to defile in order to prove its might.

Lilian tightened her grip on the sword hilt.

"Listen to your heart, Lilian. Listen how it…ticks."

The sound she had tried to shut out was now the only one she heard. Her heartbeat, but not the dull thump of muscle. Not what she had listened to with her head on William's chest. The noise she had attributed to others permeated her ears. She could not hear the rush of blood through her veins that indicated a pulse.

"You swallowed so much laudanum. A suicide, except when I found you, you were having second thoughts. Afraid to die. And you did, in my arms."

"You're mad!" Lilian nudged the sword into the dip of the Legatus' collarbone. His skin dimpled, and she drew a bead of blood.

"My people—my 'tinkerers,' if you will, gave you a new heart. A new mind, after we salvaged what we could. Your own name was lost to you. So you do, in fact, owe me your life."

And what did I really want, Marshall?

To die.

"Marshall knew."

"The same microscopic machines preventing your body from breaking down are the ones he needed you to transfer to his creation. They have dissected the metals and recoated him in synthetic skin."

"He had the Great Work!"

"Once he had you, yes." The Legatus closed one hand around the blade. "He stole that from me as well."

William groaned and writhed, attempted to fill his collapsing bellows with air. Lilian hoped for one terrible second his suffering deafened him to the Legatus' words, if he didn't know.

He must. He has never called me by another name.

The Legatus tinkered with his memories as well. But not the ones that truly mattered.

And if he knew, he had loved her anyway, though death had parted them once already.

"Go ahead," the Legatus said. "It will change nothing."

Lilian plunged the sword into his throat. He peeled away his ventilator and offered a gruesome, red-toothed grin. "Mary," he gurgled. Gloating, even now, at the power he wielded over her.

Blood drowned any words left, and the light in his eyes faded. He collapsed to the ground as soon as she extracted the blade. None of the *centuriae* had as much as unsheathed their weapons. They stared at the Everliving, whose skin rippled. His jewel eyes glowed brighter than all the lamps combined.

"A woman named Maria will rise," one of the soldiers said. "He who will be born from her is the true God."

The soldiers fell to their knees in veneration.

"Do you see?" the Everliving asked.

She did—true visions this time. Genuine prophecy. But she did not speak of the mechanical cities rising into the sky, of the way the air composition was altered to prevent oxidation—and which prevented humans from breathing without assistance. What mankind created was subject to its flaws. The price of its arrogance, its insistence on evolving without nature's guidance.

"Yes," she said. She shed the ventilator the Legatus had let her believe she needed and walked to the Tau cross. Even if she cut him down, William would not live.

He gasped, sagged, and she touched his ankle where the nail had gone in. She was glad he'd see no more of this world or of her.

"Did you…love me?" he rasped.

That the Legatus had recovered those memories was perhaps a punishment of her own, but they connected her to a humanity she'd assumed had been hers all along. To Mary, who had loved William dearly when love had mostly fled the world.

"I want mercy for you." She thrust the sword upward, just under his ribcage. His blood spattered her face like hot tears.

William deflated against the wood, but his tiny, soothed smile broke her heart all over again.

"I did it because of you." She wiped tears, blood, across her face. "I thought you were dead. Or at least, never coming back. I swallowed the laudanum. Without love, what point is there?"

"It doesn't have to end with him."

She spun around. The sword dropped from her hand.

"We can make the world as you wish it to be. If you think, in time, you could love me."

"I'm not human. Not anymore." She gazed at William's motionless form. Such human tears, though. Stopping up her throat and her nose, pounding behind her eyes and between them, and splashing her cheeks.

The Everliving held out his hand. "In time," he said.

Objectives did not matter. She saw the dark skies, the underground colonies, the world above mephitic and clacking like a giant, mechanized beetle. The human experiment had failed. The age of the machine had dawned.

Lilian curled her fingers around his. Mother and son, or husband and wife. Their clockwork hearts hummed and ticked synchronously with the desire to spread their gospel, carried in the tiny machines capable of replicating the world in their image.

ROUGH BEAST, SLOUCHING

Randee Dawn

Here's what I know is true:

There's things in life we're meant to do. Things that ain't getting done right without the right one of us doing them. You latch onto that thing you're supposed to do, figure out how it works and it'll purr on you like a cat or an engine. Me, I do that same thing? I'm gonna screw it up. 'Cause if you're doing something you really ain't picked out to be doing, you're not just wasting people's time. You're upsetting the balance.

"*An dtuigeann tú?*" Ma used to say. *You understand?*

Yeah, Ma, now I do.

"Be my entertainment, Nevada," Scott said to me, dragging a bar stool over. His hand came up covered in someone's old gum and an unclassifiable substance. "I even came out to this shithole to ask nicely."

He'd tracked me down to the Four Clover, the Mick dive where I'd been living my nights since Ma died. Needed a place to go after she kicked, and home wasn't it. When she was still breathing—if you want to call it that—I'd held the job just fine, writing hack journalism by day for a paper most folks use to line their bird cages; then at night I'd be down at the hospital ward with her hacking until the morph took over.

With Ma gone, I had a lot of free night hours. I was using 'em to drink.

"Bartender, give this guy a medal," I grumbled. I was used to my Clover routine: Stare at the same thick saggy faces and have the same tired arguments with the regulars about how the union was screwing us over, then blink at my goopy drink like it was a Magic-8 Ball until things got blurry. It was like taking a trip into my future: previews every night, starting at 5:30.

The Clover was completely not Scott's scene. Milk-fed suburbs-raised kid, former intern at my paper, doing rock band reviews at the artsy-fartsy entertainment rag these days. He glad-hands names I only read on album liner notes. I'm a relic—I not only have albums, I play 'em. Scott lives 'em.

"Look," he said. "I got one band to cover on a five-show lineup. Those opening acts are gonna suck hard. Be my plus one."

Good man, Scott. He'd come to the funeral and paid respects to my Ma, who he never met, and now it seemed he was making me his latest project. It was easy to sit in the Clover and think about the way cancer played rough with Ma late in the game, sucking the life right outta her like a parasite that never got full, and me with a front row ticket to the shitshow.

"Drinking's more my style these days," I told him. "I like this place."

"Yeah," he sneered. "You call it a Mick bar, you like it so much. Which is like me calling a deli a hymie diner."

I chuckled. Fact is, I like places that are… squelchy. I like 'em dark. The underneath of this world is true and real and never lets you down.

"Anyway," he added. "Since I'm press, we get an open bar."

That perked me up. I do have a way of getting lucky sometimes. Right place, right time.

"Not everybody's *ádhúil* like you, Nevada Sullivan. Not everybody knows their place in this world." That's what Ma would say, talking about luck while taking a huge hit off of her cancer stick. I'd sneaked a few in the ward in those last days, what the hell, she was walking dead already. I still picture her sending the smoke outta one corner of her mouth, a dragon with sass.

"Lost souls go wandering," she'd say, sometimes in her clunky musical Irish, sometimes in English. "They won't hurt you. You can care for 'em. But others, *fiagaí dorcha*. Dark hunters. They put a pin in your soul, you stand too close."

In the end, they cut off Ma's morph and she spent those last days going out hard. Not even fifty years old. Something seriously out of balance. Nobody should have to know what the one person who loves you most in the world looks like when they pull into the final terminal of life's railway station. Nobody deserves that exit.

"So?" Scott pestered. "Do I gotta get down on a knee and propose?"

———•———

We went, of course. Friends only. Scott's not my type, if you get the drift. Truth is I ain't pretty so the girls look past me, and boys don't interest me and a long time ago I stopped pressing my nose on that glass. Got used to Status and Quo as constant companions. But I said I'd go with Scott for shits and giggles and because a gal can get a little too wrapped up in her own head.

We met at this dive in Central Square that's half hummus dispensary, half live venue called The Middle East. One of the bands that night was doing a livestream for YouTube or some such shit and to say the place was crowded was like saying the Charles River smelled a little funky. It was like every yahoo in the world had come to the show and crammed themselves up front so they could slam into one another.

To please Scott, I stood there curmudgeoning the night away. Nit-picked the amateur songs and actively booed a Peter Frampton cover, negged the ugly haircuts, harped on the watery free beer, snickered at the violent "dancers" up front. They were doing something called mushing, I think Scott called it.

Then kids started filtering back from the scrum near the stage and looked at me with black eyes and dripping bloody noses and dislocated fingers and wide, insane grins. Reminded me of Ma on the morph drip, and my tough girl attitude went to crumbs.

"Claustrophobia alert," I yelled in Scott's direction so I didn't bust out crying and pushed my way to the first clear space I could find. Scott chased me down and next thing I knew we were in a roped-off, saner area in another part of the room and he was passing over another cold, nameless concoction. I put it up to my face.

"Better?"

"Yeah," I mumbled and squared my shoulders.

The view improved considerable in the VIP space; all the crazed fans were far away, looking like a hair carpet waving while the bands ground through bad blues and stumbled over simple rock chords. Then I turned around and the view got even better: I clocked this chick lounging on a moth-eaten formerly velvet sofa, one long leg bent over the other, foot bouncing. Ponytails held up some bright blonde hair and barrettes restrained the loose ends.

Scott caught me ogling. "Kat," he said. "This here's Nevada. Kat's on in a few but… maybe you two might connect."

My mouth went all dry and I pulled out a lollipop I always carry from my pocket. Looked at it, then handed it to her. Scott nearly had hysterics.

Kat unwrapped it right there, gave it a good old swirl with her pink little tongue, then tilted her head and handed it back. "Hold this for me?" she asked, kicking herself to her feet and picking up a nearby guitar.

I was sold.

"This here's Jordan," Scott gestured at a beefy, bearded guy with a bushy mane of dark hair. "Singer. Writes songs, too."

Jordan held out a meaty paw and I took it, liking him right away 'cause of his grip. Can't tell you how many guys I wanna slap upside the head for giving a gal one of those "I might break you" softies.

"Nevada!" I said, tapping my chest with the bottle.

"Heh. I shot a guy in Reno!" he chuckled at me.

"Just to see him cry," I grinned back, misquoting on purpose. You got no idea how many folks make some kind of Las Vegas joke when they meet me. I gave him points for originality.

A minute later Kat and Jordan were waving "bye" as they picked their way to the backstage. But then Jordan cut to one side, beelining to the equipment storage near the stage. A woman was sitting there, hiked up on a packing case, hands caught behind her like she was hiding a surprise.

He halted hard in front of her and they made googly eyes. Hell, I probably would too—even at this distance I could see she was a grabber, long black hair shining like asphalt after the rain. She had on a white shirt that billowed out over a wide black leather belt, her lower half encased in shimmery leather pants. She wrapped those long legs round Jordan's waist like they were the only two in the room. She was so petite, almost childlike next to his bulk.

Then she turned from Jordan, who had leaned in for a smooch, and eyeballed me. No expression on her face but those eyes—even at twenty paces they made me twitch. That intense gaze was like a long needle slowly piercing the pleasure center of my brain, only it didn't make me feel good. It made me feel tired.

She turned back and gave Jordan what he was puckering up for.

"They're up next," said Scott and I jumped. I'd forgot he was even there. "Who?"

"Blue Pooka," he said. "Kat and Jordan's band."

Worst goddamned name ever, I thought. Made me think of shell bracelets.

He pointed with his pencil as an announcer took the stage and the crowd exploded. "They've got hell of a lot of buzz," he yelled. "Gonna be *huge*."

Next to me the soundman flashed a light and darkness swallowed the room. Scott pushed past me to get a closer look and I was alone in the VIP section.

A spotlight lit up the announcer. "You know why we're here," he said by way of introduction.

"Free beer!" shouted some wit.

He ignored the funnyman. "We're making a video tonight, so everybody act like this is the biggest damn concert of your life. Act like Elvis just took the stage."

"That would be unpleasant," a firm, insinuating voice next to me purred.

Not Kat. Definitely not Scott. My mouth went dry again and I wondered what happened to Kat's lollipop. Finally I slid a glance to the side.

It was the woman from the other side of the room, the one playing tonsil hockey with Jordan just a few seconds ago. She stood next to me, arms gently folded, hip cocked to one side. I wasn't sure if the laws of physics permitted her to get across the room as fast as she had, but I wouldn't argue with facts.

"Unpleasant?" I croaked.

"Well," she said in a clear, lilting voice. "If Mr. Elvis Aaron Presley were here, don't you suppose he'd be in a rather rotten state? Even a fat man like him couldn't last long after forty years underground."

"How the hell did you get—" I began.

"I go where I like," she said, smiling up at me and that needle reappeared in my brain, a soft sliding invasion. When she blinked, I got an up-close look at those unsettling eyes. An earthy, pulsing green. Like moss, or fungus. Something that grows over dead things and consumes them.

"Greetings, Nevada Sullivan," she continued.

"How—" I stuttered again.

"You may call me Sheerie," she said, a name that reminded me of gauzy things, and nodded. "Now hush."

Lights blasted full onstage as the drums crashed everyone awake. In the sudden bright stood Kat and their drummer and bassist—but no Jordan. I eyeballed where he'd been a second earlier and there he was, scoping the area like he'd lost something.

Next to me that something waved a tiny white hand and twiddled her fingers to the right. He stopped turning 'round and made a gigantic leap, achieving the stage faster than I imagined a guy his size could move. He gripped the mic like it was a lifeline and the song kicked into gear.

Sheerie sighed with pleasure.

Now, when it comes to music there's what I like and there's what the rest of the world coughs up a hundred bucks to see. But this band, the one with the worst goddamned name ever, killed me. Blue Pooka weren't just good. It was like somebody took all the music I ever loved in my life and made me see that it was just crayon scratches. This was above all that, pure in the ears, straight out the heart type sounds. I was in that moment with that music. Some of it was heart-tearing bluesy, some of it swampy Southern rock, and somewhere buried in there was a powerful heart that made me think of the biggest, meatiest 60s Brit bands.

And while a lot of it was about how great those songs were, it was Jordan, too. He was this dervish of a frontman, whipsawin' this way and that, haulin' us all along for the ride through a forest of shiny knives.

Kat more than held her own, wielding that axe like she meant to show it who was boss, doing everything she could to keep up with Jordan. She ripped into her guitar and flipped those ponytails around and squeezed her eyes so tight her sweat looked like tears. They were a fantastic team, but there was no question of who was in charge. Kat was good. But Jordan had the "it" everybody always talked about.

Two songs in, I started feeling… off. The needle in my brain was turning me to jelly inside. Had to be the crappy free beer. I was scoping out the closest exit sign when a small hand slipped into mine and locked me in place.

All at once the music was inside me. It went looking for all my soft places and found them and pressed hard until I felt a funny flip all the way downtown. In my good spot. I froze up, then tried to relax into it. That was some kick-ass music.

But as the song went on the sensation coiled up in me and there was no release. I loved it and hated it. Wanted more and had to throw it off of me. This wasn't right. This was bad idea jeans.

I thought of Ma. And of morphine drips that come after the screaming agony. I let go of it all and the hand slipped from mine.

Sheerie looked up at me, a half smile on her lips. "Thank you," she said. "That was just enough."

I bolted for the back entrance and vomited in the alley.

———◆———

Outside it was cool and April and quiet. I could think again. Gulped the last dregs of my beer and spat them out to clear my mouth. Smoothed down those big fat black curls on my head, wiped my face and rested my cheek on the chilly brick wall and realized I was stone sober.

Inside, the music swirled on and on, muffled greatness. My head whirled and I stood there a good long while. Long enough for the music to finish and I figured I was safe and could probably go back inside, find Scott.

The back door clanged open and out tumbled most of Blue Pooka—drummer, bassist… and a welcome pair of ponytails. No Jordan, though.

An unlit cigarette dangled from Kat's rosy lips, and her skin was shiny with sweat. Two high pink spots stood out on her cheeks and she looked even more like a doll than she had twenty minutes earlier.

Her eyes went right to mine.

"We meet again," she said.

I gave her a small wave.

She handed the cigarette back to the drummer. "Believe you were holdin' something for me, Nevada."

"Lost it."

"Nah," she said, and reached across my arm. There was a little tearing noise and the lollipop—which had stuck to the arm of my leather jacket—came straight off. "Thanks," she said, inspected it, then took it into her mouth again.

"Some show," I said finally.

"Puke-worthy, I hear," she said.

Well, that was it. So much for ponytail girls. "Bad beer," I mumbled.

She looked me over. Mouth went side to side, teeth crackling against the candy. She looked over her shoulder. "Hey, Jeremy," she called and the drummer perked up. "Pack up for me tonight, willya?"

I felt like looking around. Somebody was playing a joke on me. Between Kat and whatever Sheerie did to me—that was more action than I'd gotten in a long, long while. Like I say, I ain't winning no beauty contests. But that don't always matter as much to chicks as it does guys. Go figure.

"Wanna walk?" she asked me.

"You sure?"

Kat gave me a squinty eye and started off toward Mass Ave. I followed, a pup at her heels.

———◆———

We walked but didn't say anything, not at first. Not that I could think of anything to say, especially after she took hold of my bent elbow. Eventually I just started babbling about covering the Boston city council beat and then she was telling me about how her band got going. Starter talk.

You don't get many nights like that, where there's means, motive and opportunity to take a long walk into the night and talk the talk that comes when two people don't know each other well, but are working on fixing that. It's about trying to plug into someone's wavelength but knowing at any minute you might tip and ruin it. But then it doesn't and you start trusting the night and the talk and the girl you realize you're crushing on bad.

What happened inside the Middle East—I didn't hit on that, not right off. Like a raw place you gotta get some scab over first, I itched around it. I slipped into interviewer mode. That's where I live best: I can ask anybody anything; I know the art of talking but also the craft of listening and I can hear the things folks ain't saying. I got her to tell me about where she grew up—in Lost Wages, ain't that a kicker—and why she didn't get a college edumacation (she was pre-law, then quit three years back) and what made her dress up like a little girl while she was grinding out indie music (to be determined).

"I like lollipops," she said.

I coughed. "Nice to know you didn't see that as an asshole move."

"I know a pass when I see it," she said.

We got to the bridge then and took a break leaning out over the brackish, shimmering water. She shivered, so I gave her my jacket.

"So," she asked. "Tell me about how we sounded."

By then, I had a bead on her. She wasn't asking for a review. "Blew my damned head off," I said. "But—it hurt, kinda. Music's not supposed to hurt like that."

She swiveled those big eyes at me. "Didn't used to hurt. Used to be the wildest ride ever."

"What changed?"

"Someone got a new girlfriend," she said.

"One with long black hair and green eyes?"

Her mouth twisted. "She talked to you, didn't she."

And more, I wanted to say. I thought about how things changed only when Sheerie took my hand. The music—the needle—stopped jellying up my brain and dropped into my nethers. That's when it got… weird.

"She showed up week, week and a half ago," said Kat, staring out at the black river. "Jordan and me—we were a thing, once. No more. But. I go ragging on his girlfriends and he thinks I'm angling for another chance. So I can't say anything."

"But you know she's bad news."

"She's news, anyway," said Kat. "Don't know what kind."

"Well," I said, and turned her face to me. We touched noses. "That's his bad news. Not ours."

And then we didn't have to speak again for a good long while.

———◆———

But you know how it is.

Something smells funny the night before, come morning it's like you dreamed it and by lunch—you made it up altogether. Scott didn't call me to get my opinion of the show, and I ended up putting it down to Jordan being super inspired by some chick, and me just being all worked up from meeting Kat.

That's where it might've sat, except suddenly Blue Pooka was everyplace. Rocking it every night, venues bigger every time I looked 'em up in Scott's rag. Like watching a comet streak across the sky.

With Pooka on fire, I didn't get to see much of Kat. Easy come and what have you. I don't get invested too fast. But the band had caught my eye, and I wanted to know more. I looked up what a pooka was, expecting to find out why surfers wore so many stupid shells.

Leave it to Scott to get me hooked on a band with a Mick name: This book I found in Ma's collection said you could spell it pooka or puca and it was some kind of animal spirit from Ireland. And get this: the book was authored by none other than W.B. Yeats himself. I thought he just wrote about the end of the world—who knew poets had hobbies?

Couple months later I got an invite to the band's record release party at T.T. the Bear's—a club right 'round the corner from the Middle East—and I made sure to bring my little book all about the pucas and the other folklore from the Auld Sod.

Scott was there and I pinned him down near the bar. "Buy you one," I said.

"It's an open bar," he said, rolling his eyes.

I'm generous like that. We got our drinks and I brought out the book. Showed him what I'd learned about pucas and he turned all smug.

"See you got some book larnin' done," he joked in this fake hick tone.

I made a face. "Yeah, I'm the Woodward and Bernstein of the band's name. Like I got time for *that*."

"Seen Kat lately?" he asked, waggling his eyebrows.

Beer went down the wrong way and I coughed a minute. "Nah. She's kinda busy these days."

"Well," he said, and lifted his chin to a space across the bar. There she was, standing in a small circle with Jordan—who'd clearly been doing some working out; he was slimmer and the beard was gone now—and some other guy in glasses. Kat was standing a little too close to Jordan and eventually gave me half a smile. That was it.

I tipped back the bottle. Hell, if she plays it both ways, that's how it rolls. I don't have no ground to get bent outta shape. I ain't no puca. But I can't say it didn't sting. I let Scott slip away to do his job and sat there nursing beer one, then beer two. Meantime the trio of Jordan, Kat and Mr. Glasses had grown by one—a small woman with hair so shiny dark you could see your distorted face in it.

Right after she showed up the chat turned ugly. Kat took a step back as Mr. Glasses got right in Jordan's face and started doing a lot of pointing and loud talking I couldn't make out. Then he was jabbing a finger at Sheerie. Now back at Jordan. And Sheerie again. Jordan's face narrowed, then pinched up, and finally he let a rabbit-punch fly straight at Mr. Glasses' face.

The guy dropped like a stone and the crowd gathered around them rippled out from the common center. Nobody saw Sheerie back away, then circle around the bar. Nobody except me.

She sidled up on the stool at my right, not making a sound. She picked up my beer and took a sip, then licked the foam mustache with a darting, silver tongue. "Aren't they marvelous?" she asked me. "Men, I mean."

"They have their charms," I said, watching while Mr. Glasses yelled up from the floor at Jordan and two security guys finally moved in to keep them apart.

"So they do," she giggled, and the bracelets around her wrists clinked and jingled with a high, unpleasant sound. I leaned back a bit and got a good look at her. She'd been so tiny last I saw. A child next to Jordan. Now there was something more substantial about her—as if she'd come into focus. "What do you think it was that bothered Mr. Manx so much that Jordan needed to thump him?" she asked me.

Manx. I knew that name. Matthew Manx. Guitarist in a band called Overflow. Couple summers back when Ma was starting her downhill run, their hit song "Two Seconds Glory" held me together. They were gonna be huge, break out of Beantown. Whatever happened to them?

"Beats the shit out of me," I said. "What, you know?"

"I might," she said, sipping on my beer again. I wasn't gonna touch it now. Kept thinking of those mossy, shifting green eyes and that glittering tongue. "I once knew a friend of his. From his band."

"And what happened to him? Not Manx. The friend."

"We had an arrangement," she said. "When it concluded, I moved on. I believe—" she tapped her cheek as if parodying someone trying to remember, "he went for a swim and did not return."

Then it came back to me; even through my fog with Ma I'd read it in my paper. Went off the BU Bridge. They never found the body. Once that was called doing a Brodie, but I was probably the only old fart in this bar who knew it. 'Cause Ma knew it, told it to me. Ma knew lots of things.

Sheerie spun around on her stool, her short plaid skirt riffling in the small breeze she created. She went once around, twice, then stopped hard. "You are a nosy one, Nevada Sullivan."

"Maybe you interest me."

She laughed, a sound like damaged bells. "Maybe *you* interest *me.*"

"It's my job. To get interested." At the paper I always took the assignments nobody wanted. I got my thrills pulling up worms and creeps and things nobody likes to look at. I hold that shit up to the light and grin until my face hurts.

"Writers *are* interesting," she mused. "Even if you are twice the work. Musicians are so much more… simple."

Sheerie slid to the ground and folded her arms. "I'm needed elsewhere," she said, and flicked a finger at Yeats, which was resting quietly on the bar. "Do keep reading, Nevada Sullivan. You're not there yet, but you will be." With that, she twirled once and was away from me so fast I didn't even see her go. I looked over my shoulder and she was back with Jordan, other side of the bar, helping him with his bruised fist. Manx was long gone.

I turned back and jumped, nearly falling off the stool.

"Well," said Kat, behind me. "You gonna buy a girl a drink or what?"

Or what, I thought, thinking about Sheerie. Tried pushing her aside, but it was tough. "It's an open bar," I said.

She set a hand on my leg. "Tell me something I don't already know."

———◆———

Blue Pooka played that night, even after the fracas. But somehow it just don't mean anything to say that Pooka *played.* Soon as those first chords started up, everybody peeled off the barstools and peeled across the room, locked in place like before. Didn't even take our beers.

I swore I'd never watch 'em live again, not after that first time, but I was hooked. For one thing, I couldn't walk out on Kat again. But for another, the music had me in its claws from note one. I stood in a back corner, trembling and horny, then ashamed and totally sapped after. The whole set, I was lost to the sounds.

There was a funny little silence as the last chord faded out, and everybody stirred at once, like we were comin' out of thrall. The clapping and hooting rose up in a wave until it was too loud to do anything else.

I checked my watch: They'd played for 45 minutes. It felt like five years. One minute they were on, the next they weren't, and the time between was both enormous and tiny. The show was time travel.

I wanted to see Kat just then. See if the music still hurt, and if it did why we kept coming back for more. But I waited. Scott taught me it's best leaving the band be for a couple of minutes after a show. It's intense, their ears are ringing, they're having a moment to just come down. Not that you all the way come down for hours, he told me—but in the raw first breaths after a show you're a wire wound too tight. Y'gotta return to the real world.

A cold hardness pressed up against my back and I whirled around, hair all pricked up and my throat like I'd swallowed a golf ball.

"Beer?" asked Sheerie.

She held two bottles pinched between narrow fingers and I took one mechanically. Guinness.

"That's what I like," she purred. "A woman who isn't afraid of the dark."

I can describe Sheerie, that's what I do for a living, but you can't know what it's like to be there with her, with those eyes trained on you only. The closer she got the more I felt things. Felt everything. With her right there, taking delicate sips off the beer neck like she was having tea in a Victorian lady's parlor, I was focused on the hard wood of the floor under my boots, the sick little A/C breeze making its way into our corner, the trickle of sweat sliding down my back.

But it wasn't just about feeling the here and now; I got this tightness in my gut that reminded me of being in love the first time, how desperate and hopeless and unlikely it all was. There were all the girls I didn't approach outta fear and the boys I faked it with for the same reason. It was like that needle I felt earlier with the music was back, and this time it was slipping into my soul and letting it escape, gasp by gasp.

"You're a woman men fight over," I said.

She smiled and a furnace turned on in my belly. Then it went lower.

"Not always men," she said. "Not always fighting."

"I'll bet," I said. "So what are you, then?"

She cocked her head and chuckled. "Oooh," she murmured, and her smile stretched almost too wide. "Can't we merely agree that I am a muse to Jordan? As I was before him to others?"

"'Muse' don't seem the right word."

"T'isn't," she said. "But you are less familiar with the right words than your *máthair* was, true?"

A breeze tickled the back of my neck and my curls felt stiff beneath the invisible caress; mentioning Ma proved I wasn't just standing next to some strange chick. There was magic, real magic in here and it was terrifying. It also felt like I'd just seen the world show its real face for the first time.

Sheerie finished her bottle of beer, then released her grip on it. It hung in mid-air, wobbling. The dark glass caught the light and sent shards of bright dancing around the room.

I stood there, breathing the same air as her. Was this what Jordan felt when he was with her? Was it what Manx's singer did, before he went swimming? Maybe. But there was somethin' different, too. Some-thin' more. I thought again about how with the great bands, you either wanna be the lead singer, or you wanna fuck the lead singer.

I looked at Sheerie and I knew which one I wanted.

"I bet you're a fascinating *múinteoir*," I said, the word sliding like water from me. Ma's word.

Her face brightened and the bottle spun harder. She clapped her hands together once. "Oh, Nevada Sullivan, you are delightful," she said. "I have been called many things, but I don't suppose I've ever been considered a teacher." Then she went thoughtful. "But perhaps I could be."

My throat caught. "What is comin' next?" I asked. "For Jordan. For Kat."

She winked at me. "Ah, now that would be tellin'," she said.

"Do tell."

"In exchange for what?"

"Depends," I said. "What do you want?"

Just then the dressing room door burst open and I felt Sheerie—not exactly vanish but become *not there*. The bottle fell to the floor, shat-tered. Jordan ran out first, carrying a flopped-out Kat in his arms. She had one hand curled at her chest and the other dangling' down. Her eyes flipped open at me.

"Get me out of here," she said in a creaky, old voice. "Help…"

Behind me, I heard jangling laughter, like bracelets clanking.

And like that, they were all gone.

Oh, not *gone* gone, not with Cambridge Hospital 'round the corner. Kat was laid up in the sickroom for a long while, 'til they figured out it was some kind of undiagnosed heart valve weakness. Told her she had to rest up or she'd need slicing open. I took to visiting couple of hours every day and when she asked, I read her stories. Sometimes we talked. Sometimes I brought her hot, strong tea. We learned plenty.

Took me 'bout a week of doing that to realize I hadn't thought of Ma, and her nightmarish hospital sickbed once the whole time.

But the others did vanish pretty quick, and by that I mean Blue Pooka and Sheerie. Band got signed and then they hit the road, playin' all over the country. Kat was out. Couldn't travel, couldn't do what needed doing, so they sacked her with all the grace of a bag of rocks to the head.

That meant I had places to be: Job, Kat's apartment. I started sleeping over. We were a thing. For a long time, that was all I had to pay attention to. I liked the road I was on. Things were… well, balanced.

I kept reading her stories, and damndest thing about that book, y'know. These stories weren't happy dappy crappy fairy tales with the bow tied in a knot at the end. The little folk have all kinds of names in his book, and none of 'em make you think of Tinkerbell. The one that stuck with me was the fey creature who inspired the poets while sucking the life outta them.

Kat perked up when we got to that part of the book. "It's not the whiskey that kills them young," she said in a soft voice, propped up with pillows on her ratty old sofa. "It's the *sídhe*."

That word, Irish for "fairy," sounded a lot like "Sheerie."

When I pointed that out, Kat started crying. "Jordan," she said. "I worry for him every day."

I gave her a hug; last thing I wanted was her bawling over some ex-boyfriend. 'Specially when part of me wasn't all that sympathetic. Jordan was a grownup. He knew what he was getting into, or should have. You didn't have to let a thing like Sheerie trap you, not if you weren't greedy. And could stop thinking with your dick.

That was not a problem for me, y'see.

I asked Kat later on what was going on in the dressing room right before she collapsed, and she said she and Jordan were having it out. She'd decided after that show to confront him finally, ask what the hell was going on.

"'Cause he never wrote songs like that before," she said. "You know when you got Beethoven in front of you from note one. That's not him." She snorted. "He just gave me this pat on the head and said, 'Found my muse is all.' Next thing I knew I was down on the floor and my heart felt like a rock. Figures, I crap out during our first fight in five years."

Then there came a day that we put the books aside and she asked me to read from my local rag. She wanted to hear my stories. I told her it was just local muck and ugly, nothin' to share.

"Can you write about things that are uplifting?" she asked.

"Suppose," I grumbled. But ugly sold papers. And I like having my hands dirty. The ugly feels right when I'm pawing through it. But I didn't have those words to explain, not to someone sweet like Kat.

We were flipping through the paper one afternoon to find a story of mine when we stumbled on a full-page ad for Blue Pooka's upcoming tour. Kat leaned over me and was half in my face, trying to see it up close.

The picture had us mesmerized. The band was posing in a school play yard, with Jordan front and center, all rockstar cool. He was slim and trim, clean-shaven with a fire in his eyes that transmitted clear through newsprint. The others were flat images, but his popped in three dimensions. He was almost glowing.

"Well," I said softly. "Seems like Sheerie is doing her job."

We turned to each other, noses touching. There was this electric crackle.

In a low, husky growl she said, "I don't wanna talk about *her*."

We had other things to do instead.

———◆———

I didn't want to attend the Blue Pooka show when they came back to town. But Kat sure did. She moaned all afternoon about how we were always stuck in the house, how we never went out and did anything *fun*. I reminded her of the kind of fun a person usually got at the Blue Pooka shows, and it was like her eyes glazed over. She fought me hard. I said all she wanted to really do was check in on Jordan.

"So what?" she said. "Look, if you don't want to go, fine. I'll go solo."

That was a bad idea, I just knew it in my heart. Fact was, the dumb part of me did want to go. I was just worried about what might happen when I got there. *Who* might happen.

The band set us up proper on the comp list at Avalon with VIP passes to the roped-off upstairs balcony, open bar, the works. Once inside, Kat and I scoped out the crowd below and drank our freebies, though we didn't say much for a while.

"I know you don't want to be here," she said at last. "I just have to *see*."

"Well, here's hoping your heart can take it," I said.

She didn't think that was funny. There were still some landscapes in our lives we hadn't crossed, places we weren't ready to go. We trusted each other but not enough, and I was afraid that big black hole of things we wouldn't talk about was gonna pull us apart eventually.

"I never saw Pooka play," she said, dreamy. "I was always up there with Jordan. With them. We'd start up and it was like I wasn't in control, like a windstorm had gotten inside me and all I could do was rip through every song hard as I could to make it go away."

"Yeah, well, when I hear Blue Pooka play," I said, "it's like too much. You know how some sounds can make your ears bleed, right? That music makes me feel like I'm bleeding inside my head."

"Oh, honey."

I put down my bottle and looked at her, real hard. Tried to look clean and clear at that kind little face. She was blinking up at me, and it was like this caul fell off my eyes. She was flushed, on the verge of tears and her bottle was still all the way full. A tremble had come over her, and a note of music hadn't even played yet.

"Right," I said. "Let's get outta here."

"Yeah," she said. "This was a pair of bad idea jeans."

She took my hand and we made to go.

"My writer!" a familiar voice slipped in around us, slicing through the crowd roar with a bell-like clarity. That cool, thin needle passed into my soul again and bits of me started slipping away.

We turned and there was Sheerie, beckoning with those slender, pointed fingers at us from her perch near the balcony's edge. She was still little, hair shining with a light no one could see, and her shifty eyes sparked at me again in greeting. She was captivating and terrifying at the same time. I felt more aware immediately.

I stepped toward her, but Kat caught my elbow. "What do *you* want?" she barked.

Sheerie raised an eyebrow, looked between us. Smiled. "A question with endless answers," she said. "Not nearly enough time for such now."

Kat frowned. "What did you say?"

See, Kat didn't get it 'cause Sheerie wasn't speaking to her. Or speaking in English. I got the words, 'cause it was Ma's language—like words from the Yeats book. Erse. Gaelic. That bumpy musicality. But while I knew some of that language, I was no way fluent. I should have been nearly as baffled as Kat, but Sheerie was coming in clear as a radio in my ears.

Sheerie flicked a glance at me. "You are far cannier than you give yourself credit for, Nevada Sullivan. And this one," she nodded at Kat, "is too good for you. I think you know that."

The world contracted and I felt a little sick. "Want a drink?"

Her head shook and I heard a metallic chime. "No. I merely wanted to say farewell. I shan't be seeing you for a time."

"You're leaving," I said, and couldn't keep a note of loss from my voice.

Kat goggled at me.

She nodded. "Things are concluding here."

I stepped closer to her just as the lights behind me darkened. "What happens to him when you go? Is there a long swim in his future?"

She set her open palm on the side of my face and it burned like the music. Down on the floor, the crowd went crazy. "I like you, Nevada," she said. "We shall meet again soon. I may enjoy being a *múinteoir*. We may see if you are an apt pupil."

With that, she slipped from the stool and melted back into the darkness.

Then Pooka were on the stage and it was too late to leave. Their music was a physical thing, and I had to grip the balcony rail to keep myself grounded. Kat stood rigid at my side, taking it all in with an open mouth that was half pain, half joy—she was hearing them and feeling them this way for the first time. I knew what that was like. Way too well.

Down on the stage Jordan was spinning and strumming and bobbing and weaving and singing his heart out. He was less a slimmed-down version of the hulk he'd once been than a wraith now, all bones and angles and pointed things. But we felt him, oh how we felt him—that piercing of his own soul was bleeding out to all of us, and we took it in, helpless. It was Jordan, it was Blue Pooka and they were doing what they were meant to do, doing it better than anybody else in the world.

All was balanced.

In the end, Ma was right about finding your thing and sticking with it. But she never told me you could lose that thing after you found it.

Was about a year after the Blue Pooka gig at Avalon when I heard from Kat again. After that show, she came home with me but we weren't together anymore. Something broke between us on that balcony. Coulda been me talking to Sheerie in Irish. Coulda been her thinking I bored up her formerly crazy life. Might've been it just wasn't meant to be.

Or, could've been Sheerie was right: She *was* too good for me. Heard Kat went back with Jordan in pretty short order. Not sure if they were pals more or more than pals, not sure if she was guitaring for him again. Whatever. Told myself not to care. Sometimes it worked. Sometimes I needed an extra Guinness at the Four Clover.

I dove into work mostly. Bigger jobs, investigative journo shit, the wretched and mean stuff nobody wanted to tackle. I dug up some seriously maggoty shit about a local hero coach who was diddling his teenage players in the locker rooms. I loved writing it up. They gave me an award, if you can believe it. After that it was easy to vanish into work, forget about music and ponytails and pucas.

Phone rang on my way into the office one Thursday morning deep in the dregs of November. Before I touched the ringer I knew. *Kat.*

Breathing on the line when I picked up, breathing like a person trying to get hold of herself, it was her. "Nevada," she said and tears were all over her voice.

"Where are you?" I asked. Didn't need to know the details except that.

She told me: Some fancy-schmancy condo over in Back Bay. "You hurt?" I asked.

"Not me," she said, and made a hiccupping, wet sound. "Hurry. He's not himself."

I hung up and it wasn't until I was in a cab and doing the cliché of telling him to step on it that the dime dropped. She was at Jordan's place. He'd been able to buy it once Blue Pooka shot into the strato-sphere on rocket fuel. Even I couldn't avoid watching them ascend: Remastered album release, three number ones, four times platinum. They were gonna play the goddamn Super Bowl, for crying out loud. It was like a fairy tale, watching them go from paying folks like me in beer to watch the video getting made to being hugged by the world.

But once you dance with the devil you gotta be ready to keep up the beat and not three months after that album came out the label started clamoring for the follow-up. That's where things went south, Scott had told me over beers one night: Jordan had nothing left. He spent hours locked in a room, trying to write, came up snake-eyes. He had the time by then—his dark-haired girl had vamoosed, and that's usually solid grist for the mill. Last month rumors started that the label was gonna drop the band. Call in the remaining chits. Yeah, hard to imagine how an album that sells twelve million can end up in the red, but that's the business, ain't it?

No reason why they couldn't swing back again, except I knew it wasn't gonna happen. He was used up. Done. Sheerie didn't kill him herself. She just left him behind, left him to decide how he'd do it in her place.

He went for a swim and did not return.

And I'd let Kat go back into all that muck. Now it was up to me to get her out of it. A person shouldn't have to watch her loved one go to pieces. I know.

I threw a fifty at the driver when we pulled up and didn't wait for change, bounced out of the car and caromed off the walls of the eleva-tor until I reached 24. I pounced into this tiny hallway where Kat was sitting, slouched against a front door. One small fist was knocking, but her head was turned away.

"Hey," I said. "You got nobody better to call?"

She leapt up and threw herself at me; I caught pretty good and hugged her hard. She smelled like candy, like always. "I can't get in," she said. "He won't talk to me."

"I left my lock pick at home."

She sighed. "You just know things. You know how to do things."

"Fill me in."

So she did. It was all pretty much in the gutter at this point with Jordan, she said. "He's got no music, no nothing inside him," she said. "Like he's been emptied out. And we can't seem to —" she cut off, but

I heard it anyway: probably couldn't get it up in bed, either. When it goes, it all goes and it never seems like it's coming back.

"We had a big screaming fight last night and I crashed over at a friend's place, and when I got back he had the door locked up and told me to go away," she finished.

She had no key. Lost it somewhere. Musicians.

"Super?" I asked. "He got a spare?"

She shook her head, then shrugged. "Maybe?"

"Run down, get it," I said, not wanting her here for this part. "G'wan."

She scampered into the waiting elevator and I held off until I heard it sliding to earth. Then I knocked once, hard. "Jordan," I said. "Nevada. We know somebody in common."

"Fuck *off*," he called to me. A faint, howling windy sound whooshed behind his voice.

"Sheerie," I said.

A soft scrambling of feet, then a click. The door swung open and a gush of wind swirled out at me. Before I could even get inside he was already halfway around his sofa, this big poofy calfskin thing that faced a corner wall made of nothing but windows. They were all thrown wide, and the room looked like it was ground zero for a tornado that wanted to do some interior decorating. Papers fluttering everywhere. Bottles stacked and tipped over. Clothes waving from where they hung draped on every chair.

You could see the whole world out his windows, if your whole world was Boston. And he was checking it out, staring at the outside like I wasn't even there. After a minute, he swiveled his head to me. "Sheerie," he said. "Do you know where –"

"Nah, man," I said. "She was all wrong, you know that, yeah?"

He turned 'round to me and the quilt he had wrapped around him hung open and I saw that whoever this was, it wasn't Jordan anymore. I don't even know if he was totally a person. Just a skull with a ragged beard sitting on top of an Adam's apple, a T-shirt with the band name on it hanging off him. Didn't even have pants on; his pecker was peeking hello through the bottom of the ragged hem of the shirt. His eyes were enormous and their color shifted, ever so slightly, from light brown to mossy green. But more than anything else, he just looked tired. Like someone had stuck him with a thin needle and slowly let his soul trickle out.

Whatever I felt watching Blue Pooka play, it looked like it had been in his head 24/7 for months. That never-ending sound of your brains going soft and squishy and your guts getting twisted and you having no say in any of it. "I keep lookin'," he said, eyes shifting to the window every few seconds. "I leave the window open, in case."

In case what? I wondered. *She's gonna fly in like Superman?* His brand of stupid longing was getting on my nerves. "Was she worth it?" I asked him, soft, not taking my hand off the doorknob.

"Yeah," he sighed, and a smile split his skull face. Pulled the skin back so I could see gums and missing teeth. So I could see exactly how empty he was inside. Then the smile faded. "Nothin's been the same since she left, see? It's all just… flat. All gray. All gone."

I stared out at the city. Sheerie wouldn't want a sad sack like this. I mean, she's fuckin' magic. She can make bottles twirl in in the air; she can bend talent to suit her whims. And he's waiting for her like some kind of sick, sad puppy.

I wouldn't kick a puppy in real life, but in that moment I wanted to kick him.

Go for it, I could imagine Sheerie whispering to me in Irish. *He's no good to anyone.*

Of course, neither was I just after Ma went. *I* was the sad sack in the bar, not sure where my life was heading, and Scott came for me. I could be Scott for this guy.

And just like that, I saw the roads ahead of me. Ma always made it sound like there was just one natural place, and when you found your groove you would know. But suddenly it was like I could see more than one unspooling. See, I know how to handle the ugly stuff. I can make the hard decisions. I don't scare easy. I know the questions to ask. I have the words.

I saw one road, where if I gave him the sweet encouragement he wanted and a couple pats on the head and a sandwich or two, he'd be OK eventually. He'd get some help. Serious help. And Kat with her good, broken heart would be with him all the way. Which meant I'd be sleeping solo yet again.

Then I saw the other road. The one that didn't have a Jordan in it anymore. The road where Kat came back to *me*. It was the road Sheerie might have taken and it was the one I wanted to peek under and rip up to see what was wriggling beneath.

Go with your gut, the Sheerie-voice in my head said.

So I did. I smiled, feeling warmth surge through me. I swallowed it. Ma would not approve of any of this.

But I sensed Sheerie would. She'd put a pin in my soul.

So I picked my words like you might pick arrows for your quiver and I asked him: "If you thought she was never coming back again, if it was gonna be gray forever—what would you do?"

He flinched and one hand actually reached out to the sky, as if he could grab on to it for assistance. But he didn't answer.

"Well, she ain't coming back," I said, brutal. "Not to *you*, anyhow. Welcome to your new life."

And he smiled at me.

I backed up around the door, pulled it closed. The latch fell just as the elevator bonged and Kat walked out with the super, pointing at the door. When we walked into the apartment a minute later, there was no one in the room. Just a quilt, half in and half out of one wide, open window. Draped. Dangling.

For a moment, there was silence. And then there was wailing.

———— ◆ ————

We had to hold Kat back, the super and me, from practically going out the window herself. I found a Valium in the medicine cabinet and she swallowed it and then she was quiet on the big poofy couch until the cops came to take our statements.

When we could go, I walked her out of the building and shielded her gaze from the large, shining dark spot on the sidewalk where Jordan had landed, taking out a tree branch and half an awning on his way down. He wasn't there by the time we were heading by; they'd already carted the shattered bits of him off to the morgue by then.

Official prevailing theory? Death by writer's block, side helping of despair. Dropped by label. Sad story. Familiar story. So many in the naked city.

What didn't make the papers was what I saw in his last seconds: the fact that he was just bones and skin, dying by inches. What also didn't make it was the funky little smile on his face I caught when I handed him his sentence of a gray, living death. Right before I backed off, his mouth went up and his eyes closed and then I was outta there.

I'll remember that smile for a long time. Ain't enough Guinness in the world to erase that.

Few days later they had the funeral. I went for Kat's sake. She might have been in mourning, but afterward she was also in a forgiving mood and we went back to my place after and spent the afternoon getting reacquainted. It's nice, being around her; she makes me think I'm not actually the asshole I'm sure I am. I might move back in.

But as a wise woman—a wise *sídhe*—once noted to me, I am a person who likes the dark. And to be found interesting is one of the best compliments a realist like me can expect. Sheerie is a free spirit and apt to pursue whatever interests her most next. I've been thinking hard on her last words to me. About how she might like a change from the music makers. How this time she might find a writer more to her taste.

See, I know better. I don't have to end up like Manx's pal or Jordan or whatever other sops she's come across. She interests me, too. I could learn a few things from her, if she's really willing to be a *múinteoir*. And maybe she can learn a few things from me. Remember, I like the ugly. It never lets you down.

Nobody grows up wanting to be the bad guy. People are just out there thinking they have some great purpose and it's up to them to do whatever it takes to fulfill it. They do what they're supposed to do, get on that path and move with it. Even if they have to live in the cracks to get things done. To keep the balance.

Right now, all roads are open to me.

That is what I know to be true.

DON'T PUNCH KYLE

Michael David Wilson

Week One, Saturday

One of the first things I learnt living in Tokyo: people take their train game seriously. When the doors open, passengers rush on, sometimes before others have departed. I'm often caught short and seatless because pushing past children and the elderly isn't my style. On that fateful Saturday, I boarded easily enough, but some tall guy in a black leather jacket soon shoulder-barged me back off. A couple of salarymen caught me, sparing my embarrassment and potential dry-cleaning costs. I looked back for the shoulder-barger, ready to give him a piece of my mind, but to no end. He'd merged into the blur of passengers exiting the station. I thanked the businessmen—offering some praise in the wrong formality—and stepped back onto the train. Despite the ruckus, there was still a seat free, which I quickly occupied.

The air smelt fetid inside the train: stale alcohol and bodily fluids coalesced. The bloke next to me dropped his magazine. I picked it up—the pages crinkled and warm.

"You dropped…" I noticed the magazine's cover: *BX Blackbox Magazine*, a young lady with surgically enhanced tits popping out of a red silk bra.

He snatched the magazine back and I looked dead ahead, acting as though it had never happened—occupying my thoughts with lesson plans and work and definitely not porno mags. A lady in a black suit stared at me, glaring with disgust. But disgust at what? Me, the porno mag, the bloke next to me? I shook my head, trying to diffuse the situation. But when she refused to react or even break eye contact, I cast my eyes downward.

My porno mag-reading companion had holes in the front of his shoes and scabs on his legs. A thin layer of grime coated his trousers. I turned towards him, saw him properly for the first time: cheeks like a bulldog's jowls, white patchy beard, long fingernails that curled at the ends, his hands clutched a can of Kirin Strong Seven beer, a porno mag resting in his lap. It wasn't so much the train but this one guy, responsible for the pungent stench. So *that's* how I'd got a seat.

Our eyes met and he shuffled closer, affording me a good whiff of his breath: skunks wrestling in raw sewage.

"Don't punch Kyle", he whispered.

"What?"

"Don't punch Kyle." He had an American accent which struck me as strange because I didn't see many other expats on this line, let alone expats in such a bad way.

When the train pulled into the next station, he bent over, picked up a large plastic bag full of empty cans, hoisted it over his shoulder, and departed the train.

———◆———

Off the train and walking to work I puzzled over the whole 'don't punch Kyle' thing.

I was still lost in thought when Andrew, a fellow teacher, slapped me on the shoulder. "Hey, buddy, how's it going?"

So, I told him.

"'Don't punch Kyle', what an odd thing to say", he said.

"Right. Though I figure following his unsolicited advice will be easy enough—I don't even know a Kyle. And I don't make a habit of punching people either. Matter of fact, last time I punched someone was back in Birmingham, outside Wetherspoons on Broad Street."

"Go on then, I'll bite. What happened?"

"Some no-neck skinhead in a City shirt pulling this girl's hair, yelling all sorts of shit at her—all the while she's screaming for him to get the fuck off. Skinhead's a big lad, but there are plenty of other big lads standing around smoking. I figured someone would intervene, but it didn't go further than eyes in the couple's direction."

"People these days …"

"Right! When he slammed her against the wall and started choking her, I had to do something. So, I'm all 'hey arsehole, the hell are you doing?' And I'm loud about it, thinking if I kick up enough fuss, others will help."

"But they didn't?"

"I got people's attention all right. But no one did a bloody thing, because it wasn't their girlfriend, so wasn't their problem. They were too damn drunk, or too damn scared, or too damn some other bullshit people tell themselves to justify inaction."

"People suck."

"Skinhead goes, 'mind your own business.' Casual, polite almost, even though two seconds earlier he'd been shouting at her, all red-faced, about to pop a vein. Of course, I didn't mind my business."

"How could you, under the circumstances?"

"I tried to be polite. 'Let her go', I said, though inwardly I was fuming. And for the briefest of moments I made eye contact with the girl. Saw hope in her eyes, a silent 'thank you'. Or maybe that's just what I'd wanted to see. Not that it made a lick of difference to the skinhead, so I gave him an ultimatum: 'get the fuck off of her or I'll make you.'"

Andrew laughed. "Can't imagine you like that, you're usually so calm."

"Guess the skinhead felt the same because the sonofabitch laughed in my face. Looking back, can't say I blame him. I'm this skinny geezer in a Depeche Mode shirt and eyeliner, he's this big bruiser of a bloke who likes his Stella and lives the stereotype. Of course, he stopped laughing when I socked him across the face which forced him to loosen his grip on the girl."

"Holy shit! What happened next?"

"She goes running up Broad Street, fast as anything, towards the cinema and I legged it to the city centre. You don't hang around when you've hit a guy like that, unless you want your ass kicked."

"You got away?"

"The dopey bastard had a real conundrum: go after me or the girl. He wound up abandoning her, which I suppose was in character. I got as far as the library before he caught up. The twat hit me so hard I have astigmatism in my right eye, but rather me than her."

At school I was quick to forget about the guy on the train—I had a full morning of lessons, ten until two, and a stack-load of reports to write. When the break came, a new teacher with blonde wavy hair, light stubble, and a navy-blue suit introduced himself whilst I was making a much-needed cup of coffee.

"I'm Kyle." He had an Australian accent.

"Nice to meet you, *Kyle*. I'm Tyler."

We shook hands.

"Busy day?" I asked.

"Not so bad, just finding my feet. Better than yesterday, mind—I was on my own."

"No other teachers?"

"That's right, mate. Just me at that school, Kichijoji or moji or … well, Kichi-something or other. Anyway, I'm gonna grab a drink after work if you fancy joining me, otherwise I'll be on my lonesome again."

"Sure. Could mention it to Andrew, too."

"Already did, but he's got a date with some girl."

After work, Kyle and I grabbed our jackets and made our way to The Aldgate—a small British pub in Shibuya with plenty of draught beers on tap. It's cosy inside with standing room only on a busy night—the atmosphere akin to someplace in rural England named 'Ye Olde … '. A home away from home. I ordered a couple of pints of Aldgate Ale.

After five minutes of polite conversation about school, previous jobs, and other shit neither of us truly cared about, I asked Kyle what music he was into.

"All sorts, really."

A bad start—I hated that noncommittal bullshit. But I urged him on and established we both liked rock. Within minutes we progressed from radio-friendly Kings of Leon to the gore-drenched sounds of Cannibal Corpse. As soon as we'd got onto extreme metal, it was a matter of name-dropping lesser known bands back-and-forth to see who could out-obscure the other. When he'd stayed with me for Dying Fetus and thrown Malevolent Creation, Cattle Decapitation, and Septic Flesh my way, I'd decided he was a good guy. We progressed from The Aldgate to the aptly named RockBar where they'll play anything on the stereo as long as it's available on YouTube. They care as much about licensing laws as they do the prohibition of marijuana, a permanent green haze fogging the building.

We drank, we laughed, we spoke until words and sentences slurred.

A little before midnight, we called it a night, thanks to train times. Kyle offered to pay the bill at RockBar—I laid down some thousand-yen notes, but he pushed them back insisting he'd had a good time and this was his treat.

We headed out onto the streets, arms slung around shoulders, singing songs that made no sense—practically best friends.

At the train station, Kyle pulled me close, and spoke in barely perceptible English. "Wednesday I'm at Shin-Yurigaoka. Know much about the school?"

"I don't, but my girlfriend, Amy, teaches there, so I guess you'll meet her."

He grinned. "Cool. I'll try not to fuck her."

Too plastered and taken aback to tell if he was joking, I stared open-mouthed.

"Relax, mate, it's a joke. Bloody hell—your face! Besides, blokes like us, we stick together. Truth is, I'm only here for the jay-joot, know what I mean? Now that's a flavour I really want to try."

I laughed nervously. *Another joke or …*

Kyle left me on the platform, awaiting my train home. I googled 'joot' just to be sure it meant what I thought it did—I'd been right. *Creepy bastard.*

Kyle and I were no longer best friends.

⸻

I arrived home gone 1 a.m., tiptoeing carefully around so as not to wake Amy. It went well until I stumbled into the recycling bin, spilling rubbish onto the kitchen floor. Spent the next five minutes sorting plastics and metals into their respective containers.

When I reached the bedroom, the bedside lamp was still on. Amy sat in bed reading *The Practice of English Language Teaching* by Jeremy Hamer.

"Sounds like a laugh." I nodded towards the book. "But I bet it's no *John Dies at the End*."

"Got to read a few chapters ahead of tomorrow's DELTA meeting."

"The excitement never ends. Say, I didn't wake you, did I?"

"Lucky for you I haven't tried sleeping yet, but you made a hell of a racket. Who were you fighting?"

"The recycling."

"Standard."

"Went for a drink with Kyle, the new guy at Mizonokuchi. Seemed cool at first—he's into At The Gates and Celtic Frost—but then he got weird."

"Oh?"

"Said something about only being in Japan for the women. But the way he said it and the look he gave me, made it all the worse. Like it was more than the booze talking, you know? How did he put it ... 'here for the jay-joot.'"

Amy looked blank.

"Joot means minge."

"Eww ... you know I hate that word. Hope you didn't punch him or do anything stupid—I know what you're like, especially after a drink."

"Hey—why would I punch him? I'm practically a pacifist."

"Yeah, right ... What about Rick?"

"That was a long time ago, and *besides* he was hitting on you. *In front of me.* Like I'd stand for that! Anyway, that was then, this is now. I'm basically a peacenik."

"You might have your friends fooled, but you can't fool me, Tyler. By all means, wear your mask in public, but not here."

⸺•⸺

Week One, Wednesday

I met Amy in TGI Fridays after work. We ate beef burgers and fries with an extra serving of onion rings—washing it down with unlimited soft drinks. TGIs was almost empty so we got a booth in the corner far away from other diners, just the way I liked it.

"Met Kyle today." Amy forked an onion ring around her plate. "Seemed like a nice guy—didn't say anything creepy either. Found something out about him, though ... He's loaded—his Dad owns one of the biggest retail stores in Australia."

"That explains why he's so generous with money—he wouldn't let me pay for a damn thing at RockBar the other night. It wasn't cheap either, we polished off *a lot* of whiskey."

"You let a man get you drunk *and* foot the bill? He might think you owe him something."

"Yeah, yeah." I rolled my eyes. "Only thing I owe him is the next night out."

"Be careful, Tyler. Don't want to lead him on—you heartbreaker, *you.*"

Week Two, Saturday

Kyle strolled into school ten minutes late wearing a heavy biker's jacket with a huge buckle across the front.

He picked up his schedule from reception, skimming the day's lessons. "Looks like we're both teaching Ami. I'm up first. Guess you'll have to do with sloppy seconds, mate?" Kyle winked and made his way into his classroom.

I glanced at Akari, the receptionist, ready to share a 'what a prick' moment, but instead she smiled and wished me a good morning.

There were only five minutes between Kyle's lesson with Ami finishing and mine beginning. I had no time for lesson prep, barely enough time to find out what Kyle had taught. The five energetic kindergarten kids from my previous class weren't helping. They flitted between the classroom and reception area, arbitrarily picking up and putting down items.

When Kyle approached, he had one hell of a smile on his face. "Bloody hell, mate—you won't say no."

"What's that?"

"You won't say no. Man, I'd like to smash her backdoors in—I'm telling you, nearly got a stork-on during the lesson."

"Kyle, what the *actual* fuck?"

"Easy tiger, it's all good. She might look young but she's twenty-five."

"She's your *student*."

Kyle grinned. "Relax. Back in Spain we were *all* fucking our students."

"I doubt that."

"Ah, shit, sorry mate—I forgot you have a girlfriend." He passed me the textbook. "Anyway, start from the top of page twenty-five."

When six o'clock rolled around and it was time to head home, it relieved me to hear Kyle had left early thanks to a last-minute lesson cancellation. I waited for Andrew to pack up his things before we headed to the station together.

"What do you think to Kyle?" I asked.

"He's a great guy. Got a lot of time for him—wicked sense of humour. He's won some amateur football trophies, too. You hear about his Dad? Jesus! Kyle's a lucky man, if he wasn't so nice, I think I'd hate him."

"Has he said anything *weird*?"

We stopped at the traffic lights outside the Seven Eleven. Andrew took a moment to consider. "Well, the other day we were talking about that Amanda Knox documentary on Netflix and he called it a *doco*— guess that was *a bit* weird. Keeps encouraging students with the phrase 'give it a burl', too. Never heard that one."

"Right, but anything *inappropriate*? Anything a little *off*? Or *improper* ... you see what I'm getting at?"

"Nah, doesn't sound like Kyle. He's a stand-up guy, as decent as they come. Doubt there's a bad bone in his body." The lights turned to green and we crossed the road. "By all means chat with Akari if it'll make you feel better, but she'll say the same."

Sleep didn't come easily and when it did it was broken and fitful. At three a.m. I gave in and headed downstairs, pouring myself a whiskey on the rocks. I pressed my headphones tightly around my ears and played electronic drone at maximum volume to exorcise the bullshit inside my head. But to no avail—too many voices shouting at once, competing for headspace.

Don't punch Kyle.
Back in Spain …
He's a stand-up guy.
Nearly got a stork-on.
Seemed like a nice guy … his Dad owns one of the biggest retail stores …
(I'm practically a pacifist.) What about Rick?
Blokes like us, we stick together.
I'm only here for the jay-joot.
Be careful, Tyler.
I'd like to smash her backdoors in.
You can't fool me, Tyler.

I downed the whiskey then flung the glass hard as if I was pitching. It exploded against the wall.

"Fuck you, Kyle."

As the days passed, I thought often about Kyle and the man on the train. The way he'd sidled up close, the smell of sewage, his voice—so soft it was barely there: "Don't punch Kyle." Rationally speaking it was a weird coincidence I'd met *a* Kyle that day. Weirder still he was so bloody punch worthy.

And yet I was angry with the man on the train—why hadn't he been more thorough in his explanation? Why couldn't I punch Kyle? What were the consequences? And what had been the emphasis? Not punching or Kyle? And if I couldn't punch Kyle was everything else fair game or was he untouchable? How about a roundhouse kick to the face? I couldn't *actually* execute a decent roundhouse kick, but it was worth clarifying—I could learn.

Questions mounted—an absence of answers remained.

I kept an eye out for the bearded bloke with his 'don't punch Kyle' philosophy, especially on the train, but to no avail.

Week Three, Saturday
Sleep quantity and quality continued to decline. After hours of restless-

ness I headed to the living room for an early-hours whiskey to speed-up the process. As I waited for the desired effect, I jotted down reasons I should and shouldn't punch Kyle. It wasn't the first time I'd compiled such a list and was unlikely to be the last. Reasons not to punch Kyle came up short.

Because I didn't have enough information.

Because I didn't know what was at stake.

At six a.m. I jolted from my slumber, whiskey glass still in-hand. Next to the television, ceramic blue and white porcelain lay broken, remnants of a Virgin Mary ornament Amy's now deceased Grandmother had given her. I swept up the fragments, wondering why the hell I'd done such a thing. I didn't tell Amy.

✦

I arrived at school early to ask Akari about Kyle. So far, everyone, including Amy, had nothing but praise for him. Seemed ludicrous! I couldn't be the only one who thought the guy was a grade 'A' bell-end. Then again, what if he only came out with his inane pseudo-macho bullshit when I was about because "blokes like us stick together"?

Blokes *like us*.

Jesus Christ, his reading of me was so far off the page it wasn't even in the same fucking book.

"Good morning!" Akari greeted me with enthusiasm too lively to be sincere.

I nodded in her direction then made some coffee, before returning back to her. Fresh paint perfumed the air.

"You get the decorators in or something?"

"Kyle wanted his room painted red. Says it has more energy and will bring out the passion in his students."

I clenched my fists. She had to be kidding—less than a month at the school and the arsehole gets to dictate his classroom's colour scheme, while old muggins here is in the job for years and has a hard time acquiring new board pens.

And who in the hell paints their classroom red? A fucking psychopath, that's who.

I gritted my teeth and gave Akari a smile as genuine as her enthusiasm.

She passed me my teaching schedule.

"No lesson with Ami?" I asked.

"She's taking a double with Kyle today." Akari switched on the reception computer, loading up the school's email.

"Of course she is."

"What was that?"

"I was just saying I have a gap in my schedule so don't mind teaching her."

"Don't worry, Kyle insisted—said you worked hard enough. And he's right. You always have such full-on schedules. Kyle's so thoughtful—a really great guy."

"I'll take the lesson, Akari."

"But Kyle—"

"But Kyle *what?* I said I'll take the lesson." I slammed my fist against the reception desk. Akari peered up from the computer, mouth wide open. I sighed, softened my tone. "Sorry. But about Kyle, is he actually such a great guy? Like, *really?* You don't think there's something just a little *off* about him?"

Akari shook her head—obviously she did, because everyone loved Kyle.

"While I've got you here", I said, noting her hands were clasped tightly together. "This might be an odd question, but I don't suppose you've ever had, say, a homeless guy or a drunk, tell you to or not to do something whilst riding the train?"

Her hands relaxed. Less anxious, more confused. She cocked her head to the side. "What do you mean?"

"What I mean is has a drunk—possibly a vagrant—given you advice, but in such a way that it seemed … *important?*"

"Hmm … sometimes there are drunks on the train, especially late at night and early morning. They say many things. Probably best not to listen to them."

———◆———

After completing my lesson prep, I loaded up an old episode of *The Inbetweeners*. A few minutes later Kyle swung open my classroom door with not so much as a knock—smug grin upon his face, a flick of his stupid surfer boy hair.

He peered over at my laptop: "Just checking you're not batting off … Anyway, how the bloody hell are you, mate? Pretty good I imagine— see your schedule? Well don't worry about it, you can thank me later when we hit the bar." He slapped my back playfully.

"I have plans tonight", I said then tried to think of something.

"Room for one more?"

"No."

A reasonable silence grew awkward.

"I mean, it's my mother. She's ill. Seriously, in fact. Not terminal, but it could be."

"It could be?"

"Oh yeah, sure", I said then adjusted my tone because it was too chirpy. "Like, in the future, it could be terminal. It isn't but it *could* go that way. It could develop … *terminally*." *The fuck was I even saying?* "So, I need to get back and Skype her ASAP."

"I'm so sorry, mate. If there's anything I can—"

"There isn't. There's nothing anyone can do."

He stroked his chin. "You know, if she's seriously ill perhaps you should go back to the UK for a bit, just in case …"

"Nah."

He lingered, unsure what to say. For once, I'd shut him up—no irritating comments, no stupid quips, no smug self-satisfaction. Of course, if he tracked my Facebook and by proxy my mother's I'd have to give her a WhatsApp and ask her to lay low, but it was a small price to pay.

"Ah well", Kyle said. "Better get prepping. Got a double with Ami later. Gonna work my magic, if you know what I mean."

———◆———

Week Three, Tuesday

The grass was a golden yellow in Tachikawa Park, which was where I saw him—sleeping on a bench, body covered in newspapers. I recognised his beard first and the porno mag second—guessed he took it everywhere, clung to it as if it were a talisman.

I sat on the edge of the bench next to him. Though sat is generous, there was little room, my arse half-off the bench.

"Hey", I said, gently at first. "Hey. Hey! HEY!" So, this was what my life had become—screaming at a homeless person until he awoke. He stirred, sat up. Not looking at me, he started gathering the few possessions he'd stowed underneath the bench, ready to move on.

"Oh no you don't. Stay where you are, don't go anywhere."

He gazed through groggy eyes.

"Remember me?"

He bent down and retrieved a can of beer from the floor, taking a swig. Ordinarily I might have told him that was fucking disgusting— that he hadn't the foggiest what had happened to that can since he'd been out—but from his facial expression and life circumstances, he was all out of fucks to give.

"Don't punch Kyle", I said. "That's what you told me. And so far, I haven't. But honestly, I'm not sure how much longer I can keep it up."

He didn't respond.

"I dunno if you've met Kyle but he's pretty difficult not to punch. And I'm not just talking about the shit-eating grin and the dumb haircut." I glanced at his beer, could do with one myself. "Oh, sure, at first he appears decent enough. Had me fooled for a little while, with his taste in music and all the whiskey he bought, but the truth soon came out—the real Kyle soon emerged. Doesn't take a genius to see his true colours. I mean, it's obvious—or it should be … though *apparently* I'm the only one who sees Kyle for who and what he is—which is a piece of shit."

The man shuffled down the bench, creating some distance between us. He wouldn't look at me, but I could tell he was listening.

I took a deep breath. "I wish you hadn't told me not to punch him. I mean, I don't know if I would have punched him—maybe, maybe not—but ever since you said that, it's all I can think of. I'm serious—I'm *actually* losing sleep over it." I looked him up-and-down, he was falling apart on the outside. "Must sound like the textbook definition of a first world problem to you, huh? God knows what you must lose sleep over—out in the wild, sleeping rough. At least I go back to a warm bed, a heater in the winter, air con in the summer, plenty of food in the fridge … Jesus, that's insensitive of me, isn't it? I'm sorry man it's just …" But I stopped myself, unsure what to say. I edged closer up the bench—towards him. His right shoulder twitched, a small but perceptible movement. He didn't want me near him, certainly didn't want me talking. Then again, I hadn't wanted his unsolicited advice. You don't always get what you want.

"I'll leave you alone soon, I promise. But I *have* to know, *hypothetically*, if I were to punch Kyle … what would happen?"

He turned towards me—eyes wide, glistening and wet.

"What would happen?" I repeated.

He stood up, muttering to himself.

"Please", I said.

He shook his head, grabbed the porno mag from off of the bench, then ran towards the park's exit. I remained on the bench, surrounded by newspapers and beer cans—weighing up the pros and cons of chasing after him but decided against it. The guy clearly wasn't right in the head. 'Don't punch Kyle', was just the ramblings of a drunkard—it had to be.

And yet I couldn't shake the notion that there was something more to it. Something deeper.

—◆—

Week Three, Wednesday

I was halfway through lunch when Amy called. I chowed down the rest of my tuna onigiri and answered.

"Why don't they put enough filling in onigiris?"

"Um, hello, Tyler."

"There's plenty of rice and the right amount of seaweed thank goodness, but the filling—the main event, if you will—is decidedly lacking."

"I was calling because—"

"I mean, Christ, it's as if there's a famine and Japan is rationing out all the good stuff."

"I don't think it's like that at all. Anyway, I wanted to let you know I'm going out for drinks after work with Kyle."

"Just the two of you?" I sounded angrier than intended, less than I felt.

"No, no—there's a load of us. It's to welcome him to the school. You can come, too, if you like."

"Better not, we don't have much money until payday."

"I can tell this isn't about money. Honestly, Tyler, you're so transparent." She paused. "This is about Kyle."

"It's not *fucking* Kyle."

Akari peered through the windowpane. I didn't know how she did it but every single time I lost my temper she appeared like clockwork. I gave her a thumbs-up and forced a smile like 'no big deal I'm definitely not losing my shit and shouting down the phone'. She retreated to her desk.

"Look, I'm sorry. And okay, *yes, it is* Kyle, who everyone seems to think walks on water—he's basically Jesus. But newsflash: the guy's a total fucking sleazebag. But the way you are, the way Andrew is, the way Akari is, it's like I see a different Kyle to the lot of you. As though he only says these fucked-up things to me."

"What *things?* What are you going on about?"

"*I've got a stork on … I'm gonna fuck my students … some people see a woman, I see an opportunity … The guy's a wanker, fuckable girlfriend though …* Everything he does—everything he says … He's everything I hate."

Amy laughed. "Oh, come on. Don't be ridiculous, you've got him all wrong—Kyle's a gentleman."

"A gentle—then how do you explain what he said?"

"He's never said anything like that to me. Quite the contrary …"

I hung up. Kicked the table hard, stubbing my toe in the process. I glanced up to see Akari watching so gave her the finger.

Later I apologised, blamed it on indigestion. She told me she didn't get it.

———◆———

Week Four, Saturday

Every Saturday morning, I ride the train to work—tired, hungover, sometimes both. I turn my music up loud and keep my eyes towards my phone, avoiding conversation like everyone else. Yet more often than not someone still talks to me. I'm considering a 'fuck off' tattoo on my forehead.

This Saturday's distraction was the worst. Not because it pulled me away from Bongripper's cheery number 'Doom' but because the prick pulling me away was Kyle.

"What do you want?" I said. There was no point pretending I liked him anymore.

"See the black?"

"The what?"

"The *black*. You see him? He was on the previous train. You were on it, too—only you were down the other end. I thought about walking over but you know how rammed things get at this time in the morning."

"The black *what*, Kyle?"

"The black *man*."

"Racist piece of shit." My knuckles clenched, pulse quickening.

"Calm down, mate. Sounds like you need some coffee. I saw a black on the train, nothing racist about that, mate—just a fact. You don't see blacks much in Japan. You ever seen a black on the train before?"

"Just *fuck off*. And stop saying 'a black'—what the fuck is wrong with you?"

Off the train I tried to out-walk Kyle, building to a near jog, but he kept pace.

"Look, I'm sorry about what I said, mate. I wasn't thinking—it was insensitive. We're still friends, right?"

I ignored him, focused ahead.

"I promise it wasn't racist. I promise *I'm* not a racist. Like I said, it was just an observation. You don't see many Muslims either. Is saying that anti-Islam or anti-Muslim or whatever? … Please mate, stop with the silent treatment … Speaking of observations, I feel much safer living in Japan than I did back home. Don't you? Low crime, for one."

"And I suppose that's because there are less *blacks* and Muslims, huh? Know what—go fuck yourself, Kyle."

———◆———

I didn't notice the students who'd arrived early as I stormed into the school making my grand announcement to all who'd listen. "Kyle is a sexist, racist, Islamophobic piece of shit—he's a hatemonger and if you can't see that you're all fucking *blind*."

———◆———

I sat in my classroom, notes in front of me but not reading. Deep breaths in and out as I processed what I'd just said and what my next steps were. I'd snapped, lost control, made a hell of a scene, but that didn't mean I hadn't been right in what I'd said. It was all the truth, no falsehoods. The trouble was, the Director of Studies might not see it that way and management certainly wouldn't see it like that. I'd have to backtrack, apologise, make excuses, if I wanted to keep hold of my job. And either way it might be too late. It wasn't right, though.

Kyle needed to pay.

A few minutes later Kyle entered the classroom. This time he knocked and was gentler in his approach. He put a can of Black Boss coffee and a Meiji dark chocolate bar on my desk.

"I *am* sorry about earlier", he said. "And I heard what you said about me. All I can say is you're wrong—I haven't got a prejudiced bone in my body."

I suppressed laughter—what a joke.

"I know you're ticked off but at least give me a chance. If I say anything untoward, if anything ruffles you, I'll hold my hands up, mate, and admit wrongdoing. And we won't have to see each other again—I'll request a transfer to another school. What do you say? One more chance to prove you wrong—to show you I'm not a bad guy. Can't say fairer than that, huh?"

I had to admit, Kyle transferring schools was an attractive proposition. And it'd save me worrying about socking him one, too. He was bound to screw up. And sooner rather than later—almost every other sentence was objectionable.

"I'll take your silence as a yes … As *consent.*" He grinned, goading me, waiting for a reaction. "Anyway, you have a double with Ami this week. I'll get my notes, show you where we got up to." He lingered in the doorway. "Speaking of where we got up to or should I say *what* we got up to, I went out with her the other week. She was shit-faced, like proper paralytic—I wound up fucking her … Funny thing is, I don't know if Amy even remembers."

Kyle burst into laughter, hunched over holding his stomach.

Amy or Ami? What had he said? What was *he saying?*

What followed is hazy—I rolled my hands into fists and popped him with a straight right and a left elbow. I must have got him good because he fell so quick and loose I swear he was out before he hit the ground. Problem was, I didn't stop there—I thwacked him in the gut with the full force of my Doc Martens, back-and-forth, back-and-forth, until Andrew was in the classroom, arms around me—dragging me away from Kyle and into the privacy of his own classroom where he threw me up against the wall.

"What the hell are you playing at? What are you *doing*? You've got to leave, Tyler. You've got to get out of this school. *Now.*"

Andrew pushed me out of his room and back into reception. A thirty-something student helped Kyle to his feet. With his arm around the student for support, Kyle staggered out of my classroom—lips and mouth leaking blood, hair dishevelled. "It's all right. A misunderstanding, that's all", he lisped to Andrew as if drunk. Then to me. "*Ami.* I said *Ami.* Not Amy, mate. Not your bloody girlfriend." He paused, wiped blood from his lips. Mouthed, "Amy." Winked.

If it hadn't been for Andrew and all the students I'd have gone for Kyle again.

"Go home, Tyler", Andrew said.

"No need for that", Kyle said. He removed his arm from the thirty-something, positioned himself towards the other students and parents. "Tyler got passionate, that's all. He's a good bloke really. Isn't that right, mate?"

***

Shortly after leaving the school, I received a phone call from the Director of Studies. He suspended me with immediate effect. That was it then—I'd punched Kyle and had an answer: don't punch Kyle because you'll get suspended. Well, thanks drunk bearded guy for your wisdom. Without such sage words, without such insight, I would never have envisioned that punching a colleague would lead to a workplace dismissal.

Back home, I listened to heavy metal, drank whiskey, and replayed the morning's events. I'd likely have to leave Japan if Kyle, the school, or anyone else sought legal action or went to the media. But despite it all, punching Kyle had felt good.

I prepared dinner for Amy's return: rare sirloin steaks with peppercorn sauce, sweet potato mash, and broccoli-and-onion garlic stir fry with a little brown sugar and ground ginger. When she arrived, I poured her a glass of red and asked her to take a seat. I put electronic music on, unobtrusive and easy on the ear, brought the food to the table, and joined her.

"What's this all about?" Her eyes narrowed.

"Love."

"Hmm." She carved a piece of steak.

"What? Can't I make you a nice meal without it being *about* something?"

"Oh sure, it's possible. But with you it's … *unlikely*." No malice in her voice, she was playful. "But I don't understand how you had the time to do all this. I'm normally back before you at the weekend. What happened?"

"I left early."

I had every intention of telling her what had happened but didn't want to spoil the mood and meal. I didn't lie, as such. She didn't ask, "were you suspended today?" or "did you finally punch Kyle?" Nothing like that. And I volunteered no further information. We ate a delicious meal, watched a feel-good film, and enjoyed ourselves.

I'd meant to tell Amy about my suspension on Sunday, but we'd wound up going shopping and dined at one of her favourite restaurants and, as with Saturday, it seemed a shame to put a dampener on a perfectly good day. I know it was irresponsible, childish even, but good days didn't come often.

Week Four, Monday

Monday morning things took a turn for the worse. I was eating soft boiled eggs and listening to Nevermore's *Enemies of Reality*, when Amy entered the living room towel-drying her hair.

"Guess who I just spoke to?" Her tone suggested trouble.

"I don't know."

"Head Office. They've been trying to get hold of you all weekend to discuss Saturday's incident. You need to ring them back. *Urgently.* But not before you tell me what happened."

"You won't like this but …" I stalled. Considered whether there was a gentle way to put it, if I could underplay the truth and fix things later. Too risky. "The thing is … I was suspended. You know how Kyle's been winding me up? Well I had enough, Amy. I snapped and hit the prick."

"What the hell, Tyler? He's such a sweet guy."

"He's anything but ... Jesus, if you'd heard what he was saying. I couldn't stand it, that's why I smacked him one."

"You shouldn't have done that."

⎯◆⎯

Head Office scheduled a meeting to discuss my future that afternoon. Amy delivered an ultimatum: get your job back or else. She didn't elaborate on 'what else' but we both knew there was no way to afford the rent or living costs on her wage alone.

Amy's phone lit up, a text message. She read the message and winced. "What the hell did you do?"

"Huh?"

"Kyle's face, it's all messed up."

I reached for her phone, but she pulled away. Why did she even have that bastard's number? Kyle had mouthed 'Amy', as if implicating them both. Confessional. What if *Ami* had been Amy all along? That's what he'd been trying to tell me, which was why he'd muddled the names.

"What are you texting that dickhead for?"

"Excuse me?"

"You shouldn't be texting Kyle, he's not right."

She backed up against the wall. "Tyler, you need to calm down."

"There's no truth to what he's saying, is there?"

She raised an eyebrow. "And what exactly *is* he saying?"

"You tell me."

"I think you need to leave or you're gonna be late for your meeting."

But I didn't care about the fucking meeting, couldn't think or see straight—a blur of heat, hate, and despair. I wanted the truth.

"Amy ..." I said.

"And for God sake, brush your teeth and swig some Listerine. I can smell the whiskey on you. Getting drunk in the evenings, having zero time for me, and shutting me out is bad enough, but drinking in the day—in the morning?! Sort yourself out, Tyler. Sort your-fucking-self out."

I had so much I wanted to say, especially after the wonderful weekend we'd had—a weekend in which we'd spent *all* our Sunday together. And sure, I'd had a drink here and there, but nothing excessive.

I gritted my teeth.
Said nothing.
Did nothing.
And for once it was the right decision.

The Head Office meeting lasted under five minutes.

I spent the afternoon searching the web for a new teaching position. After bookmarking twenty-plus opportunities and sending my CV out to various recruiters, I poured myself a large glass of whiskey and put on Ulver's *Shadow of the Sun*. Soon after, Amy returned home from work—two hours early.

"His fucking face, it's even worse in person. How could you?" Amy slammed her bag to the floor, shoved her phone in my face. "Look at him! Look at what *you've* done."

Kyle's right eye was swollen shut: shades of purple branched into reds and yellows—a tapestry of pain. His left was ringed and red. A flattened, inflamed, mess of a nose—thick lines extended from the bridge to his eyes. Lips scuffed crimson and cracked.

"This is bullshit", I said.

"Yeah? How'd you think I feel? How can I stay with someone who'd do that to another person?"

"You're right. But I'm telling you, that wasn't me. At least, not all of it. I hit him once in the jaw. Once, Amy—that's it. A little bruising, the discolouration around the chin, even the cracked lips—sure, I can own that. But the nose? The eyes? That wasn't me."

"Are you for real? You're going to deny this?"

"I'm denying it because I *didn't do it.*"

"Then who did it, Tyler? Who *the fuck* did it?"

"I don't know. Really, I don't. What's Kyle say?"

"That it was *you*. Andrew says the same."

"Well, Andrew knows for a fact that Kyle's face didn't look like that when he pulled me off of him. I don't know how he got all of that, but it has *nothing* to do with me."

"You're lucky you're not in prison."

"You've gotta believe me, *I don't know* what happened."

"I haven't got to do anything. You think he did this to himself? Set you up?"

"*Amy*, please ..."

But she wasn't listening. And it got me thinking ... What if he had done this to himself? What if he *had* set me up? I'd have been crazy to suggest it, but the possibility seemed plausible.

——◆——

Week Five, Tuesday

Amy started spending longer at school, often returning home gone midnight. More time with colleagues equalled more opportunities to sing Kyle's praises equalled more disbelief that I'd had the gall to attack him. Kyle quickly transformed into a martyr. He'd been so selfless—begging others to forgive the very person who'd hospitalised him was Christ-like. I learnt that after my dismissal, Kyle had gone to the hospital on his lonesome. Of course, Andrew had offered to accompany him and *of course*, Kyle had refused. Hadn't wanted to trouble him—*classic Kyle*. I figured sometime between leaving the school and arriving at the hospital Kyle had inflicted the real damage to his face, the damage I'd seen in the photographs. I wasn't sure of the how or where, but the why was glaring.

"We should consider moving back to the UK", I said to Amy.

"We?"

Hours later our relationship was over. She gave me as much opportunity for discussion as the school had. Her decision made. I got that. Expected it, even. But two weeks to find a new place when she'd known I had no money to my name ... that stung.

Week Five, Friday

I rose early and travelled to Tsudanama in Chiba Prefecture for an interview with a small school. Though perhaps small school is too grandiose, it turned out to be a couple of rented rooms in an office block geared towards freelancers. If I hadn't been desperate I'd have given it a miss—the hours long, the pay low—but eviction was imminent and Amy had already advertised for a new housemate.

I was reviewing my interview notes, drinking a drip coffee in the Starbucks nearest the station when he came in. He wore a full beard, thick and trimmed with high cheek lines and a handlebar worn down, jet black hair slicked straight back, his suit designer label—with a sophisticated sheen, stylish not tacky, in a colour catalogues would describe as 'charcoal' or 'noir' and never black.

I stared at the bloke. Was he famous? A distant colleague? Some dude I'd seen on commutes?

Then it clicked.

"Don't punch Kyle."

There was no mistaking him, only he was all cleaned up—hair dyed, clothes fresh, shoes polished. Hell, he even looked half a stone lighter.

I watched as he ordered a cup of coffee then settled at a table, at which point he took a MacBook out of his bag beggaring my belief further.

I walked over, placed my cup on his table, and sat opposite.

"It's you. It really *is* you", I said. "I don't understand, little over two weeks ago you were sleeping rough, clutching porno mags and stinking of … well, no offence, you were just stinking. But now *this*."

"You punched him", he said, a calm confidence to his voice, as fresh as his appearance.

"Yes."

"You look like shit."

I glanced down at my suit, dirt clung to the edges, a thick smudge on the chest pocket where this morning's toothpaste had landed, creases on my shirt.

"Have you even slept?" he asked.

Jesus, how rude. I sipped my coffee—*this* is *my sleep. Who needs sleep when you have caffeine?* I glimpsed my reflection. Evidently the answer was *me*.

"I lost my job, I lost my girlfriend, I lost my friends." My words slurred together, sleep deprivation taking over.

"You shouldn't have punched Kyle. Though, I did warn you." Genuine pity in his eyes, as though we were close friends and he was terribly sorry things had played out like this. He drank his coffee, sighing with contentment.

I shook my head or perhaps I thrashed it about, mental and physical sensations became disconnected, eyes itching and dry. "Huh? What are you saying?"

"First coffee of the day", he said after another sip in which he appeared even more delighted than the first.

"What are you *saying*?" I stood up, people were staring.

"Goodness, there's no need to cause a scene, dear boy. I'm simply saying you shouldn't have punched Kyle. Nothing more, nothing less."

"But that doesn't make any sense. That makes *fuck all* sense. Punching Kyle shouldn't have caused all this."

"Did it?"

"Did it what?"

"Cause all this."

"You just said it did."

"All I said was you shouldn't have punched Kyle."

I exhaled. "Look, did it or did it not cause *this*?"

He drank his coffee.

"Did *punching Kyle* cause *this*?"

He said nothing.

"Well, what about *you*? Why are you so different? The suit, the hair, the … everything."

"Oh, me?" He sounded simultaneously flattered and embarrassed. "Just luck."

"Luck how?"

"It's not exactly a riveting story, but as you're insistent, a few Saturdays ago I was collecting cans by the river, as I am wont to do, when I bumped into an old friend. He could see I was … I was … well, let's just say in a tough spot, and he wanted to help. I'm living with him at the moment and he's helping me find employment again. Matter of fact, I have an interview a little later today and I have an inkling, things will work out."

"A few Saturdays ago, you say. How many? And at what time?"

"Oh goodness, let me see. This would have been two Saturdays back and … Hmm, well, I'm sorry to say I can't give you specifics, but it was morning. I was drunk—I was *always* drunk—so couldn't tell you more than that."

"That's when I punched Kyle. Two Saturdays back, in the morning. Is that the answer? Is this a *curse*? Do I have to pass on *the curse*?"

He stood up from his seat, his coffee mug still half-full. "I should get going."

I grabbed hold of him. "*How* do I stop it? And *why*'d you tell me not to punch Kyle? Please, I *have* to know."

The baristas looked over with concern. I loosened my grip.

"I really must—"

"Is it a *curse?!*"

"A curse? Come on, this isn't a fairy tale."

"*Please.*"

"Some chap offered me 10,000 yen to say it. He seemed rather desperate, too. Said you needed to know. I've no idea why he couldn't say it himself, but I wasn't going to argue. So I said it—that was it."

"Who was this guy?"

"Beats me. The Ozzie accent and leather jacket's about all I recall. Now please, I must get going."

"What else? What was his hair like?"

"I couldn't say. But I had a bad feeling about him all-told. 10,000 yen though—it isn't to be sniffed at, not when you collect cans for a living." He walked towards the door. Turned, expression halfway between pity and contempt, and called back. "Good luck, kid."

———◆———

To my unsurprise, I didn't get the job, but I *did* get kicked out of my house a week early. The photos of Kyle, though, now they *were* a surprise. The interviewer had laid them out in front of me, as soon as I got in the room. Shots of the various injuries Kyle had sustained in and after the incident. She asked if I knew anything about what had happened to him. I was shocked. *Obviously,* I was shocked. And yet I still made a quip about how I thought this was a job not a police interview, but she didn't seem to find it funny which was fair enough. Anyway, I told her I didn't know how Kyle had got *all* those bruises, which was the truth, but she was sceptical. Said she'd contacted my previous employer and heard all about my little altercation.

After Amy gave me the boot, I stayed in a few cheap hotels. It turned out they weren't cheap enough. Soon after I was unable to pay and was blacklisted.

Things got worse and fast.

I wound up befriending some of the homeless community by the Tama River and collecting cans for small sums of money. With the pittance I earned, I'd buy the strongest beer in the nearest convini, drink it as quickly as possible, and try to forget what I'd become.

Now maybe you're wondering why I didn't call it quits and return to the UK? I might not have had much to my name, but surely the government would have preferred sending me back than have my unkempt beard, knotted hair, and questionable smell sully Japan? And what about my family? Wouldn't they have bailed me out? Possibly. Possibly not. They're a complicated bunch. But there was no way I was telling them Amy and I hadn't worked out and I definitely wasn't telling them I'd blown all my money. They'd expected both and I'd rather have been homeless, hell I'd rather have been dead than returned to their smug cunty smiles and 'told you so's'. Besides, we hadn't spoken for six months and likely no one would initiate anything for at least another six. That was just how it was.

I'd often think about the once-homeless-then-rich bloke in the suit and I'd think, too, about the guy in the leather jacket with the Australian accent who'd paid him off. I'd been convinced it was Kyle. It had to be, right? Then I was convinced it was definitely a curse, some otherworldly entity that science couldn't yet explain. Later, I decided it was both—a weird combination of black magic and malice. But the more time passed, the less certain I was. And the less real my past life with Amy became. The less real Amy became. My memory of her faded and crumpled like her photo in my wallet.

On the bright side, at least my Japanese progressed from entry level to conversational in a matter of months. Losing everything and becoming part of the homeless community isn't necessarily a language learning route I'd recommend but it worked for me. Christ, that's depressing, but if you don't laugh you cry. Often I do both. Funny thing is that in some ways I integrated more with society after losing everything. The way my beard and hair grew out I wondered if the general public could discern me from rest of the vagrants. Probably not—no one ever looked at us long enough. Afraid that if they were to give us eye contact, they might catch something.

Time passed. I don't know how much, time ceased to matter, but the length of my beard and the thick heat suggested we were deep into summer.

It was early morning, the sun not fully risen, and I dozed on the cool riverbank clutching the previous night's can of beer close to my chest: an aluminium teddy bear. I was mid-dream and it was a good one, too—it was Christmas day and me and Yuki were in KFC feasting on an all-you-can-eat buffet. Presumably part of some 'help the homeless Christmas programme'. We were offered baths, too—I don't know why there were baths in KFC but Yuki said not to question it. Yuki was my new girl and we had a better relationship than Amy and I ever had. Simpler, too. She showed me the ropes and took me under her wing, soon after I joined the community. Yuki was the first good thing to happen after Amy and the best thing to happen to-date.

The dream ceased when the stomach pain began. I looked up and saw some guy with a stubble beard, black leather jacket, and heavy boots. I figured the prick had booted me one in the stomach. "Wanna earn some money, bum?"

Not really, mate. Just want to be back in KFC with Yuki and all that chicken.

"What am I saying? Course you fucking do, look at the state of you, you fucking mug. Anyway, here's the deal, I'll give you ten thousand yen, all you've gotta do is talk to this guy, right? And you don't have to say much 'n' all, just a single line. Easy money, huh? I'll take you to him, tell you what to say, then when you're done you get your money. What do you say?"

This guy didn't look like Kyle, didn't sound like Kyle, was definitely *not* Kyle. And yet this was a near-identical predicament to the one that other bloke had found himself in. The situation that had altered his life.

And mine.

"Come on, bum, I ain't got all day. Ten thousand yen. You comin' or what?"

I followed the man from the riverbank to the train station. He pointed to a chap with short cropped blonde hair, a short-sleeved pale blue shirt, and black trousers.

"That's the mug. Follow him onto the train and tell him this …" he whispered into my ear the three words I feared the most, the three words that had changed everything.

The train pulled up.

"You have nothing to lose", the man said.

I boarded the train. Sat next to the chap, which he appeared none too happy about, but he said nothing, just engrossed himself in his smartphone—flicking through photographs, family snaps of himself, a woman, and children. All smiling, laughing, and having fun. *His* family. *His* life. Unaltered.

Nothing to lose.

That's what the man had told me. But it simply wasn't true. I did have things to lose. I had the community. I had a sense of belonging. Most of all, I had Yuki.

Three simple words. Then what? Would I get my life back? Would I get a change in fortune? A new job? A new suit? A new start?

And what of Yuki? Where did she fit into the equation? What if I lost her? Then again, this could be something special, something wonderful. If I gained a job, a home, reacceptance into society, I could transform Yuki's life, too—the ultimate thank you for all she'd done.

But what if that wasn't what she wanted? What if I lost her *because* I got rich?

I shook my head. She wouldn't leave me because of wealth.

I glanced at the chap's phone: on the screen the woman stood to the left, he stood to the right, and two children—one boy, one girl, neither older than seven years old—stood in the centre. I recognised the location. Fushimi Inari Taisha, a shrine in Kyoto, famous for its path, hundreds of gates long, each in glorious incandescent orange. If I said those words, for me, for Yuki, for us, I might destroy this man's life. Might destroy his family. His children.

Yuki wouldn't respect that.

Then again would she ever find out?

I tapped the man on the shoulder, gave him my best smile: "Hey …"

THE SOLIFUGE'S GRIN
Avery Kit Malone

Tonight, the assassin is dreaming a nightmare. Behind closed lids, he is two decades younger and back in the desert with his brother; he has dreamed of this trip often. The sky is a coruscating shatter of sunlight that causes his eyes to ache. He does not feel it on his face and arms, but he does feel the brush of the wind. His brother babbles, words sliding out all together, beads on a string, but sometimes his voice is replaced with the rush of the wind; the desert wind sweeps out from his mouth.

Things skitter from place to place amid the dust. In the shadow of a dune: solifuges, lizard-long and spider-legged. Shadows slide away and well up in other places on the sand, and the solifuges flee the open sun into pools of shadow, sometimes to Daniel's shadow, or his brother's. His brother cowers in fear, spinning round and round, eyes darting wildly at the shadows and the arachnids, and the assassin, not yet an assassin, tries to calmly explain that they seek only to escape the open light, they are only hiding, but he can't open his mouth.

His brother's face contorts and his fear-wide eyes blink over a mouth that stretches, yawning, gaping, a parody of his expression upon his death, and solifuges crawl into the shelter of his cavernous mouth.

Daniel turns from this scene and steps forward onto a precipice, scrabbling to find a hold as he tumbles downward, and he manages to grip tightly to the edge of the cliff; sand sifts through his desperate grip, falling onto his face and into the abyss below, a great dark place. Below him something seethes in that dark. He can see a vast shadowed shape, and something like two blades, gleaming. His pistol rests oddly heavy in his free hand. He could drop it and try to get a better hold of the cliff, or he could try to kill the thing below. He strains to aim behind and below, and fires. He knows without seeing that he has missed his target. The strength of his hand gives out.

He falls into the darkness and his heart is pierced twice over, one blade still stuck in him and suddenly the next, his body jerking with the force of it, and he makes a sound like a half-drowned man coming up for air and then his eyes snap open to the cool indifferent dark of his bedroom.

———◆———

Daniel's new contract is a big one. A photograph grainy from being blown-up too far taped to his mirror: he picks it off like a leaf between two fingers and stares. Close-cropped hair like wheat, deep-set shark-black eyes. A particular challenge: this man is a performer. He leads the theatre in the Old Town district, a magnificent building custom-made for his troupe and their performances. Daniel has seen it in photographs, has seen the odd spires cresting the ragged horizon of the tops of other buildings on occasion, but he has never really seen the place in person. The man, his target, one Marius Victor, is never observed to leave it.

Daniel does not wonder why anyone wants this man dead. The potential reasons are a bramble tangle of human flaws and conflicts that he does not reach into ever. His targets are inevitably affluent figures; he presumes, given his fees, that his clients must generally be, too. He does not speak with his clients. His handler slides his tasks beneath his hotel room door on a slip of paper, often with an attached photograph. He receives his pay in a similar manner. Only his handler knows his name.

Daniel straightens his tie in the mirror and observes the corvid brightness of his eyes. His eyes always gleam brightly on the night of a job. He wears a pressed button-down of a deep plum color and a pair of black slacks. His hair is combed and shining with product. He fastens his wristwatch to his arm and gives himself a final, cursory glance and then leaves, his pistol pressing hard and familiar at the small of his back.

He looks at the glossy pamphlet in his hand as he glides onto the sidewalk of a twilit street. The title of the show is "MARTIN KEENEYE

DREAMS THE FUTURE, OR, A COURT OF PHANTASMS," as told in large gothic lettering along the top of the pamphlet. Below it is a collage of scenes rendered in the deeply shadowed and saturated style of a baroque painting. These scenes include a half circle of vultures, bowing, splay-winged, a brown ram lying in their center, its baleful eyes gazing out dumbly. A man and a woman in lissome poses of dance, both dressed in sepulchral elegance, her arms raised and sloped toward him, his hand taking hers. In the deep shadows of the bottom-left corner, something faint: the suggestion of a denizen of the deep sea, Daniel thinks. Something with gleaming twists, pale where it barely surfaces from the black at the edge of the painting, slightly, oddly familiar.

The tickets are hard to come by, but Daniel does not question how his handler has obtained one. Even he cannot help a small pang of intrigue regarding the show: all sorts of rumors surround the odd Theatre of Totality, the most persistent of them claims it to be the front for a cult.

Daniel waits at a bus stop on a sleepy street corner where the traffic noise permeates the walls and alleys from somewhere distant and nonspecific, a constant, churning and faintly echoing drone. A child is kneeling in the gutter beside him, picking coins out of the filth, counting aloud with each find; an old woman waiting beside him carries a silky white cat in her arms. It regards him with clean jade eyes and flat ears and a wildly fearful growl and so he edges away and waits outside of the small plastic shelter of the bus stop.

Then the bus arrives and he boards and takes a seat beside a grimy window and watches the district wash away. The streets become clogged, and pedestrians thicken from a lonesome scattering to a throng, more and more expensively dressed the farther the bus groans and whines into Old Town. Daniel notices a young dark-haired man waiting at a crosswalk ahead of the bus; as the bus rolls near the man bends to adjust his shoelace and when he straightens, his face belongs to Daniel's twin brother: a face very nearly his own, but Daniel always knows it's him. He stares blankly at the bus window, eyes unfocused but landing directly on Daniel's face through the glass, mouth a shape of slack confusion, a suggestion of blood at its corners.

Daniel squeezes his eyes shut and counts in reverse from ten. Sometimes this happens, ever since his brother's dive from a fourth-floor window. When Daniel opens his eyes the man has already crossed the street in a stream of other people and Daniel is able to draw a breath again. Daniel has seen a great many dead faces, but he is only pursued by one.

Daniel de-boards the bus and finds himself within sight of the grand structure of the theatre, elegant steep stone with four tall spires at its outer corners, and the fifth tower, like the thumb of an upturned hand, positioned in the center of the courtyard outside. A plaque names the building the Theatre of Totality. As he gets closer he can see that the top of each of the towers spins somnolently, something like an enormous lens exposed on one side. They gleam asynchronously as the towers turn, each lens glittering the red-orange of the dying sun before becoming occluded again by the solid stone of the other side.

Daniel becomes aware that the sound of traffic is distant here, and he hears only the chatter of other guests—sharply-dressed theatre-go-ers—like a burble of water. The doors to this large stone building are closed ahead. A handful of women each dressed in the black ballerina attire of the woman on the pamphlet dance amid the crowd of guests in slow, silent circles, making their way through the crowd.

One approaches Daniel, circling him with arms raised, and then, with a bow, she flourishes a hand and extends a prim red rose to him. Smiling, he accepts it.

"What are those towers for?" he asks, waving a hand up at them.

She smiles, a close-mouthed smile, and slowly pirouettes, then dances away into the crowd. He holds the rose up to his face to take in its scent, cool and brittle. As he lifts it in the last of the day's sunlight he can see now that it is splotched with dark, moist patches; something white and small writhes nestled in the heart of the flower. Now he can smell a faint undertone of rot. He drops the rose to the pale pavement and grinds it under his heel.

Ahead of him, the doors to the theatre open. The murmuring crowd mills inside, and he is carried with it.

—◆—

The inside of the auditorium is an assemblage of velvet reds and golden detailing. Ivory statues of broad-winged buzzards and dog-sized stag beetles stand as sentinels in the cavernous foyer. Heels click elegantly on the marble floor; Daniel looks down and sees his face reflected pale-ly at him from the polished stone.

One of the dancing women, now standing still and ushering people to their seats from the maw of the auditorium, slides a playbill into his hands, whispers into his ear, "Seventy-two," and gestures inside to a row of seating.

Daniel enters the dim chamber, finds the seat with the gleaming gold placard for seventy-two, and sits, folding one leg over the other. He watches. People drift into the hushed dark quiet and fill in the spaces around him; their voices come out muted as though the room has a physical effect on them, suppressing them, making them small, making speaking more effort than it is worth.

After a long time the doors close. The audience is a smear of shadows within shadows. A spotlight bleaches a section of the stage as the curtains beneath the proscenium finish lifting away. A man steps into it from behind.

The man's light hair is slicked back, and he is dressed in a red suit and black tie. His eyes are painted dramatically, lined with thick black. Daniel recognizes him right away as Marius Victor.

"Good evening. I am Martin Keeneye, and tonight I will be your oracle," he says. The susurration of shifting feet and whispers dies abruptly. His voice is the only sound. "In this space, on this stage, there is a vision. Here is a *grand-guignol* with only one show. Here is a dream we will dream together."

Behind him, on either side of the stage, some of the dancing women emerge from the wings and dance slow circles as he speaks.

Daniel takes the time, while Marius-as-Martin continues, to eye the other patrons, or at least their silhouettes in the darkness. They are rod-straight, enrapt. Daniel's eyes traverse the dim theatre. He is memorizing details of the layout. He has already decided tonight will not be the night.

His attention is returned to the stage as a circle of men, bald and walking with a slow, stooped gait, dressed in trailing grey cloaks with collars of feathers, enter the stage and slowly pace. The light shifts red, and Daniel can see that they are not men, but actual vultures, pacing the stage, bowing with splayed wings. They murmur a song about death that enters his ears, coils around his brain, and leaves his mind scrubbed clean.

The music takes on a shrill keening that rises slowly in volume, and the vultures bow, tucking their heads beneath their wings, and they step back and back, retreating slowly into the wings. Then the light is shimmering blue, drowning the theatre in an aquarium glow.

A man emerges from stage right, and here Daniel sits up straighter: the man is Marius. He leaps across the stage, arms extended, hands raised in a gesture of supplication; lithe, with sweeping, fluid motions, he dances back and forth. Daniel leans forward and strains his eyes and sees that Marius's face is a mask of effort and concentration, sometimes giving way to what resembles a sort of cold fury. Eventually, one of the dancing women joins him on stage--it's the woman who gave him the rose, Daniel is somehow sure of it.

The music rises to a crescendo, becoming an atonal shrieking cacophony, and when it reaches its peak, the woman slips away into darkness again. Marius faces the audience, arms upraised, and the music falls suddenly silent.

"And now, the portents," he declares.

The vultures step out once more, and Daniel sees them as men one moment, birds the next. A man with the brown head of a ram walks slowly out, dressed in a simple cloth—the audience around Daniel tenses in anticipation, knowing something that he doesn't. The vultures bow again and then watch, a semicircle of statues, an image of patient hunger. The ram-headed man—and Daniel is not certain that it's a mask, he is no longer certain of anything in this room—disrobes and stand nude, and Marius appears again, a curved and gleaming blade in his hand, and he holds it out to the ram-headed man.

The ram-headed man takes the cold-gleaming blade and seemingly no sooner has he pressed the tip to his chest than his flesh splits from sternum to groin; his head throws back, eyes glassy. The audience stirs and gasps as the ram-headed man's right hand slides into the flap of flesh, pulling it wide, baring a gleaming row of pink-red ribs, a pulsing mass of lung. Marius takes hold of his opposite side, wrenching it open; blood soaks the man's legs and genitals and pools thickly on the floor. Marius crouches, peering intently at the black twitching coils of intestine, sometimes gently pushing one aside, tugging out a loop of it here and there and letting it hang, pulsing, dripping, over the floor. A woman in the row in front of Daniel is giggling frantically and drops suddenly forward, and the man beside her rushes to lift her and support her head.

Daniel has nearly forgotten his purpose, so intently is he watching. He is certain he witnesses a live disembowelment on stage. There is no question in his mind that the viscera glistening onstage are genuine. He is enrapt, and overcome with the flickering sense licking at the corners of his consciousness that he is witnessing something important, but he cannot quite grasp it.

Marius stands and turns to the crowd, announcing, "Fortune!"

The audience wakes like an animal. They stamp their feet in a rhythm; they chant out, "Fortune! Fortune!" in a joyous voice and clap their hands. In the din, the ram-headed man slowly collapses on the stage. The vultures flare their wings and pace a slow circle around him. Marius turns from him, arms outstretched, with a beatific grin, and bows.

The curtain drops.

————◆————

Here, now, is a cold place.

Daniel paces a corridor thrumming with ambient refrigerator noise. The floor is dark, gleaming metal. The ceiling is the same metal, a smooth, shining plane unbroken by any sort of light fixture, though Daniel can see in this place in a dim, colorless light, all the same. The walls, as he passes them, are endless columns of heavy square doors, stacked three high. Some are closed, but most are open, and Daniel can see the people lying in them, each cell filled with a cold blue light, each body in a thin gown, their heads lifted and watching him pass with dispassionate gazes. Some he knows are his own previous work; this is not a recognition of these people so much as it an implicit understanding. He simply knows as he passes them.

They mumble to him as they watch lying stone-still in their cells, only their mouths moving, and he can hear something that is not a person but making a moderate effort to sound like one from behind the closed doors; it follows him as he walks from behind these, moving from closed cell to closed cell, and its voice is made from odd buzzing and clicks.

He is beginning to sweat and this annoys him, but he is unable to slow his heart or think clearly in this dim tunnel, in the sea of muttered dead voices. Daniel breaks into a run; the noise of his feet slamming the metal floor echoes mockingly in the corridor. Beneath it he thinks he can hear the un-person start to laugh.

Then he breaks into a silent place. Looking around, he can see it, too, is made of the dark metal, but a pale bulb dangles from the center of it. He turns and sees the room is circular, and there is no exit. Beneath the bulb, in the center of the room, is a metal gurney, and on it his twin brother lies covered up to the neck in a white sheet. His head turns as he languidly tracks Daniel's approach. His eyes are impossibly black. Something is moving under the sheet.

Daniel walks to his brother's side, avoiding his eyes. Gingerly, he peels back the sheet, because he knows he is intended to. Resting on his brother's chest is a solifuge from the desert. Rendered visible, it circles, confused. Daniel looks at his brother's face and sees that it is now smiling.

"It's an ugly thing, isn't it? To see it?" his brother whispers. "Better not to look under covers, in the shadows…"

Daniel's eyes are frozen on the pale, gleaming creature scuttling back and forth, seeking a hiding place.

"It's not sitting on *your* chest. You could look away."

"I can't," Daniel finally says.

He wakes in his bed, his sheet tangled around his legs, bare chest sheened with sweat carried over from the dream. Eventually, he slides out of his bed and returns with whiskey from his kitchen. After several glasses he is able to ignore the dark corners and crevices of his room, the places where shadows seep and gather; he is able to ignore the echoes in his head of the corpses' low choir of muttering and of his brother's whispering enough to lie back down and be subsumed by a deep and dreamless sleep.

* * *

Daniel attends the performance again the next evening. The audience is again a sea of the well-dressed affluent denizens of Old Town—they could, he reasons, very well be the exact same audience, for all that he can discern a difference. The events onstage repeat themselves exactly as before while he watches, the bold stage lighting reflecting off of his wide, attentive eyes, with the sole exception that he is somehow sure that a different man wears the ram's head mask tonight. This detail stirs his fascination.

Daniel is surprised by his own curiosity about the performance; his obsessive need lately to understand what transpires nightly on the stage. He reassures himself that extensive research is necessary for this job. He hasn't forgotten his target.

He does not dream of his brother, for which he is grateful. In the morning, he decides he must know more about the Theatre of Totality. He steps briskly out of his hotel and passes the gangly child kneeling in the filth, collecting coins from the street, whose count has surpassed three hundred now.

At the city library, he braves the gaze of two winged stone lions and passes unscathed between them up the white steps and into the quiet cool of the building, which smells like dust and dry wood rot. A few people stand in the dim, flickering buzzing yellow light but they do not turn to him as he passes.

The librarian is a woman with a tight narrow face and tight gray hair. Her gaze is acidic. Daniel doesn't know what she might have been doing before he arrived, because when he turns a corner that allows her desk into his view, she is standing with arms folded behind her and waiting for him.

"What is it?"

"I want to know about the Theatre of Totality. I want any materials you can provide."

"Why?"

He blinks.

"Never mind," she says.

She turns and gently glides into the deep shadow of the rows of archives behind the desk. Daniel stands in pseudo-silence to the humming of the lights. When the librarian finally returns, she unfolds a newspaper and presses it down on the desk, the print facing him, and smoothes the creases.

"What am I looking for?" he says.

She jabs a thin finger down on the print, a glossy nail hovering over a line in a brief article. He can see the newspaper is the city's local press. The words beneath the librarian's finger read, "…completion of the magnificent Theatre of Totality on Sunday evening, designed by local engineer A. A. Murasin."

Daniel looks up plaintively.

"That's all?"

The librarian's scowl adds a lethal dose of venom.

Daniel returns to the street with his fists clenching and unclenching in his pockets. He realizes that he has already made the decision to return to the theatre again tonight. He wants to see the performance, is looking forward to it. He shoves that thought aside so that he can better simmer in his frustration. A little squadron of the feral dogs that roam the lonely streets after dark coalesce from nearby alleyways and stalk him, teeth bared, ripping into the evening air with their low voices. Daniel stops and turns and gives a sudden, snarling shout, and they scatter.

He returns to his hotel room, and takes his notepad and scrawls a message. He seals this in a crisp manila folder, and places it under his door, just so the edge of the folder is reachable to probing fingers slid under the door, should they know where to probe. Then he leaves again, and meanders to the theatre, abandoning the bus in favor of the long route so that he can think more along the way.

By the time he reaches the theatre again, the sun's low glare reflecting in the rotating lenses like beacon flares against a dusky sky, patrons are already filtering into the building to be seated. The last of the gleaming cars that the theatre patrons arrive in, looking like a squat, sleek beetle, peels away into the evening. Their drivers will return for them before the show is over; Daniel doubts that even one of them has ever had to walk the streets after dark.

One of the dancing women spins slowly toward him. She smiles.

"You gave me the rose," he says.

She takes his hands in hers.

"I've seen you lately. You've only just begun to attend the service," she tells him. Her eyes are either green or hazel; he isn't sure, they shift in the light.

"That's right." He notices the line of people dwindling at the door. "Say, what are you doing after this?"

She looks him up and down, still smiling.

"The diner at the corner of West Street and Hermit. Seven o'clock," she says, and then unclasps him, and twirls away.

He shuffles into the dark.

⸺◆⸺

In the diner, Daniel orders a coffee. He tips exactly three drops of creamer from the pitcher into it. He waits. One of the diner patrons up the counter from him is starting to look like his brother, so he relocates himself to a corner table and trains his gaze out the window and onto the sea of headlights that is the street.

At exactly five minutes past seven she enters and takes a seat opposite him. She orders a coffee with one sugar and a slice of apple pie, and only after the receipt of her coffee does she look at his face, humming softly to herself.

"So," she says. "Do you have a family?"

"No. I had a brother."

"What happened to him?"

"He fell from a decent height. Intentionally."

"Oh." A pause. "Was he depressed?"

Daniel shrugs, recalling asking him that very question. "He always said he just saw things as they are. Not happy or sad."

He frowns at his coffee.

"Listen, I was hoping you could answer a few questions for me."

"I'm not going to sleep with you."

"Okay."

"What were your questions?"

"Is someone really killed on stage each night?" he says. "The scene with the auto-haruspex, that's real?"

She smiles.

"It's on the stage, isn't it?" She slices off the corner of her wedge of pie. "People come because they enjoy what they see. They can enjoy what they see without thinking too much about the truth underneath."

"What can you tell me about Martin? Or really, Marius?"

She begins humming to herself again, louder than before.

"What are the towers at the theatre for?"

He sighs. Swearing, he rises to pay the bill and leave.

"Why not just enjoy it?" she says, behind him. "Come see what you'll see and leave it at that. Each night he predicts fortune. That's all people want, really."

He walks back to his hotel in the subterranean dark. Few people are out on the streets by now, and those that are brandish great sticks or knives, to beat away the dogs. Only the occasional passing car keeps him company for most of the walk. As he nears the hotel room he steps over a gleaming scattering of coins on the street and sidewalk; huddled nearby, the dogs hunch over something still and dark. A sound like a wet rag being torn, and reflective eyes lift to greet his, but he hurries past, paying them no mind, knowing that they are sated.

In his hotel room, the manila envelope is gone from his floor. In its place is a small note. It bears an address, and nothing more.

----—◆—----

The next morning, Daniel has found the apartment building in a ramshackle district. The buzzer for the unit is defunct. The front door is locked. Stepping onto a small side-street, he makes a few quick judgments to locate the proper window, and slides a rusting metal trashcan over to the wall to climb to it.

He is prepared to break the glass if necessary, but the window screen and pane slide open easily, and he pulls himself inside, crouching in the dark. Not a single light is on, and so he relies on what filters dimly through the window to help his eyes adjust.

A living room, dust-coated, layered with trash. He creeps to the bedroom. Sitting very still and facing him in the dark is a cadaverous man in an armchair. A blindfold covers his eyes.

"Murasin," Daniel says, and the man's head jerks up toward the sound.

"Who are you?"

"A guest. Easy, now. Just answer some questions for me and I'm gone."

Murasin rocks back and forth anxiously.

"Go on," he says in a quiet voice.

"You're the architect who built the theatre for Marius."

"I built the theatre. But I'm no architect."

"What? What are you, then?"

"An engineer."

Daniel cocks his head. "What sort?"

"I built magic lanterns," Murasin says. "I was a leading expert in them. Phantasms from light, the bending of light."

"Why did you build the theatre? What do the towers do?"

Murasin's mouth purses tightly.

"Now, listen," says Daniel, and he has rushed at the seated man with the ease and speed of a jungle cat, and now he leans intimately over his left ear, feels the man's trembling shoulder beneath the grip of his hand, "I don't know what your blindfold is about. I don't think you can see. And if you want to keep your other senses, I think you'd better listen here."

"The bending of light," Murasin says feebly, and then he begins to laugh, more and more riotously, causing Daniel to jump back.

He rips the white satin ribbon from his face, and two gaping dark holes draw in Daniel's gaze.

"I did this to myself," he whispers, grinning at some obscure joke.

"Why?"

"So I don't have to see. Because once you see the truth, you'll never see anything else again. No amount of tricks with light will ever cover it again for you."

"Murasin," Daniel says dangerously, and now he's drawn his gun, which he hadn't planned on, and pressed its cold mouth to the gaunt man's throat, "Murasin, tell me what I need to know."

"In my desk. A spyglass," he says. "You'll see everything you want to know. The lens is special. It refracts refracted light—it straightens it back out. You'll see. You'll see."

Daniel searches the old wooden desk, throwing a half-look over his shoulder periodically at Murasin, who continues to merely sit, wheezing and shaking. In the bottom drawer, he finds it: rimmed in brass, a rose-colored lens. Hesitantly, he lifts it to his eye and peers through it at Murasin. He sees only the same eyeless man sitting in the dark, though strangely, his vision through it is normally colored, despite the tint of the glass.

Without another word, he escapes back through the window. Murasin's laughing drifts with him outside, and far up the street, step after step, turning corners with him and still onward as he walks, long after he has left the man quaking in the dark.

❦

As Daniel approaches the theatre, he feels the familiar pit of certainty in his chest that tonight is the night. On some instinct, he has the spyglass tucked safely in his pocket, waiting for the right moment.

When the court of vultures emerges, Daniel decides to draw it out and holds it to his eye. The vultures are certainly men, he can see; they wear long, draping robes and carry solemn, hairless heads on their shoulders. Then comes the auto-haruspex, who looks fairly unchanged through his lens, except that the man's hands are behind him.

Marius walks out, knife in hand. Daniel's breath catches in his throat. Marius's shadow is not his shadow—or rather, there is something hiding inside of his shadow, something huge, larger than he, an enormous lurking shade with numerous bending arthropod legs; he can see two dispassionately gleaming fangs, each larger than a man's head, hanging over Marius's shoulder. Marius pretends to hand the ram-headed man the knife, who cannot really accept it, with his hands bound behind him. And Daniel can see now that it is not the knife, but an appendage of the creature that slices open the chest of the onstage sacrifice, and the hulking thing lowers to feed as Marius turns to the crowd and announces, "Fortune." And over the jubilant roar of the crowd, only he can see and faintly hear the tearing of meat, the wet squelching of feeding, the strangled scream-sobbing of the ram-headed man, whose hands, Daniel can now observe, are tied. And Marius gazes into the crowd, and his eye falls upon Daniel, and Daniel suddenly knows: he can see him seeing.

He sits with a racing heart until the crowd rises to leave, his heartbeat filling his ears. When he stands with the other patrons, two of the dancing women appear before him, hands folded neatly over their abdomens, and with waitress-patient tones gently ask him to remain seated. The spyglass rests forgotten already, tucked in his pocket once more, because he does not need the lens anymore to see what it had revealed.

As the last of the crowd departs, he can see around the two women, can see behind them, back on the stage, approaching: Marius, grinning; Marius, bearing a blank, blind grin beamed directly at him, his movements stilted as an automaton. And the vast dark thing lurking in his shadow, rising from it, twitching over his shoulder, expanding its fangs.

Daniel shoves past the women and bolts, racing to gain an advantage, get to somewhere he can stop to think; he runs up the stairs to the balcony, and kneels behind a pillar, drawing his gun, thumbing the safety. Over the railing beside him he sees a spiderlike leg spear up and bend down toward him, and then another, and he scrambles up from the floor, but the creature is fast. The first leg misses but the second catches him by the back of his shirt, jerks him stumbling backward, and for just a moment he is suspended by the short railing pressing at the backs of his legs before his balance shifts and he begins to fall backward over it.

Managing to take hold of a rail, he struggles to hold himself dangling from the balcony as the creature clicks and hisses underneath him, scrabbling also to keep its hold on the underside of the balcony with arthropod claws. Shouting, he kicks it in the face, hard, and then again and again, and his last few blows land on a couple of the reflective obsidian eyes, and it falls below, several of its legs folding with the force of the impact.

His right hand strains and sweats and the rail grows slick in his grip. His left hand carries his gun. He chances a look below and sees Marius—now he can see Marius clearly, unequivocally, to be an empty thing, a dumb smiling shell—and the horrible many-legged thing chittering below him in the dark, amused, waiting.

"Why couldn't you just play into the illusion, like the people here?" Marius says. Daniel sees his mouth fall slackly open and shut, a poorly-done ventriloquism; his voice comes crisply from the thing behind him. "They love it. All they want to hear is *fortune*. They need it, in fact—they need to pretend, to be told all is well."

"I can imagine they do," Daniel says, sweating under the strain of holding on.

His brother, unbidden, drifts into his mind: his brother, as he envisioned him in an image that haunted him for years, lying sightlessly upon clinical steel; his brother, stepping forward stone-faced through the window—a brief and incredible silence ended by a full, wet sound.

"But you couldn't let it alone, fixating on the suffering beneath," Marius says in the tired, gentle, reprimanding tone of a schoolteacher.

Daniel's head is spinning. The suffering beneath. The wild screaming of the ram-headed man, the gore-spattered stage. Scattered coins on the sidewalk. The glint of the feral dogs' eyes in the dark.

Gathering himself, he strains to look again behind and below him. His right hand burns and his shoulder screams with a jagged pain, a slight numbness at the edge.

He twists to aim the gun still grasped in his hand, neck aching, leg spasming uselessly; knowing it's futile, he fires. Marius laughs in a buzzing-clicking stridulation. Daniel's hanging legs grow still. His arm and his face relax. He realizes he has already made up his mind.

Just before he lets go, he wonders what his brother would have seen in the Theatre of Totality. No, he thinks to himself, there is no question.

He understands now. His brother would have seen the truth in the shadows all along. He always had.

Daniel releases the balcony rail and falls to the vast and dark and gleaming thing that rears and raises its cage of legs upward, gently, to catch him. Almost lovingly, they fold around him. His heart is pierced twice over, one great fang still stuck in him and then suddenly the next, his body jerking with the force of it; he makes a sound like a half-drowned man coming up for air.

Suspended in the air with his head hanging limply downward, he sees Marius's wild and idiotic grin upturned at him from below. Briefly, he dreams his brother's face imposed over it as he dies.

TERMS AND CONDITIONS APPLY

dave ring

I couldn't put them down, even though they were way too expensive. "We gotta go, Aaron. The car is almost here." Jo stood by the entrance of the store.

I returned the ten-eye red and black mottled Fluevog boots to the clear plastic stand.

"I guess you don't want to try those on." The goth girl behind the counter kinda had an attitude.

"I'm fine, thanks," I said and walked out.

"Are you fricking kidding me?" Jo said. "What a dick."

"Leave it, okay?"

"Whatever." Jo held up her bleached white hair to show off a fifth metal stud. The skin around it was swollen and pink. "Do you like my new earrings?"

"Yeah, they look good." I was probably letting her down by not saying something like *Yasss, queen, they look so fly* but I just couldn't.

She said something back, but I wasn't paying attention. "Who's that dude?" I asked, interrupting whatever Jo was saying. Tall and lean but broad in the shoulders, with a beard. Brown skin, dark hair. He had some script I couldn't read tattooed around his neck.

"You are so predictable," Jo said. "I'm sure he's straight though. I mean, he works at the *Captory*. There's Cassie. We have to go."

I could have argued but we had to go by the Captory anyway. I locked my eyes on the ground as we approached, to stop myself from staring, but right in front of the door, I couldn't help but snatch a sweeping eyeful from his shoes up to his face. And holy shit, he was looking right at me. As soon as our eyes met, I slid them up past him to the other guy that usually works there, Peter.

"Sorry man, that's not my thing," he was saying.

"Hey Peter," I said, as casual as I could.

"Hey man." Peter gave me the nod. I kept walking, relief running through me.

I wanted to talk to Jo about him more, but Cassie was already yammering on about all the lingerie she bought from Victoria's Secret. Since Cassie got her parents to let her start hormones and she got real boobs, she's been obsessed with them. She let Jo peek into her huge bag and started explaining where the lace would hit. The whole car ride went that way. Jo and I got dropped off together, since she lived next store to me.

"My sister says if you're not on time tomorrow she's going to leave you," Jo called out as loud as she'd dared. It was like 10:30pm. The lights were still on at her place. Not at mine, my mom was still at work.

Inside the house, dirty pots and pans filled the sink, wreckage from my mom cooking a week's worth of food for us. I filled the dishwasher and ran it, then poked around the fridge.

As usual, I didn't hear her come home because I was asleep, but at 6:30am, she woke me up with a shake. I made a noise and rolled over. She opened up the blinds and starting humming in an annoying voice.

"*Mom*," I said.

"*Aaron*," she said back, and kissed me on my forehead.

The day started like whatever. First two periods passed in a boring haze. When free period came around, I found Cassie and Jo around the corner from the smokers' pit.

"I have recently informed Harvard that I look forward to beginning my courses there this fall. Go Crimson!" Cassie said.

She must be practicing for her valedictorian interview with the school paper.

"What if they ask you about fencing?" Jo was serious.

"I don't know," Cassie said. "I don't know if Harvard will be weird about..." she trailed off.

"Oh my god, miss trans valedictorian has so many problems," I said, sarcastic.

Cassie's mouth opened and shut a couple times. Guilt hit me, just a little.

"What the hell, Aaron." Jo was pissed.

"I was *kidding*," I said. "Cass, I'm kidding. Sorry."

Cass turned away and flicked through something on her phone, ignoring me.

"Just stop, okay? We're trying to practice here," Jo said.

"I *said* sorry," I said. I sat by myself on the wall and started messing around in my journal. Their voices were like white noise. I started drawing a guy. The more I sketched, the more he resembled that dude from the mall. My hand spasmed when I drew the marks around his neck.

Something strange had been written in the middle of my scribbles: *You can be better than this*. I shivered. It wasn't in my handwriting. I didn't remember writing it. Like, I knew I didn't. The doodles around it, yeah, the ones I did with a dull blue pen that left little indentations in the paper. But these other words, they were black and glistening. I pressed my finger to the word *this* and my finger came away wet with ink.

I spun around. Now Cassie and Jo were talking to each other about some TV show. Jo raised an eyebrow at me. "You done sulking? You know that was a mean thing to say."

"No," I said, and she made a face. "I mean, yeah, whatever. I said I was sorry. Did you write in my journal?"

Cassie looked at Jo. "He is so stupid."

"Cassie, c'mon. He said he was sorry." Jo turned back to me. "How would we have done that, fuckhead? You were writing in it the whole time."

Cassie picked up her messenger bag. "The bell's about to ring. We have geometry. Coming, Jo?"

"I have to get my book from my locker. I'll meet you there."

"Fine."

When we were alone, Jo was all business. "Show me your journal."

I clenched it shut. "You sound like my mom."

"C'mon, what's the thing you thought we wrote?" she asked.

I stalled for a second, but opened it back up and showed her.

"What the hell, Aaron. I always thought you were like writing poetry or something. That isn't cute." Jo shoved the open journal into my chest.

"What?" I said to her back as she stormed off. I looked back at the page. Beneath the other thing, now it said something else: *Jo and Cassie are primadonnas.* Next to a sketch of two ballet dancers making out, all done in black ink. The back of my neck went clammy.

"*I* thought it was funny," I heard from from behind me. That guy from the mall. He was dressed in white pants and a strange, austere grey shirt with a high collar. It went down to his knees and had slits on the side. The collar opened at the neck, exposing those tattoos.

"Sorry about this." He gestured to his clothes and tugged at his collar. There was a slight sheen of sweat on his face. "I was in a meeting when you called. You'd probably like something else better." He didn't do anything that I could see, but his clothing completely changed from one moment to the next. Cutoff jean shorts exposing thick thighs, ten-eye black boots and a white undershirt that clung to the planes of his chest. He glanced down at himself and laughed. "This is what you're into, huh?"

"No," I lied. My cheeks got hot. The degree to which I now was jones-ing for this guy was out of control.

"No, no. You don't get out of it that easy. I don't mind, honestly, it's cooler. Come here," he said.

I wanted to go to him, I did. But I froze up. I stared down at my shoes, at the place where the sole had started peeling off. Something in me really wanted to move towards him, but I resisted it.

"Aaron," he said. "Look at me."

"How do you know my name?" My throat was dry like paper. My eyes flicked to my journal, the drawing that resembled him.

He'd gotten closer while I averted my eyes. "It's not as if you don't know my name, you know. Or at least the first part." He tapped the drawing's neck. "See. Although you got the end wrong."

His forearm, and the play of muscles under his warm skin, distract-ed me from his point. The broad nail of his finger pointed at my draw-ing of his tattoo. "Wait," I said, raising my eyes. "That's your name?" My fingertip went to his tattoo, unintentionally mimicking the gesture he'd made, but with skin instead of paper.

"You can call me Dhuaan." He smelled like smoke. Incense, not cigarettes.

"Dhuaan," I repeated, to make sure I said it right.

"Yeah," Dhuaan said. "Can I kiss you?"

I almost said yes. The word was smooth and cool in my mouth like a marble. I swallowed it.

"What?" I pulled back my hand from his skin. "No."

Dhuaan touched the small of my back. "Oh, I like you," he said. My spine twitched like I'd stuck my finger in a socket, but I didn't want to move away from him. "You have grit."

"Grit?" I repeated, looking up at him. Who said that? What was he trying?

"I'm not meeting my quota. Can you help me out?"

"Maybe." I felt my resistance crumbling. What was this about?

Dhuaan pulled away. I was relieved and distraught at once. "You're going to sign this."

"Sign what?" I asked. This made no sense.

Dhuaan pulled a phone out from his pocket, a brand I didn't recognize. He plugged a little attachment into it, like the little white squares vendors used at farmer's markets.

"Are you selling something?" I asked. "I don't have a lot of money."

"Something like that. You can afford it, I promise," he said. "If you agree to the initial terms and conditions, hold still."

"Okay," I said slowly. My agreement surprised myself. Why would I do this without knowing more? As the word left my mouth, I tried to pull it back. "For wh—shit!" Dhuaan had poked me with it. It didn't actually hurt, but a single drop of blood gleamed red on my fingertip.

"Sorry," he said. "It's archaic, right? You agreed, though." He scrolled through a document on his phone, filled with dense text, ticking boxes as he went. At the bottom was a bigger box. Dhuaan pressed his thumbprint against it, and the pressure left behind a swirling sigil. It was the same as the tattoo on his neck; the shape moved on the screen like a skittish colt. Dhuaan scrolled further and turned the screen sideways to reveal another box, this one wider and rectangular. It said *sign here*. He held it toward me.

"What am I signing?" I asked. I was going to get in trouble for being late; I had math next and Mrs. Kastor was a dick about those things.

"I thought you said you'd do it." He sounded hurt.

"I just don't get what this is. Some kind of weird survey?" Dhuaan sighed and hunched over. "What's wrong?" I asked. It took me by surprise. I reached out a tentative finger and held his shoulder.

He peered up at me like a puppy from an ASPCA commercial.

I shook my head. "Geez man, I'll sign for your survey or whatever." I took his phone.

"No, it's not really a—no, don't. Damn. You signed it."

I gave him back the phone. Dhuaan took it, but held it like he wouldn't mind if he dropped it.

"I thought you'd feel better," I said, uncertain.

"So did I," Dhuaan said. "What do you want?"

"Like, for lunch? What are you talking about?"

"No. Tell me three things. What do you *want*?" Dhuaan asked again. The warmth from earlier had faded.

"Oh man. Like I have to tell you right now?"

"Yeah," he said.

I thought about it. I sucked at coming up with lists under pressure. "Three things? Crap. I want those boots from the mall. And for people to stop bothering me when I don't want to be bothered. And to—"

"Hold on," Dhuaan said. He typed something into his phone. "Okay, you have a little left."

"—go on a date with you." Holy shit. I couldn't believe I said that. "A little what?"

"A little juice left in the deal before it runs out. Can't have everything." Dhuaan looked up from his phone. "Wait, what? For real?"

I started gathering up my stuff. My cheeks got hot again. "Yeah," I said. "You tell me where. When are you free?"

I glanced in his direction; Dhuaan crossed his arms over his chest. It made his biceps swell. The corner of his mouth twisted into a little smirk. "What about tonight?"

"Tonight works," I said, all fake cool. I shoved my notebook into my bag. "I gotta go to class though."

"Great," he said. "I'll pick you up at six."

"Cool," I said over my shoulder. Halfway to the school, I realized that my feet hurt. I blinked down at them, stopping short: ten-eye red and black mottled Fluevog boots had replaced my sneakers.

"Where are you supposed to be, Mr. Alvi?" Headmaster Liu asked me. She'd been putting up a sign for an after school study group night. Her clothes were as rumpled as usual, but I didn't let that fool me. She might seem like a lovely grandma but she only acted like one at open houses for prospective students. I braced myself for hassle.

"I'm on my way, Ms. Liu. Very sorry," I said.

But for some reason she only shrugged. "No problem," she said. "Do you think this is straight?"

"What?" I asked, surprised. The last time Ms. Liu caught me in the hall without a pass she'd dragged me to the office and called my mom.

"The poster," the Headmaster said patiently, pointing.

"Oh, of course," I said, and moved back so I could see it properly. It was only a tiny bit lopsided. "Just tilt the right side a bit up. Perfect."

"Thank you, Mr. Alvi. Have a good day," she said, and left me there.

I was stunned. But it went the same way with Mrs. Kastor. She didn't even blink when I walked in late. My feet hurt like you wouldn't believe though. At lunch, I took the boots off gingerly. I was right, both of my feet already had awful blisters. I side-eyed the Fluevogs, but I couldn't get angry at them. I had to leave them in my locker and put on old gym shoes.

I coasted through the day. I should have questioned it more, but I let it happen. Jo and Cassie said they were going to the movies or something, but Cassie gave me a ride home anyway without me even asking.

I listened to a bunch of music to get ready for the date. None of my playlists really worked for this situation. I had a bunch that were perfect for wallowing, and a couple for tortured journal entries, but none for whatever this feeling was. In the shower, I noticed a weird thing on my wrist. It took a few moments of rubbing at it with a washcloth before it occurred to me that it wasn't an ink smudge. It was the same sort of letters that went around Dhuaan's neck. They were only half visible and sort of hidden by the hair on my arm. They were sort of creepy.

After showering, I changed into a nice tshirt and jeans. Then into shorts, because it was hot, but then into these black chinos I had, because I had no idea where Dhuaan would want to go. I couldn't believe I was going on my first date. And that I had asked *him*. I decided I had to wear the plain black Vans that I wore to work. I looked okay in the mirror, I guess. I've always thought I was too skinny, not enough like a real guy. Or a straight guy, whatever. Even though I knew that was stupid; I mean, if someone built like Michael Sam could be gay, anyone could be. I couldn't help resenting that I'd always been so thin, no matter how much I ate. My mom always said I'd be glad for my metabolism when I was older. It annoyed the hell out of me.

I checked the time on my phone a couple times before I remembered that Dhuaan didn't know where I lived. I broke out in a cold sweat. I was such an idiot.

Then I had an idea. I got out my sketchpad and thought back to that swirling sigil that had appeared when Dhuaan put his thumb to his phone. It was hard to get exactly right, since it had been moving, but as I put a fourth shape on the page, keys jingled behind me.

"You learn fast," he said. He had on black jeans and a white tshirt.

I turned around. He was in my bedroom now. My bed was unmade and dirty laundry was piled behind the door where my mom wouldn't see it. Plus all the little kid stuff that I never bothered to take down. Trophies and posters. And—

"Is this a *teddy bear*?" he asked, with a wicked grin.

"No," I mumbled, "It's a vintage Teddy Ruxpin. What are you doing here?"

"I don't even know what that means," Dhuaan said. "But I'm 99% sure that this is a teddy bear. And that you're what, seventeen?"

"I turned eighteen last month," I said, and stepped in front of Teddy. "How is this happening? How is this real?"

"Just go with it," Dhuaan said. And I wanted to. So I did. "Tell me about the bear."

I had bought Teddy at the punk rock flea market and he'd been customized to play all the cassingles that punk bands had started putting out again. But I wasn't going to tell this guy if he was gonna talk so much trash. "If you're not explaining showing up in my house to me, I'm 100% sure I'm not explaining the bear. Let's go," I said, pointing at the door.

He eyed me with appreciation.

"What?" I asked.

"You look good," he said.

My cheeks got hot. "You don't have to say that." I thought about the last day. And all the hassle I should have gotten. "Those were like wishes, right?'

"Sort of," Dhuaan said.

I shrugged. "So, you didn't have a choice."

"This is boring," Dhuaan said. "Let's go." He took my hand. His fingers dwarfed mine.

"How are we going to get .... wherever we're going?"

Dhuaan met my eyes and my knees shook for a second. "I've got it covered," he said and swung open the door.

I don't know what I expected, but a Volvo wasn't it.

"What's the matter?" Dhuaan said, a little defensive. "They're like the safest cars on the market."

"It's fine," I said. "I thought you'd drive something—"

"What? More expensive?"

"—less beige," I finished.

Dhuaan's lip curled a little. His whole outfit became khaki.

"No," I said, my mouth cracking into a smile too. "Please. I can't be seen with you like that."

Dhuaan laughed. The shirt went white again, but he left the jeans alone. "Compromise," he said, and opened the passenger side door for me.

"Where are we going?"

"Not the movies," he said when he got in. "Definitely not the movies. Just like we are definitely not stopping by the convenience store to get cheap candy."

"You can't magic up some candy?" I asked. The word *magic* hung between us, awkward and strange, as we cut across main Street.

Dhuaan reached out through the awkwardness and took my hand again, eyes still on the road. "Magic spoils some things," he said. "Not worth it. Haribo is one of those things."

He squeezed me. I squeezed back. My palm started sweating but I tried not to think about it. A couple minutes later, Dhuaan took his hand back in order to make a turn, and after, he put it back on my thigh. I couldn't not react to it. I pulled my phone out so that I would have something to distract myself from my lap.

When Dhuaan saw my phone, he said, "Selfie time? Quick, we're at a stop light."

I would never in a million years have thought to do that. But I found myself opening up the camera. Dhuaan grinned wide and I cheesed, hard. I could barely look at myself. "Aww, that's a nice one," he said. "Hashtag date night, hashtag my boo."

"Stop," I said. "Too much, too fast. Are you even real? This could definitely be an extended hallucination. PS green light."

"I got it, I got it. C'mon, post it," he said. "I am totally real."

I hesitated, but when the picture posted, sure enough, Dhuaan was there. Within seconds, Cassie had liked it, and a second after that, posted, *Soooooo cute.* I hit the button to make the screen go dark. "Okay, you've convinced me. You're real."

We pulled into the parking lot of CVS. He leaned over and grazed my jaw with his thumb and before I knew it we were making out. Our lips mashed against each other with an urgency that I'd never felt before. He tasted good. His fingers were at my waist, half under my shirt, and whenever they connected with the skin of my back it was like lightning shooting through me. His stubble was like sandpaper; when we pulled away for a second my lips were raw.

"Wow," he said, smiling. "That was some first kiss."

"Yeah," I said. "Shit."

He untwisted the seatbelt from around my foot, ran a finger along my jaw, still smiling. I could look at that smile all day. "What do you want?"

I met his eyes. "What kind of question is that? Want like, to do next?" I wrinkled my eyebrows.

He laughed. "No, like, what candy? Haribo and what?"

"Oh," I said. "Runts. And Twizzlers."

"You're the boss," Dhuaan said. "Be right back."

I leaned back in the chair, my fingers unwittingly going up to my lips. It seemed like my whole body was buzzing. But it was actual buzzing from Dhuaan's phone. It had fallen between the seats. I pulled it out. He had 16 missed calls and a text from Vedansh. The entire text wasn't visible on the lock screen, but the first part said, "Only one soul in a week, Dhuaan? Not good enough for..." I put the phone back in the gap between the driver's seat and the console.

One soul. Is that *my* soul?

The car door opened. Dhuaan dropped a plastic bag in my lap overflowing with candy. "We shall feast like kings," he said. "What's wrong?"

"Nothing."

"No way. When I left, things were awesome. What happened?" He met my gaze. A vein in his forehead jumped.

I felt apprehensive now. I clutched at the bag of candy like it was my life. "I'm not sure about this anymore," I said.

"Where are you going?" he asked. His voice caught. "What did I do?"

Then the buzzing started again. Dhuaan ignored it for a second but then had a flash of understanding. "There's something on my phone, isn't there?" I opened the door as he started fumbling for it. "What does it say, Aaron? I can explain it."

The whole thing had me shook. I took advantage of the inability of his big hands to get in that small gap to slide backwards out of the car. "What did I sign away?" I asked.

Dhuaan cringed. "You probably won't even notice it," he said. "Probably. Get back in the car and I'll explain, honest."

"I don't think so," I said.

"But—"

"No," I said, and I put out my palm to stop him—then a wisp of smoke fluttered off my fingers. And the sigils drawn on my wrist got way darker too. One second I thought Dhuaan was going to make a scene in the parking lot and the next he backed off, all meek.

"It's cool," he said to himself. "It's cool." He got back in the car. I backed away until I the wall was behind me. I still had the bag. My phone buzzed in my pocket.

It was a text from Jo: *I can't believe you are out with that guy!*

I texted back: *He just left. Where are you?*

Jo: *Movie is about to start. East Main. Join us?*

Me: *omw*

I ran. It was stupid to run with these blisters, but I ran.

My phone buzzed a few more times while I ran. When I got to the theatre, panting, I pulled out my phone to check. I had texts from number I didn't recognize. They must have been from Dhuaan.

hey can we talk later

i know i have some explaining to do

i really like u

When I got into the theatre, Cassie and Jo were in the back row. Of course, they wanted to be told what was going on. We got shushed by the people in front of us when I started to explain so I showed them my phone. Cassie gave me a Look.

Did he try something you didn't want to do? she typed into her phone and showed to me.

I made a face and shook my head. *Not like that*, I typed. How the hell could I explain that I might have sold this guy my soul because I thought he was cute?

Afterward, when we walked into the fuscia-carpeted foyer, still blinking from being in the dark, Jo elbowed me. "Aaron."

"What?"

"*Aaron*," she said again, and pointed.

Dhuaan was coming out of a different theatre. Of course he was. We'd been going to the movies. I didn't think that he would have still gone. I crossed my arms.

"Oh, this is gonna be good." Cassie bit her lip. She only did that when she was excited.

"Yes, but we won't see it, because we're going to the bathroom." Jo took Cassie's arm.

"I don't have to pee though," Cassie said.

"Neither do I." Jo dragged Cassie after her.

I took a deep breath and started walking toward him. "But I wanna *see*," I heard Cassie say to Jo behind me. "It's gonna be *drama*."

"This isn't *Real Housewives*." Jo wasn't very convincing.

"I know," Cassie said. "It's more like the second episode of *Bachelor*."

"Come *on*."

I opened my mouth to speak when I got closer to Dhuaan, but before I could say something, someone else was there. Someone with a bad attitude, an undercut and a crop top exposing like twelve abs. They could have come from behind the *Batman Rises Again I Know, Yeah, Again* cardboard display, but I had just walked by there. So I knew they didn't. They came out of nowhere, the way that Dhuaan did.

"You're not working," they said to Dhuaan. It was halfway between a question and a statement. Sort of like they were halfway between butch and femme and I had no idea what gender they were? All I knew was that I wanted that cream suede jacket.

"What are you doing here, Vedansh?" Dhuaan said.

I knew that name. It was whoever had been blowing up Dhuaan's phone. Which maybe meant they were... whatever Dhuaan was?

Vedansh's lip curled. "I think I asked you the same thing. This isn't how we meet quotas."

"Well." Dhuaan looked away. "Maybe I have to work up to the big ones."

"Not gonna cut it anymore, kiddo." Vedansh unwrapped a piece of pink gum and put it in their mouth. "Weren't you paying attention in the meeting? You're in the big leagues now. We need you to produce something or Vadi Maan is going to cut you loose. Where's the soul you contracted with this morning? They aren't locked in yet. Can we escalate the terms?"

"There are complications," Dhuaan said finally.

"I don't have time for this." Vedansh blew out a bubble. "I'm responsible for you. Your ass isn't the only one on the line."

"I said there are complications. I need more time," Dhuaan said.

"What sort of complications?" I said. I couldn't stop myself. Both Dhuaan and Vedansh whirled around. "Because I'm about to make another one."

"Aaron," Dhuaan said. His face fell. "I want to talk but you should go."

"No, stay," Vedansh said, stepping in front of Dhuaan with a cocked head. "What has my brother told you about the contract you signed?"

My eyes narrowed. I couldn't help it. I didn't like the way they were treating him. "We were going to go over the fine print later," I said. "After dinner."

I saw Dhuaan open and close his mouth behind Vedansh.

"Really," Vedansh said. "That's not the impression I was getting."

"Well, maybe you can sort this out after our date." I said, stepping around them to Dhuaan's side. "Because that's what I was promised."

"That's true," Dhuaan said, as if he thought Vedansh might object. "Let's go," I said. I took his hand even though it was terrifying to do in public. It seemed like everyone was staring at me. I'm pretty sure no one actually was but Cassie and Jo, who were trying but failing to hide behind the *Batman* display. I might have been high on adrenaline at this point. Halfway to the parking lot, Vedansh was standing in front of us, although I would have sworn that they hadn't moved.

"I'm not sure who you think you are, but that isn't how you end conversations with an Ibdelisva," Vedansh said.

I glanced at Dhuaan.

He shrugged. "It's a hierarchy thing. I'm only an Isva." It still didn't mean anything to me.

I held my palm up, like I did in the CVS parking lot. "Aaron, don't," Dhuaan said.

"Leave us alone." I did the thing I did before, but there was way more resistance this time. A cloud of smoke billowed from my fingers; my wrist burned as the symbols there thickened and danced. Vedansh was midway through a bubble; it popped discreetly instead of all over their face.

Vedansh pirouetted like a dancer, their jacket swirling around them. "Sorry to bother you." I almost couldn't believe it had been so easy. And why had they been grinning?

Dhuaan gestured to my marked wrist. "Damn it," I thought he said. But then I realized he'd said, "Damned."

"What?" I asked. "They went away, didn't they?"

"Yeah," he said. "But you fulfilled another of the three terms."

I remembered that word he'd used. "What's an Isva? What are you?" I asked.

He winced. "I'm sort of a demon."

"Oh," I said. I thought about the different sort of demons I had heard of. "Like the Bible kind? Or like Rakshasa or what?"

"Or what," Dhuaan said. "Some of the other ones are real too, but we're different."

"You're like, terrible lawyer demons from hell," I said.

"Respectfully, that's like most demons. And we prefer to call it the Abyss."

"Oh well then," I said. "My apologies."

"Apology accepted."

"I didn't mean it," I said.

"Oh," he said.

My phone buzzed. "Oh shit." Cassie had boomeranged my little moment with Vedansh. Smoke billowed and unbillowed from my hand as the moment played out and then happened in reverse, over and over again. I showed it to Dhuaan. "Does this sort of thing get you thrown in demon prison?"

"Hashtag where's the dry ice?" Dhuaan read outloud. "No. This has like a hundred and four likes already. And Vedansh won't flag it. They look too cute in it." They did. The video captured Vedansh walking away so that both their coat and hair caught the wind perfectly.

When we got to Dhuaan's car, the reality of things started to catch up with me. "What does it feel like, to not have a soul?" I don't think I believed in the idea of a soul until I learned that I'd signed mine away.

Dhuaan started driving me back to my place without asking. We weren't that far away. "It doesn't hurt exactly. But it's also the thing that sort of makes you *you*. People without souls get boring. And sort of fade away."

"Fade away," I repeated. "Like a ghost."

"Like a living ghost," Dhuaan agreed.

"What the fuck," I said.

"I know," Dhuaan said. "I won't blame you if you never talk to me again."

We drove in silence until we got to my driveway.

When we pulled in, there was a twinge at my wrist. I held it up, and another section had darkened. "What the hell?"

"What happened?" Dhuaan asked.

"Oh my god," I said, thinking out loud. "Did the contract consider our date concluded because you dropped me off? The blood was one thing, but *this* is archaic."

Dhuaan jaw dropped and his brow furrowed. "I should have thought more about this. But I've never been on a date before."

"I can't believe it. You too?" I started laughing. "This just sucks because I really *like* you."

"That was sort of on purpose." Dhuaan's face fell, mood soured. "Makes you willing to sign things. Although I'm not really that good at enthrallment yet. You broke through most of it."

"I mean I figured that out, but I thought I liked you *despite* all that." I leaned the seat back, put my feet up on the dash and closed my eyes. I couldn't believe I was going to fade away.

Dhuaan hissed.

I shrugged. "I know it's rude, but you basically sold my soul, so I don't care."

"You're not wearing the boots," Dhuaan said.

"Oh, I'm sorry," I said. "I love them, but they gave me blisters."

"No," Dhuaan said. "That's great. That's perfect. If you're not wearing the boots, the contract isn't fully sealed."

"I'm not wearing the boots," I repeated. I wasn't getting it.

"You have to actually use the things you get from the deal, or it doesn't count."

"I took them off." I finally got it. "They're at school."

"I could kiss those blisters," Dhuaan said.

"Please don't. I'm not ready yet. Probably never. But what do we do about the boots?"

"Well," Dhuaan said. "There's still a risk of the contract being actualized if they get worn later. By you or anyone. So we need to burn them."

"No," I said, aghast. "They're beautiful."

"They're boots," he said.

"They're ten-eye red and black mottled Fluevogs," I said.

"Yeah," he said. "We're going to need to destroy them. With fire."

"What will that do?"

"It's like a loophole. The soul gets processed after all the previous terms and conditions are satisfied."

"What will happen to you? Your um, sibling, seemed pretty mad."

"Yeah, Vedansh and our boss Vadi Maan are going to be furious when they find out. But that's my problem."

"Maybe it can be our problem." I held up my arm so that he could see the moving sigils circling my wrist.

"Our problem," Dhuaan echoed. "Does that mean you're not breaking up with me?"

"Dude, we aren't even going out. We just made out a lot in your car one time."

"Oh."

"I might go out with you someday though." I took pity on him. "But I'm going to need more car makeouts first."

Dhuaan leaned towards me. "Like now?"

I kissed him again, and while I did, I made a decision.

"Oh man." He pulled away grinning. "Worth it. Lunchtime tomorrow I'll meet you at your school tomorrow with some matches."

I pulled out my phone as Dhuaan pulled out of the driveway. Would 'not being hassled' mean that I could walk out of a store without paying for shit?

I texted Cass: *I need to dish. You still with Jo?*

My phone buzzed: *We're at the mall now.*

I didn't hesitate. If I was going to have to burn those boots... *Be right there*, I texted.

What was the worst that could happen?

HOMECOMING
Erica Ruppert

I

Grace punched the accelerator as she ramped onto the interstate, forcing her aged Corolla up to seventy.

The call had come before dawn. Her mother was on morphine. She had better come soon. Grace had rolled out of bed and dressed in the dark so as not to wake Andrew. She grabbed extra clothes, her makeup and toothbrush, a towel, and stuffed it all into a canvas grocery bag. She left Andrew a note on the kitchen table, telling him where she had gone.

It was three hundred and fifty miles from Pittsburgh to Holyoak. Maybe five hours, without traffic, if she could keep up her speed.

Ahead of her the sun emerged as a white sliver on the horizon, and the sky streaked with grey and amber and salmon pink. Grace drove hard through the long rolling green of Pennsylvania, through mountains and fields and the scars of cities, and crossed the deeply cut Susquehanna River at Harrisburg. She wondered briefly at her calmness, then put the thoughts away.

Soon she was halfway home.

Home. Holyoak was only home because it was where her mother was. Grace had left it right after she graduated high school in 1977, nearly twenty years ago. The distance made a buffer against what she had been. Looking back seemed to Grace a failure, an admission that she would always be just a trash girl from the fringes of a broken town. Looking back meant she would be just as trapped as her mother.

Grace could count on her fingers the number of times she had returned to visit. The last time had been more than two years ago, for a brief, uncomfortable Thanksgiving dinner. She remembered how fast she had eaten, how she had refused the pie and coffee her mother brought out, just so she could leave. Even then, Sheila was fading. The twitch of Grace's conscience was suddenly sharp. She should have been a better daughter.

It was too late for it now.

II

Sheila had already slipped past any awareness by the time Grace reached her, her secrets kept. Sheila had refused all along to let her daughter know how fragile her condition was, how hopeless and finite. But, Grace admitted to herself, she never did ask her mother how she was really doing, or if her constant refrain of 'all right' was a lie.

The nurse who let Grace in was solid and quiet, calm as milk. She realized she had never known any of her mother's nurses by name. The woman smiled silently and disappeared into the kitchen, leaving Grace to find her way.

Sunlight flooded the house, with every shade open to let it in. Grace had not expected that. She had steeled herself for dim lights and mourning. The house was also impeccably clean, the air spiced with the faint tang of bleach.

Even her mother's room, when she entered it, was full of light. The blinds were up and the windows open, letting the early summer air wash out the closeness of the sickroom. Her mother was beyond being chilled, or disturbed by such brightness. Grace still moved as quietly as she could, taking in her mother's sunken face, her wasted body. Sheila made barely a ripple in the blankets.

Grace cleared off one of the bedside chairs and sat nervously beside her mother, speaking of trivialities to Sheila's unresponsive shell. She heard the floors creak as the nurse moved into the living room. The house was so quiet that Grace could hear her turning the pages of a magazine, passing time. Hours dragged on, slow as syrup. The nurse came in occasionally, to check Sheila's pulse, her heartbeat, her position. Sheila's breathing was like a failing machine, labored and abrupt, her mouth hanging slackly open, the rattle begun at the back of her throat.

A death rattle, Grace thought. So that's what it sounds like.

The heavy breathing went on, and on, hitching in Sheila's throat like a cough, the pauses between breaths stretching longer. Grace stared at her mother's face, watching her skin turn from pink to cool ivory, waiting for the end.

Grace held her own breath when her mother released her last.

The nurse, close enough to hear what was happening, hovered in the bedroom doorway. She waited a few moments before coming in to check for the stilled pulse, to listen for the stilled heartbeat. Then she turned to Grace and said, "I'm sorry. She's gone."

Grace nodded, suddenly empty. It was done. There was nothing more, nothing next. The nameless nurse offered her open arms, and Grace accepted. The human contact, the nurse's hand patting her back, was at once reassuring and unfamiliar. After a few seconds Grace pulled away.

Grace smiled slightly with embarrassment, tucked her hair back behind her ears, smoothed her pants along her thighs, and sat down again beside her mother's shell while the nurse marked the details of Sheila's passing on her chart and made the requisite calls. Grace touched her mother's hand. It was already cold. Sheila's skin had turned a pale yellow as the blood drained down. Grace had never seen someone die before. It felt so unfinished, so incomplete. She had expected more drama.

When the hearse came Grace stood politely aside as her mother's body was zipped into a black bag and wheeled out of the house. She followed the gurney outside, uncertain of what she should do, and stood on the porch as the calm, soft-spoken mortician loaded her mother into the back of the hearse with solemn, practiced smoothness. It looked too easy, too cleanly managed to be real. Grace felt as if she were watching from a distance. It was almost as if she were somewhere else entirely.

Once the hearse pulled away, the nurse gathered her bag and book and left Grace alone with the empty house. As she drove off, it occurred to Grace that she was an orphan now.

The sun had slipped down the sky, the light becoming more densely golden as the angle changed. Grace shut the door against the fading day and pulled every shade, letting shadow fill where light had been. The silence of the house was its own presence. She curled her legs under her on the worn sofa, picked at her nails for distraction. She added her own silence to the larger void.

III

It was the unfamiliar quiet that eventually woke her. She stretched her numb legs. She hadn't meant to sleep. She switched on a table lamp, and glanced at the wooden clock hanging beside the door. Eleven fifteen.

There were things to be done.

Dry-eyed, she stripped the bed where her mother had been, bagging up the sheets for garbage. She was glad that the mattress had been covered with plastic. She stripped that away as well, flinching at the noise of it. She found the extra bedding in the hall closet and remade the bed, tucking and smoothing the old chenille spread the way she had been taught as a girl.

Grace remembered jumping into this bed when she was very small, waking her parents when they needed their sleep, snuggling between them and being allowed to stay. It was one of only a few memories of her parents together.

She did not allow herself to linger over what was gone.

She tossed all the medications from the nightstand into the trash, the used tissues, a dying houseplant. Next she opened the closet. She would have to decide on a dress to bury her mother in, but all the rest would be trash. The idea of anyone else wearing a dead woman's clothes seemed wrong to her.

The smell of her mother's closet should have been familiar, but it was not. She remembered a different perfume, something sweeter and more floral, something young. The first scent she noted now was mothballs. She dug through the tightly packed clothes, skirts and dresses, blouses and coats, all long out of style. She tried to remember things she had seen her mother wear, but all she could imagine Sheila wearing was a housedress.

A slash of pale blue caught Grace's eye, sharp among the mostly dark garments around it. The fabric smelled of camphor, musk, and heavy roses. Grace laid it on the bed. She tried to picture her mother in it. Nothing came.

She emptied the closet onto the floor. Dry cleaners' bags rustled and slipped among the layers of fabric. There was even a fur stole tucked far in the back. She had never seen her mother wear it. She tried to imagine the mood that would have caused her to want it, or her father to get it for her. Grace petted it, the fur coarse and patchy. It had never been stored correctly.

On the closet's back shelf, behind the extra blankets, was a young girl's jewelry box painted with roses and ribbons. Inside were tucked folded love letters from Arthur Beaucher to Sheila Dinsmorte. Grace sat on edge of the bed with the box in her lap and unfolded the top one.

"Dear Sheila," it read, "I have missed you this week. Work has taken most of my time, but I will be there Saturday at seven to take you to the show. You know I love you. Art."

Beneath the letters were a few pieces of costume jewelry, a tangled strand of crystal beads and a rope of fake pearls, round clip-on earrings and two enameled brooches. Grace teased out a gold chain from the shiny nest. It was a bracelet with a single charm attached, commemorating Sheila's first holy communion. She put the charm bracelet gently back, closed up the box, put it on the bed.

She sighed, thinking of all the things she had never spoken of with her mother. But she kept moving, tugging open the night stand's drawer to stay ahead of the despair that lurked at her back.

Beneath the last few months' accumulation of Reader's Digests, Grace found a small double frame folded shut like a book. Inside was a picture of Grace at her sixth birthday, and opposite it a shot of her father. It surprised her, for it was the first photograph of him she had found.

The colors had faded with age, taking on a yellowed tone. The picture had been cut to fit the frame. Grace could just make out a sliver of someone standing next to her father. She studied the image closely, trying to fit the details of the photo to the memories she had of him. In the picture it was summer, and her father's shirt was dark around the neck and underarms from sweat. He was squinting into the sun, his pushed-back hat doing nothing to block the light. His face was creased, with shadows filling in the lines. He looked young. His smile was real.

There was no premonition of his leaving in the photo. Who had her father been, that her mother had kept him secret so many years?

Grace turned to the picture of herself as a child. Juxtaposed with that of her father, it told a fuller story. That had been the last birthday she had marked with him. She remembered that he had spun her around after she had blown out all the candles on her whipped cream-frosted cake. That was in April. By August he was gone. It was as if Sheila had tried to commemorate the last time they had been together as a family, to make something broken appear to be whole, or to preserve the last moment it was intact. Her mother was in neither picture. The two people Sheila loved most were frozen in time, separated from her, and from each other.

Grace stood the frame up on the nightstand next to the jewelry box and moved on.

She stripped the bathroom, next. The medicine cabinet still held an ancient bottle of L'Air du Temps that had evaporated to a few potent drops. Grace unscrewed the cap and tilted the bottle against her fingers. This is what she remembered. She dabbed the scant perfume behind her ears and threw the bottle out.

In the kitchen, Grace went through each cabinet, clearing out all the food. Everything, even sealed packages, went into the trash. She did the same with the few remaining contents of the refrigerator. She believed vaguely that eating a dead person's food was somehow unhealthy, unnourishing. As if the dead took its sustenance with them. She could not say where such a belief had come from, but she embraced it now. Loss made its own superstitions.

Grace finally sat down at the kitchen table, not sure what to do next. By the relentless ticking of the stove's clock, it was approaching three o'clock. She realized, now the food was all thrown away, that she was hungry. She gulped down a glass of water to trick her belly into fullness, then went upstairs to her old room to try to sleep.

It was strange to pass the night in her mother's empty house. When Grace had come back to visit she had always stayed at a hotel. Now the house felt like a stage set, impermanent and flimsy, and her childhood bedroom was as impersonal as any hotel room, just a space full of someone else's belongings. The same bedspread she remembered still covered the bed, the same abandoned toys and books still cluttered the shelves. They were at once hers and no longer hers. She did not know how to feel about them.

Grace lay on her narrow bed, staring at the wrinkled ceiling, cocooned in the rustling quiet of the night. Sleep when it came was thin and restless. She opened her eyes to raw dawn, disoriented and nervous. She did not feel real.

IV

It was barely nine o'clock when Grace rose with a headache and a stiff neck. She called her office to let them know she would be taking a week of bereavement leave, and a week of vacation following that. Two weeks, she thought, should be enough time to get everything in order, to tie up the loose threads of a life. She accepted her colleagues' offers to be there for her, to just call if she needed anything, anything at all, for the sincere but empty words they were. There was nothing her supervisor or coworkers could possibly do to help her now.

Next she called Andrew, another duty to be ticked off the list. She waited impatiently for him to answer. She considered hanging up. He picked up on the third ring.

Grace had married without informing her mother she was even seriously dating anyone. Grace told her afterward, when she and Andrew had settled into their new status of Mr. and Mrs. A. Spanner. Her mother had taken the news calmly, with no obvious sense of betrayal, and with little enthusiasm or surprise. But secrecy was her nature. Grace had learned it from her.

So Sheila never knew her daughter's marriage was unspooling around her. Sheila had never even met the man who was her son-in-law. Too late, now, Grace though. Too late to make up for anything she had not done.

Andrew was talking. She forced herself to focus.

"How are you?" he said. "How is your mother?" he added before she could answer the first question. His voice sounded hollow and distant over the phone, the connection poor.

"She's gone," Grace said. "She was all but gone when I got here."

"You should have flown," Andrew said quickly. She stayed silent, counting seconds.

"Sorry. I didn't mean it like that," he said at last.

"I know." Grace said, already drained.

It was his pattern, to react bluntly and then retract what he had just said. It exhausted her, his inconstancy, his refusal to think before speaking, the repetitive snipe and apology that was his pattern of conversation.

"Look," she said. "I don't want to talk now. I didn't get enough sleep."

"I'm sorry," he said again. "I can be out there by tomorrow night. I just have to get some things in order in the office and I'll be on the road."

"No. I can handle this myself. Most of it's already done." She rubbed her forehead, trying to ease the headache behind her eyes. She should have gone out for something to eat to stave off the coming crash. She heard Andrew breathing into the phone as he composed his response. She could tell that he wanted to push her, to win his point.

"All right," he said, a chill creeping into his voice. "Call me if you need me, I'll come."

Of course he would. He needed to be at the center of anything in her life. Her own temper flared at the thought of him intruding even here, into her mother's death. She bit her tongue, kept the peace.

"Goodnight, Andrew."

"Goodnight?"

Grace paused, confused.

"Goodbye. I meant goodbye."

He hung up. Grace didn't care.

She left the phone off the hook. She didn't want to talk to anyone right now.

She went into the living room. The house was a void around her, familiar in all its details yet still an alien space. Nothing looked quite as she remembered it, even though all the furnishings had been here when she was young. It was disconcerting to have her memories made concrete again only to show that her memory was inaccurate and incomplete.

V

Grace was unsure what to do with herself, how to fill the unwanted wealth of hours. She did not know what new power she had over her mother's things. The idea that they were her things now had not yet taken root.

She opened the blinds in the living room and kitchen, letting in bright morning sun. It reminded her of yesterday. In daylight the neat furnishings revealed their true shabbiness. Her mother had not changed anything that Grace could tell. It was as if the house were trapped in amber. Her preserved room was not the exception, but the standard.

She returned to the barren kitchen as her hunger flared into a sharp cramp. Her headache had intensified. She pressed her fingers into her eyes to ease the pain. She had to get some food.

Although she felt grimy from her night's work, Grace didn't feel like making the effort of showering. She got her bag of toiletries and washed up at the green bathroom sink, using her shirt for a towel. The taste of the toothpaste tamped down some of her hunger pangs. Her hair was too tangled to lay smooth without washing it, so she tied it back in a frizzy tuft.

She changed her underwear and top and pulled back on the jeans she had slept in.

She checked herself in the mirror. The strain of the last day cut grey lines beneath her eyes that would not wash away. She shrugged at her reflection and left the house.

The day was beautiful, richly summer. For several minutes Grace just stood in the glow of the morning sun, letting it warm her skin and ease her head. Her mind seemed clearer now she was outside. She looked at her car where it squatted on the gravel driveway. She had cash in her pocket but her keys were still in the house. She knew she would lose momentum if she went back in, and set out on foot.

Sheila's house was on Route 12, a few miles outside the town proper and too far out for amenities like sidewalks. Grace walked along the wide shoulder of the road, careful of smashed cans and roadkill. When Grace was a child she had had a bicycle for trips into town. She imagined that bike would still be in the barn, if she looked for it.

Cars passed at long intervals and swung wide as they approached to give her space. The long grass growing up along the road smelled sweet and warm. Insects buzzed in the rising heat, the white noise of nature. Her feet slapped the pavement in fabric flats not designed for long walks, picking out a rhythm over the background buzz.

Small houses were scattered widely here, set back on their lots and separated by empty fields. At this time of day the houses were quiet, the life in them gone elsewhere. Grace embraced the solitude.

Her mind was not empty, but her thoughts were so unanchored and amorphous that she felt as if she were not thinking of anything at all. It was its own kind of peace. She jumped when a pickup truck honked at her as it went by. She had drifted out into the lane.

At last she reached the outer fringe of town, and Route 12 became Kingswood Road. Houses assumed a suburban closeness, and she stepped up to a narrow sidewalk. A blister ruptured on her heel, but she kept walking down the long slope of the road, limping slightly, her shoe damp. As she rounded the last slow bend the town opened up before her.

The main structures of Holyoak remained constant, the hotel and bank and the Victorian mansions that had once belonged to the town's elite. But so much else in the tiny town was changed. She had rarely bothered to go into town when she came back to see her mother. It was uncomfortable to finally see all the changes at once.

The ancient Citgo gas station at the intersection of Kingswood and Mill Street had a small deli attached to it, now, to support the new municipal parking lot. Grace hobbled in. The slack-eyed girl behind the counter looked young enough that she should have been in school at this time of day. Grace picked a premade tuna sandwich from the cooler, paid and walked out. She felt eyes on her back. The girl did not trust her or particularly want her in the store. She was not a regular here, not recognized.

Grace had forgotten the cloistering attitude of an isolated community, even one that appeared to be growing. The cliques and fluid associations of the university were nothing compared to the ability of a small town to shut out an outsider.

She headed down the last stretch of Bridge Street where it ran short and straight toward the river. In this part of the state everything led to the river.

The only people she noticed were in either the diner or the laundromat. But it was a weekday, and most of the shops lining Bridge Street in Holyoak were for the tourist trade—coffee bars and gift shops, restaurants and antiques. A few artists had taken up residence in the apartments over the storefronts, and advertised their wares in their windows. None of these shops were ones she remembered, but these businesses had always cycled through with fair regularity, prey to the whims of the tourist economy. Grace browsed the shop windows as she walked, looking idly at the displays, wanting none of it. Let the Sunday visitors have their souvenirs.

Grace stopped before she reached the river. She sat at a wrought iron table outside a still-closed Mexican restaurant half a block up from the bridge. As she unwrapped her sandwich and started to eat, she wondered how long the place had been there. She knew the building flooded every few years.

This corner was also the stop for the bus to New York and Philadelphia. She guessed the older kids still used the bus to escape sometimes, the way they did when she was in school. Grace had never gone with them. Sheila wouldn't allow it.

Grace remembered sharply how it felt to be left behind.

She balled up the empty sandwich wrapping and stuffed it into her pocket. Her headache had faded but her stomach clenched, wanting more. She disregarded her hunger, and walked back up through town.

The businesses that served the locals were buried in the side streets. Grace turned up Race Street to find the pharmacy still in the low-slung, dingy stucco building that housed it in her youth. It took up half of Holyoak's single strip mall.

She went in, stopping in front of the bright displays to get her bearings. The carpeting was new, and the fixtures, but the layout was essentially the same as it had always been. Grace browsed slowly through the magazine rack and the greeting cards, and the surprisingly good selection of rental videos. She picked one up, read the back of the case, put it gently back.

Cosmetics, easily shoplifted, were kept close to the register and the pharmacy counter at the back of the store. Grace drifted over, drawn by the vibrant colors of eyeshadow and nail polish. She squatted down in the aisle to examine the glittery, crayon-hued display. As she leaned forward she realized that she was being watched. Not with the same urge of dismissal she had felt in the gas station, but watched just the same. She turned as she rose.

The woman behind the counter was older than Grace by at least a decade. She looked familiar, although Grace could not name her. She knew her face from her youth, part of the scenery.

"You're Sheila's girl," the woman said.

Grace stepped up to the counter. "Yes, I am. I'm Grace."

"That's right. I'm sorry about your mom."

"Thanks." Grace was not sure how else to respond. It didn't surprise her that her mother's death was already known, not in a town this small. The local newspaper office was only two doors down.

The doorbell chimed as another customer came in. Grace glanced over her shoulder.

"You don't remember me," the woman behind the counter said, drawing her back.

Grace shook her head.

"We lived down the road from you when you were a kid. Lemonte."

"Okay," Grace said. The other customer stepped up behind her.

"Never could get a real feel for you folks. Your mother was nice enough, but we hardly ever saw her after you left."

Grace tried to remember a family named Lemonte, but she couldn't. "Yes," she said, stalling. "My mother kept pretty much to herself."

The Lemonte woman reached suddenly past Grace to take a greeting card from the other customer. Grace stepped to the side, self-conscious.

"Hi, Barbara," the woman said, "This is Sheila's girl, Grace."

Grace turned at the introduction, aware of her poor grooming. Barbara was about her mother's age, but without the hunted look her mother had worn. Grace smiled weakly, already tired of being a novelty.

"Imagine that," Barbara said. "It has been a very long time since I've seen you."

Grace's curiosity stirred. She waited for more.

"I worked in the Five and Ten. You used to come in after school."

Grace studied the woman's softly wrinkled face for one she recognized. At last it came to her.

"Yes. Yes, I know you," Grace blurted. "Mrs. Tracey. You used to wait till school was out to feed the fish in the pet department."

Barbara smiled. "I did. Will you be in town long?"

"I don't know how long. At least a couple of weeks. I have to clean out the house, get things in order."

"The house," Barbara said, neutral.

"Sheila just died," Mrs. Lemonte interjected.

"Oh. Oh, I'm sorry, Grace. I didn't know."

Grace shook her head. "It hasn't been formally announced, yet," she said. "The funeral is tomorrow."

Barbara murmured her sympathies again while Mrs. Lemonte finished the transaction.

There was nothing more to say. Grace wished the women goodbye and made her way out of the store. She knew that they both watched her as she left.

Being in the town again resurrected old memories she had put away when she left, and allowed others to rehash their own memories of her and her family. Grace had not considered the impact of seeing anyone from her childhood again. She was not ready to rekindle any relationships in Holyoak.

She wished now she had driven, so she could get away.

With her head down, Grace made her way across town to the IGA.

The supermarket was small but clean, and had been here since the late eighteen-hundreds under one name or another. She went up and down each aisle, examining the stock, picking up packages of unfamiliar brands and studying each of them like some new toy. Deciding what she wanted in the house was harder than she had expected. Slowly, she filled a hand basket with a few essentials to replace what she had thrown away, instant coffee, tea, milk, sugar, bread, peanut butter, a few apples. It was more than she could comfortably carry. She did not particularly care.

The woman at the register was stone-faced as Grace fumbled in her pocket and pulled out the crushed bills. She watched impassively as Grace smoothed the bills before handing them over. The woman counted them slowly, and just as slowly made change. Grace dropped the coins into a donation can next to the register, looped her bags over her wrist, and left with a feeling of relief that she was done.

As she walked back through the quiet streets Grace felt as though someone was just behind her, watching over her shoulder. She turned her face up to the sun. She knew she should at least enjoy that, but she could not. Not here.

The plastic bags cut into the soft skin of her forearm as she made her way slowly back up the hill out of town. She shifted the groceries from hand to hand every few steps to relieve the pressure. More blisters had formed where her thin shoes rubbed her heels, and she found herself shuffling like an old woman. It did not matter how beautiful the day was. Grace was in no position to be part of it.

By the time she reached the house again the back of her left foot was bleeding freely. She wondered if she had left a trail along the road for a hunter to follow. When she stepped onto the lawn she dropped the bags, kicked off the torturing shoes and let the thick cool grass ease her mangled feet.

It took her a few seconds of squinting into the sky to realize she was crying.

The noise of passing cars finally made her aware that she was standing in the open. She wiped her face on her sleeve and brought the groceries in. The milk was already warm. She stuck it in the empty fridge anyway.

When she was done in the kitchen, she hauled all the garbage bags she had filled yesterday out of the house, and sat outside for a while to rest. She knew she should eat again but her hunger had waned.

It was beautiful here, deep in the country, with a field for a back-
yard and trees all around. Grace had let so much go when she left here.
She did not know if she could ever get it back. She wanted a cigarette
badly, even though she had quit a decade ago. She could taste the heavy
smoke, old addiction teasing out the memory of it. Her hands trembled slightly.

She got up and went back inside.

VI

She found herself glad for nightfall. She indulged in a long shower at
last, wincing as the hot water splashed over her torn feet.

As she dried herself off the phone rang. She ignored it. It stopped
after nine rings, then began again, and again, and again, until Grace
could not stand the sound of it. She wrapped herself in a towel and
padded down to the kitchen to answer.

"Who is this?" she said.

"I've been calling you," Andrew said with an edge in his voice.
"Where were you?"

Grace sighed heavily into the phone.

"I don't need this now, Andrew. I was in the shower. The funeral is
tomorrow. Can you just let me get through tomorrow?"

He barked out a short laugh. "Yeah. Sure."

And then he hung up. She held the hook down, the receiver still in
her hand. Almost immediately, the phone rang again. Grace disconnected, lay the receiver across the top of the phone, and put herself to bed.

VII

The funeral was lonely. Grace sat in the center of the front row, solitary, dry-eyed. Sheila had made her own arrangements with the funeral
home when her health first began to decline. Grace only found out the
details as she read through the folder of papers left out on her mother's
desk. Sheila had chosen a plain wooden coffin, purchased her burial
plot, selected the pattern and prayer for the remembrance cards. She
had even composed the death announcement that would be submitted
to the newspapers. All Grace did was call the funeral director to review
the details and to set the date for the viewing and burial.

There were only a handful of mourners to shuffle past her, peering
at the closed coffin before offering their rote sympathies. There was not

much else for them to say. They did not know Grace. They had scarcely known Sheila.

No one who came shared a memory with Grace, or spoke of how Sheila would be missed. She wouldn't be. She had left nothing behind. It was a small town, and although her mother had never left it, she had only isolated herself further after Grace's father had gone. The only two people Grace knew to be her mother's friends were already in their graves.

Grace folded a handkerchief into a tiny square to keep her hands steady. She was glad she had told Andrew not to come to this, to let her bury her mother in peace. He would only have issued some sort of judgment on the scarcity of mourners, criticized the casket or her mother's dress. He wouldn't be able to stop himself.

The quiet in the room was suddenly sliced by a woman keening her sorrow. Grace turned in her seat to find another face she did not recognize. The few other attendees did not acknowledge the woman, did not even glance at her as they talked among themselves. Grace could not help but stare in amazement as she continued to wail and clutch a rosary to her throat. After several minutes the funeral director, Mr. Gantz, came to the door and nodded at her. She at once fell silent, gathered her purse, and left. Gantz glanced quickly at Grace before he retreated.

Grace felt as if she had forgotten some vital part of the mourning ritual, of having committed a subtle insult she could not name. She got up to stand near the coffin for something to do.

The viewing dragged on, and the few mourners straggled out. For a time Grace was alone in the room. The soft classical music playing in the background began to tug at her attention, intruding, drawing her out of her reveries. As she slowly circled the room, examining the restful art on the walls, she saw that an elderly man had entered and was standing at the back. Grace stopped moving when she made eye contact with him, and waited for him to approach her. She held out her hand, retreating into formality.

"Thank you for coming," she said.

The man took her hand, gripped it softly. He was old, his skin falling in deep wrinkles from the squint of his dull blue eyes. He wore shabby but neat clothes, respectful of the occasion.

"I don't expect you know me. I didn't really know your mother, just to say hello. I knew your dad better. I'm Lou DeChansey. John De-Chansey's cousin. You knew him."

"Yes," Grace said, tipped off balance by this introduction. "We knew him well."

Lou gestured to the empty chairs. "Let's sit," he said. "I'm tired. You must be, too."

He settled into a seat, tugging up the knees of his trousers. Grace felt unaccountably vulnerable. She craned around, but there was no sign of the director.

"I guess you're wondering why I came," Lou said, pulling her back.

Grace nodded, slowly, uncertain of where he was steering her. "I wonder why anybody came," she said.

"This is strange country," he said. "Some strange people in it."

He paused, to see if she would follow him. Grace felt lightheaded.

DeChansey waited, reaching out to pat her hand. His skin was cool on hers. He continued.

"My cousin John was a good man, but he wanted to go another way. He and your father were as close as brothers, and they went bad together. Your mother got caught up in it through no fault of her own."

Grace looked at where his hand lay over hers, trying to fathom the conversation.

"I'm sorry to bring this up now" he said. "I know you don't want to hear it."

Grace looked up at him. His eyes were fixed on her, sharp and wary.

"No," she said. "I don't. I really don't want to hear your gossip."

DeChansey leaned forward. "It may be better that you don't, then. This way the trouble he and John got into won't go any further. Your mother knew enough, but she was smart. She wouldn't say a word. Not a word."

Grace saw Mr. Gantz at the open doorway again, listening. He dipped in when he realized Grace saw him. Gantz nodded at Grace, then turned to DeChansey.

"Lou, don't you think you've taken enough of Ms. Beaucher's time today?"

DeChansey bristled. He withdrew his hand, clenching it against his own knee. He made a show of ignoring the director.

"Forgive me," he said to Grace. "The sadness of this occasion has made me speak foolishly."

Grace nodded, but would not look at him again.

"All right then," he said. "Let the dead bury their own."

He rose, straightening his jacket. "My condolences on your mother. May she rest in peace." He brushed past the director as he left, in a small show of dominance. Grace sat stiffly in her chair after he was gone. Gantz came up to her and rested a hand on her shoulder. She shrank away from it, until he murmured apologies and left the viewing room.

Deep inside the funeral parlor she heard the heavy chime of a grandfather clock. She felt very much alone.

Her mother had wanted a full four hours. The last hour of the viewing passed at glacial speed. There were no other visitors. Grace realized the few who had come had been on their lunch hours.

To distract herself, Grace wandered in and out of the room, stepped briefly outside into the light and warmth of the empty parking lot, ventured downstairs to the disused smoking lounge where the air held an enduring acrid tinge. When she trailed back to the empty viewing room she made certain not to look into her mother's coffin. She already knew what was in it. She sat again, and waited. At last Mr. Gantz came up to her to tell her the wake was over. Fortunately, Grace thought, there would be no service. The niceties here were finished.

She thanked him for his time, picked up her purse, and walked out without a final farewell at the coffin. There was no point in it. It would only be window dressing, a show without an audience.

Grace waited in her car while the staff brought the coffin out, slid it into the hearse, and loaded the meager flower arrangements around it. She stared off into the empty sky. Nothing to see, anywhere. The subdued click of the hearse doors closing drew her back down. She pulled her car up behind it for the short trip to the cemetery.

Except for the gravediggers, she was alone at the grave as the coffin was lowered into the ground. She felt deflated, empty, as she threw her handful of dirt into the grave, her single carnation.

All that was left were ashes and dust.

VIII

After the burial, Grace drove the two blocks into the small heart of Holyoke. She didn't want company, but she was not ready to be alone in her mother's house. The day was bright. She got a cup of coffee at the coffee shop, and cradled the paper cup between both hands as she navigated the uneven brick sidewalk in her high heels. She didn't hesitate when the sidewalk ended above the river. Her heels sank into the silty bank as she made her way to an empty bench.

It was sheltered here, shielded from the street above by a screen of saplings and weeds, and canopied by low-hanging branches. Grace sat motionless, listening to the birds calling from the trees, gazing at the ripple and flash of the river. Her coffee grew cold in her hands, forgotten.

She had been there at the end, she reminded herself. That was important. But it was not enough. The void was huge. Grace's eyes ached. She wondered that she didn't cry.

As time slid by, the sounds of life in the town grew louder. Cars rattled over the bridge with people coming home. School let out, and teenagers gathered in the parking lot behind her. She heard them laughing and horsing around, heard the scrape of skateboards, smelled the tang of cigarettes. She had never been so free as they were. She had always had something to hide.

A young girl came down the path through the corridor of weeds, looking for some privacy of her own. Her eyes were rimmed black, and silver rings glinted in her ears. She stopped when she spotted Grace, not expecting anyone to be there. Grace looked up at her, met her eyes. The girl ducked her head and retreated.

Grace sat there until the sun began to sink. It got dark quickly in the river valley, with the surrounding hills hastening the dusk. She rose in shadow and climbed gingerly back up to the sidewalk. Older kids still hung out, messing around on bikes and skateboards. She watched them for a moment before her presence dampened their fun. She walked quickly through their small crowd, smiling faintly, trying not to create too much of a disturbance with the sharp click of her heels.

It was after seven. The streetlights had just come on, fading into the gathering night with their dim yellow glow. Except for the pizzeria, the shops on the street had closed for the night. Grace dumped her cold coffee into a trash can on her way to her car. As she got behind the wheel and closed the door, the weight of the day swept down and crushed her, and she began to sob.

After a few minutes she forced herself to stop, so she could see well enough to drive home.

IX

At night the house made its strange own noises. Grace slept poorly, waking at unfamiliar sounds, at fragmented dreams that roused her almost to consciousness. It was scarcely past dawn when she gave up and made her way downstairs.

The kitchen looked strange in the morning light, the lines of it somehow become crooked overnight. Grace filled a cup with instant coffee and sat heavily at the table, staring out the window over the sink. She felt as if she were floating away. With the funeral over, there was nothing in particular to anchor her here any longer. She drew patterns in the wet ring left on the table by her coffee cup.

Mourning felt strange, like a garment cut too closely. She was not precisely sad. Instead she was exhausted. She was alone with this loss. She was the only one who could bear it.

She finished her coffee and forced herself to get up, to rinse out the cup, to do something productive.

Grace went through the rooms again, assessing now. She realized that she hadn't really looked at anything here in years. There was surprisingly little accumulation. Her mother had been more prone to discarding than hoarding, but it still seemed so little to remain of an entire life. Grace tried to remember any clutter or decoration in the house when she was growing up, but she could not form a clear image.

In the living room she picked up a small glass figurine of a ballerina from its place of honor on the console television. She had bought it for her mother when she was nine, as a birthday present. She had gotten it in the Five and Ten, paid for it with money hoarded from Christmas. She remembered how proud she had been when she gave it to Sheila, how pleased Sheila had been to receive it. Grace began to cry again, hard sobs that wracked her then ended as quickly as a summer thunderstorm. Her breathing was ragged. Still holding the ballerina, Grace sat down in a floral-upholstered chair.

She had never considered her mother to be sentimental. Grace wondered what else she would find.

She covered her face with her free hand. Sobbing broke her again. The pain was immense, like being swallowed by the sea. She sat for a long while, staring teary-eyed at the empty room, watching the light move, waiting for some swell of inner resources.

At last she gathered herself. She decided it would be best to begin in the attic, and work her way down.

The attic was warm and airless, and brighter than she had expected, full of strong sunlight that fell in bars through the slatted shutters covering the small windows. The space smelled of dust and dry wood. Boxes were stacked under the slope of the roof, piles of old fishing equipment, odds and ends that had made their way up the narrow, dog-legged stairs and been forgotten.

Grace could only stand fully upright directly under the peak of the roof, wary of nails coming through the boards near her head. She pulled the chain for the single unshaded bulb wired to a beam beside her. Its light was all but lost to the invading sunlight.

She knelt to gingerly explore the boxes nearest her, expecting to disturb squirrels or a nest of mice. The dried husks of carpenter bees were all she saw of pests, though. Grey dust stained her hands. She should have worn gloves.

The first box was full of her old baby clothes, faded and brittle with age. She held up a tiny pink bonnet with a stain on its brim. Beneath it was a matching dress, delicate as a china cup. Grace mourned the child she did not have, here among the remains of her own infancy. She pushed the box aside and opened the next one.

Far away downstairs the phone rang. She ran down the two flights to the kitchen and fumbled the receiver off the hook.

It was Andrew.

"I'm in the attic," she said without greeting him.

"How is it going?"

"I don't know. I need to see what's even here before I decide what to keep and what to toss. I just found all my old baby clothes."

"Cool," he said. She could tell he was not really listening.

She bit her tongue on the flood of injured words that wanted to be spilled. She sighed.

"I want to get this done while I have the light," she said.

"Alright. When do you think you'll be coming home?"

"I don't know. I can't tell yet."

Andrew had often criticized Grace's relationship with her mother, of the long distance and weeks without speaking. He saw nothing wrong with lecturing her on how she should treat a woman he had never met. She had tried to explain, and he had told her that her reasons were wrong. It was no surprise to her that he had no sense of what she was experiencing, how complicated it truly was. He took death as a personal affront. Andrew had lost two of his high school friends since she had been with him. The misplaced rage he had thrown at Grace startled her into hiding. He threatened to leave her, accused her of being the distraction that kept him from his friends before they died. There was no compassion in him, no ability to be there for the bereaved. There was only blame.

"Let me know when you do," he said. He hung up as she said goodbye.

She dragged herself back up the stairs, and went back to the box she had opened before Andrew called.

The first thing Grace lifted from it was a folded sheet of leather, its center stiff and darkly stained. Black dust drifted from it as she opened it, wincing at the way it crackled. Beneath the leather was a fabric pouch holding thirteen carved and polished bits of what seemed to be bone, At the bottom of the box was a thin book, no more than a pamphlet, brittle pages in a faded cardboard cover.

She bent the cover back carefully. On the first page was written "To Raise the Dead" in a sweeping, messy hand, and below that "Arthur Beaucher". Her father. Tucked between the pages was a smaller sheet of paper, fuzzy with age and covered in her father's script.

"John," it said, "Whatever you convince yourself, do not try this. Too much can go wrong. Keep her safe. A."

Grace pushed the box back into place and climbed down from the attic. She carried the small book into the bright sunlight of the back yard. She sat on the doorstep and looked up at the wide blue sky before she opened the notebook again and began to read.

It took longer to get through than she had expected. When she finished, she went back and reread it, and then returned to particular parts of it. The contents of the book were one of the strangest things she had ever seen, describing, literally, the raising of the dead. Her father had clearly believed this—he had written out a set of instructions and then made copious notes about the flaws he found in the original process.

He also clearly believed it was dangerous. Grace wondered why he had not simply destroyed the record and let his findings disappear. Perhaps he had believed that someday it would matter again.

Grace closed her eyes and let her head fall forward. She was tired. Her mother had always told her that her father had left them, gone away and never come back. Now she wondered if he had a choice in it, if he had fled because of something he had done, if he had been driven away rather than left on his own.

It was not a mystery that could be solved by asking anyone in town. She knew of no relatives on either side of her family, no old friend who might know the truth of the matter. She thought of Lou DeChansey and his insinuations, but the idea of finding him and listening to his melodramatic story was too much for her. She wasn't sure what good could even come of asking.

The sun made her drowsy. She thought idly of what Andrew would have to say if he ever saw her father's notebook. She did not particularly look forward to going home to him. As barren as her life was at this moment, she was glad that she was here alone. She was glad that she had to explain nothing, could just let things happen as they would and let them be. It was already hard enough.

X

She cleared out most of the attic over the next day, bringing the brittle boxes into the living room to sort through. She realized that none of this meant anything to anyone but her. It made her even more lonely. She piled the boxes behind the house. She kept the strange notebook, leather sheet, and bones, a couple of boxes of her father's books, and a small portrait of her mother which Sheila had inscribed "For Arthur".

In her second day of solitude a knock came at the front door. Grace started. She was becoming used to silence. She ran her hands over her dirty hair to lay it in place, and opened the door.

An older woman stood before her, holding a container wrapped in foil.

"I'm sorry to intrude," the woman said. "I'm Geneva Roche. I was a friend of your mother's, a long time ago. I heard you were here and thought you might like some company."

Grace stared at the woman for a moment, then invited her in. While Geneva stood in the entryway Grace went around the room lifting shades, pushing back curtains. In bright daylight the room looked littered and abandoned.

"I'm sorry," Grace said. "I haven't been out much."

"It's all right," Geneva said.

"Please, come in to the kitchen," Grace said.

Geneva followed her in, and set the container on the table. "It's cookies," she said.

Grace set water on to boil.

"Sit," she said as she got out cups, tea, and instant coffee.

"You were still a baby, the last time I saw your mother," Geneva said as she settled in. "My husband and I lived the next farm over. My kids were a little older than you. Sheila used to watch them for me, sometimes, when I had errands to run, and I would sometimes watch you. But you were too young to remember any of that. Tea, please."

Grace unwrapped the cookies, set them in the middle of the table.

"I don't think my mother ever told me about you."

"We moved away while you were still a baby. Not too far, but far enough. It's hard, with little ones. I tried to keep in touch but your mother just stopped responding, wouldn't answer the phone…I missed her terribly. I was sad to hear she had died."

The kettle whistled. Grace dropped teabags into two cups and poured the water over them, glad for the activity, glad for the chance to step away from the unexpectedly intimate conversation for a moment. Geneva spooned sugar into her cup.

"My mother became reclusive after my father left," Grace said. "It was no fault of yours. She just couldn't handle the world after that."

"You two were lucky to have John DeChansey around. He took good care of you and Sheila."

"Did you know him?" Grace asked.

Geneva shrugged, smiling. "I knew the DeChanseys in general, and John had a good reputation."

Grace sipped at her tea. She took a cookie, broke it in half on her plate, did not taste it. "When I was small I wished he would marry my mother and stay with us."

Geneva nodded.

"I wondered about that. But I think your mother was too devoted to your father, even after he ran off."

Geneva paused, considering.

"I loved your mother," she said. "She was such a smart woman. I loved talking with her."

Grace looked away. "I knew her differently, as her daughter."

"Of course." Geneva waited a moment. "What happened after we lost touch? What was she like, then?"

Geneva was hungry for an answer, trying to fill in her own gaps. Grace could not think of an adequate response.

"She withdrew," Grace said at last. "She rarely left the house, after Dad left. It was very hard on her. The only places she would still go were the store, sometimes, and the library."

Geneva clucked her tongue, sympathetic. Grace went on, surprised with herself.

"When she went to the library she would take out books on everything—gardening, chemistry, history, and read and read. Those books were my bedtime stories, sometimes. She wanted me to go out and explore, even though she wouldn't."

Grace stopped again. She was making her mother sound better than she had been, better than Grace actually remembered her. She looked into Geneva's eager face, and continued.

"She depended on Mr. DeChansey for a lot. It was very hard after he died. It was a good thing that Mom sold off most of the farm after my dad left, because having to work it would have been too much. Just too much. She wasn't made for farming. She should have gone to school."

"Yes," Geneva said. She pressed her fingers to her lips, as if to stop them trembling.

"Did you know my father?" Grace said quietly.

Geneva shook her head.

"No. No. I don't think anyone did at all."

XI

Who had Arthur Beaucher been? Not who Grace had been allowed to believe by her mother.

Grace was only six when he left, and her memories of him were scattered things overlaid with memories of Mr. DeChansey. Her mother had only spoken of her lost husband in fragments, telling Grace that he had liked horses, and the color grey. She had never told his daughter what kind of man he was, if he were gentle or harsh, funny or somber. The disconnected details were not enough to construct his personality, or his ambitions.

Grace had known John DeChansey much better. He was kind to her. He had died the year she was thirteen. He was a farmer, and often smelled vaguely of chicken manure. He had been at their house almost daily when her father was alive. Mr. DeChansey had no children of his own, and no wife. Instead, he became an integral part of the Beaucher family.

After her father left them Mr. DeChansey still came around, a reliable presence, less frequent but regular. He made sure Grace and her mother were safe, and that repairs to the house were done. He brought them venison and eggs, and sometimes candy for Grace. He never tried to assume her father's place, but he became the man of the house in her father's absence. Her mother relied on him. Not heavily, but enough.

She remembered how sometimes her mother and Mr. DeChansey would shoo her away and close themselves in the kitchen to discuss adult matters. She would hide behind the door, or outside the window, eavesdropping on conversations for which she had no frame of reference and could not understand. They spoke of resurrection. Divination. Lost souls.

Mr. DeChansey died in a car accident one autumn dusk. He must not have seen the deer that ran into the road, only jerked the wheel away as the impact occurred. His car hit a stand of trees at a fatal angle on the driver's side, staving it in, crushing him into the console. Grace overheard a neighbor explaining the accident to her mother. She did not realize Grace was in the house until she heard her daughter scream.

Her mother did not allow her to attend the funeral.

The loss of John DeChansey's constancy was almost a mortal wound to young Grace. And it was the beginning of her separation from Sheila. Sheila did not acknowledge the rift that had opened between her and her daughter. She often commented that Grace was a difficult child, and left it at that.

Sheila did not admit her own part in Grace's difficulties. She withdrew even further after John DeChansey died. As far as Grace knew Sheila only spoke to one other person after losing him.

Anna Woodsell was Sheila's only friend, much older than Sheila and just as guarded. Her family had lived in the county for three hundred years. The land was in her blood and bones. She knew things about the area and its people that should have been beyond normal knowledge. Not foresight, exactly, but a perspicacity that bordered on it. She kept an enormous flower garden, a lush tribute to the beautiful over the practical. Grace remembered the hum of bees amongst the roses when her mother would bring her to visit.

When Mrs. Woodsell died of old age, alone in her house, Sheila was truly alone in the world. Her daughter's alienation was met with her own. Grace was seventeen, then, and fully aware of Sheila's turning away. There was nothing left for either of them, not even each other.

As her graduation approached, Grace applied only to universities in other states. She wanted to be far, far away from Holyoke.

XII

Grace fell into a loose, unproductive rhythm, alone in the house every day.

She played at packing and cleaning, but made almost no progress. She was in a strange half-life, wanting to discard all the detritus of her mother's life but afraid of erasing her.

More often she would abandon the task and wander the fields and paths behind the house. Her long rambles brought her through the back gates of the new developments that had sprung up during the last real estate boom, squatting on acres of former farmland like scattered building blocks. When she got back to the house she would sit in the back yard and reread her father's writings.

The incantation he had copied out seemed to be in a bastardized dialect of French. The instructions were in English, and fairly simple if grotesque. She thought she understood them.

But more important than understanding, she was coming to believe.

XIII

Even though it was early, Grace was in her bed, the dull headache behind her eyes keeping her awake. The crunch of tires in the driveway broke the evening's quiet. She struggled up and leaned out the upstairs bedroom window to see over the wedge of the porch roof. She didn't recognize the car, but she caught a glimpse of her husband's hair through the slice of windshield she could see. He had not called to say he was coming. She hurried down the stairs and threw open the door as he climbed out of the car.

"Andrew. What are you doing here?"

"I was worried about you. I thought you would need some company and some help."

Grace stiffened, then stepped back, her hand gripping the edge of the door.

"I have it under control," she said tersely.

"You've been out here more than a week," he said. "You don't always answer the phone."

"It takes time," she said.

Andrew reached for her, rubbing her shoulder with digging fingers when she would not step closer. She twitched his hand away. He smiled thinly, then shrugged past her to go inside.

He looked around, taking in Sheila's living room, the shape of the furniture, the patterns of rug and wallpaper. Grace stared at him with stony eyes.

"Nice place," he said flatly. "Cozy."

She did not respond to his comments.

"I wish you hadn't come," she said. "I need to do this myself."

Andrew's face flushed with anger and his eyes grew hard, but he spoke softly, as to a stupid child.

"I imagined that my wife might need me after her mother died."

Grace moved away from him, positioning herself behind an over-stuffed armchair. Her hands moved restlessly over the worn fabric.

"Please, can't I just have some peace?" she said, and started to cry with frustration. "Just go home."

She was so tired. She did not have the strength to pay attention to her husband.

"I flew in."

Grace sighed, sniffling, and fixed her eyes on the seat of the chair. She did not want to look at Andrew, did not want to have lost again. She thought briefly of telling him to sleep at the airport, to sleep in his rental car, to sleep anywhere else but here.

"I also brought you some clothes. Jeans and stuff. Underwear. I figured you didn't pack much."

"All right," she said. It was nearly nine. "But in the morning you go."

"I don't get you," he said. She only shrugged, and led him deeper into the house.

Andrew followed her into the kitchen. She made herself tea, and offered him instant coffee. He refused. While she sat to sip the hot tea he wandered through the downstairs rooms. She could hear him touching things, her mother's things, hers. She cringed.

"Was this her room?" he called from down the hall. She followed his voice, and found him sitting on the old chenille bedspread.

"Yes."

He patted the bed beside him. "Big enough for two."

"Oh, no," she said, repelled. "No."

He smirked at her reaction.

She finished the tea and brought him upstairs to her old room, to the single bed with the mended pink coverlet.

"Here," she said. "I have a headache and need to sleep. We'll fit." He did not argue.

But beside him in the dark she was too aware of the press of his skin on hers. She tried to move away, but the bed was too narrow. He reached for her hand, placed it on his groin, cupped her fingers around himself. She felt him grow hard, but she refused to respond. She let her hand rest limply on him, as if it weren't there. At last he turned as far away from her as he could in the tight space, and she heard his breathing finally deepen into sleep.

When she awoke in the morning he was gone, nothing left behind but a cup in the sink. She was glad he had left without starting a fight, yet the relief was tempered by the vague feeling that he would make her pay for it.

XIV

Grace had met Andrew Spanner in college, although they had not begun to date until after graduation. He had taken a job in environmental consulting and she had taken a job at the university as an administrative assistant. He embraced the idea of being a professional, with billable hours and a fluid schedule. She preferred the comfortable familiarity of the school. She knew the faculty and staff, knew how the system worked. She was good at what she did, dynamic in her role, safe in her office. It was the safety, she knew, that was most important.

They had talked about children often while they were dating, at first circumspectly but then with eagerness, planning their career trajectories and how many babies their paths and ages could accommodate. But after they married things began to fray. In such close quarters they fell relentlessly apart.

Andrew drank daily, something he had not been able to afford as a college student. He blamed her for his drinking, telling her that his demons were under control before she had come into his life. She withdrew, trying to protect herself, but he demanded attention. She tried not to anger him.

Just before their second anniversary Grace became pregnant. She was frightened. She wanted the pregnancy. She believed the old lie that this could be the turning point to bring her and Andrew back to where they had been, before the wedding, before the drinking, before the daily, grinding anger.

First, as ever, he blamed her. Then he grew tender, and held her, and gradually convinced her that an abortion would be the best thing for them. He promised he would rededicate himself to the marriage, to her, and they would have children when they had healed. She wanted this pregnancy, but she wanted to believe her husband.

So she agreed.

Then he was too busy with work to accompany her to the appointment. Then he was angry with her again for mourning their child, for wanting to talk about what they had done. He was even angrier that she wanted to talk about what he had promised her. She could not stop herself.

And six years later Andrew still was not ready for children, and still would not discuss it. Grace cried, and pleaded, and gave ultimatums she was browbeaten into taking back. She turned in on herself, the only protection she knew.

She wanted to love him. At times she still did. But the disappointment, the sadness, the resentment, washed it away like tides scoured a beach. What was left was far different than what had been.

XV

Three days after Andrew left she walked into town again, this time carrying the book, bones, and leather with her. She had thought long on what was in the notebook and was prepared, if not completely ready, to perform her father's ritual.

The cemetery nestled against the southern edge of Holyoke, high enough up the slope to be safe from floods. Its gates stood open, one hanging by a single hinge with yellow police-line tape around it. Old graffiti splashed the driveway.

Kids here got bored and destructive. Without cars or friends with cars they were trapped in a town that closed up shop at six o'clock. Heroin was less of a problem here than in other towns along the river, but when beer and pot were not enough to relieve the monotony the harder drugs sometimes made an appearance. Then things got broken. People got hurt.

Grace shoved those thoughts away. She was past those temptations, now.

She walked along the asphalt road that made its single loop through the cemetery grounds. The old family names on the gravestones were still represented in the community. Some families had been here for centuries, like the Woodsells.

But her roots were not that deep, the Beauchers only having come here three generations ago. Her grandfather had bought many acres of farmland, and worked them until he died. Her father had gradually sold the land off. He was interested in other things than farming.

Her mother's grave was near the fence, away from the road. The earth over it was still raw, but weeds already pushed their way up into the sun. A small metal tag marked it. Grace hadn't even considered what to put on a headstone, yet. It was one detail her mother had missed.

She frowned as she placed the leather square on the bare dirt, flattening the stiff, stained skin as much as she could. It still tented along the fold lines. She hoped it would be all right. It should be all right, she thought. It had been used before.

Sunlight fell warm on her shoulders. She breathed in the soft air, reluctant to begin. She smoothed the leather again and again, as if her hands could press out the brittle stain of blood. She looked at her fingers, splayed against the dark leather. They were shaped like her mother's. She drew a deep breath.

It was time now.

Grace closed her eyes. Even here, she could smell the sweet fragrance of the river. She forced her mind to be quiet and envisioned the design she must make. The right design, the true one, was not sketched out anywhere. It must bloom in her.

The pattern came to her in a sudden inspiration. She pulled the carved bones from her pocket and set them delicately and without hesitation on the leather, forming the shape revealed in her memory.

The magic was the act of creation. It was instinct. She placed the last bone and leaned back on her heels, studying the arrangement she had made, reading the shards of meaning in it. This was hers. It held her life and all the connections within it. It held the paths that bound her to her mother.

The dry bones on leather still needed her blood to make their connections.

She looked around, making certain she was alone. The small cemetery was empty on a bright Thursday morning. A single car passed on the road below. Then all she could hear was the rustle of leaves and grass in the breeze.

She unwrapped an old paring knife taken from her mother's kitchen, its blade honed to a fine sharp sliver. It stung as she sliced across the meat of her palm. She squeezed her fist around the blade, and shook her now-useless hand over the the bones. The dry leather drank in the spattering red. She flinched from its hunger.

Next was the incantation. Grace fumbled the booklet out of her back pocket, the cover already folded back to the right page.

The spell was short and written out phonetically. She read it slowly, afraid of the consequences of a mistake. Her voice rose and fell with the rhythm of it, the meaning of the words less important than the pattern and her intent, according to her father's notes.

The pain in her hand distracted her at first. She remembered Mr. DeChansey, and ancient Mrs. Woodsell. They had been kind to her, once. Others she only remembered as faces and nothing about them, their names lost on the fringe of childhood memory. She thought of her father, scarcely more familiar. At last she sifted through to her mother, the smell of her, the sound of her voice, her moods and manners. She summoned everything she could, to call her home. Grace repeated the spell nine times, as instructed, holding the image of her mother in her thoughts and letting the words flow through her.

Then it was done.

Her scalp prickled as if there were electricity in the warm air. Expectation grew like a weight in her chest. She waited, a witch of Endor, not knowing what or how soon anything might happen. Would the ground open, or her mother materialize before her?

The cemetery remained quiet. The sun still followed its path down the sky. Shadows grew longer around her. Nothing had changed in the world that she could see. If magic were not true, she had done no harm.

She wrapped a bandana around her hand. Then she climbed to her feet, knees aching, and walked slowly back up the road to her mother's house.

XVI

The sun sank to touch the trees in the west, but the afternoon was warm in its yellow light. Grace sat on the back porch as she had when she first found her father's journal. She opened the book and read it again, checking herself against her memory. She was sure she had followed it precisely, had not missed a word or a motion.

And she knew she did not truly want the magic to work.

Her stomach rumbled. She had not eaten today. How much of her inconstancy was hunger, she could not tell. The light was fading, and the bellies of the clouds shaded to red and violet. She went inside to eat, and to think.

XVII

Grace locked the doors that night. The day had left her on edge. Her hand hurt, the cut reopening and seeping blood when she tried to use it. She knew objectively that what she had done was irrational, but what if, what if?

What if her father had found the power to raise the dead? What if she had followed his instructions correctly? What if her mother came back?

The phone rang, shrill in the silent house.

It was Andrew.

"Hi," she said, momentarily glad for a human connection.

"Hi. I was wondering if you were coming home soon."

Her warm feelings chilled.

"I'm not sure," she said, sighing. "There's still a lot to do here."

"What, exactly?" he said. "You've been gone two weeks. More."

"My mother's been dead two weeks," Grace spat. "I'm not at my best, here, Andrew."

"I'm sorry," he said with a wheedle in his voice. "I wish you'd come home."

She could hear him moving around, papers shifting, the thud of something falling. Even now, she was not his focus.

"I don't know when I'll be home. I'm so tired."

"Okay," he said. "Okay."

She wondered if he had heard her at all.

XVIII

Grace stood at the counter, making tea. A fragment of song looped in her head as her hands moved, disconnected from her actions and the thoughts that filled the empty spaces in her mind. She mouthed the lyrics silently. Then Grace turned with her cup in her hand and saw her mother, standing quietly in the doorway between the kitchen and living room. Grace froze, lips parted on unvoiced lyrics and eyes unable to blink. It still felt as though she were alone in the house.

Her mother did not move. She was an object instead of a presence, without breath, without any transcendent spark of being. The glue holding her eyelids shut had given way. One lid had drifted upward, revealing the milky glass of a dead eye beneath. Grace could not look away.

The kitchen table stood between them. Grace placed her tea on it, the china cup rattling against the plate. She pulled out a chair, the scratch of its legs on the worn vinyl floor loud in the empty air. Slowly, she eased herself down, never taking her eyes from her mother's face. She was too bewildered to be afraid. Such things could not happen, not in this world.

But here it was, an anomaly, a piece of strange magic. It had taken three days.

Grace placed her hands palm down on the smooth table and slid them forward, leaning toward the remains of her mother. "Mom," she said, her voice even on the heavy word.

Her mother took an unsteady step forward, beckoned by her name. Beneath the heavy funeral makeup, her skin was the yellow of old ivory. Again, she lurched forward, and her hip hit the edge of the table. She stopped, inert.

Grace studied her, tamping down her own disbelief. There was black dirt in her mother's hair, burrs and twigs caught in her ripped dress. Grace would not imagine how she had gotten here, what it had taken. In this moment Grace only saw her mother, not her mother's corpse.

She got up slowly, her own limbs suddenly awkward, with no way to gauge how much her mother could comprehend, how much of her was really there. She eased herself around the table and reached past her mother's shell, pulling out the chair on that side.

"Sit down, Mom."

Like a broken puppet, Sheila slumped into the seat. Her arms hung limply down, dirty fingers crooked against the air. Grace realized her mother had no shoes; her feet were filthy and torn. They would be bleeding if she were alive. Grace brushed her mother's messy hair back with her fingers but quickly pulled away, startled at the feeling of touching a thing rather than a person. Sheila opened her mouth. A thin rasp emerged, a sigh without breath to form it. Grace twitched, and forced herself to finish stroking her mother's hair into place.

"It's alright, Mom," Grace said, to soothe herself.

Her mother's hand snaked up slowly, brushing Grace's arm, closing finally around her wrist. A thousand horror movies flashed in Grace's imagination. She waited for the teeth.

Sheila's mouth moved, awkward and disused. Her tongue flopped around in a quest for words. Grace held herself still. When her mother spoke at last it was nothingness, a sound like Grace's own thoughts as they spun in the confines of her head.

"I missed you."

Grace studied her mother's immobile face. Without the normal cues the words were as dead as Sheila.

Again. "I missed you."

There was no intonation, only a dull insistence. Grace began to cry, fear and exhaustion finally seeping into her. Her mother sat silently, unresponsive. Grace wiped at her eyes with the back of her hand, slowly brought herself back under control.

"I missed you, too."

Grace could not tell if it were the right response, She could not even tell if it were true.

Sheila sat, still as stone. The clock over the sink softly ticked down the long minutes.

Grace broke down again, overwhelmed by her mother's silent presence. Sheila remained as quiet as she had been in her grave.

XIX

Grace did not know what to expect of her mother, if a corpse could still be kin.

There was no one to ask about this. Grace had stepped off the edge of the world when her mother came home again. Reality was different than it had been.

She needed time to think, to turn the facts over in her head until she had seen every facet and combination. After an hour of waiting for her mother to do something, offer anything, she left the body sitting silently in the kitchen and headed out into the fields.

The day was clear and beautiful. Out in the open air Grace began to doubt that it had happened, that it was anything but the distraught meanderings of her own mind. How could the dead climb out of the ground and find their way back home? Such things had no place in the great clockwork of the universe.

Except that her dead mother had returned to her, at her own command. Magic had functioned to produce the requested result. What should not have been most assuredly was—or Grace herself was insane. She could not allow herself to discount that possibility. She stopped herself from considering what it would mean to have lost her mind, and simply allowed the possibility to stand.

Grace realized she had not seen any of the landscape she had walked through. She was into the second field, past the trees, following a rutted, rarely used track through the high grass. She thought she might be off her mother's land now. Not her mother's land, she corrected herself. Her land. Things had changed.

She stopped, then, to give herself the chance to breathe the clean air and feel the sun on her bare arms. These were fallow fields. Green grass came up through the lacework of last year's weeds. Turkey vultures wheeled high in the sky, sharp shadows against the sun. It was solitary here, but not lonely. At a distance she could see the backs of new houses, oversized things where families could hide from each other. She could not hear any human noise where she stood.

She turned back, following the path she had made through the grass. At least her mother's house still had its privacy, even as the rural stretches around it became the frontier of suburbia. There was still enough land to give her a buffer.

When Grace climbed the three steps to the kitchen door her mother was already there, just on the other side of the glass, pressed against it, leaning forward to get out. Her mother's slack face pressed against the door's window, smearing it with funeral cosmetics. It was a picture from a haunted house, a too-realistic Halloween decoration. What tranquility Grace had found out in the fields dissolved.

Grace turned the handle and with great patience pushed the door slowly open, nudging her mother's corpse slowly back without knocking her down. The whole process was surreal.

Her mother hovered inches beyond the arc of the door as Grace slid back into the house.

"I missed you," the empty body breathed.

The sound of her mother's words was like a caul on Grace's soul. It took away any remnants of joy. Grace brushed past to get to the sink. Sheila pivoted slowly to follow her daughter's motion.

Grace imagined that this was the reason cats sometimes startled at nothing, the terrible sensation of being watched by emptiness. A reaction would dispel it, would prove it was really her imagination. Grace turned, but her mother was still there. This was not a fantasy. The ghost was in the room.

She had stumbled onto questions that couldn't be answered. What of her mother was left, and what would remain as her body decayed? Did her mother still have motives, plans, intentions? It was all a mystery.

Grace wondered at her lack of fear. She had read enough horror novels, seen enough movies, to spark expectations and fuel her nightmares. But this was still her mother. Whatever ugliness had existed between them in the past, her mother needed her now, depended on her like a child.

Except Sheila was already dead. There could be no natural ending to this. Grace had created a strange hole in her life, the shape of her mother's empty grave.

XX

As Grace adapted herself to her mother's empty presence, she realized that Sheila could answer her questions, could pull spotty details from the cavern of her memory and give them some rough form. Flickers of ideas seemed to exist, but they were limited, and repetitive as ripples. Any response that came echoed the one before it. Her mother's mind was trapped in its place, unable to grasp the huge change in circumstances.

Grace spent her time finding ways through the mess, teasing out answers, filtering out echoes. Sheila was incapable of narrative, but each question Grace asked and asked again produced variations, and each foggy answer Sheila gave led eventually to others.

"What about Dad?" Grace asked.

"Gone. Dead. I miss him."

Grace paused. Dead, she had said. No longer simply gone. Her father had died, not left them.

If one looks, one will find.

"Where is Dad?" Grace asked again.

"Dead. Gone."

Grace repeated her question. She had time, now.

———◆———

From the slow interrogation of her mother and the scattered details she knew of her own family, Grace was able to piece together a story for her father. She wrote it down as she went, afraid of forgetting, of missing any part of it. She did not expect what she got. She often asked her mother to repeat what she had said, shading the question differently each time.

The story was fantastic. And Grace had committed some of those same acts herself, to have brought her mother back to tell it.

XXI

Arthur Beaucher had been born in this house. His father was a farmer who had worked as a field hand until he had come into a bit of money and bought land of his own. He married a local girl and produced only one living child, Arthur. The farm was more fertile than the farmer, and his father intended that Arthur continue it in his time.

But Arthur was a different boy than his father imagined.

Arthur learned how to manage the farm, but his interests lay in other places. His closest friend, John DeChansey, shared those interests. The DeChanseys were also farmers, though of older stock, and the boys' lives assumed a strange parallel. They explored together. They met people. They asked questions. They found their way to Thomas Woodsell, who knew a great deal about the darker side of the world. They listened. They repeated. They practiced.

Arthur met Sheila Dinsmorte at the county fair. She was from a neighboring town up the river, and had heard of Old Man Woodsell but not of his protégés. Arthur courted Sheila, and married her. They lived on the farm with his parents, in quarters too close for newlyweds. Arthur fought with his father, increasingly resentful of the farmwork that was expected of him. Sheila kept quiet, with Arthur's mother leaving the men to fight among themselves.

Then the elder Mrs. Beaucher died, and it was just the three of them.

John was around more and more. Evenings, after the work was done, the two young men would retire to the barn and lock the door behind them. They were of an age where the shortness of sleep did not slow them down. The elder Mr. Beaucher would shake his head in disgust and tell Sheila what a mistake she had made with his son. Sheila stayed quiet, made the meals, kept the house. She knew what her husband and his friend were doing. Not the details, which he would never share, but the broad outline. He would show her small magics that could not be mistaken for parlor tricks. At night, in bed, he would tell her about the progress he had made, what he had discovered was possible.

Through Arthur, Sheila became friends with Old Man Woodsell's daughter. Sheila had drifted away from her own friends from before her marriage. She did not miss them. Anna was at least twenty years older than Sheila, never married, still under her father's roof. Like Sheila, she had become the woman of the house. Like her own father, she explored other paths through the world. She knew plants, knew how to combine them, knew how to coax things from their roots and leaves. She knew more, too, but wouldn't speak of it.

Seven years after Sheila married Arthur, his father died, a heart attack in the snow.

Arthur became angry. He cursed his father bitterly for dying, cursed him for not seeing the wisdom of his son's ways. It was an ugly winter. Sheila tried to comfort him but the hostility between father and son had been too deeply rooted to disappear with death. John served as a buffer for Arthur's anger. Sheila endured.

Then came the February thaw, and the fire that killed the Dinsmortes. Sheila's parents and two younger brothers died in their beds. Something went wrong with the house's wiring one night. A surge, a spark, a flame, and then fire roared through the old wood frame building. By the time the fire trucks came it was too late to save them.

Sheila was devastated. She took to her own bed, staying there for more than a week. There was no funeral to be had. A mass was said for the dead but Sheila did not attend it. She was too lost even to cry. Arthur tried to be understanding, but he could not fathom how she felt. There was no solace. Even John DeChansey stayed away from her and her loss.

Eventually, when spring came, Sheila began to face the world again. Anna Woodsell came by with herbs and green tonics, brewed fragrant teas to help Sheila back into life. But Anna avoided Arthur and John as much as she could. Those two sought more than she did, and although her father advised them, Anna did not agree with his decision. She disliked the unnaturalness of what they were trying to do.

⸻◆⸻

Now it was only the three of them. Everyone else was gone. John De-Chansey had his own farm to tend, and was with the Beauchers when he could be. Arthur began to sell off parcels of his land rather than work the whole farm. Their needs were few, the house and land paid for, the equipment used until obsolescence and not replaced; properly invested, the proceeds kept them going for years.

Neither Arthur nor Sheila expected they would become parents. It had not happened since their marriage, and there was no reason to think it would. But then Sheila began to feel ill, and again took to her bed to escape the world. Anna came, and told her that she was only morning sick. She offered herbs to soothe the sickness. She offered herbs that would end the pregnancy, as well, if that was what was wanted. Sheila declined. Arthur was uncertain, but left the decision to his wife. It was she who would suffer. He had merely to provide.

It was a difficult pregnancy, ending in a difficult labor. Anna attended, since Sheila refused to go to the hospital. Grace was born after two days of labor, healthy if small. There was a sea of blood. Anna made poultices to staunch the bleeding. Arthur would come into the bedroom and watch Anna working, silent, mesmerized by the process. At last he found the courage to come all the way into the room. He placed his hand on his wife's cheek, and told her it would be all right. Then he picked up the tiny swaddled thing that was his daughter and carried her away.

He sat with Grace in his arms like a small package, sitting where Sheila could see him from her bed. When Grace began to cry with a high mewling squall Anna brought him a bottle and he fed her. When Grace was asleep he brought her back to Sheila and laid her in her arms.

⸻◆⸻

Once Sheila had recovered most of her strength, Arthur returned to his explorations. Anna stayed close to Sheila, helping as much as she was allowed. The women were each other's only friend, and kept to themselves to protect them all.

Years passed. Grace grew into a lanky girl. Sheila braved the outside world to register Grace for school. Once the formalities were done, she would go only as far as the end of the driveway to put Grace on the school bus. Her duty was discharged.

Then came the day when Arthur went further than even he had thought he could. He transcended manipulating mere matter, and discovered how to extract a semblance of life from the dead. Necromancy. Divination. Old magic, and unclean.

It was not wise to practice it, but Arthur would. John helped him, although he grew increasingly nervous. Sheila pretended she understood less than she did. Anna would not delude herself, and spent little time at the Beaucher farm. It was not a safe house to be in, any longer.

But it was Sheila's home, and Sheila's husband. She concentrated on her daughter, and did what she could to keep the growing child from seeing too much. When Arthur finally performed the ritual to call his father back from the grave, Sheila at once sent Grace to live with Anna. It had become impossible for the girl to stay with her parents, with such an unknown looming over them.

Arthur could not tell her if the spell had worked. They waited, for days they waited, until the scratching came at the kitchen door and the former Mr. Beaucher stood waiting to be let back in.

They did not know what to expect, although Arthur was convinced that his father would not hurt them. John still kept his shotgun at hand, unwilling to place too much faith in such an enormity. Sheila tried to keep on with the normal routine of the household, but everywhere Arthur went the corpse of his father shambled after. It was inexorable, inescapable. Unable to live free of his father's condemnation before, he had unearthed a way to ensure it beyond death.

Mr. Beaucher could not change or become anything more than he had once been. He followed Arthur around the farm and the house, reminding him in a horrible empty voice of his failings. Sheila begged Arthur to keep the ghastly thing away from her.

Arthur tried to lock him in the barn, but with the patience of the timeless he would free himself and find his son. Arthur chained him like a dog, but still his father worked his way loose, bits of flesh left behind. Sheila woke screaming too many nights. The smell of death was everywhere, a slaughterhouse stink.

Arthur took to sleeping in the barn to spare Sheila the unwelcome company. John stayed with him, to spare him being alone with the unquiet dead. But it was summer, and the windows were open. From her bed Sheila could smell decay on the night breeze, and hear the unnatural voice droning on and on through the dark.

The two living men spent their precious night hours searching for a way to return Mr. Beaucher to the grave. Old Man Woodsell had no answers, so they looked farther. The roots of the country ran deep, and the men followed them down. Even Sheila was pressed to help them, reading heavy texts at the kitchen table deep into the night. She missed her daughter.

For all their effort they found no answers, no way to rescind the magic and let the dead rest again.

Arthur became pale and drawn, despite the hours spent each day in the sun, tending the shrunken farm. They were all exhausted. Days dragged into weeks, the summer spinning by in a rotten haze. It was never clear who finally thought of a pragmatic solution, abandoning magic at last.

One afternoon in August Arthur and John cleared out a small storage shed and refilled it with straw and scrap lumber, locked Mr. Beaucher in it, and set it afire.

As hot as the day was, Sheila joined them to stand watch while it burned. There was no sound from inside but the snap and roar of the flames. They stayed through the night, until the embers had turned to ash. In the thin light of dawn Arthur and John raked the ashes for Mr. Beaucher's bones. What they found they crushed to powder. Then they shoveled up everything that was left, even the charred ground beneath, and hauled it down to the river where it would in time wash into the sea. They were sure now that Arthur's father would not come back.

Afterward, they went inside and slept. Sheila woke in the afternoon. Arthur rolled over, still deeply asleep. John snored from his spot in Grace's room. She called Anna, and told her in a whisper that it was over. She asked her to keep Grace for another day or two, to let the men pull themselves together again. Then she crept into the kitchen and began to cook dinner. As she stood at the stove turning ham steaks in the pan she heard the far-off crack of a gunshot. It was out of season but not so unusual.

She set the table and went to wake the men. Arthur was not in their bed. She went into Grace's room, where John lay sprawled amidst dolls and stuffed bears. She shook him gently, and as he came awake she asked him where Arthur was. He did not know.

They searched the house. Arthur was gone. They searched the barn, the sheds, the yard. The car was still there, and the pick-up truck. John told Sheila to stay at the house, and he headed down to the fields.

She already knew what he would find. She stood over the sink shaking, hair raised on her arms.

After an endless while John came back and leaned heavily in the doorway. Sweat poured from him. His hair was soaked. He was crying. Sheila stifled her own cry with her hands. There was no time for it, now.

She got a tarp from the basement, and they drove the truck down to the bottom of the field where a fringe of trees made a windbreak. Arthur lay at the foot of a young maple.He had held the gun to his throat, under his chin. His face was unscathed but the base of his skull was a crater.

Sheila helped John roll Arthur's body into the tarp. She scuffed dust over the blood and spattered meat where he had been, scattering the flies. John put his friend into the bed of the truck, and wiped his bloody hands on his jeans. He leaned against the tailgate of the truck. The sun slanted low in the sky behind him.

Sheila was past crying. Thickening blood dripped onto the truck bed. The tarp disguised how loosely her husband's head was still connected to his body. The shotgun blast had ripped his neck open. She put it out of her mind.

She heaved herself into the driver's seat and waited. John finally climbed in, and she drove them back to the house.

"What now?" she asked him, but he didn't know.

They went inside. They ate a cold dinner. Sheila called Anna again and said it would be a little longer before Grace could come home. Anna did not ask why.

Sheila told John she could not bear an inquest if Arthur's death was reported, could not jeopardize John's life, Anna's and her father's. Her own. She decided to let Arthur disappear. Let him become a mystery rather than a monster.

John helped her take her husband down from the truck bed. They brought him into the barn. It still reeked of death in there. Tomorrow she would have to open all the doors and hope it eased. She got out the branch saw. She took his head, and she took his hands. John helped her with what was left. At dawn they built a pyre for him. It took longer than she expected for him to be consumed. They had to tend the fire, adding fuel throughout the morning. At last it was done.

John finally went back to his own home. Sheila did not see him for nearly a week. In that time she found a safe place to bury what was left of her husband. She wanted him close. She wanted him alive. It was too much to manage.

When John came back to the Beaucher farm he had a box full of the writings and notes he and Arthur had pieced together over their years of study. He told Sheila he had no use for it any more, asked her to keep it for him if he someday needed to understand what they had done. She hesitated, but she took it. She did not tell him where she had buried Arthur's remains. Better only she knew.

They decided to allow word to spread that Arthur had left her, and to let it be known that she had hounded him until he ran off. She would take the blame for this. He would be an adulterer, she a harridan. He would be safe from so much worse.

And so would Grace.

The years went by. Old Man Woodsell died, then John DeChansey, then Anna. Sheila was the only one left who knew what had happened. And then she was dead, too. And Grace was no longer safe.

XXII

Another week passed before two scarecrow figures came over the wide back lawn, bodies so long dead that they were little more than bone and leather strung together with dry sinew. But they were still articulated enough to come to her. Revenants. Mr. DeChansey, Anna Woodsell. They had to be.

Grace, watching through the kitchen door, was not surprised.

They moved awkwardly, off balance like broken toys. They fell and crawled. Grace could only watch them come, disbelief abandoned. Her mother stood at her shoulder, but gave no sign of being aware of them at all.

They were coming because she had remembered them. She had

called them back into the world without even intending to. She thought of the sorcerer's apprentice, of water flowing down, drowning them all. Magic was a wilder thing than she knew. Her mother slipped her hand into Grace's while they waited. It was so cold, and so soft. Grace steeled herself so she would not pull away.

As the scarecrows got closer Grace opened the door for them. They came to her, clumsy as newborn colts. They knew her. The tall one, Mr. DeChansey, reached for her with hands of bone. He smelled of earth, of old leaves. The jaw moved but no sound emerged. There was nothing left of him to move the air.

"I'm here," she said. Bones closed on her arm, the skull leaned close. The jaw moved again. She imagined words of friendship where there was only empty air.

The wreckage of Anna Woodsell could no longer stand. She lay instead across the steps as if she had been dropped there. Grace freed herself from DeChansey's grip and her mother's shadowing presence to lift the tangled bones of her mother's friend. It was a selfish thing to have called her, Grace thought. Such an effort for her to come.

Grace carried Anna Woodsell's barely articulated body into the house, setting her gently into a chair. There was so little left of her. The fragile skull pivoted to face her. An incomplete hand rose to gesture at her. Grace leaned closer, and the hand brushed her cheek. She startled, but held herself in place. She had remembered these people. They remembered her, as well.

XXIII

Sheila's memories had opened Grace's own.

The summer Grace lived with Anna Woodsell had come back to her like a shock. She remembered the bright garden, the abundance of it all. She remembered the big, sloppy house that smelled of spices and dust. She remembered how much she had missed her mother, and how she had asked for her often. But at six, she could not understand why she could not simply go home.

It was not a lost summer, but it was a lonely one. There were no children in Anna's house. Grace had only adults to live among, and no outlet for her childish ideas.

That summer Anna treated Grace as a temporary apprentice. She taught the girl the names of the flowers and herbs she grew, the trees and weeds in the fields; roses, dahlias, asters, rue, willow, redbud, beech and oak, thistle, bittersweet, loosestrife, ivy, olive and sage. She taught Grace simple recipes and potions that could effect small changes in the world. Grace grew brown in the sun, helping Anna tend the garden and gather what was ripe, and what was needed. Anna showed Grace how to prepare what they harvested, how to preserve it, how to make it more useful. How to make it something of influence. She taught Grace how to sew a simple doll, a poppet, and stuff it with sweet grasses and strands of hair.

Grace loved Anna. She was frightened of Anna's father. He was then near eighty, tall and bent like a tree. He was not a cruel man, but gruff, used to his own ways and out of practice with children. Anna kept Grace away from her father as much as possible, waking her early and taking her into the fields, into the woods, lunch in a bag to sustain them on their long walks.

But there was no avoiding him at dinner. Anna cooked and set the table for the three of them. The old man would grumble as he ate, working out his thoughts. He often asked Anna's opinion. Grace listened without comprehending, the language and the concepts too far above her. In veiled phrases they discussed what was happening to Grace's family that summer.

It was years later that she realized how deeply involved they were. Then, she would only sit quietly, eating what she had been served, waiting to be released from the table and sent to bed. She would go upstairs to the room Anna had made up for her, and leaf through books until Anna came to tuck her in. Grace would often lie awake long into the night, listening to the sounds of the house.

Grace had never known that her father and Mr. DeChansey had been there while she lived there. She was let completely alone by her family.

It was not until she was older, approaching adolescence, that she began to hear the rumors common about the Woodsell clan. The Woodsells had always been on the fringe of acceptable society, as much by choice as by exclusion. They were an old family in the county, one of the first to settle there. They did not seek the approval of the families that came after them. Because of their solid isolationism, it began to be whispered that there were irregularities in their family relations. Inconsistencies in their religious affiliation. Rudeness to neighbors. Secretiveness. Hints of strange habits.

The insinuations had never been spoken loudly, and by the time Grace heard them they had become hazy, a pall on an old name, part of the description of the family. The rumors were almost silly in their attachment to colonial superstitions. Witches. Dabblers. Not safe to be around, not welcome in good houses.

But they were an old family. So the Woodsell were avoided, when possible, but respected when faced.

Grace found this out when the whispers began about her parents' connection with the Woodsells. Fingers were never pointed at her, although she was kept at a distance by the other children and their families. Grace was angry at them all in the consuming, illogical manner of adolescence. She was in several fights in school to defend her father, and Anna. Eventually she learned how to separate herself from her family. Eventually the whispers stopped. Grace was allowed to exist at the edge of the crowd, allowed to be free of the worst taint of association.

XXIV

The first time Grace had to leave the house for groceries, she returned to find her mother stepping stiffly onto the road. A car came by in the opposite direction. Grace pulled sharply into the driveway and her mother turned toward her. She hoped fervently that the other driver had not noticed how much was wrong with her mother.

She sprang out of the car and guided her mother into the passenger seat, half carrying her to hurry the process. Sheila's skin ripped as Grace forced her legs to bend to fit the seat. She smelled bad meat, and gagged. She climbed back in and drove up the long driveway. She wondered if her mother had fallen on the trip down.

"I missed you," her mother said.

There can be no reasoning with the dead, no rationalizing. It is only the eternal now of what lingers in their stilled minds, what remnants of their lives persist. Nothing new can impact them.

"I know, Mom," Grace said. She knew it would not make a difference.

She helped her mother out of the car. Touching her, she could feel the fragile skin slip over the soft muscles. Her mother's body weighed less than she expected. Grace picked her up and carried her through the wide-open front door. She could not believe the smell. It was exactly what Sheila had described.

Now there was no peace for Grace. The revenants followed her around the house, as slow and inexorable as glaciers. Only Anna stayed in place, watching from her chair, too decayed to move any longer. Grace locked the door to the bedroom every night, because every morning her mother and Mr. DeChansey stood in the hallway before it, waiting outside time for her to emerge. If Grace herself had died in her sleep, they would still wait for her.

It was madness to be haunted by the dead behind her. But this was her world now, one that allowed the dead to rise and demand the attention of the living. Her father had left a clear warning, but Grace had only understood it as for her mother, long ago. She had misunderstood her own responsibilities.

XXV

The phone rang, loud in the breathless silence of the house. Andrew called her each evening at seven, like clockwork. She had thought about taking the phone off the hook, but she didn't want to provoke him.

"What's that noise?" Andrew said, before she could say hello.

Her mother had knocked over a side table in the living room on her shambling path to her daughter's side. Grace steadied her, held her up, maneuvered her into a chair. She had to hold her breath until she stepped away again.

"Nothing," she said after a pause. "I tripped."

"What's the matter with you?"

"Nothing, I said. Are you going to cross-examine me every time you call?"

He hung up. She was used to it.

Grace put the phone down as her mother struggled to her feet. It rang again. It could only be Andrew. She did not pick it up.

XXVI

Grace read the entire handwritten pamphlet again, searching for some clue as to how to reverse the process, how to lay the dead to rest again. As many times as she read it, the magic worked in only one direction.

Grace went to the attic and methodically emptied the boxes of her father's things. She read through all the loose papers before turning to the books. She had expected books on magic, but there were only yellowed science fiction paperbacks. She shook them out, in case anything had been tucked inside. Nothing, and nothing, and nothing.

She heard clattering and scratching at the bottom of the stairs as her mother and the others tried to come up to her. They were drawn to her, flies to honey. She heard the sound of dry sticks falling. The thought of them crumpled on the floor disturbed her, although she knew they would not feel it. Still, they had once been people she cared for. In their own way, they still cared for her. She abandoned her search and went back down.

As she lifted the thin, fallen bodies, she thought of how it was better that she and Andrew had not had children. He was not suited to giving up himself. It would all have fallen on her, all the responsibility and all the blame. There would have been nothing left of her.

XXVII

As the days became weeks the air in the house became unbreathable, drenched with the cloying thick reek of decay. Grace wore a kerchief over her face, and sprayed air freshener everywhere, but there was no escaping the smell of death. It was nothing she could get used to. The stench permeated the house, her clothes, her hair. The only respite was in her bedroom, where the dead were never allowed to wander.

Grace figured the problem would ease eventually, when her mother had rotted to bones as the others had. Until then, Grace had to protect them, and protect herself. The day after she found a note from Geneva pinned to the front door she gathered tools and odds and ends of wood from the basement and the unused barn to secure the house. Her goal was to keep them in when they would follow her and keep out any outside eyes. It would make a cage of the house, a trap, but there was no other practical way.

She was busy sealing up the downstairs windows, nailing plywood over drawn shades to preserve their fragile privacy, when Andrew pulled up the long driveway and parked directly in front of the steps. He stretched as he got out of the car, studying the front of the house before he climbed up.

She met him at the door, hammer in hand.

"Why are you here?" she said sharply, angry that they were replaying a scene from weeks ago.

He shrugged. "You aren't answering the phone. You haven't called me. I came to see if you're alright."

"I'm fine. You need to leave."

She stepped out onto the porch, pulling the door shut behind her.

"I deserve better than this, Grace."

"Please go. I have things I have to take care of."

"I'm your husband, or have you forgotten that? I have a right to know what's going on."

He grabbed her arm, tugging at her. She leaned back.

"Let go of me."

"I'm not hurting you."

"Let me go. Get the hell out of here."

Grace pulled her arm out of his grasp, and reached behind her for the doorknob, trying to get back inside. Andrew shoved her against the door, forcing it open and following her in. She pushed him back.

"Get out," she said again, her voice rising. But he was already inside. His face twisted at the unmistakable smell of rot.

They were still in the entranceway. She tried again to push Andrew back out the door but he was stronger. He stood firm, pressing her backward toward the living room doorway.

"What is going on in here?" he said, and then he saw.

Sheila stood blankly in the middle of the room, having made it that far in pursuit of her daughter. She swayed there, unsteady on her decaying feet. Mr. DeChansey leaned against the wall just beyond the door to the hallway.

Sheila found the momentum to take another step forward. Andrew's eyes widened, disbelieving. He spun toward Grace, but she was already moving forward to intercept her mother. Mr. DeChansey slithered along the wall.

"What is this?" Andrew shrieked. "Grace, oh my god, what did you do?"

She could not think. She had to protect them.

"Andrew, it's alright," she said, knowing her words were useless.

He turned on her with raw fear in his eyes. "What did you do?"

He reached for her again, grabbed her shirt. The fabric tore in his fists as he shook her. "What did you do?" he howled again. He tried to drag her behind him, tried to bring both of them back outside.

Grace felt a strange calmness settle over her spinning thoughts. There was no way out of this. Everything was crashing down. She looked at

Andrew's open mouth, watched spittle form a thread between his teeth. He must think she had dug up the bodies. He would take her away from here. He would have her committed. Her mother would be lost.

She swung the hammer in a smooth arc, and felt the shock run up her arm as the hammer connected with his head. The sound of his skull cracking was softer than she thought it would be, a wet slump. He choked. He fell. She hit him again, and again, to be sure.

Her mother's head turned toward them like a sunflower follows the sun.

Grace watched Sheila, the gory hammer still clutched in her hand. Was her mother drawn to all the blood? A flicker of fear lit in Grace's belly. As she stood over Andrew she shifted into a defensive stance, afraid now, with no way to know what would happen. She had thought herself adjusted to the new reality, but this changed things yet again.

Then the dead lips moved, the dead voice hollowed the air.

"The cellar. With your father."

Grace stopped. "What?"

"Your father."

Grace dropped to her knees, suddenly too weak to stand. She looked down at the mess of Andrew, his empty eyes bulging open in a lopsided face. Blood soaked the carpet beneath him. Cold water will take that out, she thought, and laughed tight and high.

The dead outnumbered the living in this world.

She pinched the bridge of her nose between her fingers, rubbed her eyes hard. After a few moments Grace could think clearly again. She reached out to close Andrew's eyes, but they slipped open again. His skin was already cooling. She had killed him. She had killed her husband. The idea echoed in her mind, inescapable.

Her dead mother still stood complacently where she had been. She would not move unless Grace did. Grace watched her carefully, but she showed no signs of aggression. Grace was not sure why she thought Andrew's blood would trigger some innate violence in her mother. It was hard to separate fiction from the surreal truth. She forced the idea out of her mind.

Sheila had said her father was in the cellar.

That much would be true. The dead have no reason to lie.

Grace staggered to her feet. Andrew looked smaller in death than he had in life. The spirit was gone. She felt sorry for him now. Regret, if it would come, had not reached her yet. She went back to the windows to finish what she had begun. It was almost too great an effort.

The hammer left spattered gore on the first nail she drove in. The rest were clean. She sealed the first floor, making a dim tomb of it. She put the hammer on the mantel. Then she went upstairs, opened those windows to the warm summer air for a last time before she sealed them, too, and went to sleep.

XXVIII

She woke just before sunset. The house was utterly silent. The empty presence of the dead magnified her own living sounds, pronounced her solitude. It exhausted her. She brushed past the remains of her mother as she left her room. Mr. DeChansey had made it only part way up the stairs.

She washed her face, studied it in the bathroom mirror. The shadows under her eyes had grown darker. She was looking into the face of a murderer. She still could not feel it.

Downstairs, there was silence. Some natural light still made its way in through the small windows on the front door. Andrew lay in shadow now, his eyes gone dull and milky. Grace walked past him without pausing and descended to the cellar. She would never call him. He could stay where he had fallen.

The cellar was small and low-ceilinged, dug out after the house had been built and only under part of the original structure. The worn stonework of the first foundation stood exposed above the new cement walls Concrete slab made up the floor. It was chilly, even in summer, and damp. Stagnant.

Shelves lined two walls, full of softly slouching boxes, neatly labeled in her mother's handwriting. Grace pulled a box down from the top shelf labeled "taxes" and opened it. It held what it said it would. She flipped through the contents to see if there was anything of interest, then stacked it to the side and reached for the next box.

Her father was in the third carton marked "Xmas," his skull and the bones of his hands nestled neatly in a pile of fading tinsel. The remains had been packed gently, and did not seem to have been touched since they had been put there. Grace saw a wedding band around a yellow finger bone. If her magic had affected him, he was unable to respond.

Grace closed the box up, resealing the cardboard grave. She put it gently back in place on the shelf.

Where were the rest of his bones, she wondered. She wondered too if her mother could tell her. To have kept him here all these years, to have worn his ring as he wore hers, knowing he was gone…Sheila had loved him, and missed him. Grace could not imagine that for herself. There would be no such careful safe-keeping for Andrew.

A crack ran in a ragged line where the wall met the floor. The cement had crumbled there from the incessant dampness, creating a fractured, stuttering space where the wall and floor slabs did not touch.

Grace opened the box marked for the garden and found a trowel. She dug at the weakened cement, making the beginnings of a hole. She stopped after a few minutes, already sweating. She would need a shovel to hollow out Andrew's final resting place. She looked around, and spotted an assortment of tools leaning in a corner. There was a spade. She made good use of it.

The hole she made was shallow, but wide enough, long enough. She hoped there was a bag of concrete to be found in the house. She did not want to be remembered as having bought any when someone came looking for Andrew. When the search for him began, the authorities would find her here soon enough.

She ascended into darkness. She had been in the cellar for a few hours, and the sun was long set. As she fumbled for the light switches, she realized that neither her mother nor Mr. DeChansey had tried to follow her to the cellar. They were both still in the living room, waiting for her. Hair raised on the back of her neck. A new dynamic had emerged while she was busy elsewhere. Andrew had changed everything, upset a balance more fragile than she had known. There was not a sense of threat from them, but of a subtle change in their dependency.

"Mom?" she said. "I found him."

The response was painstakingly slow. As her mother decayed her resemblance to the living woman she had been decayed as well, and her ability to navigate the living world more precarious.

"Miss him."

"I know," Grace said. Her mother had not moved since Grace had come into the room. "Mom, why didn't you come to the cellar?"

The jaws moved wetly. "Grave. Not the grave."

Grace blinked at a sudden connection. It made sense, now. Grace felt her shoulders go down, her defenses drop. She had called her mother out of the grave and left her unable to return to it. To any grave, as

Grace understood her. It made a strangely elegant twist in the magic. Grace was surprised by it.

"I'll be right back," she said, and went to retrieve what was left of her father.

When she came up this time, her mother and Mr. DeChansey were at the head of the stairs, ready for her. She had to push gently past them, holding her breath against the foul smell. Sheila clung to her, leaving smears on Grace's arms. She wanted what Grace carried.

Grace brought the box into the living room, stepping over Andrew's corpse, and opened it on the coffee table.

The yellow lamplight gave a soapy sheen to her father's bones. Sheila pressed against her, impassive and eager, reaching with withered fingers for her husband's skull. Mr. DeChansey hung back, hovering, but not reaching past Sheila.

Grace lifted the skull into her mother's hands, then stood back. This was not about her, any longer. She imagined that her mother was talking to her father, communing with him in some way.

She took the chance to deal with her more immediate problems. She wrestled Andrew's stiffening body to the head of the basement stairs and shoved him down. The sound his flesh made as it hit each step was awful, flat and meaty. She followed him down the stairs, kicking him out of the way as she went. It was an awkward, slow trip down. Grace knew she would pay for this later, when she allowed herself to realize that she was a murderer. Until then she had to clean up the mess.

Andrew's body fit tightly into the grave she had dug for him, but it was deep enough that she could level it when he was buried. She shoveled in the dirt and crumbled concrete over him, stamped it down. She knew it would settle as his body decayed. She did not know how much time she had to hide the grave more completely.

There were scratchy sounds of movement over her head. Not ready to go back to the ambulatory dead, she looked around the cellar for cement. She was lucky. A partial bag was shoved to the back of a bottom shelf.

She went back upstairs, too tired to do more.

The box of her father's bones had been upended onto the floor, his finger bones scattered among the clots of tinsel. Sheila cradled his skull in her rotten arms like a baby. Grace could see where the back of the skull was torn away in a jagged hole. She approached her mother, but

Mr. DeChansey raised his arm to block her way. She looked at his mummified arm, at the attitude of his scarecrow body. She understood. She was not a part of this reunion.

Grace retreated to her room, to let the dead tend the dead.

XXIX

It would be an easy thing to dispose of the trappings of her life, the job and apartment in the distant city, the acquaintances, the bills. Andrew. Already, the hundred things that bound her to that life had lost relevance, as though they were hers only second-hand. It was a relief. The thousand tiny mouths that bit at her attention every day were falling away. Finally, she could think without distraction, focus on what had to be done instead of the busywork of the world. She would stay here, with the ones who needed her. She would stay here in her mother's empty house. She would protect them from the slow slip of memory for a little longer.

She switched off the lights, going slowly room by room, lingering over the details of the old furniture, the dingy paint. It was all hers, now. This would be her home, apart from the world. In the shadows it all became a dreamscape, hazy and unchanging. As it should be. She sighed as she turned off the light in the hallway, and climbed the stairs in darkness to the small second bedroom. She lay down on the sagging mattress and waited for sleep.

Sometime in the night she was half-awakened by a sound like leaves, and the shallow rocking of someone laying down beside her. She did not open her eyes, but she turned so their bodies will fit together in the narrow space. Hers was the only breathing. She drifted back to sleep to the sound of the wind in the trees, over the long grasses. It grew closer the deeper she fell.

XXX

Dawn came at last, an indeterminacy in the air, a stain of light on the far horizon. Grace stretched out her arms, her back, her aching legs. Every motion brought her up against another body. The dead huddled close to her, dry things that rustled and wanted. She remembered them, and brought them here, full of their old longings and desires.

The dead cannot change. They are trapped where they stopped. They cannot forget, they cannot forgive, they cannot absolve. Grace could not make up for her transgressions. She cannot lay them to rest again. She can only pour hope into a wound that would never heal. Her own life is a reminder to them of what they have lost, a way of knowing that what they once felt, and dreamed, and hungered for still persists, is still real. That they are still real.

She is the memory of them.

They are not lonely any longer.

AV_NEST.CASEFILE

Timothy G. Huguenin

Who would believe the things I've seen, even if I had friends on whom I could unload my heavy thoughts? My estrangement from normal society is the reason for the confessional and emotional tone in my reports. Stop chiding me for that, or fire me already. I know the Department won't permit a personal diary for fear of its discovery (yet who wouldn't assume it was fiction?—I ask this seriously). So my case reports will have to do for both our needs at once. Edit out what commentary you find superfluous or subjective, if it means that much to you.

There is no hotel in Augustus Valley. Marie, an older widow who lives in a humble trailer on Broad Street, took kindly to me on my first assignment here. Now Marie keeps a cot ready for me in her sewing room. In fact, I'm in my room as I type this—she now refers to it as my bedroom, rather than her sewing room—and I can hear her snores through the decrepit mobile home's paper-thin walls. I have become very fond of the cute old woman. I feel a little guilty that she still believes I'm a staff writer for *Goldenseal*. She has even subscribed to the quarterly magazine and places issues prominently next to her rocking chair in the living room. She must not read them, since she hasn't yet asked me why my byline never appears. Of course, I still keep my badge locked in my car's glove box and hide my snub-nosed revolver as best as I can, though women's fashion isn't well suited to concealed carry. These folks can spot law enforcement like they can pick out a doe in thick cover at a hundred yards. Sometimes I feel like they can smell the Department on me, even though they don't know it exists.

The closest thing to a coffee shop in this town is the Exxon's convenience store. A few tables crowd the corner with an everlasting pot of burnt coffee and a noisy cappuccino machine. Just two years ago, they installed a wireless router, and it is the only spot in town with free Wi-Fi. Three days ago, needing a break from Marie's well-intentioned nosiness, I was at one of those tables to work over some details from another current investigation. After some time, I stood to rest my nearly crossing eyes and refill my coffee. Setting my Styrofoam cup and a quarter next to the register, I looked around for the cashier.

"Hello, Brittanie?" I said. "Getting a refill here."

I was alone. The cashier stood outside, her four-year-old Nevaeh's tiny hand swallowed in one of hers. Her other hand hung loosely at her side; smoke curled up from a cigarette between two fingers. A few high school kids also stood around, all staring up at what I first assumed was just a flock of birds flying low in the cloudy October sky. But posters blocked a clear view out the windows, and I knew this had to be something stranger than a bunch of crows to command such attention.

I joined the group outside. The temperature had dropped at least fifteen degrees while I was inside. I zipped up my jacket all the way and blew on my hands. Brittanie stretched her free hand up and out, pointing the smoking end of her cigarette toward the spectacle.

It was indeed a flock of birds—but not all of the same kind. However, what had aroused their curiosity—and mine, now too—was not the diversity of species but what they carried: bundles of sticks, thistles, vine lengths, and various pieces of trash. A few turkey vultures dangled long pine boughs from their talons. A pair of blue herons worked together to suspend an American flag—I can only assume, as unlikely as it sounds, that they ripped it from a pole, for the short, starry end hung in strips and fluttered in the wind. Ironically enough, a bald eagle also flew among the motley flock, but instead of the flag, it grasped a scarecrow by its flannel collar. Since I know of no farms in Augustus Valley, it must have been previously decorating someone's lawn for the harvest season. Detached from any kind of backbone, its drooping, straw-stuffed limbs swayed, pressing on me the image of a dead man being carried away. The last threads fixed to its lolling head gave out as we watched, and down fell the painted sackcloth face into the trees' orange hands.

Though hindered by their payload, these birds flew steadily and stone-faced over the river, toward the mountains on the other side.

Obviously these weren't common migratory habits. I retrieved my binoculars from the Jeep and scanned the sky.

The birds flew to a treeless outcropping eaten out by a blanket of kudzu. They circled as one swirling avian cloud, lowered to deposit their various items in a heap, then scattered to find more refuse for their pile.

I knew it would be dark before I could reach that clearing. As hard as it would be to find in the daylight, it would be impossible without the sun. I internalized some visual markers in order to locate the area in the morning.

"Well," Brittanie said, finally breaking our silent trance, "there ain't a lotta things I seen or places I been in this world, but I reckon ain't nowhere else I woulda seen somethin' like that."

———◆———

I rose with the sun. Marie doesn't own a coffeemaker, so I dropped a bag of Earl Grey in my thermos and wrote her a note while I waited for some water to boil. She was used to me leaving and then reappearing a few days later, but I still like to give her a heads up.

Gone camping. Will be back in a few days.

I first drove to the Exxon and took another gander through my binoculars. It had rained softly at night before the wind blew the clouds away. Now the air was crisp and dry, clear of fog, and I had little trouble spotting the site. What yesterday had been a nearly unnoticeable heap of branches and trash now astonished me. It was hard to scale it from where I stood next to the gas pump, but I reckoned it to be at least fifty feet tall, being more cylindrical instead of the lumpish shape I had assumed. My heart jumped when I thought about approaching this curious artifact.

I oriented a topo map of the valley and spread it out on the Jeep's hood, hoping Brittanie wasn't watching through the window behind me. Sipping my tea, I compared the map to the mountain's contours and marked where the pile was with an X.

Just beyond the south end of town is a one-lane concrete bridge over a narrow portion of the Augustus River. From there, the map showed County Route 3/2 heading north again and climbing the valley. It wouldn't lead me directly to the site, but it was a start. I folded the map and got going.

CR 3/2 is a deeply rutted gravel road, and as usual I found myself grateful for the Department's unmarked Jeep Wranglers, which are better suited to off-road travel than what the State Troopers drive. I bounced along, looking for a convenient place to start hiking. I was about to park when I noticed a long-abandoned logging road cutting up the mountain. I stopped and checked the map and found no indication of it, but it was headed in the general direction of the kudzu patch. I followed this wide, grassy, leaf-littered trail for about half a mile until a large fallen tree forced me out of the vehicle. All further progress would be made on foot.

I downed the rest of my tea, strapped on my backpack full of camping gear and some food I had taken from Marie's house that morning, and checked my compass bearing with the map. Amazingly, the road/trail was still pointed almost exactly toward the site. I climbed over the fallen tree and began hiking.

Excessive windfall, as well as the steep grade, slowed me significantly. But as I had been able to drive most of the way, and had gotten an early start besides, I didn't let these obstacles frustrate me. I knew from the map that I had parked only a mile from the site. As you well know, I've trekked to locations much more remote than this (see previous case files re: Bigfoot activity in the Monongahela National Forest—I still don't know why we couldn't bring the BFRO in on that one).

Often have I documented my own feelings of nervousness and/or existential dread that escalate as I increase in physical and/or mental/psychic proximity to an investigation's subject. I've learned to trust—counter-intuitively, some might say—that revelation is closest at despair's climax. So far, that rule wasn't proving true. Elation, rather than fear, rose with the elevation, and with this arose my doubts. However, I kept on, knowing also that human emotions are fickle, prone to all sorts of misleading chicanery.

My heart charged heavy from exertion, and my hair clung to my sweaty neck, but I didn't stop. I had gotten past all of the windfall. Not twenty yards away, the land leveled off and hid itself from me. I hustled on, nearly giddy with anticipation.

The structure seemed to grow out of the ground as I neared the hillcrest. When I stood at last on level earth, I shouted in surprise (and something akin to rapture) at its magnitude.

The way the trail leveled and bent around the mountain, it seemed from that vantage as though all trees and vegetation had been strangled by the merciless kudzu, even though the patch was no more than thirty yards at its radius. As the first frost hadn't yet come to wither its leaves, the green cover made for a stark contrast to what towered at its center: branches, trash, reeds, grasses, shrubs—all layered and joined in a massive brown pillar.

It was much larger than I had first guessed. Even now I'm not sure how the birds found enough materials and built it in a single night. About twenty feet up, I spotted an entire uprooted rose bush interwoven into the structure. Below it, the old Red, White, and Blue skipped like a thread through the sticks. There was the scarecrow's flannel shirt, his straw guts infused into the pillar, his blue jeans stitching down its side. I was shocked to find his burlap face—a bird must have gone back to the riverbank and picked it out of the trees.

I felt unreasonably joyful in its presence, and I'm embarrassed to note that I spread my arms out and opened myself to it, like a toddler motioning for her parent to hold her. A sharp wind whipped through the clearing, and though it chilled my sweaty body, I hardly noticed. The pillar was singing to me.

I had forgotten to check my watch when I arrived, so I don't know how long I stood there gaping at it. If anyone had come by at that time, they may have thought I was experiencing an absence seizure. It is possible that was indeed the case. Suddenly, I sensed that the sun had moved, and my teeth were chattering from cold.

It finally occurred to me that whatever force had caused those birds to build such a thing could also be manipulating my emotions. I tried to regain a detached, objective perspective by focusing on data collection. By pacing out a certain distance and comparing my compass's clinometer reading with the trigonometric table in my notebook, I was able to calculate its height to be roughly eighty-seven feet. Its base circumference I paced out at ninety feet. I used my phone to take some photographs of the site and structure, which I will attach to this document, though you should already have access to them in the cloud.

That strange mania had not quite left me, and I retreated into the woods for a while, hoping to escape whatever influence the pillar had over me. Not wanting to set up camp on the steep trail that I had already travelled, I hiked around the bend beyond the clearing. The trail narrowed and climbed again, but not as steeply as before. I found a fairly level spot just off the trail and far enough from the clearing that the forest slightly obscured my view of the pillar—or the pillar's view of *me*, for I now felt as though it stared me down like a snake charming its prey.

Finally, I had found my trusty sense of gloom.

———————————◆———————————

There was little to note the rest of that day. By recording my observations for brief periods, then withdrawing again to my tent to settle my thoughts and emotions, I managed to keep the nest from muddling my wits to the point of uselessness. (I had already come to refer to it in my notebook as "the nest," even in my ignorance of what would follow.) These periods began as fifteen-minute stints, followed by fifteen minutes of rest in the tent, but by the evening I was able to watch for nearly a half an hour at a time before noticing the nest's effect on me.

I was about ready to call it a day around 1840 hours. The sun was low, I was hungry for dinner, and, frankly, I was bored out of my mind. I had already replaced my normal jacket with my down puffy, but sitting on that cold, hard rock had put my butt to sleep and made my shivery joints feel full of rust. I stood, set my notebook and pen down on the rock, and did a few jumping jacks. I walked a few circles around the nest and then looked out across the valley. A monstrous old house with too many gables poked up from a clearing in the mountains above town, almost directly opposite from the nest and me. Locally known as the Mallard House, this is the same place in which that nefarious quack psychiatrist we're researching set up practice back in the early nineties.

The sky above had darkened into a deep navy, while the sun squashed itself against the western ridge. The Mallard House's old gables darkened and became one with the mountain's shadowed side. The kudzu around me glowed with the sunset's last hurrah, and I turned to see the nest an almost unnatural deep red. It was beautiful.

———————————◆———————————

Long shadow-fingers played across the tent when I woke up later. I panicked for a second, thinking I had slept through until morning. My cell phone had died, and I had indeed forgotten to set an alarm on my watch. However, it was only 0145 hours; my body had automatically awakened itself. The brightness that I had mistaken for morning twilight came instead from the moon.

Already clothed and armed, I needed only my notebook and pen before going to check on the nest, so I turned on my headlamp and rifled through my backpack.

A noise froze me—something was right outside my tent. I turned off my light, drew my revolver, and listened as my eyes readjusted.

Branches creaked and swayed above me. A wind gust howled around the mountainside. My night vision returned; I again saw the shadows on my tent's ceiling—but they had grown bigger and darker.

I unzipped the tent door and exited, crouching low and leading with my gun. But I encountered neither cryptid nor spirit; the creatures that stared down at me from the branches were all well known to mainstream science. Silhouettes of various birds indigenous to southern West Virginia blackened the canopy—I identified most as raptors, but surely many smaller birds easily hid themselves, like the hundreds of spiders that go unnoticed in the forest until your flashlight catches their eyes.

Though I don't usually feel threatened by even the largest of birds, I didn't holster my firearm. I didn't like how they had all perched in surveillance of my tent. They didn't flee when I waved my gun in their direction and shooed at them with a loud whisper.

"Fine, stay there, then," I said. "I have work to do. You better be gone when I get back."

I headed for the nest, remembering that I had left my notebook on that rock. My legs wanted to run, but I did my best to appear calm and unconcerned with the eyes on my back. I compromised with a speed-walk, telling myself that the quicker pace was only to keep warm.

All that kudzu surrounding the monolithic nest looked like an alien landscape in the silvery moonlight. I smiled, grateful for it, loving it, soothed by it. You can see that I wasn't as immune as I thought at the time.

The nest had so captured me that I almost didn't notice the old man standing at its base. His skin and hair were as white as the moon shining on them, giving his gaunt frame a skeletal appearance. He was completely naked.

Afraid he may be high on meth or crack, I wanted to make my presence known while there was still a considerable distance between us. I shouted a "Hello!"

But he didn't acknowledge me. His eyes were trained on the ground in front of the nest—a gesture, I think, of subservient deference. Without a word, he turned up his palms and raised them to his shoulders. Then he shuffled slowly, head bowed, and kept moving his feet ever faster in the most soulful flatfoot clog dance I've ever seen, as though the wind itself played a hard-driving fiddle tune. Indeed, the wind intensified as the dance went on. I almost joined him, but I was stopped by a strong sense that this was a sacred, solitary act of worship that I dare not disturb.

At last he finished his jig and grabbed some branches protruding from the nest. I almost screamed—after such reverence it seemed an unquantifiable profanity for him to lay hands on it. But lightning didn't strike him down. He raised his gaze, and he began to climb.

The danger he was in broke the nest's spell over me—though in part I still might have been motivated by the offense of desecration. I shouted, holstered my firearm, and ran for him.

He climbed with tremendous speed. By the time I reached the nest, he was fifteen feet up its side. I yelled at him as turkey vultures circled in the sky directly above, but no amount of shouting would turn him back. I don't think he was at any time aware of my presence.

I considered climbing after him—in fact, I *wanted* to, and I don't think that I only wished to save him. But say I caught up with him at the top—what then? I don't think we could have communicated in any way, and I couldn't bring him safely down against his will.

Unsure of what to do, I retrieved my notebook and then stood below the nest, watching to see if he would fall, jump, or come to his senses and try to climb down. Upon reaching the top, he disappeared from my view. I half expected the vultures to descend on him at this point and tear the meager flesh from his bones, but they flew away like nothing had happened. The wind stilled, lulling me into a false sense of safety. I never considered going for help. I'm sure this pleases the Department, but it certainly weighs heavily on my conscience—even though I realize that my negligence was more a symptom of the nest's enchantment rather than any loyalty to the Department's soulless non-interference preferences.

I returned to my tent. The birds' unblinking stare missed nothing as I fumbled with the door's zipper, nearly ripping it when I shut myself inside. I woke up every few hours to check on the nest, but I saw nothing else that night. I tried to convince myself that the man had climbed down and escaped while I slept between shifts.

———◆———

The next morning and afternoon are a haze. All I can say about that day, before the sun went down, is that I wrote some exceptionally strange things in my journal. Awful, artless poetry that was both saccharine and bleak. Long, senseless stream of consciousness mumbo jumbo. As always, I've uploaded images of all handwritten journal entries to the server and attached them to this document. I cringed as I reviewed those awful notes. If at all possible, I beg of you, don't bring them up in any later debriefs when I get back to Charleston.

Again I failed to set a midnight alarm, and again I woke up at 0145 hours, my tent still surrounded by the birds. I was still wary of them, but this time I didn't pull my gun.

A gathering of crows is called a murder. Owls sit in parliaments. Vultures circle in a kettle. Power walking to the clearing, I wondered if there was a name for such a unified collective of so many diverse species.

A teenage girl stood where the old man had been the night before. She was also naked. In contrast to the man's ghastly and malnourished appearance, this girl's form was the epitome of youth in pure, unadorned beauty. While I am healthy and moderately fit, nature has stuck me with a wide, blockish frame that doesn't conform to popular aesthetic convention. Even in her peril, I envied this girl for her smooth, dark skin and fluid curves.

However compromised my mind was at the time, alarm bells still sounded from some deep, untouched place. Maybe the guilt I felt over my responsibility for the man had weakened the nest's hold on me. My heart raced; my mouth went dry. This time, I would intervene. This time, I would be savior instead of stenographer. I would run to her as she danced, get her out of this place, even if I had to knock her unconscious. I prepared to run—did I take just one deep breath? Two? Did I wait there for a full minute before acting? Did jealousy overrule my compassion, so that I wished her demise? Or was I intoxicated by the sight of that tall monument? Did my mouth water in anticipation of the girl's worship, envious not of her physical form but of her destined union with the nest?

She had no dance prepared. Instead, she raised a small, rectangular object above her head.

The wind howled.

She hesitated, but only for a second before she found her resolve. She threw it at the ground and stomped on it. Then she knelt.

Vultures began to circle.

My legs finally started to move, but it was too late. The girl was even better a climber than the old man.

"Come down!" I screamed. "Please!"

I don't know why I bothered. And—I admit this only for the sake of full disclosure in documenting these strange happenings—I was glad I hadn't stopped her.

The vultures flew away as she disappeared over the apex. I searched the ground for what the girl had trampled. Her offering was nothing so mystical as a dance.

It was just a cell phone, now smashed into pieces.

——————◆◆——————

I'm not doing my job.

My sleeping bag was fully zipped, and its hood was cinched down so that only my nose and mouth were exposed.

The Department pays me to observe and record.

Everything.

Claustrophobia overcame me. I thrashed, fumbling inside for the drawstring. I reckon I looked like a caterpillar struggling uselessly against a wheel bug's attack. I found the string, forced my head through—but I hadn't loosened it enough, and it caught around my nose for a second. When I got it wide enough to let out my shoulders, I hastily ripped the bag's zipper open and sat up. Great clouds of my breath filled the tent and condensed into thousands of droplets on the ceiling that came together and dripped back down on me. The cold immediately made my upper body ache, and I wished my cocoon hadn't caused me to temporarily lose my mind.

I haven't recorded everything yet.

My watch read 0328 hours. Not that long since the girl had ascended.

I haven't observed from the top.

I grabbed my notebook and cell phone, forgetting that it was dead. The moon remained bright and unobstructed in the clear sky, so I left my headlamp in my coat's pocket. The birds were not congregated as thickly above my tent as before; instead, they lined the trees along the path's edge. My brisk walk broke into a jog, which escalated to a sprint as my excitement swelled.

Nobody was at the nest's base but myself. It seemed to lean over me as I gazed up at its crown. I remember jotting down a few notes, but what you'll see in the attached images are just idiotic, senseless scribbles, like a kindergartener pretending to write in cursive.

Despite the supposedly scientific motivation guiding my ludicrous actions, I dropped both pen and notebook to the ground. Then, at some level remembering and believing my pretense, I picked them back up, putting my pen in my pocket and tucking my notebook into the back of my pants. My clothing suddenly felt repulsive, and I considered stripping down completely. I sensed that my euphoric feeling would increase if I conformed to the ideal previously witnessed.

But I didn't. I reckon that this rebellion was due to my ingrained, guiding distrust of positive feeling. Though this unfortunate result of my continued employment at the Department has aborted more potential relationships than I care to think of, it kept me alive that night.

Still clothed, then, I found holds and closed my hands on them. The wind picked up. The wood was smooth and felt surprisingly warm in my palms. My eyes rolled back and I closed their lids as an electric prickle coursed through me. I opened them again—I was doing this to *observe*, after all—and saw the vultures circling.

I wasn't as fast as the girl, but I was quicker than the old man. My weight seemed to decrease as I rose. My hands and feet never struggled to find secure holds. I paused only to peck a kiss on the scarecrow's rough, painted skin.

There was no fear of falling, no sense of the wind or cold, no longer any thought of my duty toward the Department. I'm not sure I even thought of my destination.

There was only the climb.

The ground below shuddered. The universe ebbed and expanded;

reality spun around the nest as its axis.

The top nearly within reach, I grinned.

One more step up and my elbows were over the edge. I leaned forward, swung my leg up, and tumbled into the concave top.

Five giant eggs sat in the nest with me. Each was at least as big as the girl, who sat next to them, curled in an upward fetal position. She was shock-still and held her hands loosely around her knees.

"Hello?" I waved my hand in front of her face. "Are you okay?"

Her corneas looked like frosted glass.

"Hey!"

Nothing going on. I poked her arm. She had taken on a semi-solid consistency so that my finger penetrated her flesh a quarter of an inch. A white, crusty substance curved under her feet and buttocks, containing a clear, viscous fluid up to its edge.

It was impossible to understand, but it wasn't hard to guess what was happening. The girl was rapidly reverting to an embryonic state. Soon she would be fully encased in her own shell, like the rest. I wondered which of these was the old man. Who had been the others who climbed this nest as I slept?

Typing up this scene made me so nauseous that I had to go sit in Marie's bathroom for half an hour before returning to the document. But up on the mountain, these things didn't bother me. All of this—the massive eggs, the nest, the vultures still circling ever faster overhead—it all felt like the most natural and correct experience in all my life.

The vultures!

Previously, they had flown away as soon as a person reached this haven. Yet there they were, flying now in impossibly fast circles.

Something's wrong, I thought. Then I felt the notebook still in my pants, and I realized my grave mistake. I hadn't left my offering below. I hadn't thrown off my impure human garb. I had profaned the ritual.

I placed my left hand over my mouth. My touch was slimy and soft. I jerked the hand away. Four of my fingers had transformed—but not into anything resembling these eggs. Instead they were black, wet, wriggling earthworms.

Drunken bliss melted away into disgust and terror. I broke off a piece of the girl's shell and sliced off my wormy fingers. I shrieked in pain. Despair formed a pit in my stomach.

My mind was finally clear.

Then the first vulture dove.

It came too fast for me to think, but my instincts saved me. Before I knew it, I had drawn my revolver, and just as the bird's white hooked beak was almost near enough to tear my face apart, I fired point-blank into its belly. Feathers and guts blew out its back as the slug exited and knocked the carcass through the air. I heard it thump into the ground below me two seconds later.

Now the others stopped their circling, and hung almost unmoving in the sky. Of course I couldn't pick them off with my gun from where I crouched, but I could take each of them on like I did the last—assuming they attacked one at a time.

But they didn't. Two came next, from either side. I dove forward and turned, slamming my back painfully into one of the eggs. Something cracked, and I hoped it wasn't my spine. The vultures collided with each other. I easily dispatched them both in their confusion.

The last two in the kettle were nearly on me as soon as I had finished with the others, and I had no time to dodge them. Fortunately, they took me on in single file. My first shot missed, but my second took them both out.

I took a moment to catch my breath. There were no more vultures, but I remembered all the other birds in the trees not so far away. No bullets left. Even given limitless ammunition, I wouldn't have the stamina or luck needed to withstand the coming onslaught. I had to climb down, *fast*—and when I took a sorrowful look at my left hand, I was amazed to find that my fingers had grown back. (Or had they never been severed at all? I doubt I hallucinated that, since my pain at cutting the worms from my knuckles played a major role in restoring my focus.)

As I reversed myself over the edge, I faced the egg that I ran into before. A large, vertical crack bisected the shell. I couldn't help but watch as it split entirely open. I think it was the old man—or had been. A hideous, unfinished creature slumped from the broken casing onto the nest's floor as goo spilled and seeped into the twigs.

I scrambled recklessly to the ground. Only a body saturated with adrenaline could have gotten down so fast without injury.

Grateful now for the headlamp in my pocket, I put it on and ran for the Jeep. The windfall that had slowed me before was hardly a problem after climbing down that nest.

Safe at Marie's, I crashed on the cot and slept until 1345 hours.

It is now 2158 hours. My tent and the rest of my gear are still up there. I'm in no rush to go back for any of it. I haven't stepped foot outside since my return last night, so I don't know if I should predict any further interference from the birds. So far, I haven't noticed anything out the windows.

I think I can handle going on with my original investigation, though it may take a few days to work out the jitters from this recent episode. I will continue surveillance of the nest through my binoculars only. I hope that isn't a problem. Honestly, I'm at a loss as to how I should further handle the situation, but I reckon it warrants sending at least a HAZMAT team along with some serious firepower. I would call this in over the phone, but to be honest, I'm not ready to actually hear myself voice any of the things I have written. Instead, I've labeled this email with a High Priority indicator so that you'll read my report immediately.

I shudder to think of those eggs, and to imagine what beasts will hatch from them. Or what creature might soon come to brood.

NOTES FOLLOW FROM INVESTIGATOR'S HANDLER:
A team was dispatched to the site the morning following receipt of this report. Upon arrival, they found that the described structure had been built over a large cavity of unknown origin, and the ground had collapsed under its massive weight. The investigator later admitted that she had not continued visual surveillance as she had promised and could not ascertain what hour the collapse occurred. Our team rappelled in without incident and successfully retrieved all necessary biological remains to be transported to the lab for further study. Four human fingers were found in addition to the other specimens. DNA testing confirms the investigator as their source, though she is missing no fingers on her own person.

All necessary evidence secured, the cavity was filled in. So far, no further abnormal animal or human activity has been observed.

Following their proper archival, all photos were deleted from the investigator's devices, and her notebook was burned and replaced, according to our protocols. Unfortunately, the investigator failed to obtain digital images of either the specimens prior to metamorphosis or the intact metamorphic encasings.

After undergoing extensive psychiatric debriefing, the investigator was given a week's paid leave, after which she resumed her prior investigation.

SU PORCU

Jason A. Wyckoff

Americans abroad inevitably find each other, whether they want to or not. It is the curse we most deserve. I take pains to avoid my brother, the ugly American tourist, with his loping arms and sighs of exasperation. Yet, to my recurring surprise, I find myself drawn to my countrymen, or at the very least, they to me.

Matt and Paige didn't know I was American before they asked me to take their picture for them, but, along with the other particulars (I was a woman in her forties with a pleasant demeanor) the fact that I was clearly not Sardinian may have influenced their choice of photographer. Upon learning my nationality, they asked if I could clarify for them the activity in the street below. We squeezed together against the metal rail amid other spectators and scanned the Carnival crowd from the restaurant's broad deck. It felt nice to huddle together; my thin sweater did little to protect me from the evening chill. January in the Mediterranean is still January. First, I asked them how long they were in Sardinia: A few days. That made it easier; I wasn't going to depreciate their experience by pointing out the dubious provenance of the current celebration.

"It's a mish-mash," I shouted above the clamor. "Many Sardinian towns have long-standing traditions for celebrating Carnival. Portu Rasposu had none, so it borrowed from everywhere else on the island. It was a small fishing village forty years ago, but it has a deep harbor. After the first cruise ship arrived, it grew exponentially. Now…" I opened my hands over the bustling street.

A mass of young people in costume frolicked on the cobblestone (which, though recently laid, was meant to evoke old-world 'charm', as were the rococo pediments above the single-window apartment balconies). Half a block to our left the wide strada emptied into the piazza. At the center of the piazza was a stand-in for what should have been a bonfire: a tower of automated lights had been erected; multi-colored beams swept the surrounding buildings in constant rotation. EDM pumped from speakers mounted underneath jutting cornices, competing with the braying of the crowd (likely equal parts native and foreign) and the incessant clanking of cowbells. Long, neon-colored plastic tubes, identical to those filled with 'Hurricanes' on Bourbon Street in New Orleans, bobbed like the horns of frolicking narwhals in the churning surf of bodies. Of course, Matt and Paige weren't asking about those (unfortunately) common elements. They were asking about the costumes.

I stretched out as far as I dared over the rail while I pointed to indicate different individuals.

"There—the big head with the long nose and the bushy beard."

"And the ram's horns!" Paige added cheerfully.

"Yes. That's the mask of *Su Corongiaiu*, recently revived in Laconi. And those white fur caps with antlers are worn by the *Corriolos* in Neoneli."

Matt laughed and observed, "I'm not sure those antlers are a great idea for a crowd."

"That one's wearing a deer head, eyes and snout and all," said Paige.

I followed her gaze. "From Sinnai. Many towns feature a particular animal in their Carnival celebrations." I pointed. "The ram in Seui. The boar in Ula Tirso." The boar saw me and waved. "They are supposed to be made from real pelts. These are probably store-bought costumes."

"Are you a tour guide?" Matt asked. I must have grimaced, as he added hurriedly, "It's just that you know so much!"

"No," I said, laughing; "though I suppose I must sound like one."

Paige asked, "Why do so many of them…" She ducked her head a little and moved her hand over her face, top-to-bottom.

I bit my bottom lip as I smiled. The subject was uncomfortable for Americans. "It's not blackface," I assured them. "It's meant to be done with charcoal. It's one of the most common elements amongst the different Carnival celebrations." I let that non-explanation be the explanation. The truth was, despite my research, I really didn't know why so many Sardinian Carnival characters employed 'charcoal-face'. I continued, "Taking it a step further, there are the black masks, worn most famously in Mamoiada by the *Mamuthones,* who act in concert with the *Issohadores,* in the white masks. One horrid, one blankly angelic."

"Good and evil?" Paige asked.

"More like 'animal and man'. There are many traditions pairing animals with hunters or herders."

Matt said, "But they don't have animal faces, the—the…"

"*Mamuthones.*" We gazed together at the anguished grotesqueries with their blocky, brutish eyebrows drawn together and their outsized frowns. "No, they're more allegorical than the simple animal analogues. They wear fur like animals, and they are slung with bells like beasts of burden, but their faces convey the very *human* suffering brought on by our lower instincts."

"Oh, you should talk to Paige about that," Matt said, grinning. I didn't get it. He explained, "Since she's the one always suffering from my lower instincts." He was quite proud of himself. Paige slapped his shoulder and rolled her eyes.

I skipped it and went on lecturing. "In Mamoiada, it's a solemn affair—at least for the *Mamuthones.* Their procession is extremely disciplined."

Paige guffawed. "Not like here."

She pointed to a group trying to right one of their comrades, whose face had gone crooked, causing him to stumble. These imitation *Mamuthones* wore furry, brown, short cloaks (over otherwise naked torsos) and had their faces covered by the dour black *visera* (from our vantage point, I couldn't be sure, but I believed them to be identical, made from molded plastic rather than individually carved). They didn't wear *sa carriga,* the heavy harness of globular bells, but instead bounced a sprig of two or three hung from a cross-body strap which knocked against their hips as they lurched aggressively—not at all like the practiced and regulated step of their inspiration. The white-masked *Issohadores* (of which there were only two, clad in tight, bright garb) acted something closer to their counterparts, occasionally lassoing a young woman with their thin rope.

"They don't seem overly concerned with symbolism," Matt cracked.

I smiled. "No, it looks like they've pretty much appropriated the roles for the usual purposes—to be the rutting beast or the dashing savior."

He reduced it, "To get girls."

"It's a goddamn travesty, is what it is," declared a man's voice behind us.

There wasn't available space along the balcony, but the older couple beside we three moved off at the sight of him. From his accent, he was obviously American, and from his demeanor, obviously drunk. He appeared to be about my age but far worse for it. He was flush, even in the cool night air; a ring of sweat bordered his hairline. His drooping lip glistened with saliva.

Slurring slightly, he enlightened us, "The real procession of the *Mamuthones e Issahadores* in Mamoiada is nothing like this. It is a solemn ceremony, rich in meaning." He gestured dismissively. "Not like this cheap imitation!"

Matt smiled; he likely found it amusing the man had unknowingly repeated much of what I'd just said, blaming it on his drunkenness. Paige and I shared a grin knowing that he likely would have shared his redundant observation regardless, as his sex is wont to do.

"Are you generally opposed to dancing in the streets, or only when people are having fun doing it?" I think he was momentarily taken aback that I'd actually responded to his interjection.

"Eh? No—I mean…this is just—it shouldn't *just* be people trying to get laid. Not that I'm *generally* opposed to that, either."

On the other side of Matt, Paige squeezed out little group together to ask me, "And do you need saving from the rutting beast?"

Matt added, "Or maybe you just want lassoing?"

I assumed he wouldn't have flirted with me in front of Paige unless it was meant to be an inclusive invitation. As Paige looked away, no longer smiling, it seemed as though the prospect was not as practicable as Matt might have thought.

"Don't worry," I said, "I can handle myself."

The other man barked something in my ear. When I turned his way, his arm was bent like a chicken wing, with his hand extended in greeting as best as the close quarters allowed. "Brent," he said. "My name is Brent."

His skin was soft, though the pads of his fingers were hard. I asked, "So you've been to Mamoiada?"

"I've been stuck on this island for years. I've seen every Carnival celebration. I've seen…I've seen *all* of them."

Before I could pick up on that curious bit of emphasis, a tumult arose to our left. The crowd in the piazza roared and lifted their arms as one. They faced the approach of something from one of the other streets and we had to wait for several seconds to see what it was. Matt and Paige and I leaned forward in anticipation. Brent straightened and drew back a bit so as to ease our view, and I credited him for at the very least not being a liar, as his blasé stance seemed to indicate he knew what was coming. Finally there emerged into the piazza a long, rectangular, metal-sided fire pit on wheels, ushered in by *La Sartiglia* (in costume only—white masks topped by flat, round black hats fitted with tall plumes, gold-fringed epaulets on tight vests over frilled shirts. In Oristano, these heroes of Carnival would be mounted on horses adorned with chains of flower-like medallions; here, the men escorted a pig on a spit over parallel rails of blue-tongued gas flames, their hidden faces doubtless slick with sweat). As the portable pit began a counterclockwise turn around the piazza, a second roar went up.

I watched Brent's hand go up to squeeze the bridge of his nose as he winced. "They just can't stop adding to it!" he complained.

The object of his disdain was a giant puppet supported by six stilts carried by cloaked and 'charcoal-faced' revelers. The puppet was a rotund man carrying a goblet. His face was beaming and rosy-cheeked; his eyes, shut in euphoric bliss; on his head rested a triangle-pointed crown. He was clad in what might have been a toga or might have been a wrap of rags.

"Dionysus?" Paige asked.

"Perhaps he was once the inspiration, but this is an imposter, at best," Brent snarled. "Carnival is a time for upendings and inversions of the status quo. So The King of the Carnival is just an elevated fool. And wherever there is a King—in Tempio, Bosa, Cagliari—the end of Carnival is marked by his death. Order is restored; the puppet is burned. *This* one will probably just go back into storage."

A third cheer reclaimed our attention. The procession of the fire pit had come to a halt in front of the elevated DJ's station. One of *la sartiglia* leapt up on the stage's lower tier and thrust a long blade skyward. The DJ barked something in Italian, too fast (and too distorted) for my limited translation skills. Then a digital swell bloomed into a frenetic breakbeat track just as the blank-face, dandy butcher hacked into the roast pig. He began to slice strips of crisp skin from the shoulder, flicking them into the awaiting sea of hands.

Matt laughed. "Are they just going to tear into that thing on the street?"

After a while I left the young lovers alone and drifted back towards the bar with Brent. Yes, he was a bit of a boor, but that made him all the more disposable, and the lascivious energy of Carnival combined with Matt's earlier suggestion had given me an itch. Unfortunately, Brent's bravado appeared limited to his haranguing of strangers with unsolicited invective, as he required much more liquid courage and prodding to finally suggest what I already predisposed towards doing. By the time we got to my hotel room, he was wobbling. His slapdash effort at foreplay involved sloppy kisses as he leaned on me for support. I pushed him down on the bed and climbed on top. His blind anxiousness to get to my breasts ran afoul of his undexterous fingers and a simple clasp, and in the two seconds it took me to release the ladies myself, he passed out cold, which likely saved me from the disappointment of trying to coax anything viable from below his wine-swollen belly. At least he had a crumpled pack of cigarettes in one pocket, and it had been a long time since I'd had any of those either, so I contented myself as best I could with the woozy spin of a nicotine high before I succumbed to sleep as well.

I was showered and dressed by the time he woke with a groan. He rubbed bleary eyes and then blinked repeatedly at the ceiling. I opened the door to the balcony and cool, salt-flecked air swept in. He drew the sheet up to his chest and looked at me for a few seconds. Finally, recognition came, and he lifted the sheet, as if his degree of nudity would reveal some important fact. As it failed to provide the answer he sought, he asked, "Did we..?"

I shot him a look.

"Dammit," he said by way of apology. He sat up and rubbed the heel of one palm into the center of his forehead. "Ow," he said, and then repeated, "Dammit." This second utterance seemed bleakly habitual; one more lost 'never again' swept into a teetering drift.

"I'll be checking out soon," I said. For emphasis, I turned towards the bureau and plunked my phone charger into my overnight bag.

"You're leaving Portu Rasposu?"

I shrugged. "I only ever planned to stay one night."

I think he cursed himself under his breath. "Where are you heading next?"

I turned to face him. He was buttoning his shirt—what buttons survived the night. I said, "It is the feast day of St. Anthony the Abbot. I thought I would go to Mamoiada to see the *Mamuthones e Issahadores.*"

He grunted. I think was grateful to seize any opportunity to think less of me. He nearly spat when he asked, "Going back on the greatest hits tour, huh?"

"I've never been," I replied.

He looked at me inquiringly. "But the way you talked last night…"

"I'm a single woman, travelling alone. Western Europe or not, forewarned is forearmed. And time is precious: I want to make the most of my holidays. I've imagined this trip for a long time."

He had got up from the bed and moved to the balcony door. He grasped the frame on both sides. "All the caution and planning in the world can't prevent catastrophe," he countered. I said nothing; he must have inferred something from my silence. "And why are you travelling alone? Does having no one to come with you mean there's no one to go back to?"

"Why are you still here?" I replied.

He missed the meaning of my question. "In Sardinia?"

He didn't say anything else. I suppose it annoyed me, so I provoked him. "Besides, I think I convinced Matt and Paige to go to Mamoiada, so perhaps I'll join them."

He scoffed. "And do what? Be a third wheel?"

I held my cocksure grin long enough for him to turn and see it. I said, "If you want to shower, please be quick about it."

I'd hit my mark; his pride was injured. "You're kidding yourself with those debutantes. They'll never leave the beach. If you want to see Sardinia—to see the *real* Sardinia—you'll need a guide."

I shot back with an echo from the previous evening. "Because you've seen *all* of the Carnival celebrations."

He worked his lips, but no sound came out. I'd demarcated the only area of interest from which I'd consider an offering. He was resistant, perhaps searching his skull for some *other* festival than the clearly specific and singular inspiration for the emphasis. But my poise indicated I would brook no dissembling. He made a fist over his heart and rolled his other thumb over the knuckles. His eyes steadied, became steely.

"Yes," he said. His voice dropped to a whisper. I almost felt compelled to glance around to make sure no one was listening. "Yes, I know of a place where the tourists don't go, with a procession different from all others." He made a face as though he regretted mentioning it; he waved his hands and frowned. It seemed to me like playacting. He challenged me, "But you haven't already read about it. How would that fit in your plans?"

I arched an eyebrow and said nothing. The argument was his to finish on his own; I stood to lose nothing.

He measured his words: "There are cultural sensitivities involved." He stepped closer. "You would have to listen to me. You would have to do what I say. Can you do that?"

"Can you stay sober?" I bartered.

He paused before compromising. "I can keep from getting drunk."

The feast day of St. Anthony the Abbot was the official first day of Carnival (Portu Rasposu's decision to begin early was in line with its spurious disposition). Though I had some misgivings about my chosen travelling companion, and I doubted he could provide a destination meriting his melodramatic tease, I wasn't terribly worried. I knew that we could visit any town and find at least some sort of celebration.

I rented a car and we drove northwesterly, into the mountains. For an hour we drove on pristine pavement, almost oddly bereft of cracks or ruts; white lines shone bright under clear sun; guardrails lined the sides of the road even when the downward slope was distant. The gradual rise of the road was almost uniformly smooth, so that the proof of it out of the side windows appeared more like the slow sinking of the island into the sea than our being lifted towards its heart. We passed through farmland, familiar enough but for the odd textures dotting the roadside in discordant counterpoint: cactus teardrops spilled over a slice of exposed rock, next to peevish tufts of prickly pine bushes, offset by the jubilant fronds of a thick-trunked palm. Sometimes a cluster of earth-red tile roofs bloomed in a valley, visible from a well-considered lookout at a turn in the road. On more than one long stretch of road, an old stone church stood alone.

I reminded Brent of something he'd said on the balcony the night before, that he'd been 'stuck on the island for years'.

He watched the countryside roll by. "I don't want to leave," he said. "You won't want to, either."

I assumed he spoke of love for his adopted home. "That's not 'stuck'," I said.

He grunted. I let the silence afterwards stew.

He sighed. "I was with a group." He shook his head as though trying to convince himself to stop there, but knowing he wouldn't. As before in my hotel room, it seemed to me like he might have been feigning this inner struggle. "Our boat went down in a storm. All souls lost."

I looked over. He turned his palms upwards and shrugged. "Well, obviously, I made it to shore. By the time I realized I was *thought* to be dead, I realized as well that if it was known that I was alive, there would be…unfriendly questions as to the…precise circumstances of our accident."

I scowled. "From the police?"

"Maybe. I don't think I'd describe every Sardinian official as 'incorruptible'. But as long as the sponsors of my group's expedition don't know I'm here to begin with, it shouldn't be a problem. Of course, if I tried to leave, then…"

"Wait a minute," I interrupted. "Before we go any further, I feel I should tell you that I work for M.I.6. I was recruited by Her Majesty's Secret Service from an Albanian circus when I was only eight years old. My American accent is very convincing, don't you think?"

"You don't have to believe me," he growled. "You asked."

I laughed. "If I understand correctly, you are insinuating that you've been exiled to Sardinia because you're a suspect in a murder plot involving—what—a hunt for sunken treasure?"

"The details around our objective, my status, and the *accident* are more mundane than your artful summation might suggest. Nevertheless, it should offer you an intriguing hint as to how I've managed to survive on the island without a work visa and no visible source of income."

"I bought our drinks last night and you stayed in my room. The hotel staff seemed not only to recognize you, but to not particularly like you. And somehow you managed to produce a sports bag without going 'home', from which you took a change of clothes which don't look much cleaner than those you removed. I suspect the truth is more sordid than 'intriguing'."

He shifted in his seat and leaned over. "Then shouldn't you be afraid to go off into the country alone with me?"

I slammed on the brakes.

He pushed himself upright, keeping his hands on the dash. "I'm sorry," he said, "that was inappropriate."

I glanced in the rearview mirror; no one was coming. I ran the fingers of one hand through my hair and bunched the ends in a fist. "I should have gone to Mamoiada."

"I'd rather you didn't kick me out of the car," he said. "Please."

Whatever I thought of him, I didn't feel endangered—though I wonder if I didn't feel a bit disgusted with myself for keeping his company, as my initial impression of not wanting to get to know him seemed valid.

I punched the accelerator.

After a minute, he coughed, and then said, "As impressive as the costumes of the *Mamuthones* are, I've always been a bit put off by them. The way those bulbous bells jut out from their dark, shaggy sheepskin wraps…it always reminds me of when I was a kid in Florida. My cousins lived on a farm and their dogs would get these ticks between their shoulders which would get so swollen…"

"Jesus, fuck, shut up."

He released the imaginary ball in his hands and dropped them to his lap. "Sorry. I was just trying to get us back on track."

"Just tell me you know where we're going."

He said, "In about three minutes, you'll want to turn left."

The road we turned onto was little more than one lane wide and had no edge lines. The rise was still gradual, but the way became more winding; flat expanses were fewer. New colors appeared: Naked, spindly shrubs added purple splotches to the roadside; white, skeletal branches reached over. But here, as before, even in winter, green predominated. As we approached a spur of tamped dirt on an elbow in the road, Brent said, "Pull off here."

I did as instructed. "What's here?" The foliage thinned at the angle; I gazed out on a narrow hollow between a looming ridge before us and a squat one behind.

"Nothing," he said. "This is where you have to make a choice."

I stared at him uncomprehendingly. I believe I hid my anxiety. I suddenly felt like an idiot. I had done exactly what I promised myself I wouldn't: I had been incautious. I was alone with a man I didn't know in a place I hadn't planned on being, out of sight from any help. Why? Because a flaccid drunk had half-dared me to be adventurous? Perhaps my assessment of his harmlessness was over-generous; perhaps his shabby banality was an affectation.

He raised one hand in a calming 'wait' gesture and added, "About what we do next." I had not hidden my anxiety as well as I thought.

"What do you mean?"

He motioned with his chin. "The village is just up this road another kilometer or so, on the far side of that ridge. If we go there now, we'll be welcomed, despite the village getting few visitors. I couldn't say that they'll *actually* be happy to see us, but they'll be hospitable—almost forcibly so, because they'll want us to stay put."

"Well, that sounds pleasant."

"As I understand it, men from the village go to perform a sacred, secret ritual away from the town, at the local *nuraghe*. You know what *nuraxis* are?"

I did: these mysterious, ancient structures made up from basalt stone bricks, with beehive-shaped domes in their centers dotted the Sardinian landscape. "Yes," I said, "I'd planned to see a few while I'm here."

"This one isn't much to look at. I've seen it—the *nuraghe*, not the ritual. The center structure collapsed. I don't think there is any 'inside' to it anymore. The outer walls are crumbling; the steps going up to it are overgrown with weeds."

"Lovely. So one option…"

"Would be to sneak out to the *nuraghe*. If we do that, we wouldn't be welcome in town afterwards. Even if we keep out of sight at the ritual, they'll be suspicious of us. And they'll probably already be locked up in their homes, besides."

"What the hell kind of celebration is that?"

"Quite festive, actually. Families and friends gather in groups and share a feast. And then they go to bed behind their shuttered windows so that they don't witness the parade of the returned supplicants roaming the streets."

"What?"

"Once in their lives—*once*—each villager will look out a window or step out on the balcony to watch the Carnival procession."

I stammered nonsensically, not quite sure what question to ask.

Brent said, "I've done it. If it's what you want to do, I'll go with you into town and I'll find us a feast and a place to stay. But I won't watch the return of the supplicants. You'll have to do that alone. But you must not go out into the streets. That is forbidden."

I gazed out over the hollow, inferring the stone circle to be off in that direction. "So what is the ritual?"

He shrugged. "I don't know, exactly. Some of the men in the village put on costumes and lead a cow and a sheep out of town. I imagine they chant incantations and march around the ruin of the *nuraghe*. I don't think the animals come back."

"A sacrifice? In this day and age?"

"Or maybe just a ritualistic slaughter. I can't imagine they waste the meat. Or maybe they leave some part behind, like the heart."

I winced. "Look, I know where meat comes from, but I don't think I really need to watch animals being killed."

"Like I said, it's one option. I recommend going into town."

"And looking out a window."

He turned in his seat, making sure to have my full attention. "It's a powerful experience. I promise you that."

I said, "Did anyone ever tell you that you have a flair for the dramatic?" He didn't respond. I laughed nervously. "Okay, then. Who am I to doubt the recommendation of my travel advisor?"

We drove on. I'm not sure what I was expecting of the village—thatched roofs?—but I was surprised: Though the pavement gave way to uneven cobblestone, and though the streets were narrow like those of a coastal town (the inland villages being usually less prone to compression), the village was, at first blush, little different from any other I'd seen in Sardinia, if perhaps more humble in aspect than some. Adjoined brick and stucco buildings rose three stories high in muted pastel tones; tall, shuttered windows led out to shallow, iron-railed balconies; silver gutters bracketed glass shop windows and let out onto cracked cement sidewalks. I saw an outdated blue and gold 'VISA' sign and a scrawl of red graffiti on the alley-side wall of a pizzeria. A few cars, compact hatchbacks all, were parked in that seemingly arbitrary way that only the locals would understand. There were quite a few people out in the streets, though nothing approaching a 'crowd'. And while the atmosphere was festive, all eyes stared as we idled past. In the rear-view mirror, I watched a few villagers laugh amongst themselves as they threw paper streamers after us, their white or red tails arcing while they fluttered to the street.

Brent chuckled. "I forgot about the streamers."

I parked the car where I thought it would offend no one. I put on a hooded parka when we got out. It was much cooler than on the coast, almost cold. We walked two blocks or so to a wide, five-way, trapezoidal intersection, abutting a small 'park'—a patch of grass and three stone benches facing a memorial obelisk. Nothing at all like the ornately planned piazza at Portu Rasposu. A group of men was concentrated in front of several folding tables. The crowd prevented me from seeing what was on the tables, but I guessed they were laden with parts of the ceremonial garb; two men each in modern clothing attended to several others wearing matching straight-legged brown trousers (which appeared to me to be made of leather) above black boots with thick heels, and black cotton long-sleeve shirts, likely meant to disappear beneath the waiting accoutrements. Two separate tables were buried beneath red and white streamer rolls, with more full bags underneath. Children grabbed one of each color and then dashed away, laughing and unfurling the streamers with seemingly indiscriminate tosses, to no one's consternation.

A middle-aged woman in blue jeans and a white Gore-Tex jacket approached us. Her hair was pulled back and up; her smile was bright red. She and Brent spoke in rapid Italian with attendant loose hand gestures. At one point as he spoke, Brent indicated himself and shook his head, and then gestured towards me and nodded. They spoke for a short while longer before Brent clasped her hands in gratitude. The woman bowed and extended a greeting to me before she turned away.

"That was the mayor," Brent said. "She's going to find someone to welcome us to feast. As I mentioned, it wouldn't be hard to get an invitation even without her intervention. I asked about the family I stayed with before, but they had to take their mother to hospice in Nuoro just two days ago."

I moaned sympathetically.

By the end of this brief exchange, the mayor had already turned back our way accompanied by a grey-mustachioed gentleman and his stocky wife, plump cheeks pink and gleaming above her black dress. We were introduced to Bertu and Efisia Piras. After a brief misunderstanding, we explained (quite urgently on my part) that Brent and I were not married and only travelling companions. Efisia made an expression of regret of the like, 'why aren't two such lovely young people married', though it seemed to me the sentiment carried as much concern as encouragement. Yes, they would be happy to have us join them for the feast of St. Anthony the Abbot. And then, in turn, yes we understood the prohibition about going out in the streets once the feast has begun—Brent had explained it. Oh, you've been here before? And so on.

The matter settled, our little group moved closer to the men preparing to leave for the ceremony at the *nuraghe*. As the attendants assisted the other men into their costumes, it became apparent that the dress of these 'supplicants' was surprisingly similar to that of the *mamuthones*—with one striking discrepancy. Each wore the long, dark sheepskin cloak, and each donned a unique black *visera*, features frozen in anguish, under a black scarf wrapped around the head. But instead of being cinched into the straps and burdened by the cluster of ovoid bells of *sa carriga*, a vest of animal bones strung in overlapping rows was draped over the shaggy cloak. I could hear the bone vests clatter as the men jumped to test them out, but only lightly, as the sound was lost in the clamor of conversation. I wondered at this development, as I could see the dull sheen of oblong brass bells still piled on the tables behind the men.

Two of the tables were by this time cleared off. Onto these, greeted by a boisterous cheer from the crowd, were set several kegs, the black bulbs of plastic taps jutting like stunted antennae. The men nearest the kegs waved their arms and one of them let out a shrill whistle, and a hush fell over the crowd. The mayor stepped between the men and turned to address her constituents. She made a brief speech, culminating with a crescendo and an upwards snap of her wrists, which was greeted by another roar. Glass mugs appeared from out of nowhere and were quickly filled with beer. Each of the attendants began passing out the mugs to the bystanders. The now fully-dressed supplicants followed after them with pleading, open hands, but the attendants ignored them, and whenever one drew near to one of the spectators who had been served, the beer-holder would turn and pull the mug away from the desperate beggar.

A man approached Brent and I and handed each of us a mug. A supplicant followed shortly behind him.

I hastily sought confirmation, "I should *not* give him a drink, right?"

Brent said, "You should not. There is no solace for them."

The supplicant drew near enough that I could see his green eyes behind the grotesque black mask. He bowed and shrugged, extending his open hands. I laughed and turned away, towards Brent, who turned towards me. We crashed our mugs together, sending a spurt of liquid over the sides. The supplicant reached as to grab the falling liquid. Having failed, he brought his curled hands to his face and rocked back in forth in lament.

When all the adults had been served, the supplicants, denied by all, turned back towards the attendants. They approached, still empty-handed. The attendants yanked the bells from the tables behind them, snapped them forward and shook them, making an awful clamor. Each cluster of bells was apparently affixed to a handle, of which the supplicants grabbed hold. When all had received their due, the supplicants jerked the bells in unison, first once, then twice, then three times.

The attendants again whistled for attention, though by then, all eyes were already forward. The men lifted their mugs and shouted, "*Su boe!*"

The crowd responded, "*Su boe!*"

The men shouted, "*Sa brebei!*"

The crowd responded, "*Sa brebei!*"

The men shouted, "*Su porcu!*"

Getting into the spirit of things, I said, "*Su porcu!*" I was glad of the timidity with which I responded, as instead, the crowd shouted, "*S'ómine!*"

The men again shouted, "*Su porcu!*"

The crowd once more responded, "*S'ómine!*"

A third shout: "*Su porcu!*"

The crowd was silent. Then I began to hear a strangely muffled keening. The sound swelled, and I realized it came from behind the masks of the supplicants. And then it broke suddenly into full-throated pig-squealing as the supplicants stretched their necks and rolled their heads from side to side. I heard the tap of hooves on brick. I hadn't noticed that a fat, brown bull and an unshorn sheep had been led to the edge of the crowd near to one of the intersecting streets. They skittered nervously at the sound. I pouted, sad at the sight of their distress, sadder still knowing their impending fates. A second sound emerged as the crowd began moaning "oh". Then that sound, too, swelled, and burst into a broad roar, drowning out the squeals of the supplicants. And suddenly streamers were flying in every direction as the drone burst into a cheer. I looked down as a child grabbed my hand and stuffed it with a paper roll. This, I needed no instruction to understand, and I hurled my streamer into the crisscrossed, wavering mass. The supplicants, bowed and humbled, fled desultorily from the harmless onslaught. They moved down a side street, corralling the animals between them. The barrage of streamers continued, but no one followed after.

As soon as the supplicants had turned out of sight, the attendants began to sing. The crowd joined in. Plentiful hand drums beat accompaniment, and I heard a triangle and a fife. An impromptu parade began moving down the street in the opposite direction from the departed supplicants. Children continually crammed streamer rolls into my free hand, which I obligingly, if inexpertly, emptied in the appropriate fashion. Every so often we would reappear in the piazza. I could not sense which direction we turned when we met each odd angle. I don't remember passing by the rental car, though.

When the streamer supply was exhausted, the procession stopped once more in the piazza. The music continued, and beer mugs were insistently refilled. Brent rolled his lips often. I think he was putting in an honest effort to drink slowly. He coughed and glanced away whenever he saw me watching him.

As soon as the first shadow of a building fell full upon the opposite side, without any other sign that I saw or heard, the kegs were whisked away and the tables broken down. Though still laughing and embracing, the villagers bid goodbye to each other in a whirl almost like a choreographed dance that lasted no longer than three minutes. Then they broke into smaller groups, usually multi-generational, and shuffled away quickly over the carpet of trampled streamers.

Bertu and Ifisia Piras found us and beckoned us follow them. We were joined by a son, his wife and three children, along with two young women I took to be cousins, one of them married. We were introduced, but the names went by too quickly for me to assign them. We walked a short block, made two odd oblique turns in rapid succession, and walked to the end of the next block, where Bertu opened a cream-colored, unlocked door and bade us enter. Ifisia led the way up the stairs—there were shops on the ground level, one a chocolatier, I think. I glanced back to see Bertu lock the door behind us with a key he put in his right coat pocket.

The common rooms were on the second floor, the bedrooms on the third. I hadn't thought to go back to the car to retrieve my overnight bag, and the Piras had not asked if I wanted to. Clearly that option was off the table. But Brent and I were shown to a small bedroom with a single bed (either our status was not understood after all or not considered to be a concern) with an attached half-bath where we could freshen up before the feast. And Ifisia indicated a dresser drawer with several old-fashioned night-dresses, anticipating my need for later that night.

The dining room was in the center of the house, with no exterior walls. When we went down, I noticed that blinds were drawn down over the already-shuttered windows in the living room. The kitchen ran alongside of the dining room. There were two doors towards the back; one opened on a sort of study or library; the other was shut.

The dining room was warm and loud. As even the children soon realized my Italian wasn't up to snuff, they soon switched to Sardinian, and I was completely lost thereafter, although they continued to smile guilelessly at me, and, throughout the meal, frequently offered me more food to add to my over-flowing plate. Despite the barrier, they were genuinely charming company, and I could at least take joy in the loving bond of common familial interactions. As the food was being brought to the table, I watched as Bertu spoke with Brent in low tones. I could tell they were speaking about me. Brent seemed to be reassuring Bertu that he understood, and that I understood. Bertu nodded at me and smiled uncertainly.

After the last platter had been set on the table, Ifisia and the older cousin took the final two seats. Anticipatory silence fell. Bertu set his elbows on the table and turned his palms upwards. I expected we were to join hands and be led in prayer, but instead Bertu began to speak conversationally, and everyone listened attentively. After he finished his short speech, we lifted our glasses and drank the toast, "A Chent'Annos!"

I asked Brent, "What did he say?"

"He was recounting the story of St. Anthony the Abbot," he replied.

"You speak Sardinian as well, then?"

He shrugged. "It's easy enough. You'll learn."

I laughed. "I'm only here for a few days."

He took a swallow of wine. "As you take pains to learn everything beforehand, I assume you know the story of St. Anthony?"

I answered, "Is that a question or an attack?"

He set his glass down and then slouched as he exhaled. "My *apologies*."

As his tone was disingenuous, I remained silent as we passed dishes.

Finally, I said, "An ascetic monk who went out into the wilderness to find enlightenment and was tempted and tormented there."

He belched into the back of his hand. "All true. But in Sardinia he is credited with bringing fire to humanity as well."

"Conflating his story with the myth of Prometheus?"

"Unashamedly—despite the obvious discrepancy in time. That is why Sardinian towns celebrate Carnival with bonfires."

"But not here?"

He ignored the question. "But while Prometheus stole fire from the Gods, in this myth St. Anthony was tasked *by* God to steal fire from Hell. The villagers here like to believe their broken-down *nuraghe* was built to mark the spot where St. Anthony emerged with the spark. And what are we to think of that?"

He looked towards the ceiling, wrapped smugly in his own thoughts and requiring no response. Too low to hear, I muttered, "Stop, thief!" I wondered again if I should have gone to Mamoiada.

At least the feast did not disappoint. The food was scrumptious. I suppose most of the meal had to have been prepared beforehand and warmed, as we were beginning to eat within an hour of returning to the Piras' home. Ifisia brushed off showers of praise.

After the feast, the children went into the living room with the younger cousin and watched an animated movie. Only once did I see any of them show any interest in the outside world. The youngest grandchild, a boy of about four, got up and stood beside the sofa, leaning on the arm. For a second, his attention slipped from the television and he glanced towards the windows. Almost immediately he ran around the front of the sofa and threw himself down to snuggle with his cousin, seated on the floor.

Liqueurs were served after dessert. Brent no longer looked to me for approval. I could see his face beginning to bloom red. The men and the older cousin smoked cigarettes, except Bertu, who smoked a pipe.

I began to feel smothered. Though the stimuli were generally pleasant, my senses had been overwhelmed for several hours: by the burble of their voices, by the cloying of the smoke, by the savory and sweet smells and tastes, by the warmth of the house and the alcohol. I felt a degree of relief when Ifisia produced blankets and pillows from the coat closet, and I understood that the children would be going to sleep in the living room where they now already began to swoon. Sliding French doors with frosted glass were closed to partition them. Of the adults, the older cousin and her husband went upstairs first. After a little while, we heard the rhythmic creaking of a bed. Bertu's son shouted disapprovingly towards the ceiling, something along the lines of, 'We have to sleep up there!' The son continued to smoke with Bertu while his wife helped Ifisia. At one point (while Brent was in the bathroom), I could tell that he asked Bertu about me, and Bertu used the same reassuring gestures as had Brent. The son looked at me and conferred a brief, solemn blessing as Brent returned to the table. Then he called to his wife, and they went upstairs. Ifisia followed a few minutes later.

Bertu said, "Okay"—that one, universal word—and he stood up from the table. He bade us follow him towards the back of the house, where he opened the closed door next to the study. He indicated I was welcome to go in, though the gesture had little encouragement in it. I nodded and thanked him. He smiled resolutely and turned to go up the stairs.

It was a small sitting room with a pair of mismatched chairs and a coffee table. Obviously, its primary function was to take advantage of the attribute waiting outside of twin, narrow doors: the balcony.

Brent pushed into the room behind me.

I grimaced. "Isn't this where we part ways?"

"I'll wait with you," he said. He dropped into one of the chairs. "If you like," he added, though no choice was implied.

"And what are *we* waiting for?" I asked. The ridiculousness of the concept suddenly struck me. "What is the point of a procession if no one is watching?"

"It's not really a *procession* as such," Brent said. "But I promise it will change you."

"You also promised that you wouldn't get drunk."

"I'm *fine*," he spat. "It's not like I'm driving anywhere. Or going anywhere."

I burned a hole through the back of his skull.

He caught my stare and lurched to his feet. He grabbed my arms and pulled me to him. He slobbered on my neck. "You don't have to worry about me," he hissed in my ear. "I'm ready this time." He slid his grip down to my wrist and forced my hand to his crotch to feel his erection.

I didn't flinch or pull away. I left my hand there, unmoving. After a few seconds he raised his head. I looked at him dispassionately. "That was a one-time offer," I said.

He pulled his lips inwards, baring his teeth. Breath whistled through his nostrils. I wondered if he would try to hit me. Instead, he released his grip, blew sour breath in my face and said, "We'll see." He stepped around me and yanked open the balcony doors. I thought he might step back, but instead he went out onto the balcony, raising his head to sniff at the night air.

"I thought you said you could see it only once," I said.

"I'll go inside when it's time. There's nothing to see yet. But listen!" He cocked an ear.

I heard nothing. As much as I wanted to just shut him out on the balcony and lock the doors, I thought that if there truly was something worth witnessing, I wouldn't see or hear it from inside. I didn't deserve to miss out just because *he* was a cad. I stepped out onto the shallow wrought-iron balcony and I listened. I still didn't hear anything.

And then I realized just how quiet the night truly was. The air was still. The ubiquitous hum of electricity continued, but even this seemed humbled, just as one is conscientiously quiet in a quiet room. But what startled me—only after noticing its absence—was the total lack of noise created by human agency. The town was celebrating Carnival, after all, and even with its unique traditions, it seemed impossible that every feast had ended congruently. Even sealed away behind doors, I should have heard the muffled bleat of raucous youth disturbing the calm from *somewhere* in town. Or from the fields beyond, from the farms I passed, from the tangled brush and squat trees, I should have heard at least one animal's nocturnal complaint, even if I couldn't classify the source. But above the oppressive tranquility, the only sound I could pick out was the faintly burbling, labored breath of the man crowding me on the balcony.

And as I stood there, straining to hear, the stillness seemed to thicken moment upon moment. The air pressed closer; sound swallowed in on itself, ever tighter, as though I found myself not in a small town on a clear night but calf-deep in snow in a field suffocated by fog. The hum was gone and my own breath spilled from my open mouth straight to my ears. I could barely hear Brent, though when I turned to look at him, I saw him struggling, bent half double, fists clenched. His eyes watered and his torso shuddered and heaved.

"I have to go in now," I think he said.

He stumbled back inside the doors and knocked them most of the way shut behind him. The doors shook with the impact but I did not hear it. I heard only my breath and the quick, rhythmic whoosh of blood in my eardrums. I was fascinated by the silence, but not afraid. What was there to be afraid of? I ascribed the 'unnatural' quiet to a strange (but obviously predictable) combination of atmospheric and geographic phenomena, or a curious accident of civic planning which the populace chose to accentuate on this, their most holy day. The loss of close sound like the rattle of the doors I guessed might be a mesmeric influence on my imagination by the stupefying calm.

The side of the building abutted a street, but the balcony looked out the back onto a scantly-lit, narrow alley. Of the street, I could see only the intersection and a few doors further catty-corner. But in the intersection, at least, yellow light fell in overlapping pools and delineated the streaks of the randomly interlaced streamers. And so my attention was arrested at the first flicker of shadow.

One of the supplicants staggered into view. Brent had been right: this was no procession. Not only was the supplicant alone, but his movements were erratic. I thought at first his steps and twists were not as random as they seemed, guessing instead that the man's ostensible anguish was interpretive performance. Or perhaps his movements were random because he was shit-faced drunk. Doubtless his compatriots, whatever the impetus, affected comparable suffering throughout the streets of the village.

Despite the 'muffling' anomaly, I could hear the clanging of the two grape-bunches of bells at the ends of his arms, which he shook fervently. But the sound was both immediate and remote—immediate, in that it seemed the source was closer, almost next to me; remote, in that the sound was small, as though compressed to fit in a fractional space existing concurrently with visual reality, but only in parallel. And it was both immediate and remote *simultaneously* in that it was direct; there was no reverberation from the surrounding brick and cobblestone. I thought for a second it might be a prank: the clappers were muted.

But, though the report of the bells lacked resonance, it was yet metallic; the plinking of the impacts yet sharp. In between the brassy rattling, barely at all, like the ticking of insects, I heard the clicking of the bone vest when the supplicant clumsily juked or hopped in a losing battle to center his balance.

He turned down the alley. I shifted as he passed beneath me. He reared and looked up, nearly falling over. With the light from the street behind him, the contours of his mask were invisible; I saw only blackness beneath his hood. For the first time I felt the chill of fear. I gasped, but immediately I laughed inwardly, recognizing the *thrill* of fear—the safe experience of 'a good scare'. The supplicant regained his footing and again lurched forward, flailing his arms. If he had seen me, I was already forgotten.

Was that all I was expected to see—that and more of the same? It was not enough. Not after waiting so long for this day. I was struck by the unfairness of the arrangement, by the inequality between what I had been promised and what I experienced as a spectator, wholly re-moved. I was overcome by the desire to go out into the streets. I would be discreet. I would strive not to offend. My feeling wasn't a compul-sion; it was little more than a fancy. But it was an idea bolstered by pique. I wanted to experience this night according to *my* desires. The distance to the ground seemed inconsequential; the restriction seemed arbitrary. It was a little feeling, but I owned and embraced the drive of it, so that it instantly became a commitment to an action which I saw no reason to forgo.

I burst into the sitting room. Brent sat on one of the chairs, his el-bows on his knees. I was surprised to see his palms clapped to his ears as if he was trying to block out the silence. He was startled and unpre-pared to stop me. I was through the interior door before he began to get up.

Inside the house, it was quiet, but the sound was less suppressed. I heard my footsteps and the clack of the coat closet latch and even a slight whisper of cloth as I fished the front door key from Bertu's right coat pocket and snatched my own jacket from the hanger.

My footfalls on the steps to the ground floor were louder still. Brent called my name from the top of the stair. He barked, "You can't go!" He might have finished, "outside", but by then I had the door unlocked and I flung it open.

I took two steps into the street and careened sideways, stunned by the force of the din. In truth, the volume of the sounds I now heard was not overwhelming, or even uncomfortably loud. But the sudden resurgence of my full utility of hearing was an assault; I felt surrounded by unseen, disparate sources bleating their war cry, now roused from their waiting ambush and drawing down on their target. Nonetheless, though I was compelled to hide, I did not want to go back inside. Instead I hurried along past two buildings and ducked into the first sunken doorway I saw. Realizing I was cold, I took my parka from beneath my arm and put it on. This acknowledgement of one sense led me to take better stock of the one recently returned.

It was night in a Sardinian mountain village. The sounds which ricocheted from stone and stucco and back again were clear precisely because of the quiet on which they intruded. Distance and direction to each source was impossible to guess. But I could visualize them: the supplicants staggered and writhed in their anguished dances, rattling their bone vests and snapping their arms as if trying to shake loose the clustered bells which encumbered their hands. The bones were the skittering ostinato; the bells were the crashing accents; worst of all was the undulating, heaving drone; the lonesome, loathsome, dissonant wail of the combined damned chorale.

I heard my name. Brent called to me. I leaned forward from my hiding place. He was still half-in the doorway to the Piras' stairwell, obviously reluctant to come out into the street. He did not scan indiscriminately, but rather looked at me directly. I saw that I had ruffled a sort of trail through the streamers covering the street. I looked at my ankles and saw red tissue coiled around my left ankle. I kicked to shake it loose. Brent called to me again and entreated me to return. I fled.

I ran to the end of the block. I flattened myself against a stone wall next to a rolling metal door. I bobbed my head around the corner. The intersection was a jagged 'Y'; a peach tree spilled over the top of a cement wall opposite me; one narrow alley curved out of sight, another split once more just a few paces away.

Brent called my name, his voice now angry—angry with fear, I guessed; the call was more direct *and* closer: he had left the safety of the doorway to chase after me. I sprang into the street and ran to the split. I went right. The street inclined upwards towards yet another 'Y' half a block away. I could just barely make out arrows tacked to a downspout, one pointing in each direction, but neither adorned with a word or a name.

Brent continued to call; I continued to run. I had no sense of where I was. I think the distance between us grew, as Brent was lingering to track the streamer rut or to guess which way I had gone at each intersection, whereas I chose each turn on instinct. The sounds of the supplicants kept steady, as if each remained equidistant no matter which way I turned. I wondered why I hadn't seen any of them since the one who passed beneath the balcony. I was more afraid that I would unintentionally turn back towards Brent. A new street angled downwards, as did the next. I turned into a courtyard, saw my mistake, and came back out again. A steep, jagged climb folded back at an elbow and the alley ended at a crumbling two-story house; a tumble of stone spread near to a section of orange plastic fencing staked to the ground. I turned back again, retraced my steps and hoped my next two turns were new ones. Nothing was familiar. I saw a downspout with two arrows but they both pointed the same direction. I passed down a terribly narrow alley and came to a 'T' next to a   metal gate beside a set of stone stairs which ran up the side of a building halfway and ended abruptly. I ran up the intersecting alley and followed it around a curve and nearly collided with the figure weaving across the street.

The supplicant turned to face me. He watched me stumble backwards. I knew he saw me though I could not see his eyes. I did not remember any of the supplicants in the piazza donning long, upturned horns as projected from the sides of this one's head. He stood mostly still, rocking only slightly as he regarded me. His arms slumped, leaving the bells to dangle noiselessly. A moan welled in his throat. And then I watched as the wide, mournful frown of his *visera* opened. His jaw dropped to reveal fathomless blackness in his maw. I covered my ears in a feeble attempt to blot the crescendo of his wretched wail.

I pivoted and ran. After a sharp turn, I nearly tripped and fell. I lowered my hands from my ears to steady myself. I heard the voices of the supplicants merge in tone, matching that of the one from whom I fled. The baying voices rolled on each other like a siren reverberating through the streets. It was louder than before, loud in all directions, so loud that I barely heard Brent calling for me.

I did not have to decide if I wanted to run towards him or to run away. I couldn't tell from which direction he called. But I heard his voice change. My name became elongated; pain intruded. The sound rose to join the cry of the supplicants but changed yet again. It added a keener note, a horrid, sustained squeal. I ran, still lost. The squeal grew louder, closer. I heard it behind me. I spun to face it. A glow flared on the walls of the buildings on an intersecting street.

I screamed then; I heard myself scream. My throat felt raw. I may have been screaming already before the burning pig skidded around the corner and charged.

I fell to the ground. It ran straight at me. I dug my heels down and kicked, slipping on the streamers. Somehow I got my hands under me, turned and sprang to the side of the road. I pressed against the stone and watched as it raced by. The pig was red coal, skin seared black; it burned from within. It was a screaming ember with charred sockets for eyes hurtling forward on cracked hooves. In its wake, the streamers shriveled like spent fuses and fell into the crevasses between the cobblestones, as though the street seeped molten lava and this ceiling of fragile land threatened to collapse into the pit.

When it had turned out of sight, when I stopped screaming, I heard the bells. The voices of the supplicants had fallen silent. Now only the bells disturbed the quiet of the winding streets. And they did not jangle haphazardly. They clanked in unison, like anklets bound to a tramping giant. And I heard them draw nearer, from the direction the pig had come.

I hurried up the street as best as my aching legs and burning lungs would allow. I came to a split. The pig's seared path was clear. I looked the other way. Up a short incline, I saw the back of my rental car.

Had I passed it before and not recognized it? It was possible. Perhaps I'd only found my way back just then. I had the keys in my jacket. And though I couldn't possibly trace my way back through the streets to the Piras' house, I remembered the drive in—and so I knew the drive out.

To my own disbelief—with the panicked detachment of a spectator—I paused. I looked down the pig's path. The sizzling streamers curled away like a carpet being rolled, an invitation withdrawn.

The clangor of the bells was suddenly keener. I turned and saw the supplicants aligned in a single row, ten of them, almost shoulder-to-shoulder, blocking the street and advancing slowly, each step accompanied by a forceful downward punch. Suddenly they stopped.

I heard a roar of wind, summoned from unknown reaches. It bloomed into a ceaseless howl echoing the supplicants' tortured lament, but in a single voice, lower in tone, louder and more expansive. And then the five figures on the left shot up into the air and gathered in a bundle. They hung there for a second, swaying limply, and then swooped down and stopped short of the ground with a jerk; the bells at the end of their dangling arms clapped as one. The other five flew up the same way, like a loose bunch gathered by an unseen hand, and then snapped down and stopped in mid-air the same way, ending with a sharp, brassy strike. They began to advance once more, hovering and lurching down, as if in the grasp of some invisible beast lumbering towards me, though I felt no accompanying tremors from what should have been prodigious footfalls.

The howl grew louder and more terrible; its source became centered where it would be if there was a mouth to be seen. And though I could still see through to the end of the street, I began to think that the gloom thickened and reared against the blue-black sky, darkest in three spots: the void of the mouth and the pitiless null of the eyes.

When the roar was deafening and all, when I could no longer hear the bells of the flailing supplicants but could only watch the compulsory prancing of their slack doll figures, then, finally, I ran—to the car.

The tires slipped repeatedly on the carpet of streamers. I can only imagine the path of mangled red and white I left strewn behind me as I swerved out of town.

When I had gone around the ridge and found my way back to the little spur where Brent and I had pulled off on our way in to the village, I dared to stop. I rolled down the window and listened. For a second I heard nothing but the agitated purr of the engine. Then I heard some other high piping sound far in the distance. I turned off the engine and stepped out.

I heard the sound again: a squeak. No, not a squeak; a squeal, far away. I gazed towards where Brent had indicated the crumbled *nuraghe* lay (and felt unaccountable and simultaneous feelings of regret and relief that I had not seen the infernal ruin). I saw an orange glow near the end of the higher ridge where it cascaded into the hollow. I heard one last squeal, clipped in the middle, and the light was immediately extinguished. The ensuing natural country quiet was sudden and profound—for I did not realize until it ceased, as though I had become acclimated to it with improbable speed during my escape, that the awful roar had not relented before cry and spark were snuffed.

I drove almost at random, and greeted the dawn in Oristano.

I decided to cut short my vacation. There was no point in trying to pretend I was unaffected by my experiences, even if I didn't understand them. I was able to change my departure date without much difficulty, but when it came to time to board the boat, I couldn't do it. I was overcome by what I can only describe as a sense of resolute disinterest. I felt completely physically capable of walking up the gangplank. There was no contracted freezing of my muscles. There was no invisible force barring my way. I just didn't want to go—and this was the totality of my attitude to the prospect.

I might have spared myself the expense of the plane ticket.

The languid sky beams with white filigree smiles, but its place is overhead; my place is down below. The waves speak their secrets in susurrate tones, caressing my thoughts with the poetry of the horizon, but the sea is there to encircle, not to traverse.

Only the ground is good. I need to feel her heat beneath me. A Chent'Annos.

(Eventually, I returned to the hotel in Portu Rasposu. No one there had seen Brent since he left with me. I kept his bag.)

ZAMALEK, THE DREAM

Mike Adamson

The sage Rhadimanes was a quietly troubled man, but had confided in none. As a senior lecturer in the Royal Academy of vast and ancient Zamalek, the city upon the river that was life itself, he could not afford to sow doubt in the hearts of those around him; for he upheld all that was best, noblest and highest of the ancient traditions of the land.

Rhadimanes was a tall man, of strong and erect bearing, hair silvering a little at his temples serving to underscore his authority as perhaps the most respected sage of the land. He taught in many fields—geography, literature, mathematics, geometry, history—a veritable polymath synonymous with the greatness of the kingdom. But in recent weeks a dream had disturbed his sleep, a tumbling cascade of images in which he beheld the realm from olden days to the present and on into futures dark and frightening, for he saw things he did not understand, and knew not to whom he might turn for elucidation.

All this he had kept very much to himself, yet felt his grim preoccupation heralded some wider meaning; thus his profound surprise when, after dismissing his final class from the courtyard gardens as evening deepened upon the eternal city, he received a visitor who seemed to know all that ailed him.

A seneschal of the School of Philosophy appeared under the blossoming nut trees, and whispered of a guest of no little importance awaiting him in the library annex. Rhadimanes made himself respectable, adjusted his robes of scholarly blue, retied his hair at the nape in the royal fashion, and at last allowed the seneschal to present him.

The guest stood at one of the long bench tables, in the last wash of daylight from high windows, inspecting a scroll laid out for student study. By his gold-worked purple robes Rhadimanes knew him as of high office, and made a fore-arm grip in honour.

"Master Rhadimanes," the seneschal pronounced softly. "His Excellency, the Duke Porphyrios, Grand Vizier of Zamalek." He bowed politely and withdrew, leaving the lofty men with a tray of wine and dates, and the silence of the cool stone hall. The sage recovered his hand with a half bow and expression of genteel welcome.

"To what does the Royal Academy owe the pleasure of an unexpected visit from His Majesty's highest minister?"

Porphyrios was just as tall and erect a man, greyer still and possessed of all the reserve and guile of one used to delicate positions. He took a goblet and sampled the best wine the academy could boast before turning to regard the stored wisdom of the scroll stacks around them, a mere fraction of what the main library had to offer. "You occupy a very trusted position, Master Rhadimanes. You are seniormost among those who educate the keenest minds of the young, and as such a key figure in the forward transmission of our knowledge...our culture. All that we are." He looked back over his shoulder. "Your recent lectures have been most stimulating, speaking of the continuity of the ages, of our obligation to preserve our heritage, build upon it for the future, and do so with unswerving loyalty to the code of justice laid down by our forefathers. Heady stuff, such philosophy, and vital to inculcate in the next generation who will uphold such laws, and make the decisions shaping the tomorrow of Zamalek." He sipped again and paced with silent tread, eying the long scroll with its myriad of characters in their neat vertical columns. "But recently a theme has emerged in your speeches. You have referred many times to..." He looked up. "Dreams."

A cold hand brushed the master's back but no flicker crossed his face. "Dreams are a powerful philosophic medium and must be taken into account."

"Just so." The silence of the hall now seemed oppressive as daylight left them and deep colours glowed upon the walls. "Master Rhadimanes, let us speak plainly. From the content of your speeches it is quite obvious you are experiencing dreams and building their import into your presentations."

"There is nothing new in this—"

"What if I were to tell you, you are far from alone in dreaming? In dreaming a very singular dream."

Now Rhadimanes' brows came down and he stared at the Vizier.

"Oh, yes." The politician paced slowly back, sipped a little more and set the goblet down. "Oh, yes." He adjusted the sleeves of his robe and spoke almost rhetorically. "A priest will tell you dreams are the window to the unconscious mind, and the silent whisper of the gods to we mortals... If that is the case, the gods are whispering rather loudly."

The sage swallowed, remembered his drink and downed half the goblet. He was lost for words, and did not know quite what trouble he had found himself in.

"Well, confusion, consternation, are not uncommon." Porphyrios took him by the elbow and steered him for the doors. "There is someone you must meet." He rapped softly and a moment later the tall valves swung apart in the hands of royal guardsmen —their hot-stamped black leather helmets and body armour, greaves and scarlet sashes told all. They stood to attention and the Vizier escorted Rhadimanes forth, where they were discretely followed by a small troop.

The academy stood by the shores of the Khandamos, the mighty tributary of the Aklamanes, around whose confluence the city had grown up. Boat stages lined the river frontage and a small galley waited at the academy steps. Torches flared in the cooling evening breeze as the party went aboard. The guardsmen cast off and oars beat briskly to take the craft out upon the flow.

"We live in a very civilised world," Porphyrios mused, staring across the dark waters at the gleaming city all about. "But not all the world is so blessed, and our king must perform an endless rebalancing of needs and wants, of trade and relations, to keep all we have secure. When his highest men of learning begin to speak of cycles in history, of the coming and going of worse and better days, of the vacillations of strong men and weak, His Majesty takes an interest. And when the gods whisper of such matters to those men of learning, his interest is redoubled."

The galley glided swiftly among other craft on the river to the meeting of the waters, below the walls of the old fortified citadel in the natural defensive position of the narrowing peninsula between the flows, where the city had been founded long ago. The great elevated earthworks and walls were a historical anachronism now, a testament to earlier times. Palm oil burned in great kraters as navigation beacons upon its walls, and the galley turned into the main flow, beat north against the gentle current, and Rhadimanes took in the magnificent view of the city.

Firelight flickered upon stone and painted frescoes, upon statuary and long avenues of palms nodding in the cool night wind from the south, and the throb of music came softly across the waters. Truly, Zamalek was in its element, bustling in the evening cool, its endless thousands of citizens in their revelry beneath the stars. Here was a glorious civilization, fully realised—and in this the sage understood the part he played—the necessity of not merely repeating those values to his students but of leading by example.

The galley moved up-stream ten minutes and came abreast of the magnificent walls and porticoes of a fire-lit edifice, a place of soaring columns and domed rooves. The craft turned into a canal, was passed through by guards, entered a circling moat and thence penetrated a watergate, to vanish beneath the mighty walls into lamp-lit cool. As the craft was tied up at her berth, Rhadimanes swallowed on an abruptly dry throat.

He had not set foot in the royal palace in years.

—◆—

The Vizier escorted him up a long flight of stone stairs into the sumptuously carved and polished granite of the palace, up two more floors, and left him in a small antechamber, a single guard standing silently at the door. The scholar sank onto a cushioned bench, and strove to still his nerves. Of what mischief could he possibly be suspected? He had done his duty loyally and unswervingly, surely His Majesty could be assured of no less…?

After a time that seemed painfully long, a royal seneschal appeared at the door and bade him follow, and he was escorted along a curving corridor by the light of many oil lamps to a small lounge and ushered within. The guard stood to attention in the corridor, and the seneschal closed the doors on their silent, oiled brass hinges. A moment later Rhadimanes realised he was not alone.

A high-backed chair faced into a hearth, unlit at this time of year, and a figure rose therefrom, to turn and stand with fists on hips. The visitor bowed low at once. "Your Majesty," he pronounced evenly.

King Theyestes was younger than himself, hard and learned, both warrior and scholar, as was demanded of a monarch. His robes were of white linen and cloth-of-gold, his sandals the finest craftsmanship, and keen eyes bored into the sage from a face of striking, dynamic planes, framed with reddish-gold hair. A dagger rode his hip, more a status symbol than a weapon.

"Master Rhadimanes," came the blunt and businesslike challenge. "Rarely do I command my scholars to the palace, and rarer still under such circumstances."

"How may I serve His Majesty?" Rhadimanes began formally.

The king waved a hand dismissively. "Relax, man. You're in no more trouble than the rest of us, if trouble it is. Let us speak as men of learning." He gestured to a companion chair by the hearth and they sat, the king first as protocol demanded. Rhadimanes was ill at ease despite reassurances. At length the king's hard yet fine features relaxed into an expression of perplexity. "Porphyrios tells me his agents have listened carefully to your philosophy lectures, and a common theme has emerged."

"Dreams," Rhadimanes ventured.

"Dreams." The king spread his hands in a shrug. "Why the importance of dreams? We all dream, every last human being from the gutter to the throne room dreams. We remember few of them, and fewer still are of any real importance. But now…" His eyes met the teacher's. "You have dreamt something important. Something that will not leave you when you wake."

"The Vizier told me others have so dreamed…"

"As indeed they have," the king murmured. He settled back in his seat, clasped hands across his middle and concentrated on some spot above the hearth. "Tell me of your dreams, Master Rhadimanes. In detail, if you would."

For a long moment he did not know where to begin, then settled into the moment and his words began to flow. "I have dreamed this dream many times, and it varies little… First I see this land as it was long ages ago, the coming of our most distant ancestors. Some say it was not long after the world's making that fishermen built the first village where these rivers unite, and throve upon the bounty of the waters. Soon they learned of the flooding rains, and the richness of the land in this great valley, and became tillers of the soil. I see these things as if they were but yesterday—our mighty forebears who first cut wood, then stone, turned the earth and bridged the flow, reared the first walls against the depredation of other lands, the first temples to the gods, forums to the law and tombs to the ages."

He spoke softly, aware he was reciting as if to a class and attempted to inject greater humanity. This was no ordinary person to whom he spoke but the embodiment of Zamalek. The king rested with eyes closed, impassive but hanging upon each word.

"Some say Zamalek was the world's first city. Though there is no evidence one way or another, we know it is ancient, and perhaps we are forgiven the conceit of believing ours was the first metropolis to come forth from chaos. In my dream I see the first potter's wheel turn, the first cart wheel likewise, the breeding of ewe and swine and ass. The domestication of the ox and the horse, and even the elephant for our greatest traction. The smiths who turned copper to bronze and brass, then worked the sky-metal into blades, and so much more. I see the sages of old as they mapped the earth and stars, created our sigillic script; and the craftsmen who learned the making of paper, that our documents should become simple to keep; the physicians who charted our bodies and learned their interaction with the world. The shipwrights who built the vessels of exploration, commerce and war… All these things make up the flesh and bones of our society, while trade, art, philosophy and the doings of prosperity are its very circulating blood."

He paused, studied the king's profile, saw no flicker of emotion, and was unsure whether to be relieved or afraid.

"But the dream strides through time as the bank-fisher wades in the waters. I see the line of kings, the pageant of history as Zamalek matures from village to town to city, to the greatest city of the known world, set within its land, its realm, and I see it continue to prosper, grow beyond its borders…" Now he frowned. "I see this city grown to twice, thrice its area, the people shoulder to shoulder in stinking warrens piled three stories high, whose effluent fouls the river for a thousand stadia…" Now he spoke softly and with difficulty. "I see poverty among those teeming thousands, dissatisfaction, need, and the people scourged with both disease and fire, sweeping pitilessly through their packed masses." He paused, breathed deeply, pondering his words. "I see fleets of ships whose building nigh-impoverishes the realm, setting forth on the heels of explorers, to bear the people thither, those who

would seek new life in a new land, and call it the daughter of Zamalek...
In itself this is no bad thing, but new realms must inevitably be taken
from those already there, and such theft has never been our way. Then,
as the centuries turn like the spokes of a wheel, shall the child compete
with the parent? Shall they disagree? Which is the true Zamalek, the
old which failed to provide for the young, or the new which rebuilt for
itself the wellbeing it was denied?" He spread his hands, a gesture perfect for an audience but unseen by the king.

"Even so, the dream is not done. I see craftsmen of great cunning
make better metals, and more ingenious mechanisms, things which
harness greater power than the water-wheels of the river or the ele-
phant-capstans of the cranes. They see strange energy in boiling water,
somehow capture and contain it, and make it move great weights. They
see rising columns of air and harness them to lift bold venturers into the
very sky itself." He breathed deeply, composed himself, took care in the
choice of his expression. "I see forests laid waste to provide fuel, whether wood or palm oil, and poor men driven by the thousand to mine tar
and pitch for the same ends—providing in the misery of their filthy
labours the energy for contrivances whose productive capacity deprives
their brothers and sisters of their very work... What I do not see is *why*
we would do such a thing."

"And how does this dream end, Master Rhadimanes?" the king
whispered.

"I almost dare not speak of it."

"I command you," the king returned, so softly the scholar almost
missed it.

With a sigh, he ploughed on. "I see a doom come upon Zamalek.
It takes many forms. The sun bursts in golden rain that sears the land
to ashes... I see a titanic snake crawl from the wastes, a cobra vaster
than a thousand ships, reared in the sky, and all before it flee in terror.
Armies stride across our land and set to it torch and sword, and none
are spared. They come not for the wonder that was Zamalek, but to
extinguish the pestilence it has become; and we stand powerless before
them for the people of this golden land have become degenerate, sloth-
ful and lazy, greedy and cruel, prizing only strong drink and sweet food,
with time neither for the sages of old nor the gentler of arts. Pain is
their elixir, torment their sport, and they revel in their own ignorance."
A tremor in his voice betrayed the depth of his emotion, his disgust for

what this insane vision suggested his world may become.

"Go on," the king whispered, relentless to the end.

"As from chaos Zamalek came, to chaos it returns. The people become as children, helpless in the face of challenge, bent like reeds in the gale to the words of any brutal enough to seize control. Plague follows in the train of madness, starvation soon after, and civil war as the strongest jackals battle for the remaining scraps. When the lions ride forth from the desert, Zamalek is ripe to fall, and goes soon enough to the mass grave that awaits it. The city burns, the dead are plucked clean by carrion birds, and in a thousand years bones lie bleached among sand dunes and ruins where once there flowered wonders." His head went forward and tears flowed silently where words would no longer come.

The king rose and turned to a side table where a covered pitcher waited, and poured fresh fruit juice. He passed a goblet into the scholar's hands and gave him time. At last he lay a firm hand on the older man's shoulder. "You are no simple dreamer, Master Rhadimanes. You are a prophet of doom." He smiled mysteriously as he sat once more. "Yet, to no greater degree than any of us. For I too have experienced this terrible cascade of the ages. And others besides." At Rhadimanes' expression he nodded gently. "Some power beyond our knowledge is speaking to us, and we must rise to this challenge. The consequences of failure..." He smiled grimly. "...seem clear enough."

<hr>

The Council Hall of the palace was lit with oil lamps and candelabra, and the banners of the noble houses giving fealty to the king were proudly displayed. The royal standards enjoyed pride of place, but this was to be an informal meeting. The king's gilded seat had been removed and a circle of identical chairs placed centrally. Each was high-backed and solidly-made, with arms and comfortable upholstery, and Rhadimanes noted silently that no provision was made for primacy here—the circle signified neither beginning nor end and placed all present on the same level. Indeed, the king chose a seat at random, away from the cardinal points of the room as if to underscore the fact he was one among many here.

Rhadimanes had met a couple of the other guests socially at various receptions, but each bore the haunted expression he had come to know upon himself in his bronze mirror each morning, and when the king bade them sit the distinguished group settled around the circle in more than a little discomfort—never had they known His Majesty dispense with protocol to such a degree. The hall doors were closed and barred by the palace guard from the *outside*.

With the sound of the bar dropping into place, the king looked around the circle of expectant faces and steepled his fingers, elbows on the arms of is seat. "My friends, we are completely alone, our deliberations shall be unobserved and, if we so decide, they shall remain exclusive to ourselves. I trust you all with important office, I am now trusting you with my life." Rhadimanes acknowledged the king's theatrical edge—he was a warrior of renown, a match for everyone else present combined with one hand in his belt; but it was dramatic to say. "We have met individually on occasions over the past weeks, and the time has come for counsel." He breathed a heavy sigh. "Perhaps we should introduce ourselves." He gestured to the man on his right and stiff pronouncements were made.

Rhadimanes was impressed. Malifre, the secretary of the Rivermen's Guild was a silvering elder with the sun-burned complexion of one who had come up from the labourers; dark, exotic Delabria was a priestess in the temple of the south wind; Klyto was a comfortable, rotund scribe with the city authorities; Vaarnek was a river captain, seasoned as the timbers of his vessel, while Theremos of the Artisans Guild was a tough little man with the shrewd look of one used to assessing problems and overcoming them. A powerfully-built, darkly beautiful woman in military uniform, General Sheringa, commander of the Second Army, sat beside Ralimaan, a merchant who exported wine... Around the dozen seats a cross-section of Zamalek society emerged, important men and women, but otherwise without pattern—merchant and functionary, soldier and scribe, commoner and royalty, acolyte and academician, it seemed every dimension was addressed. When each person had spoken, attention returned to the king, and he sat forward.

"We have one thing in common, as you all know. We have all dreamed a certain thing. I have heard it from the lips of each of you, and am satisfied we share a united vision. This is unheard-of, and we would be more than foolish to dismiss it as some curiosity. Each of us is troubled by the potency of this impression, puzzled by it. Well, we are here this evening to attempt to *interpret* this dream. To put sense to it." He gestured freely.

"Whosoever wishes may speak first. Remember, this is an open discussion, but your king's word remains law. So—who shall it be?"

First to rise was the priestess. Ebon and of rare beauty, she drew herself up, silver-worked robes of green draped elegantly over her left arm, and inclined her dark tresses to the king. "If it please His Majesty. I am the sole representative of the temples in our circle, so I bring to you the perspective of the gods… It has long been held that they speak their most subtle words to our sleeping hearts, and for more than a single person to receive the same dream has always been deemed divine grace. For we twelve to share a dream of such import is beyond anything yet known. The gods are speaking to us and it is our duty to heed them well."

She paused, her rich accent echoing thinly in the hall. "That we see the rise of our land seems to say we value our achievements, and indeed that the gods would have us esteem our forebears, praise them for their foundation of the world we enjoy. But the future the dream shows us is more than troubling, it portends the collapse of our society. Not the disease and fire, colonies and invasion…" She smiled thinly. "Correct me if I am wrong, but those things are the consequences of an earlier failure." Rhadimanes nodded at once, as did several others. "A failure of the spirit, some weakness that overtakes heart and mind, and allows iniquity to exist. Our society stands firmly upon justice, the king's law is ancient, handed down from the first dynasties, modified and adjusted over the ages to be sure, but its fundamental fairness has never been compromised. For this dream we share to come true would require the law itself to be undermined, and in that we have our hedge against a future we would avoid." She paused, drew herself again to her imposing height, and her chiselled features were lit gold by the lamps. "Brothers and sisters of Zamalek—we must not *allow* it to happen."

She resumed her seat and the king nodded deeply. "The noble Delabria speaks well. It is such analysis we seek. The dream carries with it an overwhelming feeling that we ride a turning tide, and the events are unavoidable. But that may simply be the nature of dream, that the beholder is a helpless witness to matters. Perhaps, in reality, this is not so at all." He gestured to a shaven-headed elder in bronze robes across the circle from him. "Master Prelix, of the Magistracy, would you expand upon how such an age of injustice might hypothetically come about?"

The old man was as troubled as any, it took the edge from what seemed ordinarily a very bluff and matter-of-fact manner. He spread his hands, bronze bangles catching the lamp light. "The law as it stands would forbid the treatment of any in such manner as to allow the deprivations we see in our dream. But..." He spoke with difficulty. "Ordinarily I would not say this, but in a closed session with everything at stake..."

"Speak freely, Master Prelix," the king added softly.

"The law is only ever as strong as the men upholding it." He spoke simply, but the weight of implication was like lead. He need add nothing more.

The king nodded, breathed a sigh through flared nostrils. "Then, logically, for such times to come about is the failure of administrative control. And a failure from the very throne itself." Many around the circle offered gestures, expressions of disagreement, but they were unnecessary, Theyestes was frank about it. "Not *my* failure, my friends. Nor, I trust, that of any scion to claim descent from me. But the royal line shifts and changes, dynasties come and go. And it would seem we are being warned that one day a weak ruler allows him or herself to be corrupted by the words of more powerful personalities *close* to the throne. Advisors, those who have always been held in the highest esteem, their loyalty beyond reproach, should they in fact be corrupt..." He smiled bitterly. "We know them of old to be perfectly placed to take advantage of an ineffectual monarch, and in such situations the realm itself pays the price. In the past brave people have redeemed the situation before irreparable harm was done, but..." He looked earnestly around the circle of faces. "I put it to you—are we dealing with that dreadful cycle of forces, projected into a time when new human inventiveness has already strained the land to the breaking point?"

Rhadimanes had sat quietly so far, but knew eyes went to him often, seeking his reaction. Amongst all present *he* was the polymath, the one best able to connect disparate proposals, bridge gulfs, see through obfuscation. He cleared his throat softly and rose, as the priestess had. "Your Majesty, noble companions... I do not disagree specifically with any impression voiced so far. If I may summarise my position?" He cleared his throat again and reminded himself he was speaking to peers, not students. They were listening as he had listened to them—in the hope of hearing something of practical value. "In all cases we are shown two conflicting epochs. The rise of our civilisation from its humblest origins, lost in the mist of legend, to its zenith, which seems somewhere in our own future; followed by a decline, slow and terrible, to an ultimate collapse... Among my fellow philosophers of the academy, the causality of human behaviour has long been a subject of study. We live within the forward flow of time—actions have results, consequences. *If* one thing, *then* another. The closer in the future an event lies, the more certain we may be of predicting it. If I release an object in mid air, I can be assured it will strike the ground next to me. This much is certainty. But it is also a generality. The more specific we become, the more difficult the prediction also becomes. We have been shown some very specific things at a point quite removed in time—we may be seeing Zamalek hundreds, even thousands, of years hence." He paused theatrically. "But the mere fact the vision has been gifted to *us*, by the gods, by whatever powers on high watch over us, we may take to indicate that *now* is the time it needs to be considered. It cannot be pushed off to another year, another century, accounted 'too hard' and set aside for others to wrestle with. If our philosophy of causation is correct, and we believe it is, our actions lead directly or indirectly to the outcomes we experience. Therefore, if we are to foreshadow the ends we would wish, we must identify the actions in the present leading thither, and ensure we take no other."

In the following silence, it was Vaarnek the captain who raised a hand to the academician. "What of the final extremes? The snake that fills the sky, the sun shattering above us? What possible actions could we take or omit to avoid such mystical events? Surely only the will of the gods counts on that day."

"That mayhap be the case," Rhadimanes said easily enough, still standing. "And I would be first to solicit the best interventions of the Lady Delabria and her honoured fellows. But consider this. Perhaps those elements of the vision are metaphorical. The vocabulary of dream is typically metaphor, and while the historical events we see are much as we believe them to have been, the future is another matter, as yet void of form. The falling sun, the titan cobra—are they to be taken literally or are they symbolic of things far more tangible? Forces inherent in society, in ourselves, which we most certainly *can* come to grips with." He shook his greying head. "I don't think this dream was sent to us merely to inform us of the inevitable. I believe it is a warning."

The king nodded silently for long moments as Rhadimanes resumed his seat. "The rain of fire... The consequences of our own inventiveness, run beyond control? Perhaps. The mega-serpent... The evil that hides in the finest heart?" He stared at the polished granite floor where the lamps were reflected in golden glimmers. "I had hoped that particular wickedness was of a lesser magnitude, but perhaps it shall always be the ugliest of foes, for it is our own ambition, our acquisitiveness. If we are being warned to curb our own nature, then we are set a philosophic puzzle."

Rhadimanes smiled at the king. "From the first moment we dreamed, it was inherently *that*, Your Majesty."

Prelix cleared his throat, rising. "If I may. If the fatal flaw lies in human nature, we are at grave disadvantage to address it, for few human beings possess the philosophic mettle or the depth of integrity called for. However, these are things the law has always addressed, and it may do so with discretion. No dramatic shifts are necessary to set in motion a decline toward this future we have been shown, bereft of honour, pride or valour. Merely a tiny increment here and there over long periods of time, so from day to day society is unchanging, yet across generations it may fade drastically. The law is an institution which spans such periods, its continuity is its strength, and records, properly kept, remain an absolute. I would propose an addition to the Privy Council, an officer whose duty is to review the operation of the law in its application. This officer will report regularly to His Majesty with an appraisal of the performance of the judiciary, their verity, their equanimity, in all ways the propriety of the institution. How *just* is justice? Who is served? How better may it be done?" His eyebrows rose toward his gleaming pate. "This office would remain unknown to the general public, indeed to the judiciary as well. It must operate with the greatest discretion, yet with blanket access to all public records. Perhaps this would be the first tangible step to rendering impossible the decline into corruption that must permeate a society for it to grow so ill-balanced."

"An excellent suggestion," the king agreed with a deep nod. "If I understand properly the philosophy of causation—" he looked at Rhadimanes. "—it is that the longer any measure has to act upon the circumstantial medium, the greater the effect it may have. Thus, so simple a thing as placing fresh checks and balances upon the fairness of our own administration here and now, may avert catastrophe centuries in the future."

"His Majesty has the theory perfectly." The sage nodded deeply. "By all means, we must act in the present, but also take strict stock of the effects of our actions, for we cannot rule out the possibility that un-forseen consequences of such actions lead to the very future we would avoid." He shrugged apologetically. "We cannot know all things, and must do our best within this limitation."

Across the circle from him, Theremos of the Artisans Guild at last came to his feet, his expression troubled. "By His Majesty's pleasure... Noble companions, let me first say I am as troubled as any of us by the horrors we have been cursed to witness in our sleeping hours. But I knew from the start I would be the voice of dissent here." Eyebrows rose and chins were stroked in abstract thought. "I represent the arti-sans—the builders, makers, aesthetic decorators, the inventors. I can tell you that the sort of invention we witness in our dream is not some fantasy. It is beyond our grasp, but not beyond our imagining. A ship that sails upon the air?" He threw up his hands, red robes rustling. "We know not how it might be made, but the fact we can conceive of it means we may think about it in practical terms... Mechanisms that harness boiling water?" Now he spoke as if sharing a secret. "I have seen a toy entertain marketplace crowds, a brazen sphere, half filled with water, set upon a vertical pivot and supplied with two outlets which trail in opposite directions. Place a small fire beneath the sphere, the water boils and the sphere spins upon the pivot as the steam escapes through the outlets. *That* is the very mechanical force we are talking about. It is already with us. The leap from toy to useful machine is a lesser one than that by which the toy was conceived." His eyes took in their haunted expressions as they hung upon his words. "Such things will not exist tomorrow, or next year or in ten years, but a day will come when an inventor couples such force to gearing and leverage, and machines will do work." He spread his hands, took a deep breath. "My point is that this is the natural progression of the very inventiveness that gave us the ship, the wheel, the crane. It can be neither suppressed nor denied."

The king sighed and sat forward. "You are saying that natural forc-es are at work, and given one state of knowledge, a greater state is inevitable?"

"Precisely. To stifle such development is administratively possible, but we know we exist in a state of balance with other lands. As their artisans experiment and invent, so must ours. Should a foe discover a metal which will break our swords on contact, we become vulnerable.

Was it not the discovery of smiths that shoeing horses saves their hooves upon our stone-laid roads? Where would we be without the fluid-displacement counterweights of our greatest cranes? These call for metalworking, sealing rubber, the finest carpentry, elephant-driven waterwheels to fill header tanks. None of this could have existed, and come to benefit society, if our predecessors were afraid of invention."

"Your counsel, then, Theremos?" the king asked gruffly.

"It is not the invention which is evil, but the ends to which it is put." The words were simply said but carried weight. "Let the role of the invention be to free citizens from arduous, repetitive or unsafe labour, that their skills and strengths be better employed elsewhere. The two must be bound together and always viewed in that way. If they are not, then the invention becomes its own object and the human being irrelevant."

He resumed his seat and a terrible silence fell over the group, as if they had glimpsed immutable powers underpinning society. Rhadimanes understood what the artisan was saying but in his soul feared a future in which the machine competed with the human being. For some reason, Theremos's words were more disturbing than any he had yet heard.

The king looked around the expectant faces and counted off points on his powerful fingers. "My friends, we are counselled to heed this warning; to set in place checks and balances upon our administration; to plan well but flexibly for tomorrow; and to not be afraid of our own ability to invent, but to maintain firm control over the effects of invention." He sighed again, sat back. "These things can be done in the here and now. Let us deem the matter in-hand. But—and I say this with all gravity—we are the bearers of this burden. It is our responsibility and we must shoulder it willingly. Let us continue to meditate upon these issues, but in strictest confidence. I hereby place a royal command upon each of you—that this matter will be held in absolute discretion. You may not speak of it to another soul, until or unless matters become more clear. We shall meet again in a few days, and any new impressions may be voiced then, and I suggest we meet regularly from now on. Agreed?"

Heads nodded around the circle readily.

"I know many of you have not had the chance to speak, I hope you will have substantial contributions as time goes by. Does anyone have anything they wish to add at this point?" None spoke, though every expression was intent upon their problem. "Very well. The hour grows late and I'm sure we all have other matters to attend to. The Guard shall convey each of you home." He rose and nodded around the circle. "Thank you for your counsel, and I am confident we may, together, avoid the horrors we have been shown."

At the king's call, the doors were unbarred and swung wide, and the guests filed out, the Vizier assigning escorts to see them home. But Rhadimanes was held back by a soft word from the monarch, and accompanied him along the hall to a wide balcony, open to the cool night breeze, from whose elevation they looked out across the river to the glittering lamplight of the city.

"Look upon all we have created, Master Rhadminanes," Theyestes said softly. "Look upon its myriad facets, and think of the infinite levels of causation underpinning it. Without the forester, the carpenter, the rope and sail makers, the shipright, pitch-refiner and economist, the papersmith, the scribe, the metallurgist and blacksmith, the chandler, navigator, pilot and sailor...there would be no trade upon this waterway. The same could be said of anything we see here, from the stone of these towers to the foods in the markets. A society is a web, and if a single strand should part, others will unravel. You are the philosopher, you know of which I speak."

"The great tapestry," Rhadminanes said softly. "The whole depends upon its component parts, and none of them may be discarded or the whole changes in character." He nodded with a grim smile. "If the dream shows us anything at all, it is that the fabric of society has been compromised. Someone pulled a thread and the picture that is Zamalek degraded, line by line, until it was gone."

"The dream..." The king sighed and shook his head. "The dream." He gestured to the wide city before them. "Not our dream, *the* dream. Zamalek *is* the dream, Master Rhadimanes."

"Every institution is founded in the hope and belief of its own rightness," the sage returned softly. "This city, this realm, is, I hope, all its founders could have wished for, and far more besides, that it embodies things they could not have conceived of. The duty falls to each generation to preserve that dream in its perfection, and to safeguard it from turning to nightmare. For the more complex any system becomes, the more easily it is disturbed—perverted. And Zamalek is so very, very complex."

They turned for the passage once more and the king walked with hands behind his back. "Then we shall do so, good Master. We shall dream the dream for all who are to follow, and make it our business to preserve its integrity." He smiled and offered his hand in a warrior's grip, which the academician took without hesitation. "You and I. We will see to it."

Rhadimanes felt a glow of purpose as he was escorted back to the watergate and a Guard galley set out on the dark river. But, as he sat to watch the great city flow by all around him, he saw inwardly once again the shattering sun, the flash of light upon the armour of a host stretching to the horizon, heard their bestial warcry, and the thunder of spears upon shields; he glimpsed the upreared cobra, blue with the sky in which it moved, as it undulated from eternity to bring the final downfall; and he could only shudder in his robes, unnoticed in the night.

He had never asked to be a bearer of such travail; but nor did he flinch from it, for was ever a people, an age, so challenged? It was his grim privilege to be one of the few, so very few, who stood before the march of time, and openly defied the doom that hung over Zamalek.

ROCKSHELL

Mari Ness

I still go to Rockshell, though I know I shouldn't. Each trip it is harder and harder to reach, and harder and harder to return. When I do return, I need more time to realize that yes, I am really back here: back here with coffee and cars and cell phones and the internet and working plumbing and hot water that I do not need to go down two thousand steps to reach. I used to be able to adjust in a few hours, at most, or a day. Now I need a week, or more.

And yet, when I see the shadow *move*, I rush towards it, unthinking.

❦

I was four, I think, when I first went to Rockshell. I'd been playing out in our tiny back yard when I saw it: a shadow *move*. I can't describe it any better than that: you either know what I'm talking about, or you don't. I took a few careful steps forward and fell into the shadow.

I landed in rich, green soft grass, more brilliant than anything I'd ever seen. I scrambled to my feet and looked up –

– and saw a huge red and black shape against a pale blue sky, breathing fire.

I couldn't move. I could only stare at the flames and beating wings and the fire burning towards the clouds. The word "dragon" never entered my mind. The dragons I knew from books and stuffed animals —cute, cuddly creatures—were nothing like this.

When the creature finally spiraled away I turned my gaze from the sky, to see a little girl standing near me. Darre, I would later learn, but I didn't know that then.

"Come on," she said, taking my hand. "You *know* the queen doesn't want us to play out here."

When I returned home, covered in grime and even less positive things, my mother refused to believe me. She also refused to replace the two toy dinosaurs I'd lost in the shadows. It was not the last time I would lose things of this world to Rockshell and to shadows.

The latest man I'm trying to date has not managed to take his eyes from the scars on my arms. I sigh. This one is not going to last long. I order another glass of wine, try to keep the conversation on innocuous topics like television and sports. It doesn't work.

"I know I shouldn't ask," he says, before reaching a hand across the table, "but – can I ask? What happened?"

I've still never managed to come up with a good answer to this. "Things," I say. "Nothing very interesting."

He doesn't ask if we should do this again.

No one in Rockshell seemed to want to believe me either when I returned. This time, I was taken directly to the queen, who listened to the description of my small wooden house, the green kitchen, the piano, the playground, and my mother's car with absolute bemusement.

"It's *true*," I said, tears in my eyes. I knew what happened to liars; they went to bad places. My mother had told me. I didn't want to go to bad places. Not now. Not when I had found a place with real dragons and flowers that sang and a tree that grew real candy – or, if not candy exactly, leaves as soft and chewy and sweet as candy.

"The Witch of the Plains will know," said the queen, waving her hand in dismissal.

The guards followed me and Darre from the room. I was just old enough to understand that this was unusual, and just scared enough not to care. The queen had said the word "witch." It sounded terrible. Witches, my mother had said, were just stories, but what if my mother was wrong? She'd certainly been wrong about this.

"Who is the witch?"

"Somebody," said Darre, carelessly.

I tried not to cry. "You believe me, don't you?"

"No," she said, doing a cartwheel. I tried to follow her example, and failed. "But it's a good story anyway, and that's all that matters."

Good stories *matter*.

Good stories cover up a lot of things.

It was two years before I went to Rockshell again. By then I'd almost – almost – convinced myself that I had made it all up, that I'd never been to a tall castle with a hundred towers next to a blue green sea, even if this was clearer than any of my other memories.

Still is, as it happens. I have only dim memories of where I lived here, in the real world, images and flashes, knowledge that events *happened*, but no memories of them. I know we moved from New York to Maryland; I know, because I have been told, that it took a full week to pack everything up and drive down. I know it took another week to unpack. I know my father left us shortly after that. I remember none of that. Only Rockshell, gleaming under the lights of its moons, pale pink and dark green.

Not the day my father left us.

But the day I returned to Rockshell again – that, I remember.

Good stories help you forget.

That time, when I arrived, I was all alone.

I was standing beneath a green-gold tree bright with large red apples. My eyes blinked in the light. Never, on any trip, could I become accustomed to the richness of the lights and colors of Rockshell. Two moons, pale pink and green, gleamed softly in the bright blue sky.

I was hungry, so hungry. I reached up to the apples, and grabbed two. They were more tangy and sweet than the store bought apples I'd sampled before, and even though I could already feel I'd eaten too much, I reached up to grab a third. As I did so, I heard a sound behind me, and spun around.

In the shadow of the tree stood a woman all in grey, with long dark hair that gleamed green as it moved.

"Child," said the woman.

Witch, I thought, but I did not dare speak the thought aloud.

"Yes," she said, an amused tone in her voice. "Yes, I am a witch. The question is, what are you?"

Before I could answer this question, I heard another sound, and spun again.

Darre stood just a few feet away, next to a boy slightly older than both of us. She dropped the bag she was holding and flew to me, grabbing me in her arms.

"You did come back," she told me. "I *knew* you would. I *knew* it."

"Who is this?" I managed, once she allowed me to take a breath.

"Oh," she said, stepping back a little, but still keeping a tight hand on my arm. "This is Berrien. He's kinda like you. He's from somewhere else." With that, she started pulling on me, moving me away from the apple tree. "Come *on*," she said. "We're already late, and you know the elves hate that."

I didn't know. I looked back at the tree as Darre pulled at me, but the woman in grey had already vanished.

———◆———

Things vanish in this world as well: scissors, keys, library books, shadows. I am certain, absolutely certain, I know where I left them, and yet, when I return, they are gone.

———◆———

Darre's words turned out to be only slightly true. By somewhere else, she meant that Berrien was from a *city*, not the castle. He should have been nothing but a servant. But Darre had made friends with him, and he could make blue flowers spring from his fingers. I tried and tried, but the only thing I pulled from my fingers was blood.

———————

I am certain, absolutely certain, that I can get to Rockshell again. Even if the very thought of going still can terrify me; Rockshell is not safe just now, has never been safe before this. Even if just now, it feels completely gone. I remember the other times when I waited for months, years, for the shadow, the other times when I gave up completely, only to look up, and see the shadow *move* again.

I have to be patient. Wait. Be patient.

———————

Gradually, I met more children in Rockshell: San, who drifted in and out of the castle always grinning, always playing tricks; Kendar, the prince so foreign he hadn't even *seen* a dragon until he was six; Mikko, who could shatter glass when he sang; Zylie, prettier and nastier than all of us combined. We climbed trees; explored caves, took small boats out into the great sea, sailing almost but not quite out of sight of the castle, to where we could almost see the Great Troll Islands. We helped griffins crack open their eggs, cleaning the babies once they emerged; found a batmouse for Darre's birthday; built sandcastles on the seashore as the mermaids sang to us. We found the claw of a manticore, the mountain fire flower, the dagger of Akon-Zas, four chests of faerie gold; carpets that could sail through the air. Our stories were turned into songs. We learned to sail ships, talk to the kinder pirates, play the drums, cook over fires, and swing swords.

And slowly, we all learned I could never stay for long.

———————

No one is patient at Rockshell.

———————

When I wasn't at Rockshell, I did what I could to keep up. I learned to swim. I played with plastic swords and light sabers. I forced myself to pay attention during the two weeks of archery we got in gym, and for once, stopped spending gym class looking for shadows. I made myself walk for miles.

None of it really worked. The plastic toys of our world were nothing like the shining swords of Rockshell. The bows felt completely different. The foils and epees felt *wrong*. And no matter how I practiced, I was still clumsy, still weak. And I could not force a single spark of magic from my hands. And I could never avoid the pulling shadow.

In other stories, the children who travel to magical lands become wizards, heroes, queens, kings. Sometimes they are allowed to stay, sometimes they are exiled. Sometimes they die. Sometimes they are allowed to remember; sometimes they are forced to forget.

I place a sliver of dragon bone against the scars on my arms. I am not going to forget. *I am not going to forget.*

"You *can't* come," said Darre impatiently. Behind her, Kendar nodded. Berrien said nothing; he never liked to argue with either of them. "If we knew you'd make it for the whole trip – but we *don't*. We can't take a griffin for the whole trip if she's only needed for part of it."

I swallowed. I'd never spent any time in Rockshell away from Darre, not a *long* time, anyway. An hour or two, sometimes, when she was called away for duties or lessons. An entire trip – it would be *days*. "You could – if I vanish, you could send the griffin –"

"You *know* how stupid they are. One of us would have to try to guide your griffin, and then that person couldn't help, and – And besides, once we get there, the three people that start the climb *have* to be the three people that end it. You *heard* the elves."

I was *not* going to cry in front of them. I *wasn't*.

"I'll stay too," said Berrien.

"It's really a princess and prince thing anyway," said Zylie.

"Zylie!" said Mikko, but for once, I was grateful, since I now had a reason to hit someone.

———◆———

My fists slam into my pillows. Something learned from therapy – *hit a pillow. Take a breath. Hit the pillow again.* Pillows can't hurt you, can't break your skin. *Squeeze ice if you need to, and hit the pillow again. Take deep, slow breaths.* This way, I tell myself, I will be ready. I wipe the blood from my knuckles. I will be ready.

———◆———

The blood diamonds that could save the Countess of Tanshere were over the Chasm of Karosh, a great ditch of fire, that could only be crossed with a bridge woven of magic and gold and unicorn hair, a bridge that needed at least three people to build it.

Three.

Darre and Kendar and Mikko were elsewhere. We had only Berrien and San.

And me.

———◆———

Sometimes I think about writing down the stories of Rockshell and turning them into the sort of fantasy trilogy that could end up on the *New York Times* bestseller list, or if not that, let me stay at home, hiding, whenever I need to heal from these trips. Or at the very least give me some extra cash to replace everything I keep losing on those trips.

But the thought feels wrong, and when I sit down at the computer, my fingers freeze, and I find my eyes darting everywhere, looking for shadows.

———◆———

"You must give me magic," I told the witch. "You must."

"Child," she said, shaking her head. "Magic is either there, or it is not. It cannot be given. It cannot be earned."

My jaw clenched. "That's not *true*," I told her. "You can always earn something, if you work hard enough."

The witch reached out to stroke my cheek with dry fingernails. "Child," she repeated. "Did they tell you that, in your world?"

I nodded.

"And does that world have magic?"

I started to nod – then stopped, and swallowed.

"Ah child," she said. "Go on this quest, and see what you can do without magic."

They do not *need* me in Rockshell, I am told. I am a liability. I have no magic, no *control*. I've never been here long enough to gain any fighting skills. My arrows miss the target about half the time; I tire after two minutes of swinging a sword. I have a small dagger with a hilt of diamonds and rubies that has been laced with magic, filled with power, but I never learned to control it. I will be a danger if I stay.

They love me too much to risk it, they tell me. Please, please, they say, tears running down their cheeks. Go home. Go home to where you are safe. We need to know that you are safe.

In the end, Berrien and San found the diamonds and healed the Countess. I stood in a shadowed corner, watching as Berrien placed diamonds on her hands, and San placed them on her feet, clenching my fists as I felt my world dragging me back to its shadows again.

I need to know that *they* are safe, that they will triumph. If I stay at home, I will never know.

Six months. Or two days. Or one week. Or two months. The time always varied; the ending didn't. One moment I was *there*, in the radiant light of Rockshell; the next moment, trapped in the darkness, screaming until I rolled out into the light of this world, bruised and bleeding, crawling to get back into the shadow.

———◦———

I definitely should go out. Socialize. Meet people. Real people. People who can talk about computers, sports, television, books.

People who do not believe in dragons.

———◦———

I thought they would leave me back at the castle after that, leave me wandering the hallways of Rockshell and listening to the mermaids singing. I should've known better. Kendar rolled his eyes, of course, and Mikko and San and Zylie said things, but Darre simply raised an eyebrow and took my hand, and then everything was all right.

Mostly.

———◦———

I definitely shouldn't be drinking this much.

———◦———

I was in ninth grade the first time I failed to fall into the shadow.

For once, I was speaking with a friend – well, an almost friend. The closest thing I had to a friend in this world, anyway, even if the only thing we talked about was how much we hated our teachers.

Behind her, the shadow *moved*.

I took a half step, then shuffled back.

I didn't want Lisa to hate me.

I didn't want her to think I could disappear.

I shut my eyes and swallowed and then opened them again, staring at the bruises on Lisa's arms, the ones we'd agreed not to talk about, the ones she'd gotten by accident at home, and almost, but not quite, thought about showing her my sketches of dragons.

———◦———

I should get a dog, I realize. Or a cat. A kitten. Something to hold when I am alone here, with only the TV to mask the silence. It would be easy enough; the shadow never steals me away from this world for that long, no matter how many days or weeks I spend in Rockshell.

I draw my knees up, staring at the tropical fish in the tank. In certain lights, if I squeeze my eyes, their scales almost look like those of a dragon.

———— ◆ ————

The shadow didn't appear for three months.

I got sicker, and sicker, and sicker. Lisa and I kept complaining about our teachers, but I could hardly hear her words. I kept dreaming about Darre, about Berrien, about San. I failed a math test and got grounded. I held a plastic lightsaber in my hands, trying desperately to pretend it was one of the fire swords of Lantona. I failed to turn in assignments for history and biology and got grounded again.

When the shadow *moved*, I threw myself into it so quickly that I lost three textbooks, two notebooks and a Walkman on the way. My back and legs were later covered in bruises. I didn't care. I'd seen dragons flying in the sky again.

———— ◆ ————

A coworker is trying to get me to go to church. I let her talk, nodding, knowing that I can never explain why I stopped going. It's not just that I no longer have the beliefs I once had, but that when I enter a church, other images fill my mind: a god of earth breathing water and fire; a goddess hanging in chains for refusing to submit to dragons; a goddess shifting from bird to wind to bird to fire; a god who never stops dancing; a goddess who heals with a touch.

The images *hurt,* and I do not want anyone to see me crying.

———— ◆ ————

All too soon – well before San could tell me everything that had happened – the shadow had grabbed me, and I was back, falling on the sidewalk, my arms and legs covered in blood and dirt.

When I came home, my mother glanced at my arms, and then looked up at my face.

"Do you want anything special for your birthday?"

"Magic," I said.

To my surprise, she smiled.

The magic set she gave me turned out to be several magic sets at once, with balls, rings, flash paper, card decks and various tricks with magic. I forced myself to smile. She beamed at me as I pulled out the rings, sliding them over and under and over again. When tears started pouring down my face, I told her that holding the rings hurt.

"Then you're learning," she said, and urged me to use the rings again.

———◆———

I am not going to think of how often Darre and Berrien and Kendar and San have bandaged my skin.

———◆———

After that, I ran to the shadows when I saw them, crying when I returned. Each time that I came home late, or covered in mud, or missing a backpack, my mother grew angrier. At first I was just grounded, something I never could quite mind, even though the shadow never came into my room. I had stones and feathers from Rockshell to hold, memories to cherish. Later, the punishments got worse: an end to the fencing lessons I'd just started; my toys taken away, my books taken; sent straight to bed without meals, sometimes for a day or more; bruises appearing on my arms and legs.

———◆———

My job pays enough for a one bedroom apartment near the beach with a small kitchen, a smaller bathroom, and a tiny screened in porch. I line the walls with everything I have managed to bring from Rockshell: small slivers of dragon bone; jewels taken from a wyvern's cave; a string that fell from Mykko's harp. I try to fill the porch with plants, but they never seem to live long.

At night, when the windows are open, I can just dimly hear the ocean, and that is almost – almost – enough.

------◆------

Rockshell grew deeper, more dangerous. Gone were the days of teaching dwarves to sing, of finding fireflowers in the forest to save a dying woman in the castle. Now we fought sea-monsters, spied on dragons, climbed mountains made of glass, danced in iron shoes.

My skin gained more and more scars. I was sent to school counselors, who advised me to take up sports. Another teacher suggested a psychiatrist. "She's fine," my mother said.

By the next day, my arms were broken.

------◆------

In Rockshell, I have a small suite of rooms of my very own, high in a tower, with windows that overlook the blue-green sea. I keep them as empty and bare as I can: a bed, a wardrobe, one plain chair, nothing infused with magic. I keep the plain chair by the window, and watch the sea and the moons and the sky, trying to forget both worlds, and the pain that never seems to leave my arms and legs.

------◆------

Darre seized my hand and dragged me to a corner of the castle. I winced – my arms were still healing – but did not cry out; Darre would just laugh at me. She tapped on a wall, which suddenly swung open to reveal a great winding staircase cut into the very rock. Her hand pulled on mine, drawing me into the darkness, giggling as she told me everything that had happened while I was gone.

This is Rockshell, I reminded myself. *Here, I am not afraid of the dark.*

The steps eventually led to a huge underground cavern, so huge that I was astonished that the stone and castle above it didn't fall in, until I remembered: this was Rockshell, where such things happened. The cavern held one large and two small pools, connected by tiny waterfalls; shimmering crystals lined the cavern walls and ceiling, throwing back the light Darre spun in the hand not clasped in mine.

"Elian says this was a dragon's lair, once upon a time, before Rockshell even was." She pulled on my hand again. "Come on. You've never felt anything like this." She rapidly removed her clothing and stepped into the nearest pool.

"I'm not supposed to get these wet," I told her, holding out my arms.

She frowned. "I can take care of that," she said. Red light danced on her fingertips. "Come on."

I swallowed.

The casts on my arms had just been an excuse. I didn't want to take off the dress, to remove the soft fabric so like and yet not like silk that said *Rockshell* to me, so different than anything I wore at home. And even more reluctant to remove the cotton underwear that *was* from home. If I took that off, and the shadows came –

"*Come on*," Darre said, more impatiently this time, splashing me with the hot water.

Slowly, clumsily, everything came off. A shimmering blue light hovered around my arms, repelling the water.

"Isn't this lovely?" Darre said. "Far nicer than having to heat your water yourself."

"Back home," I said, "*we* have hot water whenever we want." Darre did not respond. "We just turn the faucet –" I paused, realizing she didn't know the word – "we just turn a metal handle, wait, and then hot water comes out. Just like that. *Whenever.*"

Darre moved so she was floating on her back in the water. "You don't have to make things up, you know."

• • • —◆—— • • •

Work is getting increasingly impatient with me. I'm not answering emails properly; I'm dozing off in the endless production meetings; I'm not filling in any of the three time card systems they've created. I'm not, a production manager notes pointedly, agile. My immediate supervisor is more concerned. "Is anything wrong?" she asks. "Is there anything she can do to help?"

She means, I think, "Is there anything I need to report to HR?" but it's possible that vying with the endless machinations of Karash and Toll and Vonrat back in Rockshell has made me cynical. I shake my head. Even if I trusted her, how could I tell her the real problem in any case: that I have not seen a shadow *move* in seven months?

———◆———

I took piano lessons at my mother's insistence. I hated it. I wanted to
play the instruments of Rockshell: the harps, the violins, the flutes. If I
couldn't be a princess, I could at least be a musician.

"We have an upright piano already," my mother said.

And that was that.

———◆———

In my world, I can find no records of Rockshell. Wonderland, Oz, Narnia, a host of other worlds and magic, but never Rockshell. Never anything that sounds like Rockshell.

Though perhaps, I tell myself, just perhaps, others from this world did slip through the shadows, did travel there. Only instead of Rockshell, they found themselves in another part of that world. After all, I've never known just how large that world is; it could have a hundred lands that welcomed children from our world. And instead of coming back to this world, they stayed.

———◆———

The times never matched. Never. I would spend six months in Rockshell to find that only an hour had passed here; spend three months here to find that a year had passed in Rockshell. I was younger than my friends in Rockshell. Older. The same age. Younger again.

I had no hope of being anywhere near Mikko's ability with the harp now, or even of accompanying him when he sang. I was clumsy with the dance, with the bow, with the sword, even with pulling and taking off my clothing. I was useless, completely useless, as Zylie and Kendar noted, more than once. When I dropped a heavy sword on San's foot, I ran crying to my rooms.

The queen found me there some time later.

———◆———

I never know when the shadow will come, or where. Usually outside, near a tree, or a water, but sometimes inside a building: a crowded café, a museum, an empty library, near the produce section of the grocery store, in the house of a friend. Sometimes it comes two or three times a day; more often once a week, or once a month. Months, years even have gone by without a single moving shadow. Those are the times when the world seems to go grey around me, and I am only existing, not living.

I never know when I will be *pulled* from Rockshell, find myself going from the back of a dragon into the darkness, from a dance to nothingness, from something sweet on my tongue to bitterness. I never know how long I will float in that darkness, weeping. I only know the hardness when I tumble back into this world, slamming into the ground below me, the way that the earth shifts for the first several seconds, and I have to try not to cry.

———◆———

"Have you and Darre and Xylie been fighting again?" she asked.

"No," I said, startled. It had been – it had been – I was not going to think of how long it had been since our last fight, since trying to work out the times gave me a headache. "No. It's just –"

"Right now she is older, and you are not." The queen came to me and lightly stroked my hair: a great honor, in Rockshell. I quivered. "It was sometimes the same for her, the other way around, when you seemed gone but a day here and had months of your adventures in your world. I think she was jealous."

"I don't have adventures in my world," I said. I sounded like a sullen, spoiled child, and I knew it, but I had seen Darre dance; seen her wield a bow. Seen the way she and Berrien looked at each other, the way they looked at me.

"Are you certain? You seem to describe marvels enough. Those things you call –" she hesitated, stumbled over the words, came out with something meant to be English, "tottler costers?"

It took me a minute. "Roller coasters?" I shook my head. "On those, I always know what's going to happen."

The queen stepped back. "I'll tell Berrien to give you a dragon ride."

I clutch my third cup of coffee as I stagger out to the car. After only two hours of sleep, it's not enough, but I can't miss another day of work, ridiculous as it is for me to go in. My work – as a quality assurance tester for a small software company, where I watch my screen conduct and fail automated tasks over and over again – could easily be done remotely, but HR doesn't approve of that sort of thing.

I take another long sip of coffee. *Don't think of dragons*, I tell myself as I get into the car. *Don't think of any of it. Don't look for shadows. Not now.* But as I turn the key in the ignition, I remember the hissing sound of a dragon, and then I am shaking even as I grasp the steering wheel.

Dragon rides, in Rockshell, are a privilege given to very few. I had long since given up any hope of having one, though I could not quite conceal my longing. When Berrien came to my room I was almost shaking. The corner of his mouth twitched.

"Relax," he said. "You've flown before."

Via umbrella, yes, or clinging to a griffin's foot, or on a fairy cloud, or on a carpet magicked up by a genie. Never on a dragon.

He reached out his hand to me. "Come along. They don't like to be kept waiting."

We would be riding two of the smaller dragons, he told me. That was another shock: the larger dragons could and did carry conveyances that could fit several people at once. The queen used a particularly elegant one when she rode, large enough to allow Darre and Kendar to sit beside her. Darre had let me climb in it, once. Rockshell also had smaller, less elegant ones, that I knew Berrien and San had used.

The smaller dragons could take only one person at a time, but on a smaller dragon, you could ride while touching the scales of a dragon.

The car crash takes me by surprise.

———◆———

I could barely breathe. I could not look down. The earth was falling, falling, falling away and then the dragon *swooped* and I shrieked and the dragon *swooped* again and I was laughing, laughing, as the dragon and I became one with the wind.

———◆———

I'm undamaged. My car isn't. Both of us end up getting cited, which means my insurance rates are about to pop up, something I can't afford right now. Also, I'm almost certainly going to end up at driver's ed.

I know what I should do: go and rent a car and head into work, or at the very least get a taxi and head into work. Instead I call my boss and tell her that I'll be taking a couple of personal days. After she reminds me that I don't, technically, have any personal days left, and hangs up, I stare at my now wrecked car. If I squeeze my eyes just a little bit, I can almost believe it's a dragon.

———◆———

After that, I rode dragons as often as I could, which was not often, even in Rockshell. The dragons were not tamed – they could never be tamed – and they took riders only when they willed it. Very often they left the castle altogether, and they would never take me without someone else from Rockshell to ride beside me. But when they were there, and when I saw their eyes gleam, my breath caught, and I could only think of dancing on the wind.

———◆———

Maya is worried. "That's your third crash in – what, two years?" She takes a long sip of coffee, staring at me. "Sure you don't need your eyes checked out?"

I lower my eyes against the dim colors of the coffeeshop. She is right about one thing: I feel that I am no longer really *seeing* in this world.

But I also don't think it's something that an eye doctor can help.

⸺ ◆ ⸺

I was fifteen, or twenty-five, or something between that, when Darre and I first kissed, on top of a purple mountain, when I let my hands and fingers clumsily trail down her neck towards her breasts, when I was dragged back, screaming, to the bus stop where I'd seen the moving shadow.

⸺ ◆ ⸺

Don't go, I tell myself again and again. *You belong here. Stay here.* And then a shadow moves, and I lunge.

⸺ ◆ ⸺

(It was later, much later, before Darre and I reached for each other again, hungrily, desperately. By then, I was older, so much older, than she, and she had given herself to Berrien and San, and San, after giving me every last detail, laughing as I squirmed, had in turn dragged me to bed. It didn't matter. None of it mattered: it was *Darre*, and I held her, I held until, until the shadow *pulled* at me again.

That was the first time that going through the shadow took *time*. Before then, I'd just stepped into the shadow, and then, I'd been in Rockshell. Now, I felt myself inside the shadow, felt time passing, felt my thoughts whirling. Oddly, I could never feel my heart beat, or feel myself taking a breath. But I could feel time, endless time, and it made me all the more desperate to get to Rockshell.)

⸺ ◆ ⸺

I order more long sleeved shirts from various online stores. As I do, I look at my hands, moving painfully across the keyboard, and, although it is summer, order some leather gloves as well.

⸺ ◆ ⸺

Something *happens* in the darkness. I'm sure of it. Not on my first trip, or even on my second, but later, and definitely now. I come out, here or in Rockshell, beaten and shaken, dark bruises appearing on my arms and legs. I can't *remember* any of this, any of what happens in the darkness other than the endless cycle of my own thoughts, the *come on come on come let me through let me through* the final gibbering panic and then the bruises climbing up and down my arms and legs.

————

I wanted to get something for Darre, something to show her that my world had some magic and beauty too. It took me weeks to find anything suitable, another few weeks to save up the money to buy it, another few weeks for the shadow to appear and drag me screaming to Rockshell.

When I arrived, my hands only held tiny slivers of glass, biting into my skin. I shrieked in pain until San came running, to drag me to the healers who could stop the bleeding.

————

I stop by the mall on the way home, to buy another tiny unicorn of gold and glass. I place it carefully on one of the shelves next to the one hundred or so other tiny unicorns that I have bought over the years. They sparkle in the light of my cheap lamp, and for just a moment, I am back in Rockshell again.

————

Later, I looked down at the tiny red and white scars on my hands, and thought, *Darre kissed me.*

It was just enough to get me through high school.

————

Sometimes I tell myself that this world is real, but Rockshell is not.

Sometimes I tell myself that Rockhell is real, but I'm not.

———◆———

I earned a degree in computer engineering, more for the sake of filling my time when I wasn't in Rockshell than for the sake of anything else. It should have been in something else, but literature classes hurt me: any story, any poem, just reminded me of the *real* stories and songs I'd heard there; the ones here seemed a rough echo at best. Anthropology reminded me of all the countries in that world that I'd never seen, the hopes of seeing more lands from the back of a dragon. Music was even worse. I couldn't focus on anything in science long enough to memorize the things they wanted me to memorize, and in any case, I wasn't sure if all of it was always true – things work so differently in Rockshell.

Computer classes, though, felt like puzzles – puzzles in this world, not Rockshell. Enough to make me focus and almost forget Rockshell for a time. Enough, after college, to land a job in a Fortune 500 firm where I earned an unfair reputation for diligence and working overtime. The truth was that I didn't want to come home. I never saw the shadows there. And the longer I went between trips, the more desperate I got.

———◆———

Sometimes, when it rains here, I think I can hear the rain of Rockshell, the heavy pounding against the walls, the blue and purple streaks in the water. I close my eyes and remember laughing and dancing in the rain on the castle wall, watching as our faces turned blue, as the others sent sparks from their hands to dance in the rain.

———◆———

The darkness once grabbed me while I was on a dragon.

It was supposed to be a routine trip, a mere pleasure outing to the Isle of Kar. Halfway across the sea, I heard the cry of a mermaid, and looked down. The next thing I knew, the darkness had seized me, dragging me from the dragon's back.

Darre later told me, sobbing, that they had all thought I drowned, that no one had seen me fall, but the dragon had felt me *drop*. They knew I rarely had a chance to ride dragons; they knew I wasn't skilled. Darre assumed that they had killed me. Zylie pointed out just how much gold the castle had paid to send witches and wizards out to the sea, the place they hated most, to find me.

The darkness. Yes. The darkness.

I can't tell you much about it, only that I am in it when I am crossing over and crossing back, but in *what*, I don't know. It is only darkness and nothingness and darkness again. I cannot feel myself move, cannot feel myself breathe, or feel the thump of my heart – although it must be pounding painfully, given the way I feel once I am through. I am only thinking, thinking, thinking, sometimes of the final screams I gave when pulled from Rockshell, sometimes of dragons. Each time, I find myself thinking longer thoughts, deeper thoughts, find myself trying harder and harder to scream. I have no way of marking time. But I know that each trip is a little longer, and it is getting harder, afterwards, to breathe.

When Berrien was captured by Vonrat's forces, I stopped breathing. Kendar took one look at me and slammed me down on the nearest chair. "Wait," he said roughly. "You can't do anything."

But I could.

I could vanish into the shadows.

When I was a child, I stepped through the shadows without thinking about who might be near enough to see a small child step into a shadow and vanish, or what things I might leave behind.

Now it matters. Yes, I make decent money, but I can't afford to replace cellphones that often, and my boss keeps insisting I have it with me at all times, as if the company cannot function without me, or he can't. (Neither is true. I think he just likes thinking that he as a 24/7 hold on me. After all, the clocks in this world claim that my trips to Rockshell never last that long.)

And people, I realize, are watching.

------❖------

I forced myself to breathe. In, out, in, out. When my hands and stomach felt steady, I ran down to the stables to steal a horse. It would be slow, I knew, but I didn't have a hope of holding a dragon on my own, without magic in my hands. Or even a griffin.

"Vonrat," I whispered into the horse's ear. It might have been my imagination, but he shuddered. I kicked my feet into his sides, wishing I'd taken more horseback riding lessons, and urged him to move as quickly as he could. My hands shook. I knew what the armies of Vonrat were capable of, knew I was risking far more than just shadows. I had probably never been so terrified in my life. But I had to reach Vonrat. I *had* to.

------❖------

I'm in the middle of a particularly dull meeting when the shadow finally *moves*. I have to try not to scream.

No.

Berrien. Darre. San.

Dragons.

If I go towards it now, they will see. *Everybody* will see. They will see me – see me what? Vanish into a shadow? Fall down to the floor? I've never known what happens to me *here* when I am in Rockshell, though I've been told often enough what happens to me in Rockshell when I return here: one moment I am there. The next moment, nothing but a grey shadow, and then not even that. If I enter the shadow, is that what they will see?

I don't dare to find out. I'm on the edge of getting laid off as it is, if not worse. If I get hospitalized, for anything – falling down, even more visible injuries –

It would be different if I could stay in Rockshell.

Vonrat.

If I could stay in the shadows. Or on the back of a dragon.

Vonrat was *cold*. Or maybe I was; it was difficult to tell. I was so tired I could barely make my arms and legs move, and I *hurt*. Oh, did I hurt. The one thing I never did at home was horseback riding – too expensive, too risky – what if a shadow *moved* while I was on the horse? – and I was paying for that choice now.

But for all that, it was easy enough to offer myself up to free Berrien; I wore the token of Darre, Princess of Rockshell, after all, and had shared her bed. Many times. I told them how many, cried as I told them that I would do anything for her, including sacrifice myself to rescue the wizard she so desperately needed, not just against Vonrat, but for the wizards. They have a trace of honor, the people of Vonrat, and of sentiment, and when I told them that I could never kiss her again if I failed her, and fell weeping to the floor, they looked at each other, and dragged me off to the room where Berrien was kept, in the great stone wall at the edge of the chasm of Terrel.

"I can't let you do this," Berrien said, as they seized his arms.

I looked at the torch in the wall, and then through the window. It was very dark, down in the chasm. "I don't think I'll be staying for long."

I get another lousy employee evaluation. From the lunch conversation, I'm hardly the only one; rumor has it that the venture capitalist firm that bought out the company nine months ago is getting ready for layoffs, and this is just part of the plan.

I try to make myself care, remind myself that I need this job. I need to pay rent, pay utilities, buy food. Instead, my thoughts keep turning to dragons.

The hospital bill was terrible; trying to explain how I'd ended up with a broken arm and leg even worse. I kept my voice as low and calm as possible, even through the pain. *Berrien is safe*, I told myself. *Safe. Because you risked the shadows. Because you risked the chasm.* It was worth it. It *was*.

———◆———

I don't mean to suggest that Rockshell is all adventure, all movement, all danger, all fear. It is, but between times, it is music and song and dance and watching wild dolphins sing on the waves.

———◆———

It was months before I could return to Rockshell, before I could do much of anything beyond resting in my apartment, watching mindless television shows and surfing the internet with one hand. Months before I found myself walking to Darre's room.

"So," she whispered. "You can still return from your shadows."

"Sometimes," I said. "Sometimes."

———◆———

One day, I tell myself, I will stay there, where magic – where *dragons* – are real. One day, when the shadows come to Rockshell, I will hold on, and stay. I say this fiercely, over and over, even as I feel the cotton underwear against my skin, the cloth that no one knows about in Rockshell. I will take a dragon, and see it all – every land in that vast world, every wonder, every monster. I will know that it is real.

One day, I tell myself, I will stay here, in the world of hot baths and showers, a thousand types of coffee, air conditioning, heat, cars, planes. I will believe, finally believe, that it's not real. *It's not real.* People can't smile as they grow flowers from their fingertips, or call out to the sea and hear mermaids sing back on the wind. No one can fly on the back of a dragon. I say this, fiercely, over and over, even as three sharp stones from Rockshell dig deeply into my hands.

———◆———

After that I came to Rockshell less and less. Not on purpose: it was simply that the shadows didn't come, or I couldn't. I still longed for it, still watched eagerly for shadows. Still played games with myself when the shadows didn't come, telling myself that it wasn't real, it had never been real.

And once in Rockshell, I watched my friends age; watched lines start to appear in their skin; watched grey appear in their hair. Mikko caught me looking. "Not everyone can stay as young as you," he laughed. I watched the lights dancing in his hands, and shut my eyes against the colors.

My doctor says I look older than my real age. My legal age. It's a rather horrible thing to say, but I don't correct her, simply nod quietly when she tells me I need more sleep, more exercise, better food. She hands me a few pamphlets about eating well.

I toss them out in the first trash can I can find.

At some point, I stopped talking to my mother, although I can't remember when, or why. I just did. I didn't make a scene of it; just stopped visiting, stopped returning her phone calls and emails and texts. Eventually I stopped getting any.

Kendar held me closely when I told him, and I found myself crying helplessly in his arms.

I just realized I haven't told you about any of the *important* stuff. Like what happens when I cross over. Only things directly touching my skin make it, and sometimes, not even those. If it's electronic, or metal, forget it. I can't even tell you how many sets of keys and cellphones I've lost, forgetting that in the rush of entering the shadow. And on the other side, anything heavily infused with magic won't cross over either. That's been a problem more than once when I haven't had the chance to get back into my old clothes and the shadow *hits* and I'm wearing a dress half stitched with dreamstuff and a silence cloak. To the point where I've had to beg Darre and Kendar not to give me any magical clothing at all. Plain stuff. I try to explain nudity laws to them and they look blank. I try to explain cold, and that works a little better, until Darre, damn her memory, reminds me that I've told them that I live in a place that's generally warm to hot. And then I have to try to explain nudity laws again. Kendar can only spread out his hands and tell me, "But you're not *ugly*," – encouraging words from a former lover – and Darre can only sigh and say that she is happy that she has never been dragged to my world. Something pulls at my heart, and I have to look away. San, of course, is laughing.

Anyway.

This is why I almost always travel with a backpack stuffed with a change of clothing, a spare set of keys and a small amount of cash, and try to stash it away someplace sort of safe when the shadow appears. It doesn't always work. I don't always have time, and even when I do, I return to find that someone has found it, and either taken it away, or – these days – called it in as a bomb threat. I don't want to think about how many backpacks I've lost to Rockshell.

It's also why I've always tried to keep at least *some* clothing on at all times at Rockshell. But that hasn't always worked.

I once arrived in Rockshell to see Berrien and Darre locked in each other's arms.

I can't remember how long I watched before I turned away.

I just realized I haven't told you about any of the *other* important stuff, either: the way the colors of Rockshell are deeper, brighter, *more*. I don't think I really saw *green* until I went to Rockshell, for instance, and I know I never saw *blue*. The way everything tastes sweeter, saltier, *richer*. The softness of the clothing; the piercing sweetness of bird song; the golden tones of the five harpists, who take turns playing so that the castle will never be without music, to make sure that the castle never falls. The taste of *elaynu*, the sweet drink of Rockshell, that energizes even as it soothes.

The way when I shop for clothes, I sometimes find myself crying for the colors of Rockshell.

On the other hand, this world does have fresh, hot, amazing pizza, delivered right to my door.

When I can't see the shadow, I eat rather a lot of it.

———•———

I can help them in Rockshell. I can. At the very least, as bait, before the shadows take me, or even as a note of confusion. It's not much, but it's something. Yes. I *can* help them in Rockshell. Even if the shadows never take me again – perhaps even more. I can write letters, papers, draw maps, copy the great books. I can teach the children of Rockshell – Darre's children, Zylie's children – how to read and write, before Mikko teaches them to sing. Nothing heroic, but in Rockshell, I have already been a hero.

———•———

At night, I run the memories through over and over, savoring every word, every glance, every heart stopping moment. I remind myself who I was in Rockshell, who I am. I hear the cackle of goblins, the singing of sylphs, the curses of fairies. I see the witch moving in the shadows beneath Rockshell's forests. And for a moment, I can almost – almost – convince myself that I have fallen through the shadows, that I am there now, in Rockshell, spinning wildly in the pink and blue lights from the double moons.

It is so real, so real that I can see Darre, weaving in a bright sunny room at Rockshell, one overlooking the great forests, not the sea or the road. Weaving is not an activity I associate with her; it seems too staid, too quiet.

I say this, and she laughs. "I've gained a taste for quieter things," she explains. "Part of getting older, I suppose." She moves the shuttle expertly through the loom. "It's been a long time since I have ridden a dragon." And at that word, "dragon," I can feel the warm, smooth scales beneath my hands and my legs, feel myself soaring into the wind with Berrien and San. I can see the shadows behind me, racing, facing, as I bend over the dragon's neck, whispering that we can outrun the shadows. We can.

———•———

"You seem troubled, child."

The queen's voice was soft.

"Perhaps because everyone keeps calling me a child." I tried to make my voice light, joking. I failed. Even I could hear the trembling beneath my voice.

"You came here as a child. I think, in many ways, this is still a place where you can be a child."

I thought of Darre, of Berrien, of San, even of the times with Kendar.

"Perhaps," the queen said quietly, "it is time to put away childish things."

⋯

Work lays off another 75 employees. Our division is next. I should care about this. I should be like everyone else in our division, nervous, tense, terrified, ready to backstab a coworker at the first opportunity.

I stay in my cubicle, testing, testing, testing, my mind on Rockshell. Have the armies of Vonrat arrived? Is there anything – anything – I can bring from this world to help? How can I keep whatever it is on me as I go through the shadows?

⋯

The phrase haunted me when I returned. "Give up childish things." It was a phrase I'd heard before, I was certain, and not from the queen.

It took days before it hit me: the Bible, of course, one of many passages I was supposed to memorize in Sunday school and never did, my attention too drawn to shadows. St. Peter, maybe. Or St. Paul. One of the saints who had been in the Bible, anyway. The one who had said that as an adult, he had to give up childish things.

Give up. Give up.

Not put away.

⋯

I have not cleaned my apartment in months. It doesn't matter. Nothing matters. I curl up in bed and shake.

———◆———

"Grief is not simply a thing of your world," San once told me, turning away.

———◆———

Childish things, childish things, childish things...

A coincidence, I tell myself again. Nothing more than that. Just a coincidence. Besides, if I remember correctly, in Sunday school they told us that the Bible exists in many translations, and each one says slightly different things. St. Peter or Paul might have said give up, or put off, or both, or neither. I had too many other things to think about, too many other words to remember. I thought of other childish things: balloons, silly jokes, ice cream, roller coasters.

Joy.

The witch.

———◆———

Rockshell is in danger. I know it. They fought off the armies of Vonrat once, twice, three times – but each time the war was a little worse; each time fewer and fewer people were left in Rockshell. And it is not just Vonrat, or the countries that choose to ally with Vonrat, but all of the other monsters that roam that world or hide in its shadows, eager to destroy.

I saw it myself when I was last there: the way the colors were fading, the way everything seemed darker, dimmer. The way some of the things of Rockshell *cracked* at my touch. Something is wrong, terribly wrong, and I have to help them. I look, but I cannot see a single shadow. I shut my eyes, and try to breathe. Shadows. Shadows. And –

And I am placing a dagger edged with diamonds against my wrist, watching Darre put a slender hand over it. "Wait," she tells me, eyes brimming with tears. I am looking up at her, thinking of all the times I have failed her, thinking of how I was not here when I was needed.

"I couldn't bear it," she whispers, and then she is kissing me, and somehow, the dagger drops to the floor, and neither one of us is moving to pick it up.

No, not that memory. *This —*

------------ ◆ ------------

Berrien is holding me in his arms. We have been dancing around this for years, he and I, though we have both taken other lovers before this, and will doubtless take other lovers after this. That is the way of Rockshell: love so overpowering that few can bind themselves to a single lover, though Zylie has, and she has told me tales of others. I run my fingers up his back, waiting, waiting for his mouth to come down on mine, or for him to lead me to his bed at last.

Instead he withdraws.

I swallow.

"Berrien?"

He is now a full foot away from me. His hands slip down from my shoulders, along my arms, towards my hands, which he grasps lightly as he takes a step back. "I am afraid," he says.

"Oh, *Berrien*," I start, ready to tell him what I have already admitted to the queen, to Darre, to San. That as afraid as I so often am in Rockshell, I am not afraid of love. I step forward, raising myself up on my toes, to brush my lips across his neck.

He does not let go of my hands, though he does take another step back.

"Not of that," he tells me. "Never of that. But of knowing that you could be dragged from me, at any time, even when we..."

He does not finish the sentence. He does not have to. I can feel the pull again. I cling desperately to his hands, pull myself forward so that I can at least have this: one kiss, one moment. His eyes are shut.

And I am rolling on the ground in the small park, hearing the buzzing of airplanes above me.

------------ ◆ ------------

"Please," I said, not bothering to name my request. She knew.

"Child."

It infuriated me that she and the queen still called me *child*. I had a job, an apartment, a life. Even here in Rockshell I had proven myself, again and again. Hadn't I? I had been granted a suite of rooms, a place at the queen's table beside Darre herself. I had been touched by the Wand of Corrseth, danced at the top of the Glass Mountain of Nels, named *friend* by troll and elf alike.

"It's the—"

"Child," the witch said again. "Even Rockshell cannot do everything."

———◆———

"You're getting incredibly thin," Maya tells me, poking me with a coffee stirrer. "What's up?"

"Nothing much. Just walking a lot more. Eating better. That kind of thing."

"If it was just walking you wouldn't be skeletal," she says. "Fess up."

"I'm not *skeletal.*"

"You're skeletal. Who is she? Or he? How'd you get dumped?"

She doesn't know; she can't know. But suddenly my shoulders are shaking.

"Speaking of getting dumped, I caught this bit of this *horrible* reality show," I tell her.

It's enough to derail her, at least through the coffee. And I don't have to return her telephone calls later.

———◆———

For all of the soft blankets piled on my bed, my rooms in Rockshell felt terribly cold.

———◆———

When I sleep in this world, I dream of Rockshell, only it is all wrong. The buildings are the wrong shapes and sizes; the great city of Zytar is too close to the castle; the sea is the wrong color; the mermaids do not sing.

———◆———

When I returned to Rockshell, the castle was almost empty; I could hear the loud slap of my feet against each stone. *Vonrat*, I thought, and the queen confirmed it. Darre and Kendar were rushing to other countries, to seek their aid; San and Mikko were infiltrating Vonrat, and Berrien was speaking to the dragons. Only Zylie was still at the castle, aiding the queen, hiring soldiers, training young children how to use their magic.

I begged Zylie to let me do something, *anything*. Her eyes hardened, but after a moment, she set me to counting weapons. It was dull, pointless work: at least two other people can create new weapons just by spinning their hands. I wondered if she was doing it on purpose, to show me how useless I am. How outside the shadows, I am nothing.

At least, I told myself, I am not doing computer testing. I raised my eyes up to the sky, remembering that I would see both moons tonight, from the tiny suite of rooms that are mine, all mine, in Rockshell. It was almost enough to drown my terror. Almost.

When I sleep in Rockshell, I do not dream at all.

On that visit, the shadows grabbed me before I had seen Berrien or Darre or San or even Mikko. My hands shook; I grabbed at the stone table near me, hoping its weight could hold me. *They need me*, I thought desperately, but it was already too late.

They could be dying. All of them.

The witch is wrong. *Wrong.* Rockshell is not fading, not hurting, not dying because of me. It's in danger because I am not *there*, because I have been too afraid of what might happen to me in this world to still leap in the shadows. Even if Rockshell was dimmer in my last visit, harder to touch, harder to hold. Even if I did not hear anyone sing, even if the very lights of the moons were fainter.

In Rockshell, I am a hero. *I am.* I have saved the city of Tarn Feru from the sentient roots that were threatening the city from below. I helped save a nest of griffins and was rewarded with a touch of griffin's blood. (The resulting stain turned into a fierce burn and infection back home, which puzzled doctors and infuriated my mother.) I have ridden dragons and swum with mermaids. I have stood on the castle walls and felt the wind of the Rockshell against my skin.

In this world, I hunch in my cubicle, watching my screen, ignoring the incoming emails, wearing long sleeves to hide my scars. The witch is wrong. My supervisor is wrong. And Rockshell – Rockshell is dying.

I will not cut into my skin to summon the darkness. I will *not*.

I shut my eyes, hearing Berrien weep, and Darre scream.

I have to get there. I have to get there.

I watch the shadowless walls, a cup of chai in one hand, a shard of glass in the other. I think of *elaynu*, of dragons, of Berrien and San, of Kendar and Darre, of Mikko and Zylie, of mermaids singing softly in the amethyst waves. *I have to get there.* The shadow will come again, I tell myself. I will once again hold up my hands to a pale blue moon. The shadow will come again.

I barely even feel the pain as my hands begin to bleed.

IN THE DUST

C.M. Muller

Ina was the first to glimpse the approaching duster. She turned to her father, her expression direct as any word of warning. After confirming the sighting for himself, Henry sprang to his feet and started gathering their picnic things, calmly encouraging everyone to the car. Ina's mother moaned, lamenting the fact that she had not closed windows prior to their venturing out on this clearest of blue sky days. The storm continued its static approach, the once canvas-clear horizon now filling with the nocturnal art of some dark god whose sole motif was anti-creation. The billowing nightscape was a sight Ina had grown sadly accustomed to. It had become as common as the sky and the earth and everything in between.

Caroline was crying now—something she did a lot of these days, usually at the most unexpected moments. Imogene was clasped tightly to her chest, a blanket wrapped about the infant as if in preparation for the piercing winds to come. She moved hastily to the coupe, leaving Ina to retrieve the remaining items with her father. While a sliver of Henry's happy-go-lucky self had returned during their outing today, the blunt stoicism that had marked him like a brand for the past two years quickly resurfaced, his only words of comfort being: "Hurry up now, we might just beat the devil home …" But Ina knew the truth, knew that they were too far out to make it even halfway to the farm. Nevertheless, she nodded in kind, hopeful that she was wrong, that the storm would shift, head south or dissipate before it reached them.

Taking up the blanket and bundling it between her arms, Ina noticed her mother in the front seat of the coupe. She was staring directly at the duster, her lips shifting in silent prayer behind the glass. Then, like a lit fuse, she raised her right fist and slammed it violently upon the dash, following this with a series of curses that were loud enough for Ina to make out every harsh word. She had heard these expletives before, too many times in fact, and she hated her mother for giving in to despair, for not standing strong against the dust-laden leviathans of their new world. No one in the family had been the same since Jacob's disappearance, this was true. The loss affected each in different ways, though with Caroline it was more outwardly visible.

Ina reluctantly followed her father to the car, wishing more than anything that they didn't have to leave this beautiful spot behind. The change in weather could strike so rapidly these days, and its unpredictability both unnerved and enraged her. The storms were unlike anything anyone had ever experienced, composed of dusty topsoil gathered from the dry lands of distant counties, thick enough in its makeup to dim the light of the noon sun for hours or days on end, turning a beautiful afternoon into a nocturnal hell. That was a phrase her father often used to describe these worst bad times, and Ina wholeheartedly agreed.

After she pitched the remaining items in the back seat of the Ford, she climbed in and shut the door as hard as she could. The dust would find a way in, of that she had no doubt, but the rageful act left her feeling enervated, ready to face the storm for all it was worth. She watched her father make his way around to the driver's side, pausing near the hood as though offering a final challenge to the duster; that, or willing it to fizzle out before his very eyes. Soon enough he was behind the wheel, sweat pouring from his forehead, encouraging the temperamental coupe ahead. The razor-sharp wind was already tearing at the vehicle's hull—though it hardly mattered at this point, for the coupe had weathered many a storm and had the scars to prove it.

Ina kept silent in the back seat, waiting for her father to speak. But what exactly did she expect him to say? They had gone through this so many times before, and words never alleviated the anxiety of an approaching duster, nor did they ease the inborn knowledge of what a storm like this could do to anyone caught out in it. The Ford was gaining speed now, her father's hands clenched tightly upon the wheel, his body rigid and angled forward as if willing Nature to part this sea of dust, if only for the time it took to arrive home safe and sound. Ina thought she could hear a prayer being uttered from her father's lips, but the wind was so strong now that it was impossible to make out the words.

Caroline shifted in her seat. "Ina, would you—" she began, the remainder of the thought forgotten, swept away as if by a tendril of wind. It wasn't difficult for Ina to fill in the gap, however. She reached into the picnic basket at her side and withdrew three cloth napkins, handing two to her mother and keeping the third for herself, balling it in her hand and making ready to cover her nose and mouth. The coupe provided one layer again the onslaught of dust, the cloth another. Neither was ever enough.

Ina could not help but recall the fate of the Whitman family, caught as they had been in a similar storm last year, none surviving to tell the tale. Sheriff Henderson had discovered their Dodge half buried in a drift at the side of the road, their front window shattered and each member of the family riddled with briars from the thistles that had exploded into the interior like so much buckshot. Incidents such as this were regularly reported in the county newspaper, but the Whitman story had chilled Ina the most, the horrific details having carved a memory as deep as those killing briars. She could not help but wonder if her family faced a similar fate. The Whitman's terror was now hers to hold.

Imogene was crying, her screeching intonations muffled only slightly due to her close proximity with Caroline. Now that the Ford was moving at a quicker pace, Ina could hear the scraping sound of the chain and drag-wire Henry had affixed to the coupe months ago, which not only grounded the vehicle but prevented stalling. A static charge had already started fizzling her hair, creating a tickling sensation that was the storm's single delight. The sky was darkening rapidly now, and the winds rocked the Ford like a flimsy vessel on rough seas.

They were still miles from home, and Ina could not help but wonder if they would ever see it again. She tried picturing the farmstead in her mind, but it wasn't clear at all. No matter how hard she tried, she could only imagine the dust and dunes of a landscape turned to further wasteland. She shifted her focus instead to her brother Jacob, to the inevitability that she would soon be joining him. What could possibly exist on the other side of this dust-coated Reaper?

Full dark arrived quick and hard, forcing Henry to bring the Ford to a halt. As he cut the ignition, darkness as dense as ink infiltrated the coupe. The rocking continued, giving the impression that they were still moving swiftly down the road. The scouring wind muffled Imogene's cries, as well as Caroline's desperate pleas to a higher power. Ina could not make out the outlines of her parents or the seat in front of her, even though it was no more than a hand's length away. It was as if everything had disappeared, as if she alone existed in this murky limbo. She was thankful, then, when her father's voice pierced the veil.

"It's gonna be okay … it'll soon pass."

Ina held onto this pronouncement as though it were a talisman. She kept the rag at her mouth, not daring to let any portion of it part from her skin. Dust was still rapidly accumulating inside the coupe, its density like a tightening, gritty caul. Ina hoped that her father was right, that the darkness would soon lift—but she also knew that these storms were anything but predictable. They could last minutes or days.

She heard her mother's voice, a storm of its own that contained hardly a recognizable word. Its intonation, however, was familiar—its subject matter the end times. Ina imagined her father sliding a hand across the seat, through darkness and dust, to clasp Caroline's own in an attempt to still her hysterics. Ina thought again of the Whitman family, what it must have been like when their windshield succumbed and death had come pouring in. Like an ill-lit scene in a moving picture show, Ina watched in her mind's eye as a perfect vortex of debris-filled wind stripped away their lives and sent them to that timeless place Jacob now called home.

Ina wasn't certain how long she had been caught up in this reverie before she heard a heavy banging on the door opposite to her own, along with what sounded like a muffled cry for help. Due to the force of the wind, she knew that it would be impossible to open the door, but she couldn't resist sliding across the seat as if making ready to do so. She placed her ear to the rattling window, but heard nothing beyond the roaring, grit-filled ocean of wind doing its best to strip the coupe's skin and get at its more precious meat.

Ina tucked deeper into herself and tried to think of brighter, more hopeful days, of memories filled only with joy. But her thoughts kept returning to Jacob, lost as he had been in a storm such as this, perishing alone. Part of her wished she could join him, use some inner strength to open the door and allow the storm to usher her into the void. But she had her family to consider—they needed her just as much as she needed them. There was nothing she could do now but wait and listen and hope that the storm would give up before she did.

"It's loosening," her father muttered after a time, his voice clearer now.

Ina could just make out her parents' silhouettes, and the coupe had ceased its rough-sea rocking—clear signs that the weather was shifting. What had not changed, what had become even more pronounced, was Imogene. She still seemed caught in the horrors of the storm, and Caroline could do little if anything to placate the newborn.

Henry engaged the windshield wiper, creating a bright swath across the dust-coated glass. Light flooded into the coupe, and after her eyes adjusted, Ina had a clear glimpse of the road ahead. It looked like nothing she remembered. Drifts of fine soil were cast everywhere, leaving only a snaking bit of roadway that disappeared and reappeared like a half buried serpent. Ina turned around, finding a small opening in the darkened back window. Through this camera obscura she was able to glimpse the tail-end of the storm as it swept south. It was one of the most frightening and beautiful sights she had ever seen, and it was a miracle that her family had survived, that the windows had not blown in, that the dust had not filled their innards like taxidermy for the sheriff to find.

"Henry!" Caroline called. "Someone's out there, caught in the drift!"

Ina turned, following the direction of her mother's trembling finger. Her father was already making his way outside, pushing at the door with some effort due to the collected dust. He trudged as best he could across the sandy, uneven landscape. When he arrived at the figure half buried in the soil, he dropped to his knees and pulled a child—like some overgrown, deformed vegetable—from the earth. He clasped the youngster to his chest and then ran back to the vehicle as quickly as the dustscape would allow. Ina soon determined that it was a young boy her father was carrying.

Caroline spoke, as though awakening from a dream, her words giving name to the portrait now blossoming in Ina's mind.

"Jacob," she cried. "Oh, dear god, Jacob … "

———◄►———

What awaited them at home surprised no one, least of all Ina. They had endured numerous storms, and the far-reaching dust never failed to breach the walls and roof of the farmhouse, painting nearly every surface in a fine powder. No matter how diligent they were—caulking or taping susceptible areas such as windows and doors—the dust always managed to find a way in. The attic was the worst. Often, after a duster had passed, Ina would stand in the living room and watch mesmerized as sheets of grit streamed down the walls with the consistency of a waterfall. It was almost soothing (if you could get past the mess it made), like watching sand fall through an hourglass.

In the weeks and months between storms the clean-up never seemed to end, and while Ina did her best to assist in each recovery, she sensed a growing fissure working to split her mother's fortitude. She had heard of two other women in the county who had taken their lives because of the stark impossibility of keeping a clean home, so it was important to Ina that she did what she could to keep her mother in semi-good spirits. Jacob's disappearance had cut another thread in the stitchwork of her sanity, as had the dust pneumonia that currently afflicted Imogene. There seemed little that Ina could do to brighten her mother's despair. The picnic, which had been her idea, had certainly helped for a time, but even that in the end had been a failure. The only nostrum now that had any chance of affecting change was Jacob's return. Caroline was with him currently, sitting beside his bed in the only dust-free room of the house.

While it was clear that Jacob was alive—his breathing was as steady as any of their own, save for Imogene—he had yet to respond to their pleas. According to Henry, the boy was in a coma, and that seemed as good an explanation as any. He had been lost to a duster over a month ago, his body never recovered. But how could he have survived for so long on the open plains? Had the sands somehow sustained him, preserved his body like a cocoon? It was a ridiculous and fanciful notion, but one to which Jacob himself would have subscribed. He'd always been the imaginative one, the storyteller of the family, and Ina had little doubt that he would have achieved great fame through his stories. She still had a few of them that he'd written, tucked safely in the box beneath her bed.

But what to make of this new Jacob's eyes? They never closed, and were as black as a duster's heart. Ina had heard survivor tales of others caught in a storm, their eyes layered with so much dust that they were eventually struck blind. But with her brother, it was different. She had stared at those weird eyes most of the way home, experiencing a prickling of fear as she did so. When they arrived at the farm, her mother's first task was to clean Jacob's face with a wet cloth, then dowse those obsidian eyes in the hope of renewing the blue they once contained. But the more she tried, the brighter those orbs shone, as polished and unblemished as black marbles. In time, Caroline had dropped her head in despair and wept, departing the room.

How could this possibly be her brother? If it weren't for the eyes, Ina might well have been convinced of a miraculous resurrection. She thought of summoning her father, mostly because she did not want to sit here alone. But he was currently removing drifts of dust that had collected in the kitchen and living room, and someone needed to remain at Jacob's side in case he woke up. Ina tried to think of something witty to say, certain that she'd be able to penetrate the depths of his trance, but she felt numb, her thoughts a broiling duster of confusion. Eventually, she leaned in close and whispered simply, "You in there, Jake?"

Her brother's steady breathing continued, and there was nothing in his deathlike demeanor to suggest he had heard her voice. Most unnerving of all was that he seemed to be staring intently at the ceiling. While it was obvious that he was not awake, Ina had a feeling that Jacob was completely aware of his surroundings. She had always felt a strong connection to him, almost as if she could read his thoughts. They were the exact same age, born on the same April day. But now there was a blank slate, nothing inside him that she could decipher other than this almost supernatural alertness. She placed a hand over his own, surprised by the warmth. His pulse, when she found it, startled her.

"How'd you do it, Jake?" she asked. "How'd you make it through?"

A moment later Caroline returned to the room and demanded that she and Jacob be left alone. Imogene was nuzzled against her bosom, coughing in her sleep. Ina was grateful for the reprieve, and she quickly withdrew to help her father with the dust. Part of her wished, however, to remain, for she sensed that Jacob would soon awaken.

It had taken all afternoon and much of the evening to restore the house to a livable condition, though it was by no means free of dust. Caroline had remained in Jacob's room all the while, leaving Ina to fend for herself when it came to preparing dinner. She fashioned a plate of casserole and biscuits for both her father and herself and then brought a helping to the other room. Her mother seemed intent on spending the night with Jacob, and so Ina offered to take responsibility of Imogene.

"But you look so tired, dear," Caroline said, her tone uncharacteristically buoyant. "You really should try and get some sleep. Tomorrow's a new day."

While Ina wanted nothing more than to stay and ask after Jacob—there were so many things she needed to know—she knew better than to question the wisdom behind the words. She stepped momentarily to her mother's side, kissed her lightly on the cheek, and whispered that she loved her dearly. Maybe she would be able to speak with Jacob tomorrow. Surely his dark slumber will have lifted by then.

Sleep was hard to find most nights, but that evening Ina found it impossible to drift away. It didn't feel right knowing that Jacob (or the thing that so closely resembled him) was in the next room. She couldn't resist placing an ear to the thin adjoining wall, listening for further signs of life, waiting for Jacob's call. More than once during the long night, she had snuck to the threshold of his room, merely to see if he was still there. If she was truthful, the real reason she could not fall asleep was because she was terrified of losing him again, knew that if she did not remain attentive he would disappear and be forever lost in that dusty world from whence he had been reborn.

Now, Ina stared at the ceiling and listened to the wind as it intensified against her windowpane. A storm was close, but she felt paralyzed (as though caught in a dream), unable to rise and warn her parents of the approaching duster. At some point—minutes or hours later, she could not tell—she became aware of a presence looming quietly at her side. Someone was studying her, and she knew intuitively that it was Jacob. She reached into the darkness and, in turn, a dust-coated hand clasped her own. And in the next impossible moment …

—◆—

… she is flying, soaring through the dark as dust-grit scours her flesh. There is no pain, just a tickling sensation as though being misted by cool water on a sun-scorched day. There is darkness here, though she can see through it all, see farms, cattle, cars, and all the various other detritus that litters the land, including country folk caught out in the storm. Jacob is inside her, or she is inside him, it's hard to say. They soar with ease through the raging maelstrom, and in the distance she sees a town. She tries to speak, to ask Jacob what is happening, but she exists only within vision, an impossible perception that allows her to see everything, even the kin-like things that careen as they do through the currents of the storm, things drawn toward a sustenance she can only feel in the pit of her (or Jacob's) stomach. There's playfulness in their flight, but also the seriousness of the hunter. Their arms and stout jaws seem to elongate in the stress of the storm, and at one point a group of them break free and shoot like arrows toward the earth, in the direction of town and whatever sustenance lies therein. One of the things appears at her side before its descent, its obsidian eyes curious, pausing long enough for her to catch a glimpse of its sleek, humanoid face. It shares a knowing smile before it disappears, replaced by another layer of darkness that blinds her. In the void, she becomes aware of a familiar, pleading voice …

——◆——

"Ina … Ina, dear … wake up. "

She opened her eyes and saw her father crouching before her, his concerned expression lit by the weak glow of an oil lamp. He clasped her by the shoulders, giving her a slight shake as she slowly resurfaced from whatever possession had afflicted her. How long had she been away? (More to the point: *had* she been away?) She noticed her mother standing next to Henry, smiling but tearful. The lamp's flickering flame cast her features in a ghostly light, as though at any moment she might disappear.

"*Jacob* … " she moaned, her voice desperate. She withdrew into further darkness and continued to weep. The wind seemed much louder now.

Ina turned her attention to her father, waiting for him to explain.

"Jacob's gone, honey." He rose to his feet, encouraging her from bed. They stepped into the kitchen, to the dinner table where the oil lamp was set. Wind howled under the door and against the windows and roof. Ina knew she had to tell her father what she had experienced, to explain that Jacob lived now in the storm, in the dust. She knew that her parents were not prepared for such fantasy, that they would be angered by her crude rationalization of Jacob's disappearance. In all honesty, how could her flight through the dust be construed as anything other than a dream? Even now, back on the ground and safe in her parents' arms, Ina found it impossible to believe that her experience held any merit in reality.

Caroline, who still kept to the shadows, could not stop weeping. "I *won't* do this again, *won't* lose him again," she said, nearly hyperventilating. Ina watched her, wondering if she should go to her, comfort her. She wondered if it would help, or if her mother was lost for good. Suddenly, Caroline's focus shifted to the door, and she strode quickly to it, grasping the handle, ready to invite the maelstrom in. Henry was quick to act, but not fast enough. The door exploded inward and plumes of dust burst inside, flooding the space like grain into a bin. Caroline didn't get much farther than the threshold before she was thrown violently back, falling to the floor near the table. Henry struggled desperately to close the door, succeeding only after Ina pitched in to help. With her back against the heaving slab, she was left staring at the pitiful spectre that was her mother, and it made her sick to her stomach.

"*Jacob*," Caroline repeatedly moaned, crawling toward the door, wanting to be free, wanting to step beyond where death would gladly have her.

Within an hour the storm was gone, the sun returned to its mantle of blue. Caroline was on the porch with Imogene, scanning the newly shaped landscape in search of Jacob. Ina remained inside, preparing breakfast after she and her father had cleared as much dust from the kitchen as possible. Her mother rarely helped with cleanup anymore, convinced that it was no longer necessary, no longer a worthwhile endeavor. Henry, on the other hand, remained resigned to a fault, rarely if ever shedding a complaint. To him, the cleanup was simply another labor, as essential as ministering to one's (now-defunct) fields. Most of their crops had been destroyed by locusts or jackrabbits, two scavengers who alone seemed to thrive on the apocalyptic plains. Too bad there wasn't a market for dust, Henry had often joked, because then they'd live as kings. Ina knew that deep down her father hadn't really adapted to any of it, even if his stoic veneer told otherwise.

After breakfast, Henry rose from the table and announced that he was going out in search of Jacob.

Ina turned from the sink, washrag in hand. "I'm coming, too."

Henry shook his head. "You're needed here," he said, not waiting for her to respond. He merely nodded toward Imogene and Caroline, his unspoken suggestion being that they needed looking after and he was entrusting this all-important task to her. Then he was off, leaving Ina with a mother who seemed lost, capable at this point of little else but staring numbly at the contours of their dusty world.

"I'm going out there with him," Ina said, glowing with a defiance she doubted Caroline even recognized. No motherly rebuttal ever came, and in the growing silence Ina backstepped from the table, hurt that she was not being listened to, that her mother was not even aware of her disobedience. She worried about Imogene, wondering if her mother would properly see after her, but in the end she convinced herself that all would be fine, that the tableau would remain unchanged until her return.

Outside, she paused momentarily at the edge of the porch, sighting her father in the far distance. She bolted after him, feeling as though she were floating atop the land, over soil that had drifted so high that in certain spots it bridged the top of a barbed wire fence. She stilled an impulse to glance to her right, at the thing she had just glimpsed in the corner of her eye. The recently deceased cattle deserved better, and Ina didn't understand why her father allowed them to rot for so long. She increased her pace as best she could along the dream-slippery landscape. Now and again, jackrabbits would burst from their hiding spots, their wild energy reminiscent of the night things she had glimpsed in the storm. Just last month, she had witnessed the cruelty of the jackrabbit drives in town, watched as hundreds of the penned creatures were clubbed not only by men but by boys her age and younger. She hadn't been able to watch for very long, and was angry at her father for days afterward for taking her to see such wholesale slaughter. A plague of these verminous creatures had spread far and wide since the storms had begun, so Ina could understand the need to be rid of them, but that didn't mean she had to take part or even like it. The thing that disturbed her most was the savageness of the participants. It made her regard her neighbors in a new, more disturbing light.

Her father had stopped and turned in his tracks so that he faced toward home, arms akimbo, as if this gesture would be warning enough to send Ina scurrying back. But it didn't deter her in the least, and when she finally arrived at her father's side neither of them spoke. She surveyed the disorienting landscape for any sign of Jacob, knowing all the while that he would not be found, and when she looked into her father's eyes, she knew his assessment was not far off from her own. She shielded her eyes with her hand and continued to examine the land, vague memories resurfacing of a time when it had looked so different, when the surface of the world she had been born into had not contained a sea of sand but rather a genuine and undulating land filled with a plethora of prairie grass. The past seemed more like a dream these days than memory, for Ina hadn't been much older than Imogene when the transformations had first begun. Even under such worsening conditions, Henry had no intention of ever giving up on the farm. Her ever-hopeful father, whose unwavering mantra was that *next year* things would improve, *next year* a decent life-sustaining crop would produce, *next year* the land and their hearts would heal. Always *next year*.

Ina's own abiding and desperate hope was that her father would finally come to his senses and move the family to town. It would be so much better there, with friends, amongst folk fighting this new world together. The isolation of their farmstead would not have been so bad had the land been healthy, but Henry's refusal to leave, his stubborn and impractical outlook, would not be swayed, no matter how rationally Ina might plead. So for now, they would plod ahead *together*, make do *together*, until things improved. They need only remain steadfast and hold out for a bit longer, *one more year*. The rains would come, *next year*, and when they did this land would produce a bounty never before seen. Ina half believed her father when he spoke so grandly. She trusted that he knew things she did not, though she had to admit that this trust had nearly eroded, like a house made of dust.

"Time to head back," her father said, his voice low. Ina heard other words, just beneath the surface: *Jacob's not here. The land has him now. For good.*

So she trailed Henry's long strides toward home, and when they arrived they found Caroline sitting on the porch steps, gazing despondently at a hastily-erected mound of dirt a yard or so out. A portion of Imogene's face and doll-like hands were visible, but the rest of her was covered by dust. Henry bolted forward, and as he ripped the child from the makeshift grave, Ina could tell by its drooping limbs and reflecting skin that it was as lifeless as the dust that made up this cruel, cruel world.

Henry was having difficulty starting the coupe, so Ina stepped out to help him swipe dust from the exposed engine. Caroline sat inanimately in the front seat, Imogene swaddled tightly in a bright blue blanket at her side. The blanket was as beautiful as the sky and seemed already a part of it. Ina felt numb and clumsy and useless as she assisted her father, daring not to speak over his cursing whispers. She had never heard him use such words, ever. And hearing them now made her feel that the end of everything was near to hand. She suddenly felt alone, with no one to lean on, no one to lead her from a fast-approaching doom.

In time (seemingly due to Henry's harsh language alone), the coupe fired up, providing a boon to Ina's despair. As they made their slow trek toward town, her father seemed a bit more himself now, at least outwardly, but the silence in the car spoke volumes. He was holding on by a thread, and Ina prayed that the coupe held its course, for she sensed that were it to break down, her father would quickly follow suit. And then she'd be stuck in the middle of this wasteland with no one but a ghost mother to keep her company. She needed her father, needed his strength, but there seemed little she could do to resurrect him. At times during the journey, she thought she heard Imogene crying or coughing inside her blue cocoon, and for long periods she nearly convinced herself that her kid sister had been cured of dust pneumonia and was merely sleeping. Caroline had not shifted an inch the entire while, had not checked to see how Ina or her father were doing. She merely stared blankly ahead, blind to all but her thoughts—if indeed she had any at this point. Ina could not help but imagine the coupe as a casket, her mother embedded within.

As hard as she tried, Ina could no longer hold back tears. She turned and did her best to disappear into the corner of the dusty back seat, covering her mouth as her body juddered uncontrollably. She was embarrassed by the crying fit, for she had always thought herself strong, beyond the weaknesses of her mother. After a time, she thought she heard her father speak, perhaps asking if she was okay. She couldn't tell because her ears felt plugged with cotton. When she glanced his way, the only thing she noticed were his limp arms making minor adjustments to the wheel. Ina returned to her corner and slumped against the window, staring out of it like the rest of them.

She wasn't sure how much time passed.

As the coupe downshifted and wobbled into town, Ina studied the residents and business folk going about their business. Hope returned to her, and she wished with all her heart that her family would never have to leave this place, wished that their farm was already layered by so much dust that it would never be found. She was happy to leave the past behind and to bury old memories. A new life awaited them here, and she sensed that she would never again face loneliness among such folk, that these people were different. They had waged their war on dust and won. Ina smiled, hoping to catch the attention of a few of these hope-filled souls. She'd been to town before, of course, but the place felt different this time around. Like a sanctuary.

Halfway down the street, Henry parked the coupe in front of Doc Parson's. Ina had only visited the elder's office on one other occasion, after breaking her wrist a few years back while attempting to plow for the first time. She liked Doc, whose sage demeanor never failed to put a positive spin on the tragedies of life. If anyone could make things better in this world, it was him. His name printed across the front window in bold gold lettering was like a nostrum, making her feel exquisitely lightheaded.

"Wait here," Henry ordered, withdrawing from the vehicle and walking stiff-legged toward the two-story brick building.

Ina leaned over the front seat and lightly clasped her mother's shoulder. "It's gonna be okay, Ma," she said. "Doc'll fix things up, you wait and see."

When her father returned, Doc Parsons was at his side. Each helped Caroline from the car, and soon enough the trio was headed back to the office. Ina reluctantly followed, confused as to whether or not she was expected to carry Imogene. She left the bundle behind and hastened toward the office, hardly able to still her emotions.

———◆———

Caroline had been taken to the hotel across the way, where she was presently resting in the relative quiet and comfort of a dust-free room. Doc Parsons had given her a sedative, stating that he wished to keep a close eye on her for the next few days. Some funeral men had already taken Imogene away, leaving Ina petrified to know what would become of her kid sister. She hoped her mother could summon the strength to return to this world, to shake the darkness that had enveloped her for so long. First Jacob, then Imogene, and now her mother: all lost, torn from her life. How much longer before Henry joined them and left her truly alone? Doc Parsons had given him some pills, though Ina wasn't sure what they were for. Her father hadn't moved from the chair next to the bed, clasping Caroline's pale hand all the while.

To counter the encroaching darkness, Ina imagined scenarios of her mother's awakening, her previous depressions shed like dusty skin, and all of them moving forward together, rediscovering the joy that had eluded them for so long. Ina could not help but be cautiously optimistic about their future. As much as she desired Jacob's return, she also knew that whatever life now ran through his veins was not natural. He had been changed by means she could not fathom, his transformation more fantastic than any of the stories he had ever told or written down. His new existence terrified her, but at the same time she longed to relive that incredible flight through the dust, no matter how otherworldly it might seem. There was a freedom associated with it (and a beautiful one at that), and her exposure, while frightening at first, made her realize that there was also a kind of purity there, a purity hidden inside all of that dust.

Ina leaned against the room's single window, through which she was afforded a clear view of Main. She grew mesmerized by the activity below, vehicles and citizenry moving to and fro. On the farm the only things imbued with such spirited resolve were jackrabbits. Ina turned briefly to her father, wanting to ask him if they were planning to stay for good, but now wasn't the right time. His focus remained on Caroline, and for now that was good enough. Ina made a mental list

of the things she wished to discuss with him, the benefits of city living, and the fact that she planned to apply herself to any sort of work
that became available, no matter how menial. She had no desire what-
soever to go back to the pointless upkeep of their farm. Nothing but
death awaited them there. A purposeful life could be had in this town,
and she had a sudden longing to be out there in the midst of it all.
She turned to her father, who was already staring in her direction. His
blank countenance spoke volumes, but his simple nod was acknowl-
edgment enough for Ina to act.

She approached the bed, lightly grasping her mother's hand. "I'll
be back soon, Mama," she said, remaining there until thoughts of life
and death (and something that might exist in between) threatened to
overwhelm her. She broke free and hastened from the room, clamber-
ing down the stairs and out the front door to the wooden sidewalk that
stretched unevenly along Main. She wandered for blocks, trying but
failing to unburden herself of dark memories. Eventually she stopped
on the porch of a general store, stunned by the sudden realization that
she had not encountered a single soul since leaving the hotel. She studied her surroundings with a clearer eye, taken aback by what she did
not see. Where was everyone? Cars were parked on either side of Main,
with no concern as to their placement. The sky was darkening as well,
as though evening were setting in. But that was impossible, because
she'd left the hotel at just a little past noon. She was sure of it.

Ina heard a voice summoning her from across the street, but due
to the growing darkness and wind, she had difficulty locating the individual in question. She stepped into the street and was halfway across
when she noticed a beckoning silhouette. A few more steps and the
woman became more fully defined. She was leaning out the double
doors of the movie theater, demanding Ina to her side.

"Child, quick. It's nearly upon us."

The wind blew more forcefully now, but it was only as the grit of the
approaching duster flooded into town that Ina knew she was in trouble.
The town was hardly immune; why had she thought that it ever was?
It was the same storm-ravaged place it had always been (and always
would be), and she needed to find cover, and quickly. She turned to her
right and gazed at the mile-high wall of dust that was already obliter-
ating the horizon, a mountain range come to life. It seemed somehow
more ominous than any of the previous dusters she'd seen. She felt

paralyzed, stuck like a statue in the middle of the street.

The woman in the theater was calling more forcefully now, but Ina could no longer make out her words. The storm was the only voice now, uttering the command that mattered most. Ina turned, intending to run to the theater, but was startled to discover that the darkness had swallowed it whole. She shifted herself to face the storm, overwhelmed by an emotion she was not expecting: beauty. The storm was beguiling, inviting. It was, after all, Jacob's new home, and he was up there now, soaring carefree through all that dust. Without another thought, Ina began walking into the storm, toward Jacob, struggling to keep herself steady as the stinging winds tore at her skin. But she did not fear. It felt as though her brother and the wind and the darkness were all a combination of one thing, and she grew anxious to learn this new progenitor's ways.

In the full dark, something clasped Ina's hand, and while her first impulse was to pull free, she knew that it could be none other than Jacob. She allowed herself to be led forward, and it felt more than anything as if they were running again, she and her beautiful twin brother, sprinting carefree along the prairie of their childhood and into a brighter future. She noticed that her vision was changing—it had to be, for she was able to decipher the outlines of things previously hidden from view, glimpse the world through a newer, more sensitive lens.

She could even see Jacob, so close to her side. His black eyes shone, his old skin stripped and the new one rich and glowing with life. The sensation of running soon transitioned to the exhilarating buoyancy of flight, and while Jacob was no longer holding her hand, Ina sensed his closeness and knew that from this moment forward she always would.

About the Authors

MIKE ADAMSON holds a Doctoral degree from Flinders University of South Australia. After early aspirations in art and writing, Mike returned to study and secured qualifications in both marine biology and archaeology. Mike has been a university educator  since 2006, has worked in the replication of convincing ancient fossils, is a passionate photographer, a master-level hobbyist, and a journalist for international magazines. Short fiction sales include to *Little Blue Marble, Weird Tales, Abyss and Apex, Daily Science Fiction, Compelling Science Fiction* and *Nature Futures*. Mike has placed over 120 stories to date. You can catch up with his writing career at 'The View From the Keyboard,' http://mike-adamson.blogspot.com

RANDEE DAWN is a Brooklyn-based author who writes about the glam world of entertainment by day and the seamy underbelly of the real world by night. Her short stories have been published in outlets and anthologies including *Children of a Different*  *Sky, Where We May Wag, Fantasia Divinity* and *Samhain Secrets*. She is the co-editor of *Across the Universe: Tales of Alternative Beatles*, and co-wrote *The Law & Order: SVU Unofficial Companion*. Her nonfiction articles have been published in *Variety,* the *Los Angeles Times, Today. com* and *Emmy Magazine*, to name a few. In a previous incarnation she covered the indie rock world in Boston – some of which pops up "Rough Beast, Slouching." Her work – from the glam to the gory – can be found at RandeeDawn.com.

Raised in Oklahoma, **J.W. Donley** currently lives with his wife and son in the Pacific Northwest where the foothills of the Cascade Mountain range meet the Salish Sea. He enjoys writing in the weird, horror, and fantasy genres. Growing up he loved reading R. L. Stine's *Goosebumps* books as well as classics like Frank Herbert's *Dune*, and Tolkien's *Lord of the Rings*. In college he discovered Stephen King's *Dark Tower* series, which in turn led him to King's short stories and later to books like Mark Danielewski's *House of Leaves* and authors like Clive Barker and Laird Barron. When he isn't writing or reading, Joe enjoys landscape photography, hiking, and fiddling with his fountain pens. You can follow his adventures, writing and otherwise, on Twitter @jwdonley and at JWDonley.com.

Timothy G. Huguenin lives in the dark Allegheny Mountains of West Virginia. His short fiction has appeared in publications such as *Hinnom Magazine, Beneath the Waves: Tales From the Deep,* and *Anthology of Appalachian Writers Vol. XI*. His third novel, *Schafer*, is coming 2020 from Bloodshot Books. You can find out more about him and his writing by visiting tghuguenin.com.

Jennifer Loring's short fiction has appeared in anthologies such as *Tales from the Lake* vols. 1 and 4, *Nightscript IV, Not All Monsters, Arterial Bloom,* and online in *The Literary Hatchet* and *City. River. Tree.*, among many others. Longer work includes four novels and several novellas. She holds an MFA in Writing Popular Fiction with a concentration in horror fiction and is currently working toward a PhD in Interdisciplinary Studies - Humanities & Culture. Jenn lives in Philadelphia, PA, where she and her husband are owned by a turtle and two basset hounds.

Avery Kit Malone is a tired doctoral student. He enjoys cats and wandering dark, quiet places and if you find him in a corner of your basement, please gently move him outside with paper and a plastic cup, and remember: he's just as afraid of you as you are of him. His short fiction can be found in *Pseudopod, Novel Noctule, Grimoire, Unspeakable: A Queer Gothic Anthology,* and other venues. Find him on Twitter: @dead_scholar

C.M. MULLER lives in St. Paul, Minnesota with his wife and two sons—and, of course, all those quaint and curious volumes of forgotten lore. He is related to the Norwegian writer Jonas Lie and draws much inspiration from that scrivener of old. His tales have  appeared in Shadows & Tall Trees, Supernatural Tales, Vastarien, and a host of other venues. In addition to writing, he also edits and publishes the journal Nightscript. His debut story collection, Hidden Folk, was released in 2018.

MARI NESS lives in central Florida. Her fiction and poetry can be found in many places, including *Tor.com, Clarkesworld, Lightspeed, Uncanny, Fireside, Nightmare, Fantasy, Apex* and *Strange Horizons.* For more, visit her website at marikness.wordpress.com, or follow her on Twitter at @mari_ness. 

DAVE RING is the chair of the OutWrite LGBTQ Book Festival in Washington, DC. He has stories featured or forthcoming in a number of publications, including *Fireside Fiction, GlitterShip,* and *A Punk Rock Future.* He is the publisher and managing editor  of Neon Hemlock Press, as well as the editor of *Broken Metropolis: Queer Tales of a City That Never Was* from Mason Jar Press. More info at www.dave-ring.com. Follow him at @slickhop.

ERICA RUPPERT writes weird horror, dark fantasy, and the occasional poem from her home in northern New Jersey. Her work has appeared in magazines including *Unnerving, Weirdbook,* and *PodCastle,* and in multiple anthologies. She is, as ever, working on a loosely-planned yet persistent novel. 

MICHAEL DAVID WILSON is the founder of the popular UK horror website, podcast, and publisher, This Is Horror. Michael is the author of the novella, *The Girl in the Video*, and the novel, *They're Watching*, co-written with Bob Pastorella. His work has appeared in various publications including *The NoSleep Podcast*, *Dim Shores*, *Dark Moon Digest*, *LitReactor*, *Hawk & Cleaver's The Other Stories*, and *Scream*. You can connect with Michael on Twitter @WilsonTheWriter. For more information visit www.michaeldavidwilson.co.uk

JASON A. WYCKOFF is the author of two short story collections published by Tartarus Press, *Black Horse and other Strange Stories* (2012) and *The Hidden Back Room* (2016). His work has appeared in anthologies from Plutonian Press and Siren's Call Publications, as well as the journals Nightscript, Weirdbook, and Turn to Ash. He lives in Columbus, Ohio, USA. Married. Cats.

DIM SHORES
weird horror
strange science fiction
dark fantasy
limited-edition chapbooks and anthologies
dimshores.com